Evelyn Anthony began writing in 1949, penning
a string of successful historical novels before she
turned her talents to spy thrillers for which sh[...]

Evelyn Anthony is ma[...]s
in Essex.

Acclaim for Evelyn Anthony

'A superb and captivating storyteller' *Daily Mail*

'Eminently readable' *Guardian*

'One of today's most popular and gifted novelists'
Publishers Weekly

'Evelyn Anthony knows how to thrill and chill'
Observer

'Spine-tingling . . . demands to be read'
Oxford Mail

'Recommended without reservation . . . the pace
never slackens, the energy never falters'
The Sunday Times

'Evelyn Anthony is a master of the art of
storytelling'
Woman & Home

'Brilliantly convincing' *Evening Standard*

'Thriller-writing at its best' *Irish Times*

THE DOLL'S HOUSE

Evelyn Anthony

CORGI BOOKS

THE DOLL'S HOUSE
A CORGI BOOK 0 552 14054 6

Originally published in Great Britain by Bantam Press,
a division of Transworld Publishers Ltd

PRINTING HISTORY
Bantam Press edition published 1992
Corgi edition published 1993

Set in 11/13pt Linotype Sabon by
Chippendale Type Ltd, Otley, West Yorkshire.

Corgi Books are published by Transworld Publishers Ltd,
61–63 Uxbridge Road, Ealing, London W5 5SA, in Australia by
Transworld Publishers (Australia) Pty. Ltd, 15–25 Helles Avenue,
Moorebank, NSW 2170, and in New Zealand by Transworld
Publishers (NZ) Ltd, 3 William Pickering Drive, Albany, Auckland.

Reproduced, printed and bound in Great Britain by
Cox & Wyman Ltd, Reading, Berks.

For my daughter Kitty
with my love.

I

Rosa Bennet's husband was in a bad mood. She knew as soon as he walked in and went straight to pour himself a drink, after a brief 'Hi', and a peck on her cheek. She was busy getting dinner, anyway it was useless trying to talk to him when he was in that frame of mind.

They sat opposite each other in the dining room. He looked up and said, 'This is good. I love sole.'

Then he went on eating, sipping his wine. She hadn't been late, for once. She'd cleared her desk and hurried home to be there when he got in. He hated coming back to an empty house. The trouble was he often did these days.

She looked at him. He was the same man she'd fallen in love with six years ago. Good-looking, fair and blue eyed. A sportsman, intelligent, full of energy and enjoyment of life. A marvellous lover and generous to a fault. They'd been so happy when they were lovers. And for the first three years after they got married. But she hadn't been so successful then; she was still on the bottom of the career ladder at the Foreign Office, while he was a top-salaried high flyer in a big City Investment Bank. She hadn't been a challenge to him.

I wish I could talk to him, she mused in the silence. Really talk, instead of arguing . . . If things were different I might even have been able to hint at the job . . . I'm excited and pleased and I can't share it with him. I can't share it with anybody else.

She heard him say, 'Had a busy day putting the world to rights?' and knew he was being sarcastic. She ignored it, as she did so often.

'Quite busy. How was your day, darling?'

'Rather quiet,' James muttered. He felt for a bone and laid it like a reproach on the side of his plate. 'Bloody recession just goes on and on. I had a drink before coming home just to break the monotony.'

She tried to be sympathetic.

'I know it's bad,' she said. 'But it's the same everywhere. It's world-wide.'

'It's my little world I'm worried about,' he spoke sharply. 'I leave the global issues to you. Any more in that bottle?'

She poured for him. For a moment their eyes met.

'Sorry, Rosa,' he said suddenly. 'I didn't mean to be bloody to you. It's been a lousy day. Poor old David got fired this morning. It's not going to be easy to find another job at forty-four. Most firms are shedding staff, not taking anyone on.'

'I am sorry.' She meant it. She knew David Hughes slightly. He was a nice man, with three sons at a smart public school, an expensive wife and a heavy mortgage on a house in Brompton Square. He'd ridden on the crest of the boom wave like everyone else. She couldn't imagine what he would do.

'Did you take him out for a drink?'

James Bennet nodded. 'Yes, we had a wake in the local wine bar. I left him to it.'

He finished his fish.

She brushed the hair back from her forehead. He knew the mannerism so well. She had thick, red-brown hair that turned copper in the sun. She'd been a lovely girl when they met and she was a lovely woman now. More sophisticated, self-confident.

He'd been crazy about her. She was fun to be with, glorious in bed. It had been a magic time for them both. He was ready for marriage. He'd thought she was too and, in fairness, he hadn't listened when she tried to explain about her job at the Foreign Office. So she had to work hard, he knew that . . . So she had to travel, she'd already been on a jaunt to Vancouver and made trips to the States in the first few months they were together. He didn't mind. He had a career of his own and it wasn't exactly nine to five! It had seemed so simple, a perfectly balanced partnership.

It had seemed like that to Rosa too. Now that things had changed, she spent a lot of time thinking back, trying to see what had caused the rift.

It started with her promotion two years after their wedding. James hadn't been enthusiastic about it and she was hurt and surprised.

By contrast, she took a keen interest in his job, and was lavish with praise when he did well. But he was lukewarm when she talked about how interesting her work was, or spoke well of her boss.

At first Rosa explained it as a twinge of male jealousy, and made an extra fuss of him to compensate. It was so unlike James to be grudging, let alone mean-spirited. She had refused to accept that he resented her independence and achievements in her own right.

It was a phase, she insisted, and it would pass. They were so well matched, so happy together normally. They had a charming house, plenty of money, a wide circle of amusing friends. They were a golden couple; the first time she heard them described like that by a friend of her mother's, she had laughed.

All they needed, the friend went on repeating, was a baby, and Rosa's mother joined in. A baby, a dear little boy or girl – how lovely. It would be such fun to be a grandmother.

Nobody listened when Rosa tried to protest that she was only twenty-six, and there was plenty of time.

They didn't know, and she was too proud to tell them, that James had been making a major issue of starting a family ever since she got the job of personal assistant to her head of department, Sir Hugh Chapman.

She reasoned with him, asked him for time; he refused to admit that she had a right to her job and a few more years of independence.

That was when the rift became a chasm between them, which neither could bridge. He accused her once of being selfish and immature, unwilling to take on the full responsibility of married life.

She countered angrily with a similar charge; he was selfish and chauvinistic, and jealous . . . at last the word was spoken, and although the ugly quarrel was made up, it changed things subtly between them afterwards. If she had extra work or stayed late at the office he sulked, and often drank too much which made him sarcastic and aggressive.

But he was miserable because he loved her, and Rosa knew it. He wanted her to himself, without competition.

There were times when she almost gave in and resigned. It seemed the only way to bring them together. But at the crucial moment, Rosa drew back.

What he was demanding was unfair; his jealousy of her success was unfair; if she capitulated, she knew she would never forgive him or respect herself. And pregnancy would have been a disaster because it had been forced upon her.

She tried to explain that to him, once. But James only looked hurt and said that if she loved him, she'd want his child.

And she had faced in misery, that what he really wanted was a different woman with a different view of marriage. Perhaps neither had got the other into true focus before they committed themselves.

But they were committed, and Rosa believed that like everything worth having, marriage had to be worked at. Time and determination overcame most difficulties in the end. And she still loved him. She was firm with herself about that.

She no longer discussed her work with him; he seldom asked except to attack the Foreign Office for incompetence on some broad issue which was directed obliquely at her. On the surface they lived together, but they circled one another in growing tension when they were alone.

James watched her; she had eaten very little and she looked pale and downcast. He felt guilty and it irritated him.

She wouldn't give up; she kept on trying in little ways, like cooking a dinner he especially liked, and bearing his ill humour with patience when he longed for her to retaliate and shout at him.

She was still trying, but he wasn't. He had given up.

He pushed his plate away. She got up and began to clear the table. He sat there, without making any move to help. He felt heavy with resentment.

If she was tired it was because she chose to be. She didn't have to work. He'd been clever, unlike his unfortunate colleague. He'd made a lot of money and he'd kept it. And he was very good indeed at his job. There'd be no wake in the wine bar for him. They could have been so happy. It hurt to think like that, so he stopped.

'Would you like coffee?' she called out.

He'd refused the fruit salad she'd prepared and he didn't want coffee either. He wanted a drink.

'No thanks. Can't you leave that till the morning? Isn't Vicky coming in?'

He was trying to pick a fault. Why couldn't she come and sit down while he had his whisky, instead of frigging about in the kitchen when there was a woman paid to do it for her. He was always criticizing her these days. Often to her face. There were times when she exploded back at him. That made it easier for him.

He switched on the television and slumped down

in an armchair with a large whisky and soda. Rosa came in and joined him.

After a while she said, 'I'd like to watch that programme on Hungary – it's ITV. Do you mind?'

He pulled a face. The whisky was getting to him; he'd eaten so little.

'Can't you ever leave your bloody work in the office, darling?'

Rosa stifled a surge of temper. She was hurt by the relentless needling. She said crossly, 'I thought you might find it interesting. But if you'd rather watch that sitcom rubbish!'

He switched channels. 'I don't give a shit about what happens to the Hungarians, or the Romanians or any of them! The Communists had the right idea.'

'I'm glad you think so.' She wasn't going to hold on much longer. 'Just why are you in such a filthy mood, James? It's not all because of David getting fired.'

'Poor bugger,' he muttered. 'He said he'd have to take the boys away from Harrow. I told him to sell the house and clear the debts. He can't let his kids suffer. I told him, "They're your first priority." '

His glass was empty; Rosa hoped he wouldn't refill it.

'There are other good schools,' she pointed out. 'He didn't go to Harrow; he didn't have to send his children there. They seemed nice enough boys, they'll understand.'

'If you want to watch this crap,' he said rudely, 'why don't we stop talking? You wouldn't know how David feels. You don't have children.'

'As things are,' Rosa got up, 'it's just as well. I'm going to bed, James. You may have spent time getting pissed and working yourself up to have a row when you got home, but I was very busy and I rushed through all day to get back in good time. Now I'm tired.'

She went out and stopped herself from banging the door. He had been in a foul mood. No children. That was his weapon and he used it constantly. Going upstairs her anger drained away. He wouldn't follow her and make it up. She wouldn't wait for him and hold out her arms and say, 'Don't let's fight, darling. Come here.'

She undressed and spent some minutes looking at herself in the bathroom mirror. Dark rings under the eyes, a look of strain round the mouth. She was unhappy. So was he; he wasn't unkind by nature. The James Bennet she fell in love with was warmhearted. He was disappointed and she was the cause. He wanted what she couldn't give him and she had tried to warn him from the start.

She loved her job. She wanted to succeed in it. She didn't want to give it up and have children and stay at home. And if he resented her career at the Foreign Office, what would he say if she told him about the new post she had been offered – and accepted that afternoon. She had transferred from Diplomacy to Intelligence.

She went over the long interview in her mind, the image of the unhappy woman in the mirror blurring out of focus, hearing Sir Hugh Chapman saying persuasively, 'You have exceptional talent, Rosa. That's why we want you. And you'll benefit from the experience. It'll enhance your future career prospects when you go back to a normal job. I can guarantee that. And the Brussels posting is among the most important.'

Second Secretary at the British Embassy. Eyes and ears in the heart of the European Community. An established diplomat who'd excite no suspicion of her other role. How complimentary Sir Hugh had been, praising her ability to the retired Air Marshal who was head of 'C' Section.

She hadn't hesitated for long. It was only for two years at most. She and James could spend weekends together. It might be a good thing if they were apart during the week. Lots of people lived like that: the wife in the country, the husband in a flat in London, coming home on Friday night. Brussels was no further than a couple of hours commuting by train in terms of time. It was such a challenge, such an opportunity.

If we were getting on well, the thought whispered to her while she considered, it would be different. I mightn't want to go. But even if I turned it down James wouldn't be satisfied. He wants total surrender.

She went back to see Sir Hugh that afternoon and said she had decided to accept and join 'C' section. And that was that.

She didn't have to tell James for some time. She'd undergo a basic course in Intelligence work in London before she was ready to take up the appointment. It had sounded so interesting she couldn't wait to start. And it was vital too, a challenge she couldn't resist. England was part of the Community, but with more enemies than friends in Europe. So much depended upon knowing what those enemies were saying and doing to undermine the English position. 'Forewarned,' her new employer said in his dry way, 'is forearmed, Mrs Bennet,' and it didn't even sound like a cliché.

She saw herself in the glass again and made a resolution. She would make up the silly row with her husband. She'd been unreasonable considering what had happened at his office to a colleague who was an old friend. She got into the double bed and switched the side light on. Her hair fell loosely to her shoulders and she was naked. When the door opened she called out to him.

'Is that my bear with the sore head?'

It used to be their private joke, the prelude to a reconciliation if they had a little quarrel in the early days. He came into the room and saw her, sitting up bathed in the soft light. She opened her arms and the full breasts excited him. She said softly, 'Come on, bear, come and make it up with me.'

He came and suddenly he wanted her so badly it made him rough and urgent. They made love several times during the night and fell asleep close together as if the present had become the past.

And each made their resolution. 'It'll be all right now. It was just a bad patch. I'll try harder from now on.'

*   *   *

'I thought I'd drop in as I was passing, just to say goodbye.'

Harry Oakham said, 'I'm glad you did. Sorry you missed the lunch. It was a great send-off.'

Sir Eric had sent his apologies; pressure of work had prevented him attending the farewell party at St Ermin's Hotel up the road. A lunch with plenty of drink, speeches, some of them funny, tributes to Harry Oakham on his retirement from the Service. A great send-off, as he'd said. 'A pity,' Sir Eric had repeated, that he hadn't been able to join them.

Oakham looked relaxed. He'd made a speech of his own. One of the guests had been thoughtful enough to take it down and send it round to Sir Eric. It had been witty and mercifully short. On such occasions old spies were known to grow maudlin which was embarrassing. But Oakham wouldn't bow out on a nostalgic note. Sir Eric Newton had been his superior for thirteen years and he knew Harry better than that. He had missed the party, but he made a point of coming in to say goodbye in person. So, on the afternoon of Oakham's last day in the office, he had come along to shake his hand.

'Any ideas about the future?' he asked. He wasn't really curious, but it was polite to show interest.

'I thought I might do something in catering,' Oakham answered.

Sir Eric was surprised. 'Really? That doesn't sound much in your line.'

'It's just a vague idea, nothing definite. I'm not in a hurry to commit myself. Plenty of time.'

'Yes, of course. Time to stand and stare for a

change, eh? And don't forget, Harry, if you need any help, anything at all – just get in touch. How's your wife looking forward to having you at home?'

He made it sound jocular. It was on Oakham's file that the wife played around and they weren't happy, but it was a remark he'd made to a lot of married men retiring early in the past few months. It just slipped out.

Oakham didn't even blink. 'With any luck,' he said, 'she'll get so fed up, she'll leave me.' He laughed, which Sir Eric found uncomfortable.

But then Harry Oakham was that kind of man. You never quite knew with him. But he seemed to have taken it all in good part. He was relaxed, he didn't complain or quibble about his pension and gratuity. He took it all with that slight smile that seemed to mock himself, the Service and everyone in it.

'Well,' Sir Eric Newton got up; he was a short, wiry little man and Oakham stood a head taller. He held out his hand. 'Good luck, Harry. Enjoy life, won't you? You've earned it.'

Oakham opened the door for him, closed it on him. His desk was clear. Everything was packed up. He'd given in his keys, his ID card.

He'd hated every moment of the farewell lunch. He'd listened to the humbug being talked and the bursts of clapping, and made his wry, amusing speech to more applause, much of it prompted by the amount of booze they'd put away. After twenty-eight years of service, twenty of them in active field work, Harry Oakham had been retired.

The lunch had been on the first of April, the Fool's Day. Thanks very much old chap, thanks for the best part of your life and all the times you nearly lost it. And don't let's talk about the lives you took, that's best forgotten. We've given you a slap-up party and told you how splendid it all was and waved you goodbye to a golden twilight.

He walked out of his office and closed the door with a snap. He stood waiting for the lift to come and take him down and out of the building for the last time. At his floor a young woman got out; she smiled briefly at him. He didn't know her. He didn't linger in the reception hall; all his goodbyes to the staff had been said in the pub the night before. He'd held his private party there with Frank on the desk and Pat who'd looked after the security and the old girl who'd cleaned his office since he first got behind a desk.

There was nothing to do now but wave as he walked out into Victoria Street. He moved with the spring of a man who was fit and younger than his fifty-two years. Hardly a grey hair on his head, eyesight and reflexes as sharp as ever. But not needed any more. Harry Oakham, retired spy. Times had changed; how often he'd heard the same platitudes spouted in the last few months. Men with his skills and his experience were an anachronism now. His department was being closed down. The Ministry of Defence would take over the building.

Officially the Department hadn't existed since the war ended in 1945. Unofficially it had been in operation since 1961. He'd been interviewed in the shabby office complex down the street from the Army & Navy Stores. He'd been an early recruit. For the last eight years he'd been desk-bound.

He stopped to light a cigarette. Before that the Cold War had been bloody hot for people like him. Now it was all over. Peace on earth and good old Gorbachev. He waited by the kerb, smoking. He saw a taxi, its orange light glowing and raised his hand. It slowed, stopped and he got in. He leaned back in the seat.

'The Arts Club, Dover Street,' he said.

The driver peered at him over his shoulder. He had a surly face.

'The sign says "No smoking",' he challenged.

The sign was polite, unlike the driver. It said simply, THANK YOU FOR NOT SMOKING. Harry Oakham tossed the cigarette out of the window. Never call attention to yourself. Never get involved in a public row. Keep a low profile. He'd been teaching that for years. Old habits die hard. Or don't die at all, he thought.

He was out with a pension and a cash payment and references that said he'd spent the last twenty-eight years as a reliable middle-grade Civil Servant. He'd even been given a list of contacts friendly to the Service. One of them would be sure to give him a job. Something to supplement the pension.

The taxi drew up in Dover Street. He paid the exact fare. The driver looked up and glared at him.

Oakham smiled. 'I thought it said, "Thank you for not tipping",' he said and swung away and into the club while the man was still swearing at him.

He was well known at the club. He'd been a member for many years. He liked the atmosphere. It was friendly and relaxed. Publishers and artists patronized it. There were good paintings in the upstairs rooms and usually an interesting exhibition in the handsome bar. The staff knew him, but he didn't encourage other members. It was a good place for meeting contacts. You wouldn't expect two professionals to be working out an assignment over lunch.

He ordered a whisky and soda at the bar and took it into the big reception room. There was a painting of the actress Evelyn Laye by the door. He often spent time looking at it. What a beautiful woman. She reminded him of Judith. But that had been a long time ago. Judith had had the same wistful look, the wide eyes of astonishing blue. He still couldn't think about Judith without pain.

A voice beside him said, 'Hello, Harry.'

'Hello, Jan. Sit down, I'll get you a drink. Scotch?'

'Please. Water, no ice. Thanks.'

Jan was very punctual. He had a name nobody could pronounce so everybody called him Jan. And he was never late. Except once. He was late for ten years because he was in prison in Cracow. The sentence had been life, but he was released when Poland became a democracy. He'd come back to England. England was his home, it was the only country he knew. He came home to be taken care of; they'd stood him six months in a convalescent home and then invalided him out. The psychiatric report said he was unstable after his experience. He had been one of Harry's men. When he came out of the nursing home, Harry paid for him to go on holiday to Scotland with his girlfriend. Scotland was good for the soul. You get a sense of perspective in the glens. You see that you're small and the world is big and nothing's that important. Jan was braver than the cowboys, because he had to be in place ahead of them and that meant a greater risk of being caught.

Harry had seen the medical report and chucked it into the waste-paper basket. It hadn't stopped the Service from ditching Jan. Not long after, Jan's girlfriend left him for someone with a City job and a smart little pad in the Barbican. Jan went to work for a Polish charity.

Harry came back with the drink. 'How are you?'

The Pole shrugged. 'I'm fine, very busy.' He had an engaging smile. 'Busy doing nothing much, but I get paid and I get by. And today was your last day, Harry?'

Jan hadn't been invited to the lunch. Oakham had registered that with silent fury.

'Yes,' he offered Jan a cigarette; the Pole refused it. His lungs were damaged. He had to ration his smoking very carefully.

'I'm now officially retired. I can catch my train back to Woking and sit on my arse till I get a coronary from boredom. Or take one of those part-time jobs a grateful department fixes up. Cigarette money's what they pay. And they've done you a favour. No thanks.'

He was letting the bitterness show; Jan knew him so well. Too well. He was a dangerous man when he was angry.

'What *are* you going to do?' he asked.

The answer surprised him.

'Get rid of Peggy.'

Jan had never liked Harry's wife. They'd met a couple of times; he thought she was stupid and he knew she was unfaithful because Harry made a joke of it.

He said after a pause, 'It's about time. I don't know why you put up with it.'

'Because I had other things to think about. I don't want to live with her. She certainly doesn't want to live with me.' He grinned. 'She'll jump at the chance to get a bit of cash and go off with the lover boy. Whichever one it is at the moment. I need a refill.' He picked up his empty glass. 'Finish that up and have another. Then we'll get down to business.'

'What kind of business?' Jan spoke in a lower tone.

'Money business,' Harry Oakham said. 'Big money, for both of us. We've been together for a long time. Good times and bad, eh?'

Jan nodded, swallowed the last of his drink, looked up at Oakham.

'Yes; we worked well together, didn't we? You always stood by me, Harry. I'll never forget that.'

'It was mutual,' Oakham answered. 'Now we're both off the hook. We don't owe anyone a bloody thing. I've been planning for my retirement. I haven't been sitting on my hands, Jan, waiting for the kick in the backside. I've got a proposition. We'll talk about it later, over dinner.'

*　　*　　*

'Well,' Harry asked. 'What do you think of it?'

Jan wiped his mouth with his napkin. 'You really want my opinion?'

'I've offered you a partnership, what do you think I want?'

'I think you're crazy,' Jan said.

'Meaning you're not interested,' Harry said flatly.

'Of course I'm interested. I like crazy ideas. That's why the Department threw me out. But never as crazy as this one. I'll go in with you, Harry. All the way. But one question . . . '

There'd been a little pulse jumping in Oakham's neck when he thought Jan was going to turn him down. Now he smiled at him encouragingly.

'How are we going to get that kind of money?'

Oakham beckoned the waiter. 'Coffee and two Armagnacs, please.' Then he leaned forward. 'I've got the money.'

The Pole stared at him.

'I told you I haven't been sitting on my hands. I put out feelers and I got a response. I met our bankers two weeks ago.'

'In England?' Jan sucked in a deep breath. 'You took a risk like that?'

'No risk,' Oakham said blithely. 'I took Peggy's ghastly nephews on a boat to Hampton Court. The contact was made on that trip. The kids stuffed themselves with ice cream and I talked terms. We've got a guaranteed capital and they'll provide the money we need to set it up when I've got a team together. No money's passed till we can give them the experts. So it's up to you now. How long do you think it'll take?'

Jan frowned. 'To get in touch, not long. But to get them all together in one place – I don't know, Harry. They'll need convincing it's not a trick.'

'You were always good at talking people round,' Oakham said. 'You'll do it. Hook Rilke, and the rest will follow.'

'You really believe it? You really believe you can bring this off?'

'*We* can bring it off,' was the answer. 'They owe us, Jan. You gave them ten years of your life, and what did they do? Chuck you on the dust heap. I started in this game at twenty-four, fresh out of university. Full of ideas about saving the world from the Reds. And where's it got me? Out on my ear. I nearly bought it a dozen times, and then there was Judith.'

'I know,' Jan said quickly. 'Don't talk about it.'

'They bloody well owe me, too,' Harry said, 'And I'm going to collect. So are you. Thank you.' He spoke to the waiter. He poured coffee. 'We know Rilke's in Berlin, still living with his mother. See him first. When can you go?'

'Any time,' the Pole answered. 'But you'll have to finance me. Aid for Poland doesn't pay enough for travel.'

'Don't worry about the cash, I've got enough to fund us while we put the operation together. I'll open an account at the Midland for you tomorrow. What's your local branch?'

'Gloucester Road,' Jan answered.

He lived in a dingy bed-sit near the tube station.

He had never invited Harry to see him there. He was too proud.

'I'll put a decent float in,' Harry went on. 'Get yourself some new clothes, look prosperous. Book into a good hotel and don't stint when it comes to softening Rilke up. He's got to believe we've got backing, substance. If he thinks this is just an idea off the top of my head, he won't listen.'

'Can I mention the bankers?' Jan asked.

Harry considered for a moment. High-level people needed high-level counterparts.

'Libya is backing us,' he said. 'Gaddafi's a nut, he spends money like shelling peas. Rilke knows that. That'll do to start with. How about one for the road?'

'I'll be pissed,' Jan protested.

'So what? Tomorrow, my old friend, you get things moving.'

Harry Oakham caught the tube to Waterloo. He hated travelling on the underground. It was dirty and sleazy like so much of London. And dangerous too. He sat in the train as it moved off and thought he'd enjoy someone trying to mug him. He'd give them more than they bargained for. He wasn't drunk, he was smouldering inside.

His timing was right; it never failed him. He caught the last train home. The carriage was empty. It smelled stale and there was an empty can and some refuse under his seat. The can rolled by his foot as the train jerked into motion, and he stamped on it savagely, crushing it flat.

Twenty-eight years. He started with such high ideals; too late for the war but just right for the next phase in the conflict against a new and terrible enemy. Soviet Communism, swollen with power, strengthened by the weakness of Western political leaders. A tyranny as cruel and contrary to decent values as the horror of Nazism.

Harry saw himself as a soldier, and he brought a soldier's dedication to his job. He'd loved the danger, the challenge of going into the field. He knew what it meant to be afraid, only fools claimed to be without fear, and consequently they didn't last long. But it fired him with excitement, brought out the very best in a nature that was naturally daring, and with quick reactions. He hated the enemy, but he loved friends like Jan. The thought of Jan suffering in that hell-hole at Cracow had tortured him, and there was nothing he could do to help him.

He lost colleagues during those years of action, men and women he came to know, not all of whom he liked, but most he respected.

That was the hard part for Harry. But he endured it and offered himself for the next dangerous mission with extra zeal. And then he lost Judith and the world became a dark and bitter place. Seeing the portrait of the lovely actress in the club had brought her so vividly to his mind that night. She seemed very close to him while he was with Jan. It was a ghost that wouldn't lie quiet until he too was dead. He'd made a refuge for himself in his work; he asked for and was given the highest risk assignments and he seemed in possession of a charmed life. He couldn't get himself killed, but he performed a bloody service for his masters without a single doubt or qualm. He believed in the cause, because it was all he had left. And then the betrayal started. The compromises, the evasions, the politicians with their slimy hands on the controls, manipulating good men for their own advancement. Harry had watched in disbelief as he and those who served with him became unsavoury . . . a relic of an ugly era that was safely past.

The bureaucrats at the Treasury started cutting costs; he knew for a fact that two agents in Bucharest were sacrificed through lack of funds, when a decent bribe was needed.

Then the redundancies, or retirements, as they called it, began pushing the numbers down, impairing efficiency. Almost, Harry thought sometimes, as if it were a deliberate policy aimed at closing the section. Regardless of who got hurt. His anger grew inside him like an ulcer. It gnawed at him with impotent rage.

Jan's treatment was typical. They'd regret that; he'd sworn to set that right and he was going to do it. Now he had joined his old friend on the rubbish heap, and they expected him to take it like a good Civil Servant and retire gracefully into a world he'd never lived in. Put away the knife and the gun, and join his local golf club for excitement. Put his hands to a gentle use.

He looked down at them. They were clenched together. He relaxed, spreading his fingers. They were strong but sensitive and the gold signet ring on his little finger bore a rubbed crest.

The Oakhams of Dedham in Suffolk. The Army, the Church, the landed squirearchy going back for generations. There was blood on his hands, but he felt no shame. He didn't care. Towards the end his cover was blown, and he'd only just escaped capture by the very man he was now planning to recruit. Hermann Rilke, former head of East German Security. The big fish he was sending Jan out to hook and reel in.

The irony of it amused him. He'd played his part to the end, and nobody suspected that Harry Oakham was anything more dangerous than a middle-aged ex-operator with a maverick streak.

The train pulled in and he got out. It was very late. But the night was clear. He set off to walk home at a brisk pace. He had cat's eyes; darkness didn't bother him. He'd covered miles in hostile countryside in the old days, steering by the stars above him.

He swung into the road; it was well lit, tree lined. The pre-war semi-detached houses looked exactly like each other, all had pretty front gardens. He opened the front gate, found his key and put it in the lock.

If it all works out, he thought calmly, I'll never have to open this bloody door again. Or go upstairs to find she's asleep because she's shagged out after someone else. Not that I give a damn!

He undressed and climbed into the bed. Peggy lay breathing deeply beside him. I don't hate her, he thought, as he drifted off to sleep. I hate myself for putting her in Judith's place. But then grief made me a bit mad. It's not much of an excuse, but it's the only one I've got.

'What sort of course?' James Bennet asked.

Rosa hated lying to him, but it couldn't be helped.

She said lightly, 'Everyone's gone overboard about the EEC and all the changes coming. So the Chief's decided to have some of us go on this seminar. It's only a week, darling.'

He made a real effort. 'I could come and stay at a hotel on the weekend,' he suggested.

'Oh, I wish you could,' she said quickly. She laid a hand on his knee. 'I'd love it, you know that, but honestly, darling, it would be terribly boring for you. We'll be flat out working; it's a very tight schedule. I won't have a moment of free time.'

He shrugged; she could see he was angry. She smiled encouragingly at him. 'We could slip away for a few days when I get back. Go somewhere for a weekend like we used to – remember the sweet little hotel at Fordingbridge where you tried teaching me to fish?'

He knew she was trying to make amends; he knew how hard she had been trying since that night when they had tried to recapture the past.

He tried to admire her for the effort; he even tried to respond, but it only made him feel guilty and resentful.

He remembered the Fordingbridge hotel only too well. She had burst into tears trying to take a hook out of the fish's mouth, and he'd laughed and hugged her for being so soft-hearted. They'd been so happy before her bloody career came between them.

They were driving along the Embankment on their way to a dinner party with one of his colleagues. A very senior colleague, and it was an important invitation. He and Rosa were being inspected with a view to his promotion.

Rosa had been enthusiastic, anxious to do him credit. They were slowing down for the turning and she looked at him.

His face was set and unsmiling. Still angry about the course. She'd dreaded having to tell him, even more because of the timing. But it was mandatory. A high-security seven days at Branksome with lectures and practical training that had nothing to do with EEC regulations.

Instead, she had concentrated on this dinner, on the prospects for his career. He must be in line for a partnership, she suggested, and he'd admitted grudgingly that it was possible.

She had bought a new dress, skipped lunch to get to a good hairdresser, and hoped that he would be pleased. He hadn't even said she looked nice when she came downstairs.

'Let's do that,' she said. 'Let's go off somewhere.'

'I don't know,' James said. 'Depends on the office.'

He pulled into Cheyne Walk and parked the car. Rosa walked ahead of him up the steps of the handsome Georgian house.

She looked very good, he admitted. She'd chosen a long silk dress that showed off her figure, and wore her hair twisted up into a sleek knot. A minimum of jewellery, although he'd given her some striking pieces. It wouldn't do to outshine the senior partner's wife. Rosa, the perfect diplomat, he thought, and felt suddenly angry.

'What date is this course?'

She turned, reaching for the doorbell. Oh God, she thought, perhaps he won't remember . . . 'The seventeenth, just for the week.'

He didn't say anything. The bell rang; she pressed hard because she was nervous and she could hear it shrilling inside the house.

Then the door opened and a white-coated Filipino ushered them into the hall. James introduced her to the host and hostess.

'Philip, I think you've met my wife.'

They shook hands and the older man smiled down at Rosa.

'Of course, you came to one of our dinners last year. My wife Joyce.'

'How do you do.' Rosa had a charming smile and the older woman liked her handshake. She couldn't bear a limp paw.

The party was successful; it was a dinner party for twelve, and the food and wine were chosen with originality and care.

Rosa admired the splendid flower arrangements, and knew she'd said the right thing because the hostess admitted she always did the flowers herself. The house was elegant, with fine furniture and expensive pictures.

James looked round him, mellowed by after-dinner brandy. This was the future he planned for himself. He would end up as senior partner in the firm, he was sure of that. He'd give smart parties for business colleagues with a beautiful wife at his side to support him.

They'd have a splendid town house and a place in the country for weekends. And children to make it a real family.

He was an only child himself and he longed to give his children everything that he'd missed in his own isolated upbringing. Prep school at seven, boarding school at thirteen; parents who shunted him off to stay here and there because they had other things to do than amuse him during the holidays. He'd grown up tough, determined to prove himself and to shape his own life differently.

When he met Rosa he couldn't believe his luck that she was unattached. So bright, ravishingly pretty, sexy, loving. He'd cast her into the role of wife and mother and swept her into marriage.

She was charming with people; the senior partner's wife had singled her out. Rosa didn't make other women jealous. In spite of her looks she posed no threat and instinctively they knew it. She wasn't interested in flirting. He thought furiously, she wasn't interested in anything but her career.

The seventeenth for a week. He wasn't going to say anything, but the nineteenth was their wedding anniversary. She'd be away on her course, too busy to spare him an evening. Too busy to remember that on that date, five years ago, she'd promised to love him and share his life.

He'd bought her a pair of diamond earrings. He'd booked a night at a famous country hotel just outside

Windsor and planned to surprise her on the morning. James never forgot birthdays or anniversaries. They mattered to him because quite often dates like that had been forgotten when he was growing up.

'It was such a good party,' Rosa said as they drove home. It was nearly midnight and London was quiet, the streets empty of traffic. 'She does everything so well,' she went on.

'Yes,' he answered. 'Joyce is a great asset. He's lucky this time round.'

'You never told me he'd been married before.'

'I didn't know her. She went off with someone else, I think.' His tone closed the subject.

Rosa was driving; he didn't want to risk it after drinking brandy.

'Did you enjoy it, James? You seem a bit tired, darling.'

'It was good fun . . . ' He yawned and let the sentence fade.

He hadn't remembered their anniversary. Rosa felt light-headed with relief. He would have said something. Afterwards she'd remind him and think of something special to make up for it. After all, their second year he'd had to go on a trip to Hong Kong . . .

'Well, I thoroughly enjoyed myself,' Rosa said. 'They were terribly nice to both of us. I'm sure you'll be offered the partnership. Why don't we go and celebrate?' He turned to look at her.

'Why don't we go to Annabel's for a drink? It's not that late, it's only ten past twelve. It'd be fun.'

She was smiling at him expectantly. She hadn't

remembered the date. She'd spend their wedding anniversary with her Foreign Office friends. She was so unaware of what she'd done, he could have hit her.

They used to go to the chic night-club twice a week when they first met. Drink champagne and dance together; it was their foreplay before going back to his flat to make love. But not now.

He settled back and closed his eyes. He said, 'Sorry, Rosa, but I've got a hell of a lot of work tomorrow. We'll do it another time.'

When they got home he went upstairs without his usual nightcap and turned his back on her when she got into bed.

2

Hermann Rilke let himself into the apartment. It was different from the spacious, comfortable duplex on Potsdammen Platz he'd shared with his mother for the last fifteen years. But the accommodation ended with the job and his pension didn't run to more than a modest three-bedroomed third-floor flat on the Eser Strasse. It was a noisy street in an unfashionable suburb of what used to be East Berlin, and his mother hated it. She complained about the central heating, the stairs, the surly attitude of the caretaker. And, of course, the loss of the official car. Rilke made excuses. She was old, she wasn't prepared for the drop in their living standards. He didn't mind so much, he was ascetic by nature. He had simple needs. But he minded for his mother. Even when she blamed him he was patient.

She heard the front door open and called out to him.

'Hermann?'

'I'm here, Mutti,' he called back.

He went into the sitting room, hanging his jacket on a hook in the front hall. He was very tidy. His mother had brought him up to be neat and he was obsessive about order. In the old days there was hell to pay if any object on his desk was a centimetre out of line.

36

He bent down and kissed his mother on the cheek. She had white hair and she smelled of face powder and cologne. That smell was his earliest memory of her when she held him as a boy.

'There's a letter for you,' she told him. 'Came by messenger. It's over there.' Rilke took up the envelope and saw that it was addressed with his name and his old rank.

'What is it? Who's it from?' His mother always wanted to know everything.

'I don't know,' he answered. 'I'll open it and see.'

'I suppose you didn't get the job?'

'No,' he admitted. 'They wanted a younger man.'

He'd trained as an accountant before he joined the Security Services. Sometimes she wished he'd never changed careers.

'I don't know how we're going to manage if you don't get something soon.'

She had bright blue eyes and they focused angrily upon her son. What a fool to get himself dismissed from that wonderful job in the Ministry. Losing their nice apartment, the car, all the privileges that made life so comfortable. Now nobody wanted to employ him. The world was so changed since the two Germanies had merged into one nation. And not for the better in Frau Hilda's opinion. The stability, the discipline had gone. Now it was anarchy, with people running round doing and saying anything they liked . . . and how rich those Westerners were. She would always separate them in her mind. And her son had been such a devoted servant of the East German State, he couldn't fit into the new system. That's what he'd told her. He couldn't compromise his ideals.

Not realizing the consequences, she'd agreed with him. Now she blamed him. He was a good son and he'd always looked after her, but she still scolded him as if he were a child.

'What's the letter say?' She raised her voice, demanding an answer.

There was no signature on the single sheet of paper. Just a code word. His sallow face had become even paler.

'Someone wants to see me,' he said.

'A job? Decent money?'

'It doesn't give details,' Rilke answered, taking his time, not listening to her.

He read the letter again. 'Contact me at Hotel Prosser if you are interested in a substantial sum of money. My room number is eight-seven. Between six-thirty and nine this evening.' And the code word at the bottom: 'Freedom'. He had reason to know it. Only the British with their unpleasant sense of humour, would have given such a name to that particular operation.

'Well, it must say something,' his mother insisted.

'I've to ring them this evening.' She looked irritated and he compromised. 'It mentions good money.'

'Then take it, whatever it is,' she snapped at him. 'I won't last another winter in this wretched place. I had one cold after another from January on. I'd like a cup of coffee, Hermann. I was too tired to make myself lunch.'

'You mustn't miss meals,' he said anxiously. 'You know it's bad for you.'

'Bring me some biscuits then,' she said. 'And don't forget to make that call!'

She drank the coffee and ate the sweet chocolate biscuits. He'd gone into the hall to telephone. She wouldn't hear anything.

He came back and said, 'I'm going out for a while. I'm meeting someone. I'll be back in good time to make your supper. So don't you worry. I'll tell you if there's good news when I come home.'

She reached out a hand and squeezed his affectionately. She smiled up at him.

'You're a good boy, Hermann,' she said. 'It's about time you had some luck.'

Peggy Oakham looked at him across the kitchen table. He'd been at home for nearly three weeks and she didn't know how much longer she could stand it. She'd set the cereal, orange juice and toast on the table and he'd opened the morning paper. She'd kept busy, and managed to slip away and see her friend a few times, but it was nerve-racking, having Harry at home all day. He did nothing so far as she knew but read, watch television and make phone calls. He hadn't mentioned getting a job.

She buttered toast for herself and thought how miserable she felt. Ten years of misery. He wasn't deliberately cruel; he just treated her as if she was the worst mistake he'd ever made. They'd nothing in common, she realized that now, but when they first met he'd seemed such a sexy man, with a nice voice and lovely manners.

She'd had a lot of boyfriends. Working in a restaurant made it easy to meet men. She let Oakham pick her up and take her out. It wasn't long before she went to bed with him. She was a romantic girl who always bracketed sex with being in love, even when it was short-lived. He was different. He dressed differently to most of the men she knew. He had a job in a Ministry, she wasn't too sure what he did, but it was important and he had to travel abroad a lot. They married very quietly in a register office. She'd been disappointed about that, she'd imagined a white wedding with bridesmaids and a white Rolls to take her to the church, but he'd been married before and he didn't want that sort of thing. She finished her toast. His paper rustled as he turned a page.

It was the first wife that started the trouble. She was jealous because he wouldn't talk about her. He kept her private, and it made Peggy feel angry and left out. It wasn't her fault she'd died. He wouldn't talk about that either. If he still minded, then he couldn't love *her*, she reasoned. She had begun to nag, to pick at the subject like a sore.

And then one day they had a row and she went too far. Oakham had started to shake her. He shook her till she screamed.

And then he said, 'You ever say anything like that about Judith again and I'll break your bloody neck.'

He'd never been violent again. He'd just stopped sleeping with her and put the barriers up. So she'd looked round for comfort. She needed it. She couldn't live in that vacuum. She was a warm person, a human being, not like him.

And over the years she got careless. If he knew he didn't mind. He didn't care enough to mind, and that hurt too. I hate him, Peggy thought. I really do.

She said, 'Are you going out today?'

He went on reading the paper for a moment and then looked at her over the top.

'Yes. I'll be away for a day or two. You won't mind that, will you? Give you time to play some bridge.'

She had a sympathetic girlfriend who covered for her when she was seeing the current boyfriend. She'd say, 'I'll be round at Madge's, she wants me to make up a four.' Once, when Harry checked up, Madge had said brightly, 'We're just in the middle of a rubber – Peggy'll call you back.' Harry knew what she was doing and it wasn't playing cards. And Peggy knew that he saw through the lie. She went pink.

'Why didn't you say anything? Where're you going?'

The paper was folded and put down.

'To Suffolk,' Harry answered. 'I've heard of a job.'

Now the pink had turned to an angry red.

'Suffolk? What sort of a job? Why do you never tell me anything? I'm not moving to bloody Suffolk.'

'I haven't asked you to,' he remarked. 'Don't start shouting, Peggy. My cousin Liz told me about it. It sounded rather interesting.'

Cousin Liz; she bristled, remembering the snobbish cow in the big house who'd looked down her nose at her when they were introduced. His family had made her feel small, she thought bitterly, measuring her up against the first wife, putting their noses in the air.

'Well, that's nice for you,' she said. 'Never mind about me. What sort of a job?'

She was on the defensive, hating to ask, but the money was important . . . the pension was a joke and she didn't even know how much redundancy he'd got.

'Catering,' he answered. 'There's a job in a local hotel. I'm going up to see it and stay with Liz and Peter. I knew you wouldn't want to come.'

'Stay with your stuck-up bloody relatives? No thank you! What do you know about hotels? It sounds a waste of time. If you want to go on a jaunt, why don't you say so? Catering!' she sneered, reaching for the coffee pot.

'If I take it,' he ignored the jibe, 'it wouldn't suit you to move, would it?'

She snapped back, 'No, too right it wouldn't,' and then felt he'd tricked her into saying it. 'Why don't you look for something round here? Go down to the Job Centre, *do* something instead of sitting round all day? Oh God, Suffolk, I ask you!'

She pushed her chair back. She didn't want the coffee, she didn't want to sit there trying to pierce the armour-plating. She couldn't rile him, or hurt him.

She stood by the table and said suddenly, 'Why did you marry me?'

He was looking at her and he shook his head. 'I honestly don't know. Look, I'm going in about ten minutes. Nothing may come of it, so don't work

yourself up. I'll let you know when I'm coming back.
I don't want to muck up your social engagements.'

He left the kitchen.

'You shit,' she said under her breath and started
stacking the dirty breakfast china. Her eyes had filled
with tears. I'll ring Dave the minute he's gone, she
told herself. We'll go out somewhere and have a
meal and come back here . . . 'The shit,' she whispered again, and wiped her eyes.

He packed lightly; how often he'd chucked a few
things in a bag and flown off, or gone with nothing
but what was on his back . . . under the wire, over
the Wall . . . now he was making the trip for himself.
He left the house without seeing his wife. She'd be
on the phone to the lover before he was halfway
down the road. It was a lovely day and he whistled
as he drove to Heathrow. It was going to work out.
He was confident, excited. Jan had called him the
day before. It was all set. Geneva was the meeting
place. He had booked on the eleven o'clock flight.
For a moment his thoughts turned to the sordid
squabble in the kitchen. She'd fallen into the trap
so easily. She wouldn't move to Suffolk. She'd said
so, and there'd be no change of mind when he put
the terms in front of her. He would be generous. She
could have the house and the rest of his savings. He
didn't feel mean towards her, just a huge, wearying
indifference, with the faintest tinge of guilt because
he'd married her in the first place. She'd have settled
down with a different man, maybe cheated once or
twice, she was very oversexed, but with children
she'd have made the best of it. No children for

43

him. He'd been firm about that. A widow was bad enough, but he wouldn't leave any orphans . . . thank God, as things had turned out.

The man had finished dressing. He smoothed his hair and cleared his throat before he spoke to the woman lying on the bed.

'How about tomorrow? I've got a business lunch, but I'm free for two hours in the afternoon. Please?'

She was very beautiful. She reminded him of a magnificent animal; a lioness, he thought, staring down at the naked body, arms stretched up behind her mane of thick blonde hair. She smiled up at him, and slowly raised herself off the bed. She wanted him to plead, to beg. She knew how much he liked that.

'Just two hours,' he wheedled. 'I'll bring you something very nice. Something special.'

He came close and caught her hands.

'Don't make me kneel,' he whispered. 'Don't make me crawl, darling.'

Suddenly she dug her nails into his hands. He gave a cry of pain and let go. That was part of the game. He looked down and saw that she'd drawn blood. 'You bitch!' he mumbled.

She had turned away from him slipping on panti-hose and a silk shift, sliding her feet into high-heeled shoes.

'I can't see you tomorrow, Gustav, I'm going away for a few days.'

She sat down at the dressing-table and began brushing her hair. She watched him through the mirror. She hated him, but then she hated them

44

all. The masochists like this one who wanted to be bullied and humiliated before they could get potent, the other type who liked to be rough, the mummy's boys who had breast fetishes and paid to sit on her lap and fondle and talk baby-talk. Even the straight ones who wanted good sex and tried to please her. But they paid. They paid big money for Monika. And Monika paid out big money for protection. Not to a pimp. There wasn't a pimp born who could have run her, and the idea made her laugh. Another kind of protection. From the hit and run driver, the professional waiting round the corner with a knife. More and more money and no guarantee that it would be enough in the end. The client was sucking at his palms.

'I'm bleeding,' he reproached her. 'Why did you do that?'

'Because you bore me,' she said not turning round.

'Don't say that,' he pleaded, enjoying himself. 'I only want to please you. Let me come tomorrow . . . please.'

She stood up. She was very tall. She towered over him.

'My money,' she reminded him. 'You owe me Gustav. You're not coming again till you pay me.'

'I've got it here,' he fumbled in his coat pocket, took out an envelope. 'Cash, darling. Count it.'

'I can't be bothered,' she shrugged and threw the envelope down unopened. 'You wouldn't cheat me. I'd never see you again if it was one franc short. You know that.'

He adjusted his tie, buttoned his jacket again.

'Are you really going away?'

'I told you.'

He was jealous; he knew she had other clients but he didn't like to think of sharing her with anyone. He'd been coming to see her for over a year.

'Are you going alone?'

She draped a heavy gold necklace round her neck and fitted earrings into her ears. She looked at herself in the mirror.

'I'm going to visit my mother in Grasse,' she said. 'Now goodbye, Gustav darling. Your time is up.'

She opened the front door and stood waiting. He paused for a moment.

'Two days. That's Thursday then. I'll telephone. I saw a nice brooch in Boucheron's window.'

'I don't want a brooch. Think of something else. Surprise me.'

She smiled down at him.

'I will,' he promised, and hurried out. She saw him get into the elevator and then shut the door.

There was another man coming in an hour. He always took her out to dinner first. And she insisted on a top restaurant. The Tour d'Argent, Maxims, sometimes the Grill Room at the Ritz. She had to be seen, to be on display. And to look exactly what she was: one of the most expensive *poules de luxe* in Paris. The grovelling Gustav, whose name dominated the biggest fashion store in the Rue St Honore, was a noted bully and tyrant to his staff and his family. Tonight she would dine with an even richer businessman, pretend to listen while he talked about his business and himself, and then go home and bear with his equally boring sexual activities.

At ten o'clock the next morning she would be on the flight to Geneva. The note had enclosed an airline ticket and the name of a hotel.

It wasn't the few sentences with the magical promise of money that had persuaded her to use that ticket and go.

There had been no signature. Just one word. 'Freedom.' That was why she was catching the flight.

Oakham enjoyed flying. He had no nerves, his imagination was untroubled by what might happen at thirty thousand feet and five hundred miles an hour if anything went wrong. He'd flown in everything, from twin seaters bouncing like toys in turbulence to the heavy military aircraft that spewed you out on the end of a parachute. Concorde had been the best. A trip to the States on a job where time was the prime factor and he'd been allowed to travel in style for a change. One of his best operatives had been so scared of flying that he vomited before getting on a plane. He'd disappeared in Amsterdam, of all the bloody places to get killed. He'd been a good man too. Amsterdam was as dangerous as it was dirty, full of human refuse and the rats that fed on them. Geneva was beautiful. He loved Switzerland, he loved the cleanness, the mountains, the majestic lakes. He'd done a lot of business in Switzerland when he was assigned the desk job.

He took a taxi to the Hotel d'Angleterre. It was smart but not over-expensive, a place patronized by the better-paid business executives. He registered under another name; it matched the passport he carried. He hadn't handed everything back when he gave in his keys ... He went up to the third floor and looked round the room.

'This is very nice,' he said to the boy who'd brought up his luggage, and gave him a good tip. It was comfortable, it had a pleasant outlook. He tried out the bed. Excellent.

Jan was due in that afternoon. Oakham unpacked, had a hot shower and went down to lunch. He was spending money, but it was his own money this time. No tight-arsed Civil Servant looking at every item on his expenses, querying this and that. He was going to have money to spend. Money to burn if he felt like making a bonfire out of it. He wasn't going to fail because he had never failed in his profession, except once. He didn't mean to think of Judith. She floated into his mind before he could stop her. The blonde hair swinging like silk round her shoulders, the blue of a summer sky in her eyes as she looked at him and laughed. They'd laughed such a lot together. He thrust her away, back to the graveyard of old memories.

At four o'clock Jan came up to his room. Harry let him in.

The Pole said, 'We're in business.'

He grinned at Oakham; he looked excited. 'Big business. I got Rilke to come with me.'

'Well done,' Oakham said in admiration. 'That's our ace. Well done.'

'The others will be here tomorrow morning. I said

we'd meet at eleven o'clock. I said to ask for the D.H. Co. representative. Which is me.'

'I've booked a small private room for the conference. Lunch served privately. The hotel have provided a screen and a video. It all looks very businesslike. Have a drink, Jan, old fellow. Scotch? I'll get something special sent up. How about a bloody good twelve-year-old malt, eh?'

'Fine by me,' the Pole said. Oakham was moving round the room, ordering the drinks, smiling at him. He was always restless when he was keyed up. Jan had seen him like it before an operation. Like a big cat scenting an unsuspecting kill.

'Water ... No, plain water and no ice,' Harry was saying into the phone. He turned and grinned at Jan.

'Don't want to spoil the flavour, do we – nothing like a good malt. Now, tell me about Rilke! How the hell did you persuade him to come *with* you?'

'I told him you wanted to talk to him first, before the others. I laid it on, Harry. How important he was, how senior. You know what a vain swine he is. He couldn't resist it. He expected to meet you tonight. He didn't like it when I said it was tomorrow, early morning. He's booked into the Alexandre. I said I'd take him out to dinner and we'd go to some club afterwards.'

'He'll want boys,' Harry remarked. 'Don't let him get too shagged out. He's got to have a clear head tomorrow.'

Jan grimaced. 'Don't worry, I'll look after the little swine.'

Oakham said easily, 'Some of our gays were bloody good. Forget the prejudice. Give him a good time and don't stint on the money. I want him sweet and greedy when we meet up.'

When the Scotch arrived he filled their glasses and they raised them in a toast.

'Here's to the future.'

Georg Werner kissed his twin sons good night. He was a loving and dutiful father and a good husband. His wife, Erna, watched from the doorway. They were good boys, she thought, and they loved their papa coming to read to them and settle them down for the night.

He closed the door and they went downstairs together.

'How long will you be gone?' she asked.

'I'm not sure,' he answered. 'Two days, maybe less. Depends on how the meeting goes. I'll telephone you.'

She smiled at him.

'They haven't sent you anywhere for some time now. The break will do you good. You get so bored being stuck in the Ministry.'

He put his arm round her as they went into their sitting room. It was a large, light room, well decorated with modern pictures and Italian furniture. His wife had taste. He was proud of how she looked and how she managed his home and the children. She was right. More so than she would ever know. He hadn't been sent abroad for a long time. He'd been given nothing important to do beyond his minimum brief.

No chance to shine, no hint of promotion, and he was still in his forties. Everything had changed. He had wasted the best years of his life for nothing.

'I'll get us a drink.' His wife went to the bottles ranged on an angular, black-glass table. 'Why don't I come to the airport with you? Surely the car can drop me back?'

'I'm not taking an official car,' Werner explained. He took a vodka on the rocks and sipped it. 'It's a confidential meeting, I told you. I've ordered a taxi. Come and sit down and tell me what you've been doing.'

The twins had come out of school to go to the dentist. Albrecht had been brave, little Georg had cried. She'd had lunch with two women friends . . . He wasn't listening. He was glad of the vodka and finished it quickly. It helped settle his nerves. He could still pull back. It wasn't too late.

He hadn't been contacted for such a long time it shocked him when he got the message. Something had come up which he should consider for his own sake. The airline ticket, the address of the hotel, and the code word.

It wasn't Freedom, in his case.

Harry had gone into the small conference room early. He sat at the table. Everything was set up. A screen and video, notepads, pencils at each place, mineral water and cigarettes. A discreet bowl of fresh flowers on the side. Small but impressive. A professional scene set up for people who were supreme professionals.

Five of them. He'd picked very carefully. His Libyan banker had nodded as he named them, while his wife's awful nephews slobbered their ice creams.

Hermann Rilke. That was one to conjure with. Head of the East German Security for the past sixteen years. An expert in counter espionage and interrogation. His success rate among Allied and American agents had been awesome. His name inspired pure terror among his own population. Rilke was a committed Stalinist, the confidant of Honecker, a protégé of Adolph Gorst, his former chief.

A vicious man who enjoyed inflicting pain. Jan had called him a swine. He could imagine how Jan had hated entertaining him, indulging his perverted appetites. Jan was a good old-fashioned prude at heart.

Oakham thought of him with affection. Traces of the strict Catholic upbringing remained in him. It was a hellish religion. It never let go completely . . . He hadn't been affected by his family's mild Anglicanism. He didn't give a damn about Rilke's private life. Rilke's skill and availability were what interested him.

Vassily Zarubin. The brilliant young tactician, the KGB schoolmaster who set their recruits the final exams. He was in his late thirties but his heart was with the iron men of the Soviet past. His father had been a stalwart of the old tyrant, Brezhnev. He was retired and the son had taken his job and done it even better. He played chess at masters level for relaxation.

Georg Werner, good-looking, sociable, a charming post-war West German diplomat. He'd been a Communist sleeper in the West German Foreign Ministry for the last twenty years.

Then there was the Israeli, Daniel Ishbav. Oakham had hesitated about him.

He had worked for Mossad as a specialist in kidnapping. And then taken Syrian money to finance his love of women and gambling. He'd kept both sides going, betraying and counter-betraying to keep the balance till a captured Syrian agent led Mossad to look inside their own ranks. Daniel had got away before they reached him. For two years he had been hiding in Iraq; now Iraq wasn't safe any more and he had slipped into England via Turkey. His money was running out; Harry knew about him because London had been keeping an eye on him. They didn't want his specialist skills offered to an organization like the IRA.

And then, Oakham grinned to himself, the only lady in the happy band of international brothers. Monika Van Heflin. A handsome name for a very handsome lady indeed. The Venus Fly Trap was her nickname, and she enjoyed it so much, she went out and bought herself a plant. So legend said. The sixties had spawned some aberrations among the prosperous middle classes in Holland as well as Germany, Italy and Japan. The children of the affluent and respectable took to murder and subversion, cloaking themselves in a crazed Communism. The Red Brigade had recruited Monika at seventeen. She was a student in Amsterdam, the pretty blonde daughter of a fashionable psychiatrist. She had specialized in killing men after she had slept with them, Monika could bring death and terror to selected targets who were otherwise well protected.

She was a beautiful woman; Oakham had seen photographs of her. But not recently. The terror groups had dispersed. The leaders had been caught, imprisoned, and were now forgotten. Monika had eased out in time. She had worked for the criminal element in Paris – some said for the French Secret Service itself, and done discreet jobs for the CIA. For the last few years she had lived off the highest level of prostitution, protected by the organizations who had used her. The whisper was that the protection was coming to an end.

A rich diversity of talents, nationalities, ages, loyalties – all very different. But they all had one thing in common with Harry Oakham and each other. Which was why they were coming to Geneva to meet him.

Jan had brought Rilke up to the conference room early. Harry came to shake hands with him. He'd never met the man, but he'd seen photographs. And he'd debriefed some of his handiwork. What was left of them. Rilke was short and wiry, with dark, angry eyes set deep in his head. His forehead bulged outward. He had a sallow skin, pockmarked with old acne scars, and a thin moustache above narrow lips. He had what Harry described as a wet-fish handshake, which surprised him.

He said, in excellent English, almost without accent, 'Good morning. I've followed your career with admiration, Mr Oakham. It's nice to meet you face to face.'

'It's nice to meet you too,' Harry answered. 'I've been following your career too; trying to catch up, but not very successfully. You were too good for us.'

He was a vain little skunk; Jan was right. He smirked at the compliment.

'From a professional of your standing, that's high praise.'

'Take a seat,' Harry suggested.

He must have learned his English at the Potsdam special language school.

He didn't waste time on small talk. Rilke had only been given fifteen minutes before the others were expected.

'Jan has briefed you on the general idea. I'd like your comments.'

Rilke poured a glass of water. He did it deliberately. The message was clear. I'm not committed to anything. I'm not going to ask any questions till you've given me more information.

'Ploekewski discussed a general principle,' he said. 'But it was very loose. No specifics. Just enough to interest me. But I want to know much more before I stay for any meeting.'

Oakham had expected him to make conditions. But he wasn't going to have the time.

'I have my own position to consider.'

Harry changed tactics.

'And what position is that?' he asked pleasantly. 'I understand that you have been honourably retired.

Or dishonourably, I should say. After all your years of brilliant service, you've been kicked out. And nobody's been anxious to employ you. You've taken quite a drop in living standards.'

That stung. Rilke's cheeks reddened.

'I chose retirement,' he snapped back. 'I couldn't work under the new system.'

He stubbed out his cigarette. Jan flashed a warning look and Harry laid a hand on Rilke's arm as he began to push his chair back.

'Don't walk out till you see what's on offer. I can promise you, you won't regret it.'

Rilke looked at him. 'I'm not committed. Or compromised in any way?'

'No more than any of us,' was the answer. 'Damn,' he protested, as the telephone rang. 'We've wasted time.'

Jan answered the call.

'They're here,' he said to Oakham.

There was a man ahead of Georg Werner at the reception desk in the Hotel d'Angleterre. He heard him ask for the same contact name, the D.H. Company, and Werner drew back.

He was younger than Werner. Very spare in his ill-cut suit, tall and dark with broad cheeks and black eyes that hinted at Eastern blood. Armenian probably. He'd spoken with a Russian accent.

Werner followed him across the lobby and stood waiting for the lift. He felt nervous; he kept pulling at his jacket as if it didn't fit properly. The lift came level with them and the doors slid open.

The tall Russian got in, Werner on his heels. Just before the doors closed a woman came hurrying up, followed by a small swarthy man who caught Werner's eye because he wore a bilious tie in greens and yellows. The lift was closed and Werner pressed number three. He glanced round him at the others. He smelled the woman's expensive scent.

The Russian said, 'I'm going to the third floor.'

The small man with the garish tie grunted, 'Me too.' The woman nodded; she had a lovely face, expertly made-up.

When the lift stopped all three got out. Georg Werner stood hesitating, looking up and down the corridor.

It was the Russian who took the initiative. He had that kind of authority.

'The D.H. Company is room twenty-one,' he said. 'I think it is down on the right.'

He didn't look round to see if they were following. He knew they were.

'I can tell you who's joining us,' Oakham said. 'Vassily Zarubin.' He saw the German's eyes narrow at the name.

'A German diplomat who's been one of your sleepers since he left university – Georg Werner – Deputy Under Secretary of the West German Foreign Ministry that was, and someone outside your theatre – an Israeli, name of Ishbav, ex-Mossad, ex-Syrian spy. Ex-everything by the sound of him. And a lady. I didn't want to be sexist about this.'

He laughed. The door opened and Jan appeared.

They were all on time. Punctuality was part of the code. They glanced at him, and then at Rilke and each other. He saw Georg Werner stiffen and turn pale. But Jan had closed the door. There was no going back for Werner, just because he'd come face to face with Rilke. The woman came in last. She was tall, with a cashmere throw emphasizing her height, expensive clothes and a pervasive scent that wafted towards them as she moved. Jan introduced her to Oakham first.

'This is Monika,' he said.

'Hello,' he shook a hand in a soft glove.

Unlike Rilke she gripped hard. She had a lovely face, but so had many women who could afford the presentation. What made her different was that every man in the room, except Rilke, felt like sex as soon as she came near them. She had a pleasant, rather throaty voice with a slight accent.

'Hello, Mr Oakham. Gentlemen.'

She smiled at them and sat down where the Pole indicated.

Harry took his place at the head of the table.

'Before we begin our meeting, would anyone like coffee? Or a drink?'

No-one wanted anything. The atmosphere was tense. Rilke lit another cigarette. Vassily Zarubin smoked a Russian cigarette that made Jan cough. They waited, and Werner picked up one of the pencils laid out with a notepad in front of him and tapped it nervously on the table top.

Harry Oakham stood up. He didn't smile.

He said, 'I'd like to welcome you. I'm glad to

see you here, and I won't waste your time talking a lot of balls. You know who I am and I know who you are. We're all in the same business. We've been on different sides, but we're on the same side now. I'll put my position first.'

He looked round at them. Rilke; the cold-eyed Russian; the suave diplomat fiddling with the pencil; the dark Israeli in the gaudy tie, who hadn't taken his eyes off Monika.

'I was recruited from the Army,' Oakham said. 'I joined our Security Services when I was twenty-four. I went through the training and it was tough. But so was I. I did a lot of personal jobs, and I headed several teams. We had assignments in East Berlin, in Bonn, in Poland – Jan was with me over there, and I operated in the United States once or twice. Without the co-operation of our American allies, I might add. I didn't rate their discretion too highly. I was given a job and I did it. Nobody forced me; nobody forced any of *you*. We all chose our professions. We knew the risks. Some of us thought what we were doing justified the things we did. I put my life on the line for the best part of twenty years. I lost friends. I made a lot of enemies too.'

For a moment he mocked them, his old opponents sitting listening to him.

'For the last eight years I've been desk-bound. I didn't take the personal risks any more, but I had to send out other people who did. In a way, I found that harder. But – it was my job, so I did it. This must sound familiar to all of you. Not all of us were action men. But Daniel was, for instance.'

He turned to the Israeli.

'You organized the snatches for Mossad. Everyone knows what the PLO did to an Israeli agent if they caught them. The Jehalil Sons of Allah dismembered you piecemeal while you were still alive. And Monika—' She smiled at him when he looked at her across the table. 'Monika was an idealist. It wasn't a very pretty ideal and it inspired people to do some very ugly things. But you believed in it. You killed for it, but you risked a life sentence in one of those West German women's prisons where most of the high-risk political prisoners end up committing suicide.

'And you, Herr Werner?' Oakham paused.

The others were staring at the Dutchwoman. He regained their attention.

'You've been a Soviet sleeper since you joined the West German Foreign Ministry. You had a good career, a promising future. But you'd given your allegiance and you went on living an indefinite lie, waiting for the summons to serve, didn't you? You weren't an action man, Werner, but it takes a special kind of courage to lie low for years, waiting to be caught out . . . We knew all about you, of course. We got a tip from an East German source and we passed it on to Bonn. They didn't do anything about you. They'd have picked you up the moment you were activated. Didn't you ever feel the eyes on the back of your neck?'

The German shook his head. He was pale instead of flushed.

'So that's what we have in common round this

table. We're professionals. Experts in our different fields. Jan was my co-ordinator. They call it logistics now. Rilke – you made an art out of interrogation. You reached refinements of technique that nobody had ever thought of. Zarubin – you've never had a public face, but you didn't need one. You play the Intelligence game like you play chess. Like your father did before you.

'We've given long and faithful service according to our skills. If there was a dirty job, a political foul-up which wasn't of our making, a mind-blowing Intelligence problem to be solved, our masters dropped it in our laps. And we did what was wanted.'

Oakham poured some water into a glass and drank it. They were watching him; the tension had risen. But he sensed a growing empathy. He was touching sore spots with a sympathetic hand. He had got the audience on his side by making them feel he was on theirs.

He leaned towards them, palms flat on the table. His voice was soft. 'But times have changed, haven't they? We're all going to be one big happy European family. It's Love Thy Neighbour now. The Americans are opening hamburger chains in Moscow. Information's being dished out like crates of tinned peaches. The Germans are one nation, cuddling up after the last fifty years as if there'd never been a Berlin Wall. The Cold War's over, the Eastern Bloc is just a lot of countries dissolving into the chaos, people shooting each other in the name of democracy. Most of them couldn't even spell it. But we're told there's a rosy future for the world.

'It's a nice picture. But where does all this leave us?' He raised his voice. 'I'll tell you. We're not part of that picture, my friends. We belong to the bad old days. We've got dirty hands, when everyone else is showing up clean. So my department is closed down. I got a farewell lunch, a visit from the Deputy Chief and a pension. That's me. After twenty-eight years. How about you, Rilke? Early retirement? They kicked you out. They don't want to be reminded of people like you. Werner, you're blown, your career's finished. You'll be thrown on the rubbish heap. If they want to be nasty they'll make it very difficult for you to get any kind of decent job. And they will be nasty, believe me.

'Colonel Zarubin, you're a marked man. Too hard line, too close to the enemies of glasnost. No promotion for you. Demotion, instead. Already happened, hasn't it?' he asked the Russian. 'Lost your top post at the Institute to a new man. Ten years older, but he's got liberal leanings. He wants the KGB to be accountable. You'll be joining your father soon, sitting on a park bench like Khrushchev, mercifully allowed to live . . . Daniel, your life isn't worth twenty-four hours' insurance. Your pals in Mossad will be given you as a present before long. And Monika—' He shook his head a little. 'Time's run out for you too. You bought a lot of it by working for some funny people and they've been bleeding you ever since. And you know too much about them.'

Her blue eyes glittered at him; she drew the cashmere round her shoulders.

'I can look out for myself,' she said.

He shrugged.

'If you say so. But the fact is that every one of us is finished. Some have a pretty low-grade future, others don't have a future at all. We have a saying at home – it's typical of English humbug – out to grass. You haven't heard of it? It's what we do with our old horses when we haven't any use for them. We turn them out into a field and leave them there to die of boredom. And we don't have to feed them either.'

'We send ours to the slaughterhouse and sell them for meat,' Monika remarked.

'I think it's kinder,' Harry Oakham said. 'Well, I'm not ready for retirement! Nobody's putting me out to grass. I want my share for a change. Our masters,' he used the term with contempt, 'may not have any use for us, but there are others who have. We've got plenty to offer and I've got people who want it. I'm going into business and I'm inviting you to join me.'

It was the Russian who spoke then. 'Supposing it's true – what you've just said about us – what kind of business?'

'The terror business,' Oakham said lightly. 'That's what we've been trained for and that's all we know. Only this time we operate for money. Lots of money. We can name our price, Colonel. I've already named mine and it's been agreed. Now it's your turn.'

'Who's prepared to pay?' Rilke demanded. He sipped mineral water and wiped his lips with a silk handkerchief. He was a fastidious man.

'I've spoken to the Libyans,' was the answer. 'They'll finance the operation to the extent of buying the cover and meeting the costs of setting it up. I asked for four million in sterling and they didn't hesitate.'

There was a hiss of breath among them, a movement of surprise. He really had them now.

'They've agreed to pay this out?' Daniel knew the Libyan set up better than anyone in the room. Gaddafi gave money like turning on a tap and letting it run, but he wanted value for it.

'Yes,' Harry nodded. 'For the services we can offer, it was cheap at the price. I did some negotiating in advance on behalf of the rest of you. One hundred thousand in sterling paid into individual numbered accounts in this delightful city. That's the retainer. Afterwards we'd get paid by results. All subject to the risk and complexity of the job involved. I think I got a bloody good deal.'

Vassily Zarubin laughed. He hadn't smiled before, but then he laughed. 'I think so too. I like it.'

'Rilke?' Harry asked.

The German pinched his lip; he had irritating mannerisms, Harry noted.

'In principle, yes, but I want to know a lot more of what's involved. What's the cover that's going to cost so much money?'

'We'll come to that in a moment. Werner – how do you feel about it?'

Werner had been turning the pencil over and over in his fingers. He looked at Oakham. Suddenly the pencil snapped.

'What a fool I've been,' he muttered. 'All those

years wasted. All for nothing. What use would I be to anyone now?'

'We need brains, sophistication. I can hire muscle, Werner, but you're still in your job and you can get information to us that might be very useful. You'll run on for another year; that's the plan anyway. If we're given a high-level target, you have access to embassies and ministries all over the world. You could draw the map for us. Believe me, we need you. Are you interested?'

The man was shaken, angry and frightened. He needed gentle handling.

'Yes,' he answered. 'Yes, I am interested. You're right. I am owed something. I'm going to think of myself now.'

'Good,' was the calm response accompanied by an approving smile.

'Daniel?'

The Israeli shrugged. He glanced at the blonde woman and she stared coldly back at him.

'One condition,' he said. 'I don't go to the Middle East. Otherwise yes, what have I got to lose?' He answered his own question. 'Nothing I'm not going to lose already, if you're right about the lousy British. I'll join you, Mr Oakham.'

'Harry,' he invited and gave him the welcome-to-the-family grin he'd given Werner. 'Monika?'

She was likely to be the most difficult. The fires weren't burned out in her, they still smouldered. She just might tell them all to go to hell and stalk out, the Red Brigade fist metaphorically clenched in the air.

'What would I have to do?' she demanded. 'I've

got money, I can earn as much as that retainer if I want.'

Not quite, Oakham judged, but he wasn't going to argue. He just nodded and said, 'No doubt, but you've got to be alive and there's not much chance of that without protection. If you join, you'd use your old skills. We all remember Julius Ritterman.'

She preened in front of them. It was a clever thing to say. It established her status. Julius Ritterman was found strangled in a flat in Munich. A tall blonde girl had been seen dining with him in a smart restaurant. 'Death to the Capitalist Swine' had been scrawled in red ink and the paper stuffed into his mouth. He had been president of a leading West German Investment Bank.

'That would be amusing,' she showed her white teeth in a smile. 'I've been very bored. Men can be very boring. Count me in, Mr Oakham.'

'I'm delighted.' He was gallant, making a tiny bow towards her. 'And now, if Jan will set it up, I'll show you the cover and explain it as we go along. Anyone like some coffee?'

Nobody did. They were poised, intent on the next phase.

Jan switched on the video. The room was very quiet except for the slight whirr of the machine. Oakham commented.

'What you're seeing is an estate agent's video of a property that's for sale in England.'

A handsome, red-brick Tudor mansion came on the screen, set in a rolling park. There were shots of the interior, designer decorated, a luxurious indoor swimming pool. More exteriors, including a fine lake. Rilke was scowling, Vassily Zarubin's face was a mask, Werner was fiddling with the broken pencil ends.

'The asking price is three million,' Oakham explained.

Werner spoke up. 'It's a hotel, it says so. I don't understand.'

'It's going to be our headquarters,' Harry's voice was level. 'A well-established luxury hotel. Would anyone think of looking for our organization in a place like that? And it's got all the potential we need. The extra million is for contingencies. What the Libyans want is training facilities for some of their specialist groups. The IRA have expressed interest through them. There are others – you know them.' He shrugged, dismissing speculation. 'We'd provide that service, but our main activity is carrying out high-risk operations that nobody wants to touch themselves. That's where the money lies. Nice place, isn't it? I quite fancy living there. We'd be very comfortable, don't you think?'

Rilke muttered, 'It's brilliant cover. Mad, but brilliant. Did you think of this?'

Oakham nodded. 'Yes. I know the place. I was born in that part of the world. And the beauty of it is, it's a legitimate business. We'll all have positions on the administrative staff – I'll settle the details later – we'll be salaried employees of the consortium that has bought the hotel. All taxes paid up, proper accounts, whiter than white. No fiddling with anything that could catch the Revenue's eye.'

The video ran on, lingering over the grounds, the different aspects of the house. Jan had suppressed the sound-track.

Daniel asked, 'We don't know anything about hotels. What about staff?'

'They stay on,' Harry answered. 'That's part of the deal. Don't worry about details, it'll be worked out.'

'Documentation for us? Who's going to provide that?' Zarubin demanded.

'You are,' Harry said. 'Use your own facilities; you know best how to cover your tracks.'

Rilke nodded in agreement.

'The facilities need extending, if we're going to run courses,' the Russian remarked. Training, physical as well as mental, was his speciality. 'You could build an assault course – there's enough land?'

'There are over two hundred acres,' Harry assured him. 'Some hotels run war games at weekends. It's quite a popular pastime. We'd do the same. One for the customers and one for real. But I emphasize again, that's secondary, not primary. I said yes because my contact seemed so keen on the idea. But it's got to be very selective and very limited. If we pull off one or two big operations, we can phase that out completely.'

'I'd be happier,' Daniel put in. 'I like the country hotel, it's very good for me, I'd be safer there than in my lousy room in London. But having people come and go who know about us – I don't like it.'

Harry Oakham smiled at him. It was not friendly.

He was rocking the boat; it wasn't the moment to cast doubts.

'You've been on the run too long,' he said. 'It's made you nervous.'

Daniel's face reddened. 'Cautious,' he snapped back. 'Nobody's been after *your* hide.'

'They will be,' was the answer. 'But they won't know where to find it. Or yours. Opt out if you don't like the deal, but make up your mind now!'

The Israeli didn't hesitate. He had no option and that grinning bastard knew it. He hated the English, he thought. Smug, superior, still carrying colonialism in their hearts . . .

'I'm in. I said so,' he stated.

'Good.' Oakham relaxed, beaming friendliness at him. Daniel was not deceived. He looked round at them. The video had run its length. Jan switched off the machine.

'Any more questions?' he invited.

'How long before we become operational?' Rilke asked.

He was excited and committed. There was a gleam in the cold eyes. His mother could have a luxury flat, all the comforts again.

'Three months. I'll have everything ready in three months. Jan and I are flying back after this meeting. He'll be the co-ordinator. He'll keep in touch with all of you. But I'll expect you to join me in England exactly three months from today. Now, why don't we have a drink to celebrate? Champagne?'

'Why not?' Werner threw the pencil ends aside. He smiled at Harry. 'I stay where I am and feed you information when you need it. When they do throw me out I'll be a rich man. I'll drink to that.'

Bottles were brought up and opened. There was an air of excitement; old enemies found themselves on the same side. Zarubin downed his drink. Oakham leaned over and filled it up again.

'Here's to the future,' he said. 'From now on, it's going to be rich with promise. Especially rich. I give you all a toast. To Doll's House Manor Hotel!'

Harry Oakham stopped the car at the pub just off the main Ipswich road at Higham. He looked up at the sign; it brought back memories. The Swan. Swans used to process majestically down the river at Dedham when he was a boy. The village children threw bits of bread, scared to come too close to the fierce, hissing creatures. Harry fed them by hand. They didn't frighten him.

The pub was gloomy, with a low ceiling and black painted beams. There was the familiar smell of beer and tobacco smoke and a faint whiff of frying coming from the back.

The Lounge Bar was full of locals, eating chicken and chips or shovelling down plates of a revolting mess calling itself chilli con carne. Harry had eaten the real dish in Mexico. He ordered a simple Ploughman's lunch: a hunk of fresh white bread, Cheddar cheese, butter and pickled onions. He shoved the limp lettuce leaf and tasteless tomato wedge to one side. The real ale was very good and strong. He let the taste lie on his tongue. There was a group of tourists perched at the bar. They'd be on their way to his old village, to see the place immortalized by Constable. It had changed dramatically in the last ten years, he knew. It was peppered with antique shops and tea rooms, crammed with cars. It had been a quiet place when he was a boy, growing up in the old rectory. His grandfather had been the vicar of Dedham, the younger son who had followed the tradition that consigned the second born to the Army or the Church as a career. Harry remembered him vaguely. He was very old and inclined to wander round the village at odd hours. Someone always gently guided him home. Harry's father had bought the rectory when the Church Commissioners sold it just before the last war.

His widowed mother had offered it to him before she put it on the open market. But Peggy had refused to move from Woking.

I'm not going to be buried alive in the country! What would I do all day? He could hear her saying it. Judith had been brought up in Devonshire; she was a country girl who loved to ride and walk the dogs. He'd given her Labrador away after she died. He couldn't look after it properly and it needed someone to love it and make up for losing Judith. No, he'd agreed, Peggy wouldn't fit into village life, he hadn't bothered to argue. It was all part of that terrible initial mistake. So the rectory was sold. Times had changed and now only his cousins were left. They had turned the big house into flats and lived on the top floor. He hadn't seen them for years. Sometimes a Christmas card arrived, and he sent one back if he remembered. That side of his life ended effectively when Judith died. She would have been the link with his past.

He'd taken her to see the family tombs in Dedham churchyard one hot summer day after they'd been to Morning Service. His mother liked to go to church. And he'd pointed out where his father and grandparents were buried, and the older gravestones, weather-worn with time. It had been a scorching August that year. She was bare-legged and bronzed, her blonde hair bleached to silver gold. He remembered how she held on to his arm and shivered.

'I hate graveyards,' she'd said suddenly. 'I'm cold, darling . . . Let's go.' She was so soon to lie there herself.

The deal was done. The contracts had been exchanged and the Doll's House Manor Hotel now belonged to a consortium based in Switzerland. There'd been some publicity about the sale in the Sunday newspapers. Harry had welcomed the discreet publicity. He knew country people well enough to expect rumours and gossip to circulate for a time about the new owners. But it wouldn't last long.

There was no talk of planning permission for a golf course or anything that might lead to local opposition. It was all very quiet and dignified.

Armed with his list of associates, Oakham had met his Libyan contact on the river boat plying to the Tower of London one evening after he got back from Geneva.

He hadn't queried anything when he saw the names. The banker was very experienced on covering deposits abroad so that they couldn't be traced. He believed in legitimacy up front.

The sum needed to improve and equip the hotel for its special purpose would come to Oakham through a firm of reputable London accountants who thought they were working for the Swiss consortium in Basle.

Oakham was the middleman. The bills were submitted to the accountants and settled by them. Not one penny would slip into anyone's pocket *en route*. Harry was determined about that. You didn't cheat men like the banker's boss, and live to enjoy it.

Harry went up to the bar to pay his bill. The landlord glanced at him with sly curiosity. He wasn't a tourist. He could have been anything in his shabby tweed jacket and twill trousers.

'That'll be two fifty please, sir. You visiting these parts?'

It made Harry smile. Nosey bastards, Suffolk people. But not too keen to talk about themselves.

He decided to play along for mischief's sake. 'I'm going to Doll's House Manor. It's not far from here, is it?'

'About ten mile, I'd say, sir. Just been sold to some foreigners, I hear. Nice place. You staying long?'

'I hope so,' Harry smiled pleasantly at him and scooped up his change. 'I'm the new manager. Good afternoon.'

He drove out on to the main Ipswich road; there wasn't much traffic. He turned down a side road. The air smelt sweet of fresh grass and hedgerows. The sign loomed up ahead of him. Doll's House

Manor Hotel. It was Barrington Hall when the Lisle family lived there. The change of name signified its change of status. Because of the remarkable doll's house itself.

It was a long drive, with a fine avenue of beech trees leading up to the red-brick mansion. The sun shone and the colour glowed. Rose-red Tudor brickwork with the dark diapering on the façade. He'd come to the Lisle children's parties. So long ago.

He drove up to the sweep of gravel in front and stopped the car. On his first inspection the gardens had shown signs of creeping neglect, the woodwork needed painting, a crack inched up one of the main walls in the south wing. Times were hard and the hotel was losing money. The owners had been trying to sell it for over a year without success. The dramatic drop in price came at the right time for Harry Oakham. It was a bargain. The Colonel in his desert palace had made a good investment. Not that *he* cared about a financial return. The gardens were trim, the woodwork gleamed with fresh paint, signs of exterior neglect had been put right. He hadn't spared the money either. A house like that deserved to be treated properly. He liked the idea that he was supporting a vanishing social phenomenon with the Colonel's money. It amused him.

A young man in blue porter's livery came running down the steps and opened the car door for him. Harry got out.

'Are you staying, sir?'

'Yes. Bring in my bags, will you?'

He walked purposefully up the flight of stone steps

into the reception hall. It was high and cool, with the faint mustiness of its age.

A pleasant girl sat behind a counter and looked up, smiling at him. Fresh flowers were banked in the hall. She got up and said, 'Good afternoon, sir. Can I help you?'

'I'm Mr Oakham. The manager's expecting me. Tell him I'm here and I'd like to see him in about fifteen minutes.'

She blushed. 'Oh, yes, I'm so sorry. I'm new here. He did mention you were coming. You're in the Stuart suite, Mr Oakham. It's up the stairs and the first on your right. There is a lift if you'd rather.'

She was still pink in the face. He was the new owners' representative. Why hadn't the manager told her what he looked like . . . ?

'No thanks, I'll walk,' Oakham said.

'Dave,' she turned to the boy. He'd stacked Oakham's luggage in the hall. 'Take the gentleman up, will you? I'll ring through at once and say you're here, sir.'

'Thank you,' Harry gave her a smile that made her feel better. He hadn't seen a girl blush for a long time. He liked it.

Harry Oakham walked up the broad staircase. He remembered it well from his childhood visits. He ran his hand over the smooth banister, the wood polished by centuries.

The boy was humping his luggage ahead of him.

It was there, on the top landing, walled in by glass. The doll's house. Built into the wall at the head of the stairs. He paused to look at it.

75

Large enough for a child to play in, to look out of the windows at whoever came up the stairs. It had been there for four hundred years, and nobody had thought to move it. It was quite a tourist attraction. He wondered what they said about it in the guidebook at reception. Protected by its glass from the pollution of the modern way of life, it would last as long as the house stood.

He hadn't been afraid of it, though the children he played with used to scamper past. He was not afraid of the doll's house, any more than he retreated from the menacing swans when they sailed up aggressively to challenge him on the river bank. He paused, his eyes a little narrowed, and touched the glass front with a finger. It was screwed tightly into the wall. His finger moved lightly, tracing the head of the screws sunk deep into the glass and down into the brick beyond it. The outside wall was invisible from the grounds; it was buried behind chimney breasts and pitched roofs. If the doll's house was more than a façade, it must go back some feet. A very thick wall must have been built to accommodate it. Tomorrow, he decided, I shall go up on the roof and take a look. Just to satisfy my curiosity. After all, they trained me not to take anything at its face value. For nearly thirty years I've lived with things that weren't what they seemed.

There was a plaque by the side of the glass front. He read it and smiled. It hadn't been there when he was a boy and he lingered on that landing taunting the others with cowardice.

> This doll's house was built for the Lisle children in 1598. It is a unique example and reputedly made by a carpenter on the estate.

He quickened his step, seeing the young porter waiting for him at the top of the stairs.

'This way, sir, through the door here.'

It was held open for him, and Oakham passed into a wide corridor. All the rooms had been given names with an historical association. The Stuart suite was the most expensive; the bedroom was reputed to have been slept in by James I when he visited the house in 1610. Not much of a recommendation, he thought, remembering his history master's neat description of the first Stuart king: an unsavoury sovereign. It had made all the boys laugh.

He tipped the boy and closed the door on him. He looked round. There were flowers on the table, fresh fruit in a ribboned basket. Lavish curtains and a handsome antique bed.

Not much like the seedy doss-houses and safe flats where he'd spent so many dangerous days and nights when he was active.

In the last few years when he left his desk to travel, it was second-class accommodation with a tight expense account. Some stingy bastard scrutinized the items and queried them down to the last glass of beer. The office was mean to its servants, and their meanness to him was going to cost his former masters dear.

He knew the manager would be coming up to

welcome him. He and his assistant were a pleasant, efficient couple and had run a first-class hotel. They'd be eager to please him. They had no reason to suspect that he had come down to sack them both. It was time to bring the dolls into the doll's house.

3

Rosamund Bennet's marriage broke up on the Fourth of July. There was a private party at the American Ambassador's residence in Regent's Park. Rosa had met him and his wife several times and thought them a charming couple. They formed the same opinion of her. She arrived early, hoping not to get home too late. It was a lavish party, in the splendid neo-Georgian mansion given by the Woolworth heiress, Barbara Hutton, for the US Ambassador's home in London. A band of US Marines played in the large reception room.

Her name was announced and she shook hands with her hosts.

'Nice to see you, Rosa,' the Ambassador welcomed her. His wife said something complimentary about her dress and moved to the next guest.

It was more of a personal invitation than the big official party in Grosvenor Square. Rosa was surrounded by familiar faces; she was caught up very quickly by people glad to see her. She was elegant and charming, rather a rarity in the Foreign Office female complement.

'Hi there, Rosa! I was looking out for you – how are you?'

A hand grasped her lightly by the elbow.

'Hello, Dick.'

Dick Lucas was a regular on the diplomatic circuit. He was a US Naval attaché, a popular and attractive bachelor in his mid-thirties.

Whenever possible he monopolized Rosa. The message was clear enough; she chose to disregard it. But she liked him. He was amusing and his persistence was flattering. He always took her refusals in good part. He tried plying her with champagne, making her laugh with bits of gossip.

'No,' Rosa resisted. 'No more for me, Dick. I've got to drive.'

'OK. I'd offer to take you out to dinner, only I know you'll say no.'

She laughed. 'Then why do you keep asking?'

'Because one day I might get lucky.'

She always came alone. He had been surprised to learn she was married when he asked about her.

The husband was an investment banker. Nobody showed much interest in him. Rosamund Bennet was very bright and destined for big things in the Foreign Office. She was Sir Hugh Chapman's protégé.

Dick Lucas had always admired Rosa Bennet. She had style and class. He watched her edging her way out through the crush of people. She was a very attractive woman, but she was a loner. She was dedicated to her career. Too bad, he decided and went in search of a dinner companion. The party was full of pretty women who wouldn't turn down his invitation.

Rosa hurried out of the residence into the grounds. US Marines were calling for official cars. She found her own car and drove out into Regent's Park.

Damn, I'm going to be so late again, she worried as she turned into the Marylebone Road. The traffic moved like sludge. It inched forward a few yards and then halted again. It took twenty minutes to go down Baker Street, and Park Lane was another frustrating crawl. It would be nine o'clock before she reached Fulham Road.

James would be furious. There'd be another row. She felt sick with the anticipation of it. Things had got so much worse between them in the last two months, after she'd missed their anniversary. He had reproached her bitterly when she got back from the course at Branksome.

She couldn't tell him why she had so much work to do, why she was in the office on a Saturday, why their arrangements had to be tailored to the greater demands on her time. She couldn't tell him what she was really doing. Once or twice she had been tempted, hoping that if he knew the training involved in her transfer to Intelligence, he would understand. Support her for a change. But she didn't risk it. He was jealous, and nothing was proof against that. Sitting in the line of traffic, Rosa felt they'd reached a crisis point. Brussels would be the catalyst. She hadn't dared to tell him that she would be going there in two weeks' time. But she couldn't delay any longer. She'd gone to the Embassy party, meaning to leave early, and get home in good time. James was busier now the economic situation had improved, she'd planned to be there and have everything word-perfect by the time he came in. Meeting Dick Lucas had combined with the congealing traffic to make her late. Very late, on this of all evenings.

At last she got to the intersection and turned right down the pretty street with its smart Victorian villas where they lived.

The drawing-room lights were on. James was home. She paused in the stationary car and checked herself in the driving mirror. She looked tense and anxious. It made her angry suddenly. Why had he changed into a jealous, carping man who saw her career as an affront to his own self-esteem?

She got out, locked the car and went into the house. James was sitting in front of the television with a drink in his hand. He turned round and looked at her as the door opened.

She said quickly, 'I'm sorry I'm so late, I left the party early, but the bloody traffic was a nightmare. I'll get dinner started.'

'Never mind about dinner. I'm not hungry anyway. Get yourself a drink and sit down, Rosa. I want to talk to you.'

She knew that hostile look. Maybe she imagined it was colder than usual.

'Please, not another lecture. I can't stand it. I'm not going to row.'

'I'm not going to row either,' he answered. 'We do nothing else, and I'm as sick of it as you are. It doesn't change anything. I snarl at you, and you end up crying and I feel a shit. It's time we stopped, Rosa. I'll get you a drink. Sit down. Glass of wine?'

He wasn't being sarcastic; he wasn't going to shout at her, or lose his temper. He was coldly angry, but it was different.

'I don't want anything,' she said. 'What is it, James? Is something wrong?'

'I'd say so,' he answered. 'Wrong with us. It's not working, is it?'

'No,' she agreed. She felt miserable. 'No, it isn't. But I don't know what to do. All I want is for us to be happy like we used to be.'

'If you really wanted that,' he spoke calmly, 'you'd chuck your bloody career and settle down to being a wife for a change. We'd start a family. We'd live a normal married life.'

'I told you I didn't want children just yet,' she protested. 'I was honest with you from the start. You said you didn't mind.'

'I didn't expect it to go on and on. Year after year. All I know is, I'm not important to you, Rosa. Your job, the people you work with, but not me. I tried to go along with it; I went to those fucking Foreign Office parties where nobody even bothered to talk to me because I was just the husband. Not one of the gang. Most evenings I come home to an empty house. Last year you went off in the middle of our holiday because you'd been called back, some crisis or other. I've listened to all the excuses and tried to fool myself it would get better. Just once you'd put me and our marriage first. You never have.'

He tilted the drink, making the ice cubes clink.

'That's not true,' Rosa tried to say. 'You've made it so difficult for me – I feel I'm being torn in two! You want me to give up my job. Would you give up the Bank if I asked you?'

'We'd hardly live on your salary,' he brushed it aside. 'So don't talk balls.'

He finished his drink, put the glass down and said, 'I've met someone else. I want a divorce.'

She stared at him. He wouldn't look at her. She pushed the hair back from her forehead.

'You're not just saying this to hurt me?'

'You must think I'm a complete shit. I wouldn't do a thing like that. It's true. I've been seeing someone for a while now. I may as well tell you, she's pregnant.'

'Oh my God. That's charming!' She got up and stared down at him. 'That's really charming.'

'I think so,' he answered. 'I think it's wonderful, if you want to know. And she doesn't expect me to marry her, it's not like that. She'll have the baby and we'll live together if you want to make things awkward. She doesn't care and I don't either. We'll get married in the end anyway.'

'You must really hate me to do it like this,' Rosa said. 'I suppose that's what jealousy does to people.'

He reddened angrily. 'I'm not jealous – I just wanted a wife, not a fucking Foreign Office mandarin. But I don't expect you to believe that. And I don't give a damn whether you do or not.'

'Who is this woman?' Rosa couldn't help herself. One of their friends, a colleague at the Bank? How could she have been so blind, such a fool, turning herself inside out while he was cheating on her, making her career the excuse . . . ?

'No-one you know,' he answered. 'She's a financial journalist. She came to the office for an interview

84

for *The FT* and I asked her out to lunch. It just happened, that's all. She's quite a high-powered lady in the City. But she's ready to give up *her* job.'

'Good for her. I think I'm going to be sick.'

Tears spilled down her cheeks. He didn't move.

He said, 'You blew it, Rosa. We had everything going for us, but you blew it. So don't blame it on her. If we'd been happy I wouldn't have looked at her. Or any other woman. I've packed a bag. I'll move out tonight. I think it's best to cut short the aggro, don't you?'

'Yes, for Christ's sake, just go.' She turned her back to him and said, 'I'm going to Brussels as Second Secretary. I've been trying to get up the nerve to tell you for the last six weeks. It doesn't matter now. You can have your divorce. The quicker the better. I'll ring my solicitor in the morning.'

'Thanks,' she heard him say. 'It wouldn't do your career much good to have a messy fight. I thought you'd see it that way.'

The door closed. She didn't move. She heard his footsteps in their bedroom above. She heard him come down the stairs, and then the slam of the front door. His car starting up outside. The noise of the engine dying away so quickly.

The room was very quiet. The whole house was quiet. They had no pets, not even a cat. An independent career couple without ties. Then suddenly it wasn't quiet any more. She could hear every creak in the woodwork, a murmur in the water pipes. She realized she was shivering with cold. The central heating came on in the evening; she and James insisted on a warm house. But she was freezing. She went into the kitchen. It was gleaming white, a showpiece full of labour-saving gadgets. They hadn't had a dinner party for months. She'd been too busy. The dining room was hardly ever used.

'Coffee, hot coffee,' she said out loud. 'Pull yourself together. It's not the end of the world. You've been miserable as hell. So what are you crying about, you bloody fool?'

She switched on the percolator and sat down at the table to wait. She drank the coffee slowly. She didn't feel any warmer. Five years and they were part of the divorce statistics. Everything they'd shared, all the hopes and enthusiasms when they first fell in love had ended in that decisive slam of the front door as her husband walked out to someone else.

She was twenty-nine, on the brink of a brilliant career which could end with a top Embassy. So her marriage had failed. It was a casualty along the way she'd chosen. James had asked the impossible. Give it all up and settle down to a domestic life with shopping at Marks & Spencer and taking her children to school as the highlight of her day.

Rosa got up, washed the coffee mug, replaced it on the shelf with all the others. It was his fault for wanting her to live in his shadow, waste her intelligence and talents. A double first at Oxford, rapid promotion in a job that fascinated her. And she was expected to throw it all away.

She went upstairs to their room. There was no sign of his leaving. No cupboards gaping, no half-open drawers. It was as if he had never shared it with her. She ran a hot bath and lay soaking in it, trying to think of Brussels and the challenge ahead of her. Concentration was her forte; she could shut out anything and beam in on her subject to the exclusion of everything else. But it didn't work. Was he right, was I really as selfish as he said . . . ? Did I love him? God knows in the beginning, yes, yes, I was crazy about him. But not for a long time. You can't love someone if they make you feel guilty. You end up by hating them. As he hates me. Because I'd spoiled it all.

She got out, dried herself and got into the cool bed. Her head was aching and she felt exhausted. Rosa Bennet, the great success, the rising star. 'God!' she mumbled, slowly drifting into sleep. 'God! What a terrible failure . . . '

Air Marshal Sir Peter Jefford left his desk and came to meet her. He was a tall, thin man with greying hair and a neat moustache, impeccably dressed in the dark suit and discreet tie of a senior Civil Servant.

He had been head of Intelligence in the Foreign Office for three years. He was not a warm person, but he took Rosa's hand and pressed it sympathetically.

'Come and sit down,' he said.

She was one of Hugh Chapman's protégés, and Hugh only picked out the best. She'd caught his attention from the start by her top marks in the Foreign Office exam, and he'd recommended her to Jefford. A stint with 'C' Section would be very useful, and he felt she would make a significant contribution. Jefford had monitored her progress in the last weeks.

She had mastered the basic training of gathering information very quickly, and she had a natural instinct for what was relevant. And a phenomenal memory. Her reports were excellent. She was a quick pupil, dedicated in her attitude, emotionally stable, a woman other women accepted because she was no man-eater. And attractive to men. Good company, charming and easy to talk to. Tailor-made for Brussels.

'I got your memo,' he said. 'I'm so sorry.'

'Thank you, Sir Peter. I felt you should know as soon as it happened. It's very kind of you to see me, it wasn't really necessary. I know how busy you are.'

She said all the right things, and he liked her modesty.

'And it's definite? Your husband won't change his mind?'

'Very definite,' Rosa answered. 'I had a letter from his solicitors this morning.'

She sounded very calm, but she looked pale, and there were signs of strain around the eyes. Sir Hugh had briefed him about the husband before he sent for her. A difficult customer with a chip on his shoulder about his wife's career. She'd be better off without him.

He said kindly, 'It must have been a terrible shock to you. You'd no idea it was going to happen?'

She shook her head. 'None at all. We hadn't been getting on well for some time. He wanted a family, I wanted to wait. He didn't like me working, that was the real trouble. But I know marriages go through bad patches and I thought it'd work out. I was just gearing myself up to tell him I was going to Brussels on the night he left me.'

'And is that why he left?'

'No. I never got a chance to mention it till afterwards. He just said he'd met someone else and wanted a divorce.'

Peter Jefford noticed her hands clenching as she spoke. She had taken off her wedding ring.

'She's pregnant,' she said.

He paused for a moment. 'How very untidy. I'm sorry this has happened to you. Would you like a cup of tea? Vera will bring us some.'

'No thank you. Would you mind if I smoked?'

There was a box on his desk. He offered it.

'I thought you didn't smoke. No, of course, I don't mind.'

'I've taken it up again,' she explained. 'Just temporarily.'

He leaned back in his chair. 'It's an old story, I'm afraid. It's usually the other way round. You know, the wives get bored, they don't like the travelling, or the new posting . . . It's understandable but it doesn't make our job any easier. So what are you going to do?'

'I'll give him a quick divorce,' she answered. 'I don't want to be vindictive, especially as there's a child on the way.'

'That's a very generous attitude,' he remarked. 'And I'm sure it's right. Any financial problems?'

'No, no problems. James made the house over to me when we got married. I've got a small income from my father's estate and my salary. I don't want alimony or anything like that. After all, it was mostly my fault.'

She put the cigarette out. It was stale. The box had been filled a long time ago and forgotten.

'I don't think you should blame yourself,' he said. 'His attitude seems to have been most unreasonable. I hope you'll put the whole thing behind you as quickly as possible.'

'I'll try,' she answered. 'Thank God, I've got my work.'

He leaned towards her across the desk. 'How long will it take you to sort out the details?'

'Not long; neither of us wants a fight. I'm meeting my solicitor at the end of the week. Would it be possible to postpone going to Brussels for . . . say ten days . . . just till everything's tied up?'

'Yes, of course it would. But in fact,' he favoured her with an appraising stare. 'In fact I wanted to talk to you about that. Nothing to do with this domestic business, something most unusual has come up. Sure you won't join me in a cup of tea?'

Rosa said quickly, 'What is it? Don't you want me to go to Brussels?'

He shook his head. 'No, it's just that we've got a problem and I think you might be just the person to help solve it. Now, why don't you join me for lunch? There's someone I'd like you to meet. We'll go to my club. You know Boodle's, don't you? The food's excellent.'

'Sir Peter,' Rosa stood up, 'just tell me one thing. It's not my divorce, is it? I'm not being sidetracked?'

'Good God,' he laughed. 'If divorce was a bar

to promotion we'd have no-one in the Service but cleaners! Certainly not! Actually, I think it'll be an advantage. One o'clock at Boodle's, ladies' annexe. And don't worry. This could be more interesting than Brussels. If you think you can do it.'

'Now,' Harry Oakham said, 'I'd like to introduce the new administrative staff.'

They were all gathered in the handsome Great Hall; the chef, the under-chef, the housekeeper, the restaurant manager, the receptionists, the old man who looked after maintenance. The student waiters, mostly Italian, with a few earnest Germans, even the cleaners, had been asked to come in and hear what the new general manager had to say.

Everything must be open, no hole-and-corner stuff that might cause comment among the experienced members of staff.

He asked Hermann Rilke to step forward.

'This is Mr Brandt, our financial auditor.'

Hermann nodded at the audience, managing a stiff smile. Harry went on, 'I know it's unusual to have someone actually living in close proximity, but as you know we're owned by a Swiss consortium and that's how they like to do things. Mr and Mrs Brandt have come over from Zurich to join us.'

He turned slightly towards Monika, who played her part, and smiled pleasantly. It had amused Oakham to bracket them as husband and wife. Rilke didn't think it funny. Monika did.

'An assistant auditor, Mr Daniels, is expected in

the next few days. He'll be living with Mr and Mrs Brandt in Croft Lodge.'

Harry injected a little light-hearted joke. 'Two auditors to see we get things right – we've got to watch our profit margins – or we'll be in trouble! But that's how it's done in Switzerland. Sergeant Stevenson and his two lads are old friends of mine from the Marines. They'll help you with any maintenance problems, look after the grounds and be general dogsbodies around the place. We plan to start water skiing and wind surfing on the lake, and they'll take care of clients who are interested.

'I want to emphasize that if anyone has any problems, come to me, or Mr Pollock, who you all know by now.'

He gestured towards Jan. Jan was good with people; Harry sensed that the young staff liked him. Harry smiled at the faces turned towards him.

'I'd like to say how well everyone has co-operated with us in the takeover of the hotel. We were sorry to lose John Ford and Michael Roberts, but they know they're always welcome to come back and see us. And I'd particularly like to thank all of you who've made my job so easy.

'John and Michael were a hard act to follow. We couldn't have done it without your help. This is a great hotel and we're all committed to keeping its standards and reputation as high is it was before the change-over. We're going to build on success. And that means a share in the profits for everyone who works here. That's another thing the Swiss are keen on: incentive. Mr Brandt is going to establish a bonus system based on the annual turnover and profit. So you'll be working for yourselves too. Now, we'll be starting a new season tomorrow, and I want it to be the best. Thanks for listening to me. Good night and see you in the morning.'

There was a clatter of applause. He knew how to handle people. Jan watched him pausing for a moment like an actor, immaculate in his dark jacket and striped trousers, the distinguished-looking hotel manager giving a pep talk to his staff.

Rilke grunted. He wasn't a man who gave other men praise. Or enjoyed seeing them centre stage. But Oakham was right to integrate them publicly.

They had taken over Croft Lodge, a small house on the estate, and Rilke had been given a free hand to set up his own special unit on the upper floor. He'd enjoyed doing that. He was impatient for his work to begin.

Oakham had dismissed the staff. He turned back to the little group. He called them his 'Dolls', which irritated Rilke and made the murderous Dutch-woman laugh. The Israeli, Daniel, would be next to arrive, followed by the Russian, Vassily Zarubin. He was officially dead. Werner had forwarded an item from the Soviet news agency, Tass, reporting the car crash in the Crimea. Major Vassily Zarubin, only son of the distinguished KGB General, Josef Zarubin, had been killed. Vassily had buried himself with his father's help and was already making his way via Turkey. Rilke had tried to score a point with Oakham.

'And what role in the hotel management is our

Russian friend going to fill? How do you propose to disguise him?'

Oakham was amused by the attempt.

'I don't,' he said in his carefree way. 'Vassily's a Russian author, writing a serious biography of the saintly Vaclav Havel. If you want to hide something conspicuous, Hermann, put it where everyone can see it. That's what I was taught anyway.'

He grinned at Rilke, mocking him. 'Let's go and have a drink; then Jan and I have to be on duty. See our guests are happy. We're fully booked for dinner!'

He led the way to his own house. The ex-Marine Sergeant Bill Stevenson, and his pair of goons followed. Rilke knew the type. He'd used them himself when he wanted something violent done, with muscle and no brains involved. Brutes with criminal tendencies who'd lend themselves to anything for money and excitement.

Stevenson had been dismissed from the regiment for savage bullying of recruits; his assistants both had dishonourable discharges for various offences. Rilke objected to drinking with them as if they were equals. But he wasn't in charge. Oakham was.

He didn't like that either.

'It went off all right, didn't it?' Harry asked. Jan and he were on their way back to the hotel for the early evening rounds.

'It went fine, you handled it very well.'

'Our friend Hermann was looking bloody sour – anything up?'

The Pole shook his head. 'He's like that. He's a miserable little swine. He only smiles when he's got some poor sod under interrogation. He's bored, and he's not the boss. He'll cheer up when the action starts.'

They crossed the top landing and Jan glanced at the doll's house behind its wall of glass.

'I hate that thing,' he muttered. 'I don't know why you keep it, Harry.'

Oakham had told him the legend of the Lisle stepmother who had starved one of the children to death during the father's absence. His revenge was to build the doll's house and place his daughter's skeleton in the window, so the murderess saw it every day of her life. She had gone mad and drowned herself in the lake. Jan had shuddered in horror.

Harry paused on the upper landing. He noticed that the glass front needed polishing. He lingered because he knew how much Jan loathed the thing; he couldn't resist teasing him sometimes.

'When I was a little boy I used to come here and play with the children; the Lisles were living here then. They were scared stiff they'd see the skeleton in the window. There's supposed to be a curse on it. Anyone who tries to move it, drops dead. They all believed in it.'

Jan said, 'I'll move it, I don't believe in curses.'

'Oh yes you do, you superstitious old Papist! Besides, it's a plus for the hotel, the only one of its kind. Probably a listed building.'

He laughed. Jan turned away.

'It's obscene. Let's go down.'

He sounded troubled and Harry came up to him and clapped him affectionately on the shoulders.

'Come on,' he chided, 'it's a lot of nonsense. People make up stories about old houses like this. I don't believe a word of it, never did.'

They came down the stairs and into the main hall. He mustn't pull Jan's leg like that. There were raw nerves close to the surface; he mustn't forget what Jan had suffered.

'Let's start off in the cocktail bar,' he suggested.

It was an established nightly routine to go round, greeting the guests, making new arrivals feel at home. He rather enjoyed it, and surprisingly, so did Jan. Jan had perfected a little bow when he said good-evening. It was very dignified. But as they crossed the hall, one of the receptionists came after them. It was the pretty girl who blushed. Harry had a soft spot for her.

'Excuse me, Mr Oakham, there's a call for you. A Mr Harris.'

He stopped.

He said to Jan, 'You do the rounds. I'll follow on.'

Mr Harris. Alias Hakim, his Lebanese contact. He went into his office, closed the door. There was a scrambler fitted to his private telephone. He lifted the receiver.

'Put Mr Harris through please, Jane.'

He pressed the switch and the line was safe from eavesdroppers.

'Oakham,' he said. 'Is that you, Hakim?'

They didn't bother much with small talk.

'I've got a proposition for you.'

Oakham lit a cigarette.

'What kind?'

'I want to meet with you.'

'You'll have to come up here. There's a pub at Dedham, the Old Mill. How urgent is it?'

'Very urgent. Tomorrow.'

'All right, twelve o'clock in the bar.'

There was a pause.

'It's a secure place? I prefer London.'

'I prefer the Old Mill. Don't worry, hang a camera round your neck and look like a tourist. Whatever the proposition is, you know it's going to cost you.'

'We know,' was the answer.

'And I want half the fee in advance,' Harry stated.

Always get your money first with the Lebanese.

'OK, OK. Tomorrow. Twelve o'clock.'

The line cleared.

Oakham sat still. Then he drew an elaborate doodle on the pad in front of him. He had known Hakim for a long time. He negotiated – for murder, kidnapping, blackmail, any act of terrorism for a number of organizations. He only used the best.

Harry had made sure he was approached as a potential customer. A proposition. Whoever was employing Hakim wanted to hire him and his associates for something nasty. And dangerous.

He tapped the pen lightly, screwed up the paper, and threw it into the waste-paper basket. He never wrote anything down. He didn't need to. Years of committing things to memory had produced a computer in his head. Rilke had clients booked in at the beginning of the month. Three choice specimens from Ulster. Eager to sit at the master's feet and learn how to torture another human being into submission. But this would mean action. Something for him, maybe. Excitement stirred his blood. It always sent the adrenalin running, and it was never tinged with fear.

He went out, locking the office door and went to look for Jan. He'd been a sod, goading him over the doll's house. Harry gave himself a mental kick for being such an insensitive fool. He loved Jan, as Jan loved him. He'd tell him about Hakim. That would lift his spirits. He'd give him dinner and a few drinks. They'd speculate on what tomorrow would bring. Just like old times. He found the Pole coming out of the main dining room.

He said, 'Everything all right? Happy customers?'

'Fine, no complaints.'

He was still looking strained.

'Then come back with me. I've got some good news. Things have started moving.'

Rosa arrived at the ladies' annexe of Boodle's in St James's at exactly two minutes past one. Peter Jefford was waiting for her in the bar. A man was sitting with him. He had said one o'clock; they had drinks on the table; they had been there for some time.

'Rosa, this is Jim Parker. Mrs Bennet.'

He was a nondescript type, medium height, bland features, hair growing back into premature baldness. He had shrewd grey eyes.

'Now,' Peter Jefford said, 'what would you like to drink? Jim and I are ahead of you; we got here early.'

'White wine, please.' She settled into a chair, crossed her legs.

The man Parker was looking at her, and it wasn't in admiration.

The drink came, Jefford said something about the traffic.

'They're digging up the road by Hyde Park Corner. It's absolutely chaotic. Why on earth can't they do the work at night or in the early hours instead of blocking up the whole of Knightsbridge?'

Parker had produced a packet of cigarettes. Rosa took one. He lit it for her.

'Thank God someone else smokes,' he said. 'People look at me as if I'd got AIDS when I light up.'

'Jim works for the Service,' Jefford explained. 'The Senior Service, and I don't mean the Navy.' He smiled slightly. 'His job is to keep an eye on all of us, in a way. Isn't it?'

'You could almost call it personnel. Welfare.' He glanced at Rosa. 'Sir Peter tells me you've joined 'C' Section.'

'Yes,' Rosa answered. 'I thought it sounded very interesting.'

'But you're a career diplomat, Mrs Bennet. This isn't going to be permanent.'

'No, it's an interim posting.'

There was a pause. She sipped her wine.

Peter Jefford said, 'I'd like you to explain our problem to Mrs Bennet. But first I'd like to fill her in on your role, Jim, if that's all right.'

'Absolutely.'

'Jim's job is to clear Intelligence officers for security when they retire. Or leave for any other reason. He liaises with Special Branch if necessary. It's a routine job nine times out of ten, but a very important one. Jim is quite a bloodhound.' He acknowledged Parker with his slight smile. 'He's picked up several high-risk cases. And he thinks he's got another one. Now, Jim, you carry on. But first, let's order lunch.'

She was very good-looking, Jim Parker thought. Classy, self-possessed. Not a type of woman who appealed to him. Too brainy, too competitive.

Jefford felt she'd be suitable for this particular job, but he wanted to try her out for weak spots before he agreed. She'd be under his direct authority if she took it on.

'What do you feel about spies, Mrs Bennet?'

'I don't know. I've never met one.'

'You've met lots of them but you wouldn't have known it. You think it's an honourable profession? Or a bit grubby? Seedy – like those Len Deighton characters? Or the tortured intellectual types – you know, Smiley, and all that lot?'

'I don't read thrillers,' Rosa said. She didn't like his manner.

'Just as well. They're a load of old rubbish. So you don't have an opinion. So why did you join 'C'? That's spying.'

'I understood it was Intelligence.'

'Nice name for the same thing. Could you answer the question for me?'

'I told you, I thought it would be interesting. And helpful to my career.'

'So the idea of listening in and reporting back didn't bother you?'

'Not if it was in the country's interests, no. Why should it?'

She had answered sharply. For the first time she saw a gleam of approval in the stony eyes. A very brief gleam.

'So you feel it's all right if it's done out of patriotism?'

'Yes, of course. I don't understand what you're getting at, Mr Parker.'

'What do you think about assassination?'

She was caught off guard. She stared at him.

'What sort of man goes in for that, do you think?'

'Some sort of psychopath,' she retorted.

'But suppose it had to be done. In the country's interests, like you said. What about that?'

'I don't know,' Rosa answered. 'I can't make a judgement. I think I'd rather not know if it was necessary.'

'You're not the only one who feels like that,' he said.

He lit another cigarette. He was absorbed in the game of question and answer.

'We had a section in the war; very brave men and women, ready to kill for their country. Nobody had scruples about them then. Afterwards it was closed up. The war was over, we couldn't have dirty hands officially. Unofficially, it was business as usual. Now it *is* closed up. They're rather an embarrassment.

The Americans still go round knocking people off and calling it eliminated with extreme prejudice.' He laughed. 'They do murder the English language, don't they! Anyway our licensed eliminators, if I can use the jargon, are disbanded. Golden handshakes – well, silver handshakes really – pensions, help with jobs, tokens of appreciation all round. One of their best men, a section head called Harry Oakham recently gave in his keys. Fifty-two, and starting a new life. Which is where I come in, Mrs Bennet. My job is to follow him up for a full year, just to see how he's adapting. To make sure he's not getting into trouble. Financial or otherwise. To give a helping hand, if need be. Or a word of advice. Like Sir Peter said, I'm a sort of welfare officer. After-care. It's all above board, quite open. I keep in touch once or twice and then fade out. I don't actually fade out until I can give the final clearance. That can take a long time. I'm not happy about Oakham.'

'I think our table's ready,' Peter Jefford said.

'What sort of man is he?' Rosa asked. Jefford had ex-cused himself before the coffee, leaving them alone.

Parker spooned sugar into his cup.

'I could give you details on his file. It wouldn't tell you anything about him, not what he's really like. He never minded killing; that's certain. But he never got a kick out of it. That's certain too. That kind don't last. They're certainly not kept on and promoted in peace time. Very brave, physically and mentally like rock. Never got caught. Loyal to his field workers. Liked the action, hated the desk job. It all sounds like someone out of those bloody thrillers, doesn't it? Only he isn't. I went to see him; I had my welfare cap on. He wasn't there. So I talked to his wife instead. Let me tell you about that.'

'It's good of you to spare the time, Mrs Oakham.'

She'd got a part-time job as receptionist in a local estate agent's, and luckily for her visitor, this was a free afternoon.

'My name is Parker,' he'd announced, 'Jim Parker. Your husband and I worked in the same department. I'm in Welfare now, that's why I'm here. We like to keep in touch with our old colleagues, see they're all right.'

She had offered him tea, and he sat drinking it with her in the tidy little sitting room.

'Oh, don't worry about him, Harry'll always be all right. He knows how to look after himself.'

Jim Parker took a chocolate biscuit which he didn't want.

'We didn't know he'd moved,' he said. 'We went to your old house. The new people gave me your address. I must say, I was surprised not to get a call from him. Normally our chaps keep in touch. No thanks, no more tea.'

'He's gone off to work in some hotel in Suffolk,' she said. 'I couldn't face it, so he upped and left me. Not that I'm sorry, Mr Parker.'

'Jim,' he suggested. He looked sympathetic. 'That must have been very hard on you. I can't see him in a hotel.'

'I can't either. I never really knew what he did, not

even after being married to him for all these years.'

'Well, it was confidential,' Jim Parker explained.

' "I decode signals," was what he said. "Very dull." Were you in signals, Jim?'

He noticed how easily she had slipped into first-name terms; she was smiling at him, and her skirt had ridden up several inches above her knees.

Oakham's wife was known to be a bit of a tart, but it hadn't posed a problem. She stuck to the local talent among their own circle. Married men looking for a bit of fun on the side, the odd divorced man. Like the steady she was shacked up with at the moment. Oakham didn't seem to care.

Parker said, 'Do you keep in touch?'

'No. We're getting divorced and there's nothing to keep in touch for. I don't care if I never see or hear from him again. He was a rotten husband.'

She bit her lip and pulled the skirt down.

'I'm sorry,' he said again. He leaned towards her. 'Would it help to talk about it? In what way was he a rotten husband?'

She shrugged. 'He treated me like I didn't exist. I don't know why he married me in the first place. We went to bed together, I wasn't expecting anything out of it, and he suddenly proposed. After three weeks. I was in love with him, Jim. I'd never met anyone like him. He was different.'

'Different?' he prompted.

'Romantic,' she gave a mirthless giggle. 'Sent me flowers, talked to me like something out of a book. He was something special to look at too; very sexy. I couldn't believe my luck. Of course we were from different backgrounds. His family were stuck-up bloody snobs, if you want the truth. They turned their noses up at me from the start. His mother was a frosty old cow.'

She frowned, lost in some remembered hurt.

'I wasn't like the first wife. Judith, her name was. They thought the world of her. You know — he wouldn't talk about her to me? Wouldn't mention it. I tell you it drove me up the wall. She was dead, that's all I knew. Naturally I was interested,' she excused herself. 'Who wouldn't be? She'd only been dead about a year when he met me. But no. She was too bloody precious to talk about.'

'That's very odd,' Parker admitted. 'Not easy for you either.'

He could imagine how jealous she had been. She was the type that would nag and nag . . .

'He never loved me,' she said suddenly, and her mouth drew down in bitterness. 'He was just lonely when he met me. Trying to get over *her*. He just made use of me.'

'But he did marry you,' Parker said.

Romantic, sending flowers, paying poetic compliments. Using her. Not quite, not in the way she meant.

'That was the worst thing he could have done,' Peggy Oakham said. 'He ruined my life, Jim. One day he just turned off me; we'd been married about eighteen months. "I don't want to sleep with you any more." That's what he said. "You go your own way, I won't mind." It was so bloody cruel, the way he said it.'

'And did you go your own way? I wouldn't blame you after that.'

'I had boyfriends,' she admitted. 'I'm not a cold bloody fish, even if he was. I did it to hurt him at first, to make him jealous. But he didn't care. He had his work, his travelling. He used the house like a lodger. I said something rude about Judith once when we were rowing. You know what he said to me, Jim? He said he'd kill me if I ever said anything about her again. I was scared, I can tell you. That's the only time he lost his temper. Just that once. From then on, he froze me out.'

She didn't say anything for some minutes. She pulled a paper handkerchief out of her sleeve and blew her nose. He felt sorry for her. Cruelty can take many forms. What Harry Oakham had done to this ordinary, rather stupid woman was more damaging than blows.

'What happened when he left? What did he say to you?'

'He'd been away,' she answered. The paper hand-kerchief was screwed up and pushed back into her sleeve. 'Gone up to Suffolk to see about a job. He knew I wouldn't live in the country. I said so before he went. But he took the job all the same. He just came home and said, "I'm going to manage a hotel, Peg. It's a good opportunity and I've taken it." I did lose my temper then. I told him what I thought of him for doing it without saying a word to me, just as if I didn't count. "You don't like the country. The job doesn't include a wife." That's what he said. He was such a bastard. I started crying. He sat down and said, "Come on, let's talk sense. No point you upsetting yourself. You can have the house. Sell it if you like. Keep the money. And all the furniture and stuff. I won't need anything. I've a few thousand saved. You can have that too. But I want a quick divorce. No hassle, or no house. You'll be better off without me anyway. You could marry the boyfriend if you like. I'm going to pack now." He was leaving, walking out that same day!'

Parker made a muttering noise of sympathy. Ruthless, the file on Oakham noted. Without moral scruples in the course of duty. Not only duty, it seemed. He changed tack.

'Are you all right for money? I'm sure the Department would help if there was any hardship.'

'No, I'm fine. I've got a job. The house sold well. I've got a nice bit on deposit after buying this flat. Thanks, Jim.'

'Are you going to get married?'

She shook her head. 'Not me,' she said angrily. 'Once was enough. My friend would like to, but no thanks. I'm all right as I am.'

'I wonder why he chose to go into catering? He hadn't taken any course in it had he, after he retired?'

'God, no,' she dismissed it contemptuously. 'He never boiled himself an egg if he could help it. Never washed a cup. He said he was going into management. Made it sound very upmarket.' She sneered at the idea. 'But he was like that. He loved being grand. He liked putting me down because my dad was just an ordinary working man.'

'It sounds to me,' Parker remarked, 'as if you've had a very raw deal. What was the name of the hotel?'

'He didn't say. He just came down that day with his bags and said, "Have you thought about it then? A quick divorce and you scoop the pool?" I said, "Don't worry, I can't wait to get rid of you!" He looked pleased. Smiled at me. "Good. Very sensible." And then you know what he did? He kissed me on the cheek. "Sorry it didn't work out. You'll be happy with another fellow. Good luck, Peg." And he went. Closed the door and got into his car and drove off.'

She lapsed into another silence. Parker shifted slightly.

'Was it a big hotel, or a pub? What part of Suffolk, did he say? I ought to go and see him, have a word. It's Department policy. Not that he deserves it from what you've told me.'

She sighed; she'd opened the wound, but it hadn't drained. In his view it would fester for the rest of her life.

'Dedham, where his family lived. Near there. That's all I know. Everything was done through his solicitors. It's all over now anyway. I never want to see or hear of him again as long as I live.'

Parker stood up. 'Thanks for putting me in the picture,' he said. 'This is all confidential, of course. Don't worry about that. And I hope things work out for you.'

He shook hands with her. She must have been

startlingly pretty with blonde hair and those big blue eyes when Oakham met her.

'Goodbye then.'

'Goodbye,' she said. 'If you're round this way any time, give me a ring. We could go for a drink.'

'I'll remember,' he said. 'It'd be nice.'

'Let's take a turn round the Park,' Parker suggested. 'It's a nice day.'

Rosa and Parker had left the club; Jefford had signed the bill before he left. They walked down to St James's Palace and on into the Mall. Sightseers drifted in little groups, gaping at the sentries, taking photographs. A cluster of Japanese waited uncertainly outside Clarence House. The Queen Mother was not in London, but it didn't make any difference.

'I like this park,' he said. 'There's a seat, why don't we sit down?'

'What do you know about the first wife – Judith?' she asked.

'She was a lovely looking woman. Naturally we ran a check on her when he said he was getting married. No problem there. Same background as him. County family, tweeds, dogs, horsy – she'd done some modelling in London. Not surprising when you saw the photographs of her. They'd only been married two years when she was killed.'

'What happened?' Rosa asked.

'Skiing accident,' he said. 'They were on holiday in Verbier. She went a bit too fast, hit a bend and turned over. She broke her neck.'

'How awful,' Rosa said. 'And he was there?'

'Right behind her. Brought her down himself.'

'And then he married someone so completely different. And made her life a misery. There's something out of balance, isn't there? He's not quite what he seems . . .'

She was considering slowly, trying to put a personality in the empty frame with Harry Oakham written on it.

'There was a Pole who worked with him,' Jim Parker went on. 'They were in the field together. He set the target up, Harry did the business. They were very close, those two. The Pole got arrested and did ten years in a State security prison in Cracow. Dreadful place. When he finally got out, Oakham looked after him. Paid for a holiday, tried to keep him on in the Section. But the medical reports were bad. He'd had a rough time and he wasn't reliable, or stable enough to employ. Oakham kicked up hell about it, but somebody got the Pole a job with a charity that kept him going and out of mischief. I used to keep an eye on him. Oakham met him regularly, subsidized him if he needed a bit of extra cash. He was very loyal, very protective. So that's another side to him. It doesn't fit with the sadistic bastard his wife talked about.'

'No,' Rosa agreed, 'it doesn't. He must have hated her. Or himself for marrying her. Why are you worried about him? Have you seen him?'

'Yes, I saw him. Like she said, he's managing a hotel near Dedham.'

'And what was wrong with that?'

'Nothing's wrong with it,' he said, 'except it was

like seeing a tiger curled up in a cat basket. After I'd talked to the wife and made a few enquiries round his old colleagues, I went up to Dedham to find him. What worried me was the Pole. He'd disappeared. Walked out on the job and the lodgings and vanished. The landlady said he'd gone back to Poland. I had a gut feeling I'd find him with Oakham. It's a very pretty place, Dedham. Do you know it?'

'No,' she answered. 'I've never been there. Constable country, isn't it? I've always thought he was rather a dull painter. But I don't like landscapes much.'

Parker took out his cigarettes. He was easy with her now; she felt she had his confidence. I'm being briefed, she thought suddenly. Sitting in the park where nobody can overhear, and he's briefing me.

'Can I have one?' she asked.

'Sorry, here,' he apologized.

'It's a nice drive up to Suffolk,' he said. 'I did it in under two hours from London.'

Jim Parker had booked himself into a pub called the Old Mill. He didn't know that part of England; his family came from Sevenoaks. His father had been a successful dentist. He was very disappointed when his son opted for the Civil Service; luckily there was a younger brother willing to take on the practice. Jim Parker wasn't married; he never had the time to settle down, and not much inclination. A couple of steady girlfriends kept him happy without any commitment. He hated strings. And he didn't have a high opinion of marriage. He'd seen too many break ups. The Old Mill was a nice pub, comfortable and unpretentious. Dedham was too full of tourists to please him, in spite of its quaint houses and the charming countryside. He didn't like crowds of people either. He went up to the bar for a drink and to chat up the barmaid.

And then he saw Harry Oakham. He'd been sitting in a dark corner with a man. He moved with the long strides of the predator among the fat pigeons perched around him. Parker didn't move or attempt to follow him. Oakham would spot a tail a mile off. He sat and watched the man he'd been drinking with instead. He waited twenty minutes before he left the pub. He was reading a newspaper, killing time. Parker didn't recognize him when he came into clear view. Parker had ordered a beer and drank it slowly while he waited. Now he elbowed his way close to the barmaid.

'Excuse me,' he said. 'Wasn't that a bloke called Oakham who went out a while ago? Tall, dark bloke?'

She raised pencilled eyebrows at him. 'Don't know. Never heard of him. Sorry.'

Parker shrugged. 'Thought I recognized him. Worked in the same office for a bit, but it's a year or two now. I heard he lived somewhere round here. I'd like to look him up.'

He smiled at her encouragingly. She was a surly girl and she didn't smile back.

'Bob might know,' she suggested. 'I don't come from round here, but he does. Bob?'

She called to a large red-faced man polishing glasses further down the bar.

He came over and said, 'Yes, Betty?'

'Gentleman here asking about somebody called – what was it?'

'Oakham,' Parker prompted. 'Thought I recognized him – he was in here earlier and I just missed him.'

Bob was a Suffolk man and he regarded strangers with suspicion. Strangers started at the boundary with Essex, or any other county.

'There's Oakhams living in Dedham,' he remarked after a pause. 'Been here for generations. My grandad used to work for them before the war. You could try up at Bruton Hall. It's flats now, but some of the family's still there.'

He knew Harry Oakham well enough. He'd said 'Good morning' when he came in. He wasn't going to identify him for anyone who wasn't even local. He didn't look like someone an Oakham would be friendly with. He went back to his place and started on more glasses. Jim Parker decided to try the barmaid again. It might be the shortest route.

'Any big hotels round here?' he asked.

She stared at him.

'What's wrong with this then?'

He wouldn't be put off. He grinned at her. 'Nothing, nothing at all. It's very nice. Very friendly.' He couldn't resist the sarcasm, but she didn't see it. She probably thought she *was* being friendly.

'It's just that I've got a lady friend and she likes candle-lit dinners. Bit more romantic than a pub. I'm taking her out tonight.'

'We can run to a candle in a bottle,' she retorted.

'But if you want to spend a lot of money, then try the one at Barrington. You'd have to book, it's very classy. And pricey,' she emphasized. 'Doll's House Manor. Big old place – just been sold. Bob said the last owners were going broke. But it is good,' she added grudgingly, 'if you like all that fanning around. I hope the girlfriend's worth it.'

'Oh, she is,' Parker enthused. 'Thanks a lot. I'll run over and take a look at it. I'll have a half pint of draught bitter and have something for yourself.'

She said, 'Gin and lime would be nice, thanks,' and managed a brief smile.

4

When Harry came into the bar of the Old Mill, it was crowded. He stood for a moment looking round, said 'Morning' to Bob who'd been there when he was old enough to order his first pint after a cricket match, and looked for Hakim. Hakim was a pro; he wouldn't be conspicuous. Harry shouldered his way to the bar, ordered half a pint of Pimm's No. 1 and took his time while the surly barmaid made it up. Lots of tourists, some locals, nobody he knew. He'd been away a long time, but Bob remembered him. Bob would. His family had worked for the Oakhams for three generations. Harry was touched when the first time he went there the old man leaned closer to look at him and said, 'It's Mr Harry, isn't it? How old are you, sir?'

He sipped his drink, checked his watch. He was a little early, it was a few minutes before twelve. Then he spotted Hakim coming in, glancing round him quickly, going to the furthest and darkest part of the bar and sitting down with his back half turned to the room. He had a newspaper under his arm. He opened it up and started reading. It was his recognition signal. Hakim had a sense of humour. One of his scant virtues, Harry thought. The *Sporting Life* was his joke at the expense of the English. And like most Lebanese he loved to gamble. Horses, dogs, anything. Oakham saw another waitress come up to Hakim and take an order. He waited, letting Hakim stew for a while longer. Never show eagerness. Never hurry a deal. Hakim would see it as weakness. The Lebanese finished his drink, wiped his mouth with a white handkerchief and looked round. Oakham left the bar and went over to him.

Oakham sat down opposite to him. They weren't friends. Nobody was Hakim's friend.

Oakham said, 'No trouble getting here?'

'No.' The Lebanese was surly. He disliked country pubs. He was a city rat by upbringing and inclination.

'What's the proposition?' Harry Oakham didn't waste time.

'We've got a target,' Hakim said. 'It's an elimination job.'

Harry sipped his Pimm's.

'With extreme prejudice?'

'Don't talk Langley crap,' the Lebanese hissed at him.

Oakham liked to needle people. Harry smiled benignly back at him. The CIA preferred to wrap up ugly deeds in long words.

'All right, you want some bugger's neck broken. Is that better? Who is it?'

Hakim lowered his voice so that Harry had to bend to hear him.

'Prince Abdullah Al Rashid,' he muttered.

Oakham finished his Pimm's. It was too sweet for his taste.

'No deal,' he said. 'We don't go into Saudi. Nobody would get near enough to spit on him.'

'He won't be in Saudi,' Hakim said. 'He's coming to London on a private visit. Staying at the Regis Hotel. Two weeks' time.'

Harry's eyes narrowed, peering at nothing. Hakim knew that look. He was encouraged.

'What's he coming for?'

'Eye trouble, the usual. He likes to gamble. And he likes blondes.'

'What chance of getting to him outside?'

The Lebanese shook his head.

'No chance. Bullet-proof car, armed bodyguard and Special Branch crawling round like fleas.'

Oakham pointed to Hakim's empty glass.

'Gin?'

'Yes, with orange. Thanks,' he added.

Harry came back with the drink and a glass of bitter. The Lebanese grimaced.

'How can you drink that filthy stuff? Not even iced . . . '

'Well, you know what they say about gin and orange – tarts love it. Which reminds me – where does he go for the girls?'

'He doesn't, they come to the hotel. He uses the same agency every time.'

'And he likes blondes,' Oakham mused. 'Where do you get your information?'

'We have a sympathizer quite close to him,' Hakim answered.

'Not sympathetic enough to do the job for you?' Harry asked.

'No. You lose both arms and legs before they behead you in the public square at Riyadh for a crime against the Royal Family. This is our only chance. Are you interested or not?'

'Depends on the money. What's the offer?'

Hakim had been given an open-ended cheque. The Arab Prince was his father's favourite son. An ardent pro-American after the Gulf War, a bitter enemy of the Muslim fundamentalist movement. Iran had wanted him dead for a long time. But not in Saudi and not by the hand of one of their organizations. The ideal solution was assassination in Europe, in scandalous circumstances that would outrage Muslim opinion.

They were ready to pay anything to achieve that aim.

But Hakim was a Lebanese and bargaining was like breathing. He named half the expected sum.

'Five hundred thousand sterling.'

Oakham shook his head. 'Don't fart around with me,' he said pleasantly. 'Three quarters of a million is the price.' He moved his chair as if he was about to get up and leave. 'Not a penny less,' he said, and he was on his feet.

Hakim gave up. 'Agreed. Sit down, sit down. But there's a condition.'

'Three quarters for the elimination – conditions cost more.'

'We want some dirt to spread around,' Hakim said. 'A scandal they can't hush up. Drink, drugs, something the papers can have fun with . . .'

'You want us to smear him as well as kill him,' Oakham murmured. 'I see. That will be another two fifty thousand.'

This was not the back-street bazaar plotting of the rival groups in Lebanon. This was a top assignment, masterminded and directed from Tehran. The death of their arch-enemy, coupled with a private visit to the forbidden flesh pots of the West . . . Nice stuff.

'Well?' he asked, and after a moment Hakim nodded.

'Agreed. A million for the whole job. But nothing on account. I can't move on that. Payment by results for that kind of money.'

Oakham made a quick judgement. He decided not to push too hard. 'Fair enough. You've met me, I'll waive the deposit. Now I think I've got something to work on. But I'll need very detailed information from your end. Call me tomorrow. Around six-thirty.'

He got up, finished his beer. Hakim opened the newspaper. They didn't say goodbye.

Two girls had come to the edge of the lake with a bag of crumbs; they were throwing them to the ducks. There was a lot of splashing and scrambling.

Jim Parker said, 'I like ducks. Especially the ornamentals. Carolinas are pretty. I tracked Oakham down from the phone book. I rang up and introduced myself. He wasn't very welcoming. But he was like that, apparently. Never got on with officialdom. I said I was in the area and would like to drop by and see him. Welfare and all that; wouldn't take up much of his time. So far everything checked out, Mrs Bennet. He was the manager of this hotel, all I had to do was drive up and have a chat, sum up the situation and ask about his friend Jan.

'Which is exactly what I did. And there was the tiger in the pussy basket, all snug and curled up, and purring.'

'And you weren't satisfied,' Rosa said. 'You felt something was wrong.'

'Everything was right, that was the trouble. You see he didn't know what my job really was. We do have a Welfare Department and they do offer a service to retired staff. Oakham knew that.

'So when I went there I expected him to be offhand. Mind-your-own-bloody-business attitude. That's what I got over the phone. But it was different when I saw him. The hotel was a magnificent place if you like old buildings. Tudor brick. The sun was shining on it as I drove up, and it was quite a drive. Lovely grounds, everything well kept. I remembered the girl in the pub saying the last owners were nearly broke. That place had had a fortune spent on it, and very recently. Whoever bought it, didn't penny pinch. And out he came, morning coat, pin-striped trousers, and a big smile on his face. "Hello, nice to meet you. Do come in." '

Jim Parker. Welfare. Just popping in to make sure he was settling down in the new job. Harry Oakham hung up. Then he picked up the house phone and dialled Jan's office. He wasn't there. He was in the dining room, the receptionist said, she'd just seen him go past.

'Ask him to come and see me right away.'

Welfare. Yes, he knew they did the good Samaritan bit and looked up the boys and girls when they'd kicked them out on their backsides. Very caring of them. Then he paused. It wouldn't do to be antagonistic. Whoever this little creep was, he'd better send him away happy. The door opened and Jan came in. He looked worried.

'What's the matter, Harry? Something wrong?'

'There's a bloody Welfare nosey parker on his way over.'

'For Christ's sake,' Jan said, 'why do you let him come here? What does he want?'

He was agitated; Harry noticed how worked up he was getting.

He said coolly, 'Don't be a bloody fool, Jan. It's routine; we'll have a drink and I'll tell him I'm settled and enjoying being out of the game, and he'll go home and put it on file.'

'All right, all right,' the Pole was pacing up and down. 'How did he find you? Why is he checking up now?'

'Use your head, can't you? Think straight. I'm on some computer print-out that says refer to records, non-urgent, and they finally get around to me.'

'That's right,' Jan muttered. 'They came to see me regularly after I left. The same old bullshit. How're you managing? Anything we can do? When they'd kicked me out with a lousy pension and they'd fixed me up in a job that paid cigarette money!'

His face darkened with rage. 'They're bastards, Harry. You look out for this sod. You be careful.'

Oakham said gently, 'I'm a bastard too. I'll handle him. Don't worry. You just calm down and don't worry about a thing. Trust me.'

'I do,' Jan said simply. 'You're the only one who stood by me. I'll never let you down, Harry.'

'Don't talk rubbish. We take care of each other. We always did.'

Jan said, 'For the last six months Welfare sent a woman, a very tactful lady. Last time she called I told her to fuck off. She didn't mind. She knew I'd gone funny in the head. Very tactful lady. If they ask about me, you say I went back to Poland.'

'OK,' Oakham nodded. 'You're right; we've got a job coming up. We don't want to make waves.'

Jan's eyes brightened. 'Hakim?'

'Yes. Look, stay in your flat, keep out of sight till this bugger's gone. If he asks about you, I'll say what you said. You went to Poland to find some relatives. I'll make it sound final. They'll close the file with luck. I'll phone through when he's gone.'

He left his office and went out to the main reception hall. The creep was due in the next few minutes if he'd followed the directions, and as he looked through the windows, he saw a car coming steadily up the long drive, slowed down by the speed humps on the way. It stopped and a man got out. He was dressed in trousers and a sports coat, with an open-necked shirt. About forty, Harry judged, ordinary looking, going bald.

Wipe out the cool reception when he rang up. Be friendly, show him how well you've adjusted to your new career. Send him off with a warm glow.

He came out on to the steps and said, 'Hello, nice to meet you. Do come in.'

The man held out his hand.

'Jim Parker. I hope this isn't a bad time? You're not too busy?'

Oakham had implied that it was inconvenient at any time when he suggested calling. Now the response was different.

'Not at all. Come into my office, we can have a drink together.'

It was a well-furnished, even luxurious office by Parker's reckoning. The manager did himself well. He sat opposite Harry in a leather armchair. Gin and tonics arrived. He lifted his glass.

'Cheers,' he said.

'Cheers,' Harry echoed. 'Now, what can I do for you?'

'Well,' Parker sounded a little smug. 'I'm really here to see if there's anything I can do for you. That's my job, you know. We're very conscious of how difficult it may be to adjust after leaving the Service. And you were with it a long time. Twenty-seven years, wasn't it?'

'Twenty-eight,' Harry smiled at him. 'I haven't found any problem. I was behind a desk for the last eight years. This is a little different, but it's interesting. I've always liked the idea of catering, running a service business.'

'Oh yes? Yes, it's the growth industry these days I'm told.'

Never boiled an egg. . . Never washed a cup. The words of the wife came back to him. He leaned forward.

'How did you find this job then?'

Harry gave a little chuckle. 'Through influence,

I'm afraid. I'm a local lad you see. I was born at Dedham and I've got family still living there. They knew the new owners and recommended me. I was here on trial for the first couple of months, but they seem to think I've done a good job and I'm permanent now. It's a great place; nice staff, reasonable salary, all accommodation and food provided. And a few perks besides.'

He was elbow-nudging when he said that. Cheerful, friendly.

Parker nodded. 'You seem to have fallen on your feet. Good for you. By the way I went to see your wife.'

'My ex-wife,' Oakham corrected. The smile was still on his face. 'Why was that? Nothing wrong with her, is there?'

'Oh no, she's quite all right. I went to your old house and the new owners gave me her address. She told me you'd got divorced.'

Harry raised both hands in a gesture of regret.

'Well, it was better to make a clean break. She had another chap. It hadn't mattered while I was working, but when I left the office I began to mind. I expect she'll marry him. I hope she does. I wasn't all that good a husband, too wrapped up in my work. We hadn't any children either, so there aren't those bones broken. It's bloody when children get involved. You married, Jim?'

Parker noted the Christian name.

'No. Never got round to it. Tell me, didn't you have to take some catering course or something to get a job in a place like this?'

'No,' Harry shook his head, his eyes full of amusement at his own cheek. 'I just took up where the last manager left off. I've changed a few things as I found my way round, but it's really a case of man management. And I've always been quite good at that. I ran all sorts of people in my old job. I like people.'

'And it's doing well? I saw lots of cars in the car park. Must be expensive to stay here.'

'It is,' Harry agreed. 'Very expensive. But we give value for money. Come and spend a night some time.'

'Not on my salary,' Parker said.

'As my guest,' Harry countered. 'I mean it. I'd like to show you round, but I am a bit busy this afternoon.'

It was a dismissal accompanied by a bribe. Parker didn't get up at once. He frowned and cleared his throat. He looked worried.

'I've been trying to trace an old colleague of yours, Harry.' He dropped in the Christian name this time. 'Jan Ploekewski. He's disappeared. He wasn't too stable, as you know. I've tried everyone who knew him but he just packed in his job, walked out of his room and disappeared. You haven't heard from him have you?'

Harry Oakham got up.

'He hasn't disappeared! He went back to Poland after Solidarity took over. I had dinner with him the night before he left. He was in great form, very excited about going. He said he'd make a new start among his own people. He was born here but he always said he never felt English. I had a postcard from him some time ago saying he was travelling around and wasn't planning to come back. There's nothing to worry about. I think he's found his niche in life. I hope so. He was a good man.'

He opened the door and Parker followed him out into the reception hall. They came down the steps together; the sun was shining. Parker looked back at the building.

'Must be very old,' he said. 'Has it got a history?'

He was lingering on purpose, Oakham decided. Didn't like being ushered out till he was ready. He knew that type. Officious, petty, cloaked in good intentions. He hated the Parkers of this world. He was gracious when he answered.

'Yes, it has, it was a Catholic stronghold in Tudor times, priests' holes and the rest of it. It's supposed to be haunted by a child who was murdered – all good rousing stuff but we don't put it in the brochure.

'I mean it, Jim, come and stay a night. Just give us a ring.'

He opened the car door and Parker got in.

'Thanks, I might take you up on it. Glad everything's turned out so well. And by the by – if you do hear any more from Ploekewski, here's my telephone number. If he's really gone for good we ought to close the file.'

He waved as he drove off. Harry turned and went inside.

He locked the piece of paper in his desk. Close the file on Jan. He'd feed them something later on.

*   *   *

'Look at the time, I must be off,' Jim Parker said suddenly.

Rosa got up with him. He'd left the story hanging, driving away from the hotel, and she said, 'But you haven't told me half enough. Is that all, just that intuitive feeling when you met him? It doesn't seem a lot to go on, if you don't mind me saying so.'

'I don't mind at all,' he answered. 'But it's interesting, isn't it?'

'The tiger in the cat basket,' she murmured as they began to walk back towards Birdcage Walk. 'It sounds like a good title for one of those thrillers you don't like. And where does this leave me, Mr Parker?'

'It leaves you in Birdcage Walk, Mrs Bennet, and if you hurry, you can catch that taxi I see cruising along. I'll ring you tomorrow. I could come and see you and we can go on from there. If you're really interested.'

She felt irritated with him.

'Of course I am,' she said. 'You don't need to ring. I'm meeting my ex-husband for a drink at twelve and then I'm at home for the rest of the afternoon. And evening.'

'Three o'clock then? I know the address. See you then.'

He turned and walked briskly in the opposite direction. She took his advice and hailed the taxi. She was having supper with friends that evening. People were being very kind once they heard she was alone.

*   *   *

James Bennet had suggested neutral ground for their last meeting. There was a wine bar on the corner of World's End where he'd dropped in once or twice. He suggested they wrap up their marriage between twelve and one o'clock. He was waiting for her when she came in; he looked relaxed as he got up.

'Hello, Rosa.'

'Hello, James.'

She looked rather pale, he noticed. His girl was blooming with pregnancy.

Rosa sat down; she lit a cigarette.

'Started again?' he asked. 'I thought you said you'd stopped last time.'

'You're looking well,' she said.

'I'm fine. Busy, things are picking up at last.'

'I'm glad.'

'How about you? How's the office?'

She heard the edge in his tone. He was still bitter. She'd agreed to everything he asked, but he hadn't forgiven her. Perhaps he wasn't as happy as he made out.

'I'm on leave,' she answered.

'When do you go to Brussels?' He signalled for the waiter. 'What will you have? Red or white?'

'Nothing thanks. I may not take the Brussels job. I want to get my affairs sorted out. There'll be other opportunities.'

'Don't expect me to say I'm sorry. If it hadn't been for your bloody job, Rosa, we wouldn't be sitting here now, saving money on lawyers.'

She looked at him and said quietly, 'Are you sure about that? I'm not any more. It didn't take much to pull us apart, did it? We made a mistake getting married. Let's leave it at that.'

He drank his red wine, looked at her over the glass.

'You'll meet someone else,' he said. 'If you haven't already.'

'I haven't,' she said flatly. 'You were the one who went shopping, not me. Why don't we stop sniping at each other and get this over and done with? I don't want to argue.'

'You never did,' he said. 'If I step out of line, Bella gives me hell. I find it easier to live with.'

'Lucky for you,' she shrugged. 'I don't want to talk about her. You've got the papers?'

He opened his briefcase.

'They're all here,' he said. 'That's a list of stuff I'd like to take. See if it's OK with you.'

'It's mostly your furniture,' she said, pushing the list back at him. 'I don't need to see it. When's the van coming?'

'I don't need a van,' he said irritably. 'What did you expect me to do? Strip the bloody house? There's a desk and my mother's two pictures. I think she ought to have them back. Odds and ends of books and the hall chairs. I'm not sticking on them but they did come from my grandfather originally.'

'You take them,' Rosa said. 'Please, James, whatever you want. Here, let me sign this damned thing.'

It had been her idea to renounce alimony. Oddly, he had needed some persuading before he agreed to let her sign away her right to part of his income. But once the decision was made, he had got the documentation drawn up and told the lawyer briskly that he and his wife didn't have to meet in his office to tie up the loose ends. The lawyer had annoyed him by a shaft of sarcasm.

'Nice to think you're on friendly terms. Maybe you shouldn't rush into divorce?'

James didn't react.

He took the papers back from her, glanced at them to make sure all was in order – Rosa knew he couldn't help being meticulous – and put them away.

'So what are your plans?'

'I haven't really thought,' Rosa answered.

It was like talking to a stranger; he'd been her husband, her lover, now he was a stranger, asking about her plans.

'If I don't go to Brussels, I might take a holiday somewhere. James, if we've nothing more to sort out, I think I'll go now.'

He called for the bill. She didn't want to wait, she wanted to say goodbye at the table. The pain of a final parting or the pain of failure; she didn't know which it was. But the pain was very real. He opened the door for her.

'Rosa,' he said, and he held her arm for a moment. 'You mind, don't you?'

'Yes, of course I mind.'

He said, 'I know I've been a shit, I'm sorry. If ever you need anything, any help – just let me know. Promise?'

'Thanks. I'll remember.'

'Don't forget,' he insisted. 'I hope things turn out

well for you. Maybe we'll be friends. You'd like Bella.'

'Goodbye, James.'

He let go of her arm.

'There's a taxi. Hey!'

It drew up alongside them. The driver leaned out and opened the door.

'I'll walk,' she stepped back. 'You take it.'

'All right, I'm running a bit late. Bye, Rosa!'

The door slammed; he looked through the window, raised his hand briefly and sat back out of sight. It was all over. With regrets, she could see that, and a little sadness because he had been disappointed in his hopes. But with a clean page on the ledger. It was a clean page for her too.

Parker was late. She laid a tray for some tea and put out biscuits and wondered if something had stopped him coming. There was no message on the answer machine. She looked at her watch. Three twenty. Then the bell rang and he was on the doorstep. He didn't apologize, he just said, 'Hello,' and followed her through the hall and into the drawing room. He looked around him.

'Nice house you've got. How did the drink go?'

She stared at him.

'Drink?'

'With your ex,' he said. 'Shall I sit here?'

'It went off perfectly well.' Her tone was curt.

He had no right to ask about her private life, and then she realized that in his world he had every right. And now it was her world too.

She said, 'I'm sorry. I didn't mean to be offhand. It wasn't too bad. We didn't argue about anything. He's been very generous in fact.'

'Guilty conscience,' Parker stated. 'But you're getting over it?'

'I've got over it. Well, very nearly. I'll make some tea. Do you like milk or lemon?'

'Milk please,' he said. He got up when she came back. 'Let me take that. Do you live here alone, Mrs Bennet?'

'Why don't you call me Rosa? On this table, thanks.'

She poured tea for both of them and he took two biscuits.

'You get a lot of oddballs in our Service,' he remarked. 'They have to be, I suppose, to do it in the first place.'

'Are you an oddball?'

'I expect so. Now, war is one thing, but to do what Oakham did in peacetime is not the same at all. Quite a few operators resigned after the war. They couldn't kill in cold blood – well, without the flags and the bugles in the background. He came into it young, twenty-four, out of university via a City job. Insurance broking. Bored to tears, he said he was, when he was interviewed. He wanted a challenge, something to test him.

'He had a long training, psychological checks all the way, he was pushed to the limit physically and he held up mentally when some of the same intake simply cracked up. He was killer material, that's what they decided. But even so, he went the long route through surveillance and the cipher school.

'Explosives and radio communication. Bugging. The lot. He did the equivalent of a copper on the beat before they moved him up. And then sideways in what we call Department "F". "F" for Freedom.'

'What does that mean?' Rosa asked.

'Freedom from the cares of this world,' he said. 'I think it was some snide old pansy up at Cambridge who thought that one up. Giggle, giggle.'

'I don't find it funny.'

'I don't either. Can I have another biscuit? If you wonder why I'm telling you all this, it's for a reason.'

'I'm sure,' Rosa nodded. 'Help yourself. More tea?'

She poured for him.

'I want to paint a picture of Harry Oakham for you. And it's not easy, but I've got to try. If you take this on, you ought to know what you're up against. Oakham wasn't quite right and I knew it, but I couldn't put a hand on my heart, and say this is why. And I had to do that before I put in a report. So I stayed on at Dedham over the weekend and I did a bit of snooping.'

He went out for a walk after breakfast on the Sunday morning. It was warm and sunny as he strolled round the charming village, glancing through the gift-shop windows and boutiques. The ancient church stood proud in the main street, its four-pointed tower dominating the skyline. You never heard bells on a Sunday any more, Parker thought. Not where he lived anyway. The scene reminded him of the small country town where he grew up; his father went regularly to Morning Service, while his mother prepared the ritual Sunday roast for lunch. He had two sisters and a brother. The sisters had married and moved to opposite parts of the country, the brother was a dentist in his father's practice. His mother was alive, but old and too confused to live alone. He tried to visit the residential home as often as he could. He'd drifted apart from the others.

He watched the groups of people walking up the short path to the church, and on impulse he followed and took a seat at the rear. The smell was familiar. Like this one, the church at his old home dated from the thirteenth century and there was a musty smell that made him think of dead birds when he was a boy. He didn't follow the service or join in the hymns. The sermon didn't impinge on his own thoughts. The service ended and the last notes of the organ wheezed and died away. There hadn't been many worshippers. The church was soon empty. Harry Oakham must have come here when he was a boy. Oakhams had lived here for generations. He remembered the old man in the pub, looking at him with the countryman's suspicion. *Try up at Bruton Hall.* Harry Oakham's family were old-fashioned gentry. But he wouldn't be the first of his kind to set out as a freebooter. To dip his hands in bloody mire and wash them clean at the Arts Club before dinner.

He got up and wandered round the church. There were memorials to the Oakhams on the walls. An

Oakham among the list of vicars. Harry's grandfather. That was on his file. A small stained-glass window in the Lady Chapel with a sentimental Christ cradling a toyshop lamb and two fat angels gazing up to heaven. Given in memory of 2nd Lieutenant Arthur David Oakham, the Suffolk Regiment, killed on the Somme, 10 September 1916, aged twenty. His name liveth for ever more.

Parker paused by it and walked back to the entrance. A man in a cassock was waiting to close up. He smiled at Parker and said, 'Good morning.' He had a gentle, friendly face. A good shepherd of his flock. Parker remembered his father saying that about their own vicar. He shook off the nostalgia, and started to walk round the churchyard, looking at the tombs. It was at the back, guarded by a low rail and a tall granite headstone. No weeds had insinuated themselves through the coverings of granite chips. The flower vase was empty, with a film of spider's web across the top. Nobody had been there for a long time.

Judith Elizabeth, beloved wife of Henry Oakham. Born 1953, died 1977. She'd died very young. He stood looking down at the grave. It was all in Oakham's file. Killed in an accident at Verbier. Standing there made it real for the first time. Dead, only two years after they were married. And then, following the zigzag of unpredictability, Oakham had married the woman Parker had interviewed. He'd lived in the modest little house like a stranger and abandoned everything immediately he left the Service, to end up in a luxury hotel on his old home ground. In an improbable job for which he was unqualified. A lethal weapon, disarmed and hung up on the wall . . . Man management. He was good with people. He'd got the job through family influence.

The sign said BRUTON HALL, and he set off up the long drive. It was well kept, the surrounding parkland post and railed, with a few cattle browsing in the distance. The house stood at the end of an avenue of fine old lime trees.

Generations of them have lived here, he repeated. But times have changed. There were cars in the forecourt, the unmistakable signs of a big house commercially broken up into flats. He went to the main entrance, a stone portico protecting a handsome door, and looked up the list of flats and the names beside the numbers. He found 'Oakham' on the top floor.

He pressed the bell and waited. There was an intercom.

A voice called through to him, 'Yes?'

'Mrs Oakham?'

'Who's that?'

'My name's Parker. Is that Mrs Oakham?'

'No, sorry. They're away. I'll come down.'

A middle-aged woman in trousers opened the door to him. It didn't open fully because she had left the security chain slotted in. So much for Britain in the 1990s; even in rural Suffolk fear of the stranger prevailed.

'Mr Parker?' She had a nasal voice that rose on the last syllable.

He said, 'Yes. So sorry to bother you on a Sunday,

but I was really looking for an old friend of mine. Harry Oakham. I'm staying in the village and they told me to come up here and ask.'

She slipped the chain and opened the door to let him into the hall. It must have been a very large house before it was converted.

'Isn't he working at some hotel near here? I think Liz mentioned something. The name rings a bell. He's some kind of cousin of theirs. I'm just a friend. I'm dog-sitting while she and Peter are fishing up in Scotland.'

'Did they say which hotel it was by any chance?'

'No, I don't think so. I think they said he'd rung them up or something. Sorry to be so vague about it, but I got the impression they hadn't seen him for ages. I can leave them a message if you'd like to give me a number, they can telephone you. They'll be back next week.'

He smiled, shrugged the offer aside.

'No, don't bother, I was just staying a couple of nights and I thought I'd try and look him up on the off chance. Thanks very much.'

The door closed and he turned and started walking back. A Ford Cortina gleaming with Sunday polish sped past him and drew up in front of the house. One of the flat owners. The friend who was dog-sitting had a voice like Joyce Grenfell. Looked a bit like her too. She'd got the impression Oakham's cousins hadn't seen him for ages. Oakham had said 'family influence'. His cousins were friends of the new owners, they'd got him the job.

Parker went into his office on Monday morning

and wrote a memo for his immediate boss. One lie wasn't much to go on, but it was all he had beside that nagging instinct. His boss had learned to respect that. The investigation was initiated.

'The trouble is,' he explained to Rosa, 'we can't put any of the pros on to this. There's always a chance Oakham would spot them. Even know some of them. It's a small world and it's not that secure. He's only been out of it for a few months. We need a new face. Somebody who doesn't carry a label he'd be able to read. That's why we approached Sir Peter Jefford to see if he had anyone he thought could take it on. He suggested you.'

Time had gone by very quickly. She got up.

'Have a drink, I'm going to. What would you like?'

'What's on offer?'

He was pleasant to her now; she quite liked him.

'Pretty well everything. James left me a cellarful of wine and there's stacks of spirits.'

'He was generous, wasn't he? I'd like a Scotch, on the rocks.'

'I'm a vodka lady tonight,' she said. 'Won't be long.'

He lit a cigarette while he waited. She was impressive. She listened, she didn't interrupt to show how clever she was. He liked that. He was beginning to like her. If she was as good as he hoped, she'd pick up something. If he was right and there was anything to pick up. It wasn't much to go on. A lie, making himself out the big fellow with the family that could snap its fingers and put him in a top job. It had grown into a bigger lie when enquiries established the new owners as a Swiss consortium based in Geneva. They weren't friends with anybody.

Rosa Bennet would fit in to a hotel like Doll's House Manor. She had a perfect cover and for a change it was the truth. She was having a holiday, picking up the pieces after a divorce. Two or maybe three weeks staying in the country. Reading, doing the antique shops, touring a bit. And looking for any little detail about Oakham's position that didn't add up. Depending on what she came up with, the boys from Special Branch would take over. She wouldn't be in danger so long as she was careful.

She came back with the drinks. She smiled at him.

'I found a special Chivas Regal. I didn't put in too much ice.' She sat beside him. 'Where would I fit into all this? I don't quite see a role for myself.'

'First thing,' Parker answered, 'I want you to do is think about it. Think very carefully before you make up your mind.'

'I could if I knew what was involved,' she retorted. 'I'm not a mind reader, Jim.'

'You'll have to learn that too, if you're going to be any good. Lovely Scotch. You'll have to go down and stay at that place. Keep your eyes open, try and get on terms with him if you can. Talk to him, trail your coat a bit. You're a very attractive lady. You're divorced, you're at a loose end, taking a bit of time to get yourself together. And be very, very careful not to make him suspicious. You know the kind of man he is. What he's capable of doing.'

She didn't answer at once. She drank some of her vodka.

'When you say trail your coat . . . you mean sleep with him?'

'You'd have to judge that,' he said. 'Might not arise at all. Or it might. I can't guarantee how far you'd have to go. But I don't want an answer now. And if you turn it down, you'll most likely be doing the right thing. Nobody'll think any less of you. I certainly won't. So take forty-eight hours. Don't rush it. Then ring me. If it's yes, I'll give you a last briefing and a contact number. If no, then we'll just have a drink together. Or some lunch if you like. I'd better go now.'

'Rosa, darling, why don't you go off somewhere in the sun?'

Her mother looked up from her tapestry work. She was a woman who couldn't sit idle-handed. She had to be making something. She thought it was a pity her daughter didn't take up needlework, it would have helped her relax.

'You do look so strung up,' she went on. 'Now it's all over you ought to get away as soon as possible. Pass me the scissors, will you, they're on the table.'

She was fond of her daughter, but they had little in common. She had been a widow for four years and made a busy, satisfying life for herself. There were lots of activities in the village and she took part in all of them. She hadn't time to be lonely, she said.

'I'd rather go somewhere in England,' Rosa said. 'I don't know why you're so dead set against

Spain.' Her mother threaded a silk through her needle. 'Sally and I had a wonderful holiday last year.'

She went away with friends, and adored travelling. She was convinced that a bit of sun would do Rosa the world of good, and had spent most of the weekend recommending her own favourite resorts.

'The thought of the Costa del Sol gives me the horrors!'

Rosa got up and handed her the scissors.

'I'm not going to Spain or Majorca on a package tour and I do wish you'd leave it alone, Mum. I'm going to a nice quiet hotel, in easy driving distance, where I won't be bothered by people.'

The weekend was becoming fraught. They had always argued in a mildly irritable way. Her mother had been horrified by the break-up of her marriage. She had always liked James, who liked her, and she thought her daughter had thrown away a very good husband, with money and prospects, and would live to regret it.

When Rosa first telephoned and told her what had happened she had said so forcefully, 'You're being obstinate and silly! Why should this other woman walk off with him? Oh, don't start all that nonsense about a baby; she only did it to catch him! If I were you, I'd try and get him back. This job of yours is all very well . . . '

Rosa had cut short the conversation, and didn't come down to see her until the legal details were finalized. Now it was over.

Her mother said, 'If that's really the kind of

holiday you want, then I won't try and persuade you to do the sensible thing. I think you'll be bored to death, you know what you're like. I'll make us a cup of tea.'

Rosa watched her go out to the kitchen. She was a woman who moved with a purpose whatever she was doing. She had always hurried through her life as if everything she did was terribly important. Rosa's father never hurried.

He was quiet, self-contained, a reflective man who enjoyed silence and his own thoughts. He had been Regius Professor of History at Oxford, till he retired after a minor heart attack. They had one son, older than Rosa. He and she were opposites too. He was sporting, unimaginative. He went to Australia instead of university and settled down to live there. He had an Australian wife and a brood of children who were allowed to run wild in the house when they came on a visit. Rosa had nothing in common with any of them. Her parents were pleased to see them and openly relieved when they went home. Rosa was the academic child, the brilliant student who came down with a double first from Lady Margaret Hall. Her father had been very proud of her achievement and encouraged her choice of the Foreign Office as a career. Her mother had been much more gratified by her marriage to James Bennet.

'Here we are. There's some nice sponge cake. Have a slice. Where are you going then, have you found somewhere?'

'Yes I have. I saw it in one of the colour supplements. I thought it looked a lovely place. It's called the Doll's House Manor Hotel, just outside Dedham.'

'Sounds desperately twee to me,' her mother said. 'Rather a cottagey place.'

'It's a big Tudor house,' Rosa refused to rise. 'And it's got a lake. Plenty of places to see if I feel like driving round. It's just what I want.'

'Oh well,' her mother sighed. Such a silly thing to do, going away in England. You could never count on good weather. But then she and Rosa had always liked different things. 'Never mind. Maybe it'll do you good. Fancy calling it the Doll's House Manor. I still think it's twee. Like your Wendy House – you and Philip were terribly destructive. You were always breaking each other's toys.'

'We were always fighting over them,' Rosa reminded her. And about everything else too. 'I don't remember the Wendy House. What happened to it?'

'I gave it to the church jumble sale. You'd both gone away to school and it was taking up space. Perhaps it was a pity to give it away. The grandchildren might have liked it.'

'Mum, darling, they'd smash it to matchwood in five minutes.'

'Yes, I suppose so. I do wish they were brought up a bit better. They are sweet though.' She always ended by saying that.

'They're absolutely dreadful and you know it,' Rosa said.

Her mother smiled; she never minded what she called plain speaking.

'Yes, darling, I know they are, but I do love them.'

She finished her tea and stacked everything neatly on the tray.

'One good thing about this wretched divorce, you were both so civilized about it. I was worried you and James would start throwing accusations around. It seems so clinical the way you did it.'

'Yes,' Rosa agreed. 'So's losing a leg.'

Her mother looked up quickly. 'What, you're not regretting it, are you? It's not too late if you are . . .'

'I'm not regretting it, and anyway it's not up to me. James wanted the divorce. He's getting married as soon as the decree comes through.'

'Yes, darling, I know, but I'm sure you could get him back if you really wanted to. He was so madly in love with you, I'm sure he still is.'

'I'm afraid not,' Rosa answered. 'He couldn't wait to get rid of me. It's wishful thinking, Mum. It's over and done with. And don't worry about me, I'll be fine. I've adjusted very well actually. I expect it was because you and Daddy were so happy that I thought marriages didn't go bust.'

Which was true. They had been happy for over forty years. Chalk and cheese and perfectly suited. She got up.

'I'll go and pack, Mum. I'd better go before the traffic gets too bad. You know what it's like on a Sunday night.'

Her mother took the tray out and washed up. She put the sponge cake in a tin. She sighed. Rosa was a lovely girl, she'd always been pretty even as a toddler. But she'd made such a mess of things. If only she hadn't been clever like her father. And so ambitious. Young women were so different now, so independent. But she wouldn't find another James in a hurry. They had that charming house, plenty of money. She could have been set up for life. She went back to the sitting room and took up her needlework again.

Upstairs in her old room, Rosa cleared her small case. The room was much as she had left it on the morning she got married. The same pictures, the same quilted bedspread, faded over the years, matching the curtains. They were faded too. She'd been happy there, growing up. She'd expected to be happy when she walked out in her wedding dress to start a new life. Now that was over. She paused, looking round her. She had come down on the Friday after seeing Parker. He'd taken her to lunch in a trattoria in the Fulham Road.

'I don't run to smart clubs I'm afraid,' he said. 'But if you like to eat Italian, I know a good place.'

He didn't press her for an answer.

They had a drink and considered the menu; she put it down and said, 'I'm going to take up the job, if it's still on offer. I've thought it over carefully, and I'd like to do it.'

He looked at her over the menu.

'Good. I hoped you would. Now, what would you like to eat? I can recommend the spaghetti *alle vongole* if you fancy sea food.'

She was to book for a fortnight, ask for one of the best rooms. Act normally, but be friendly to the staff. Get to know the layout of the hotel. And get to know Oakham. Don't expect a quick response. Maybe no response at all. It was all problematical. 'You need luck,' Parker told her as they drank their coffee. 'Luck is the one slip someone makes, the one coincidence that shouldn't happen. You're going to need luck.'

'And if nothing happens, if I hang around and I can't pick up anything? If he's genuine and the job's genuine?'

Parker shrugged. 'You'll have had a couple of weeks' free holiday in a posh hotel. But my guess is, it won't turn out like that.'

She had two telephone numbers. One was to a supposed girlfriend in London. She could telephone from the hotel to that number, saying she was all right, enjoying her stay, and the wording would convey that she'd found nothing suspicious. The other number could only be used outside from a secure phone. It connected directly with Parker.

'And one other thing,' Parker had added, almost as an afterthought, though by now she knew he liked to slip in an important point towards the end, 'if you run into anyone that looks like this, let me know.'

He showed her a snap of Jan Ploekewski. She studied it, as she had been taught, memorizing the features.

'He was an old mate of Oakham's,' Parker explained. 'Polish, but born in England. Jan Ploekewski. He's gone missing. I mentioned him, remember?'

She nodded. He'd asked Oakham about him. Oakham said he'd gone to Poland.

'You think he could be with him? In the hotel?'

'If he is,' Parker signalled for the bill, 'then we *are* on to something. They always worked as a team.'

He had turned to her in the street and shaken hands.

'Let me know when you're booked in,' he said. 'Mind yourself. Good luck.'

She'd driven down to her mother to spend the weekend and started the cover story going. She decided to ring up and make the booking when she got back to London. Monday would do. Clouds were coming up on a rising wind; she saw them through the bedroom window. It looked like rain. She picked up her case. It's like leaving it all for the second time, she thought suddenly. There's a finality about shutting the door of my old room, walking downstairs and leaving the house where I was born. As if I may never come back again.

She hurried to find her mother and say goodbye. She was very stern with herself for that twinge of superstition on the drive back.

5

The Russian, Vassily Zarubin, and Daniel Ishbav arrived on the same day. Daniel came by train to Ipswich and Hermann Rilke drove to the station and picked him up. There was a natural antagonism between the two men. Daniel looked shifty and ill at ease.

Rilke glanced at him and said, 'Hurry up, the car's over there.' In the car he said, 'You'll have to get some proper clothes. You're supposed to be an auditor, you're my assistant. You look like a street trader.'

'Fuck off,' was Daniel's response.

He turned and stared out of the window. He'd had a rough three days, dodging from one escape route to another in case he was being watched. It had made him nervous. He'd twisted and back-tracked till he was certain if there were watchers, he'd shaken them off, and finally ended up at Ipswich station. He wasn't in the mood to take any critical shit from that German bender. Street trader! It had stung, as Rilke intended.

'What's the place like?' Daniel demanded.

'You saw the video,' was the answer.

Rilke was furious at being sworn at by such a little reptile. They drove in silence till they reached

Croft Lodge. He felt he filled the role Oakham had allotted him very convincingly. But that unshaven, grubby little Israeli . . .

Daniel looked round him. 'You live here?'

'Yes,' Rilke hissed at him. 'Harry'll be along to see you. This is your room. We live in the same house, I'm sorry to say!'

He left Daniel and hurried off to his own quarters. They were large and led directly up to the top floor which had been converted to his requirements. Nobody ever went there except Rilke. The door at the end of the stairs was double locked. He and Harry Oakham had the only two keys.

It was very well furnished; Daniel was pleased with the comfort and especially impressed by the big modern bathroom. He was tired and he felt sweaty after the journey. He stripped off and stood under the hot shower, soaping himself. He tied a towel round his waist and wandered out into the bedroom. It was a lot different from the dingy rented hideaways he'd been living in for so long. There was a built-in TV and a mini bar, a sofa and a comfortable armchair, a good-sized single bed, plenty of cupboard space – he hadn't many clothes to put in it, but never mind – nice decorations. It was luxury, he decided. He rummaged in the hold-all for a clean shirt and some jeans.

There was a knock on the door and Harry walked in. He came up and shook hands; he laid another on Daniel's shoulder in a double welcome.

'Daniel – good to see you! No trouble getting here?'

'No trouble,' Daniel assured him. 'Nice place. How's it going, Harry?'

'It's going well.' Harry sat down. He pointed to the mini bar. 'Let's have a drink. I'll tell you about the set-up. All the staff have been told about you. You're Mr Daniels, and you're assistant to Hermann. He's Brandt, by the way.' He grinned. 'And Monika is *Mrs* Brandt.'

Daniel sniggered. 'Jesus! Do I have to work with him?'

'You work with me,' Oakham answered. 'Everything else is just a front. I have my own house adjoining the hotel because I'm the manager, but I usually come over and join you in the evenings. At all times you keep away from the hotel, unless I want you to show yourself. Rilke and you are resident financial auditors and these are your offices and living accommodation. Jan has his own flat in the stable block. There's a cleaner who comes in every morning, and you cater for yourselves.'

'I can't see myself in an office with Rilke,' he protested. 'Are there really offices?'

'Complete with computers, word processors and the hotel financial files. Rilke trained as an accountant, so he knows a bit about it. I told you, everything is normal, authentic. You'll get kitted out with some formal working clothes. I've got plenty of cash if you need some. You'll have the use of a car. Come and go as you like. I don't have to tell you to keep out of trouble and keep a low profile, do I?'

He grinned at Daniel in his friendly way, slightly

mocking the Israeli who had spent so much of his life running.

'Zarubin's due in at lunch-time. He won't be staying with you. He's a guest; he'll have a room in the hotel.'

'Why?' Daniel was curious. 'What's he supposed to be?'

'An author, working on a book. Writing a biography of Vaclav Havel. He's finishing it off down here in peace and quiet. I've briefed the hotel staff about not disturbing him; I gave them a long spiel about him this morning.'

'You think of everything,' Daniel remarked. 'Every detail.'

'We wouldn't last long if I didn't,' was the retort. 'You make yourself at home, here's five hundred pounds and the keys of your car. It's a grey Volvo 340; it's in the staff car park. Do some shopping. Ipswich is a good place when you get to know the one-way streets. Get a dark suit, some plain shirts; you know the idea.' He glanced at the trainers on Daniel's feet. 'And some shoes,' he added.

'I'm coming over tomorrow at seven thirty. I'm expecting a call about a proposition. I'll have the details and I want everyone here for a preliminary briefing.'

Daniel's eyes were sharp. He had a dark, predatory face.

'There'll be something for me? Already?'

'I think it'll be right up your alley,' Oakham said. 'See you tomorrow.'

*   *   *

Vassily Zarubin arrived at Stansted Airport at ten in the morning. He had travelled via Turkey, on to Cairo and then flown to Naples; from Naples on to Paris. He'd used different passports each time. Different nationalities. Romanian, Austrian, Swiss for the last leg of the journey. No visas because he was always in transit. The flight from Paris to Stansted was in a thirty-seater jet. He watched the descent into England with interest. He spoke the language fluently, but he had never been further West than Warsaw. The lack of fuss and officialdom surprised him. He was through Customs and Immigration very quickly. He inspected the new airport on his way. It seemed very large for so few passengers. There were no queues. He hired a car from Avis. The banner claim, 'We try harder', made him smile. He bought a map and worked out a route. He didn't drive fast because of the English right-hand drive.

It was very pretty country, very green. Like a picture-book, with its small fields and little villages, clothed in warm brick. The English were a tidy people. But then the country was so small. Almost claustrophobic compared to the huge expanse of his own country. Nothing in view but the horizon itself in parts of the great steppes. He imagined that at the end of the horizon, a man might just step right off the earth and fall for ever.

He had said goodbye to his father. It was an emotional moment, they were very close. Close in aims and ideals. He loved his father as much as he admired him. He had believed in his ideals and fought hard for them. Now he was defeated, swept away on the flood tide of historical change that had rolled over Russia. Retired into a decent obscurity. Oakham had said the same fate was ahead of him. The hard liners had lost.

He drew up at the roadside, checked his map. He was afraid he'd missed the turning. But no; it was further on. He traced the line with his finger. He looked at his watch. He'd bought the watch at Charles de Gaulle Airport. All his possessions were new. His clothes, even his razor and toothpaste. He'd been stripped of his identity down to the labels on his underclothes. He had been safe in Turkey when the car crashed and blew up. His father had called on old comrades for help, and help had been given. He was dead. He didn't exist.

He slowed, following the route, watching for the signpost. Then he saw it. The painted board by the roadside.

Doll's House Manor Hotel. His new home. He turned cautiously and found a pause in the line of traffic when a car slowed and allowed him to cross into the drive. They were polite people, the English. Nobody would have given way for another motorist at home.

He hit the first speed-bump and swore as the car bucked. He was careful to go very slowly after that.

When he called from Paris, Oakham had said, 'Get here around twelve fifteen. I'll be watching out for you.' He was ten minutes late, but he saw Oakham come out and down the steps as soon as he opened the car door and got out.

'Good afternoon, Mr Zarubin. Welcome to the hotel.'

They shook hands, Harry bowed slightly to him.

'Come with me please, I'll get your luggage sent up, sir.'

Vassily followed him, a boy in blue livery was hurrying down to unload his suitcases. By the reception Harry paused.

'If you'll register, sir. Thank you.'

Vassily signed.

'If you give reception your car keys they'll put it away for you. Jane?'

The pretty girl behind the desk smiled at Vassily; he smiled back. He handed her the keys.

'Thank you.'

Oakham was by his elbow, solicitous, deferential.

'I'll take you up; we've given you the Denmark suite. I think you'll find it satisfactory. This way, sir.'

Jane watched them go. He was a very famous author. Writing a book on the President playwright who'd been imprisoned by the Communists. Jane was a simple girl who didn't bother too much about politics, but even she had been affected by what the Romanians and the Czechs had done.

He was much younger than she expected. Rather handsome in a way, she decided. She liked his deep voice and the accent. Mr Oakham had emphasized what an honour it was for them to be chosen by such a distinguished man. He was to be shielded from noise or disturbance, his meals sent up if he preferred not to use the restaurant. If he wanted secretarial assistance, the hotel would provide it. Jane was a shorthand typist. She hoped he might ask for her. The sitting room of the Denmark suite had been fitted out with a desk, a filing cabinet and a word processor. Harry had explained that the publishers were paying for everything.

Mr Zarubin found it impossible to work in London. He had sought political asylum seven years ago and taken refuge in England. Jane thought it was a romantic story even before she saw him. Now she couldn't wait to describe him to the other girls.

Inside the suite Harry and Vassily Zarubin faced each other.

'How are you? For a corpse, you look pretty healthy! You must have had a hell of a detour getting here.'

'It was long,' the Russian admitted. 'You should have been a stage actor. You were very good downstairs. I like the bow.'

'I bow to all my guests, especially the ladies,' Harry laughed. 'It's expected. You'll find everything you need, I think. Help yourself to a drink. What do you think of England? First time isn't it?'

Zarubin was stretched out on the sofa; he'd poured a helping of vodka into a glass and was drinking it neat. There was no mini bar in the Denmark suite. A tray of spirits and mixers was provided courtesy of the management. He glanced up at Oakham.

He said, 'It's small. Pretty if you like small places. What am I supposed to do all day with all of this?'

He gestured towards the loaded desk in the corner. Oakham sensed antagonism.

He said, 'Work out a curriculum for your first assignment. Rilke's got three clients coming in at the end of the week. Belfast shit. Get yourself settled in and take a walk round, the grounds are nice, and I'll call through to you around seven. We're having a meeting I'd like you to sit in on. I'll come and collect you.'

He left Zarubin alone. He walked down the stairs rather slowly. He was right about the antagonism. Zarubin was the youngest and probably the toughest of all of them. He would need careful managing. It would be quite a culture shock for him to be shut up in a country hotel, play acting for a lot of employees.

Harry Oakham took the call from Hakim. He didn't say much; he listened and asked questions.

On the other end Hakim demanded, 'When will you carry out the contract?'

'When I've worked out the details and had a dummy run,' Oakham answered.

'He's only here for a week, and he could change his mind and go early.'

Hakim sounded anxious and impatient.

'Then we miss the job,' was the reply. 'I'm not going into anything without the proper preparation. You wouldn't like it if we cocked it up. You call in when he arrives — or if he changes his plans.'

He hung up on Hakim who had started to argue.

At seven he fetched Zarubin. At seven thirty they went to Croft Lodge to meet the others.

They'd gathered in the sitting room. Jan offered drinks, watching the door for Oakham. He was nervous and ill at ease. The snoop had been got rid of, Harry was confident and dismissed his fears, but Jan couldn't stop worrying. Once the snoops got on to you, they didn't go away without finding something. He knew all about snoops; they wore ordinary clothes so you didn't notice them, and then they grabbed you and suddenly they were in uniforms and they opened the door into hell . . .

Oakham came in. He smiled at them.

'We're all here, good. Jan, you've been looking after everybody, now how about a Scotch for me? Thanks.'

'What's going on?' Rilke demanded.

He had noticed the Pole twitching. The Russian, Zarubin, had stretched himself out in a chair, legs stuck in front of him, glass cradled on his chest. He was watching them all in turn.

'We've been offered our first big contract,' Oakham announced. 'A one-off job. And, let me tell you, the money's very big.'

'How big?' Daniel demanded.

He wore his new suit and he'd shaved. Cruelty was Rilke's vice, greed was Daniel's.

'A million, in sterling. Nothing on account, so we've got to get the job done or we come out with nothing.'

There was a brief silence. They were all professionals and they were there because they were greedy. Bill Stevenson, looking as out of place as a prize fighter at a tea party, would have done it for fun. He yearned for violence, the way Daniel yearned for money.

It was Zarubin who asked the question. 'For that money it must be a killing. A difficult target?'

'Quite difficult,' Oakham agreed. 'But not impossible.'

He paused for effect. He's a showman, Rilke thought, sneering inwardly. He wants us to jump when the ringmaster cracks his whip.

'Prince Abdullah Al Rashid.'

'The Saudi?' Daniel stared at Oakham. 'That's not a contract, that's suicide!'

'He's coming to London,' Oakham said. 'He'll be staying at the Regis Hotel. Seeing an eye specialist, playing a bit of roulette and banging blondes.'

'In London,' Rilke remarked. 'It might be possible.'

'It *is* possible,' was Oakham's retort. 'We'll have inside information on his movements. So we can plan with certainty. I've worked something out already.'

'Who's the paymaster?' Rilke asked.

He was hunched forward, concentrating on Oakham.

'My guess is Tehran, via the Lebanon. I know the contact well. He's reliable and he's got the backing for this. It makes sense after all. Abdullah's pro-America and anti-fundamentalist. They wouldn't want him succeeding his father. The Crown Prince has heart trouble. Abdullah would be the next King of Saudi. And he's the old man's favourite; he has a lot of influence.'

'What's the plan?' Zarubin asked him. He was excited in spite of himself. It would be a challenge to get near such a target. He was guarded at home like the crown jewels and surrounded by bodyguards when he travelled abroad. It would need brilliant planning and attention to detail. His special talents.

'There's a contingency,' Harry went on. 'I screwed another fifty grand out of them for it. They want a public scandal. They don't want a Muslim martyr, they want him smeared. So we're going to have to kill him and throw mud at the same time. Which brings me to the rough plan I worked out.' He turned to Monika. 'You have the starring role, my dear.'

Dick Lucas saw her walking down the King's Road. He eased into the kerb and pulled up just ahead of her.

'Rosa! Hi there!'

She stopped, saw him and waved. He got out of the car and came up to her.

'Hello, Dick.'

'Where are you going? Can I give you a lift?'

'I was on my way home. I thought I'd walk.'

'Why don't I drive you?' She'd last seen him at the American Ambassador's party. She'd hurried off home to James, worried because she was going to be late for dinner. Very late for everything as it turned out. 'Come on, I want to hear about Brussels,' he urged.

He took her arm and helped her into the passenger seat. He put the car in gear.

'Where to?' he asked. 'Where do you live?'

'Marcham Road. I'm not going to Brussels. I'm in the process of a divorce.'

He glanced quickly at her, surprised.

'That's tough. I'm sorry.'

They drove in silence for a while.

'Take the turn off to Fulham,' she directed.

'Why don't I give you dinner,' he suggested. 'I was always asking, remember? You could tell me about it.'

It was Rosa's last night in London. The night before she went down to Suffolk. Suddenly she was grateful for the invitation. She didn't want to spend the evening alone.

'I'd love to,' she said. 'Thanks, Dick. Where shall we go?'

'There's a good French restaurant just close by: World's End. I go there a lot. I'm sure we'll get a table. Shall we try it?'

'Why not?' She looked at him and smiled.

He smiled back. He was nice, uncomplicated.

He was well known at the restaurant. He was warmly greeted and given a good table with a view of a little paved garden at the back. It was lit up when it grew dark.

'This is very nice,' Rosa said. 'I'm so glad you suggested it.'

'I'm glad I saw you walking,' he answered. 'You want to talk about what happened?'

'Not much to say really. It was a shock because I wasn't expecting it. My career was the trouble. James, my husband, wanted me to give it up, stay at home and have a family. When I wouldn't, he found someone else who did. So I said no to Brussels and stayed in England to get the divorce sorted out.'

'So what's the next plan? You should have called me. I've got a great shoulder to cry on!'

'I'm sure you have,' she smiled a little. 'I'm taking a holiday. Two weeks or so; I'm due for leave anyway. Then I'll get back to work and see what's on offer. My boss's been so good about it.'

'Sir Hugh Chapman, isn't it? Nice guy. Why don't you get sent to the States? I'm due home at the end of the year.'

She said, 'You're not married, are you, Dick?'

'No. I had a lady in mind, but she didn't like the Navy. So we agreed to put it on the back burner while I did my tour in England. She didn't wait that long. Three months after I left she married another guy.'

'Did you mind very much?'

'I did at the time. Then I just kidded myself it was hurt pride. After a while that's all it was.'

'You were lucky!' Rosa held out her wine glass to be filled. 'Anything's better than a marriage breaking up. You feel such a failure. And there's hurt pride in it too. But I asked for it. He said I put my career first and nobody likes being second best. So . . . he found himself another lady.'

'And you haven't found another guy?'

'That's the last thing I'm looking for, believe me.'

He changed the subject. 'So what are you doing while you're on leave?'

'Staying in a hotel in Suffolk.'

She told the story to everyone. Parker had emphasized the importance of establishing that.

'Somewhere I can be quiet, take long walks, read, relax and bore myself to death.' She laughed. 'That's what everyone says I need. Then come back to the office and see what the future holds. But it doesn't hold another relationship, I can promise you that. From now on, Dick, it's going to be work. I never was much good at holidays. I was always fretting about what was going on in the office. It used to make James furious. Last holiday we went skiing and I was called back. After a week.'

'Well, we live in stirring times,' he admitted. 'Global peace all of a sudden and then the Gulf War. I've loved my time in London. I've put in for a sea posting, but I don't think I'll get it. I have a hunch I'm going to be behind a damned desk back home. Why don't you try for the States? Seriously, I mean it!'

'Washington isn't exactly a Naval base,' she said gently.

He was nice, very easy to talk to. Just what she needed that night.

They got into his car and he drove her home. No relationships, no ties. She was firm about that.

At the door she said, 'Come in and have a drink.'

The house had seemed so empty these last weeks. Neat and tidy with one meticulous woman living there. No dents in the cushions, no meals to cook or dirty dishes to clear away. No footfall, except her own. She opened some good brandy and gave them both a glass.

He said nice things about the way she'd done the drawing room and settled into the sofa beside her. They could catch the late news on television, she suggested. He thought that was a great idea. Then it was very late and time for him to go.

In the narrow hallway he held her face and kissed

her lightly on the mouth. 'Rosa, why don't I stay the night? I'd like that.'

'I'd like it, too. But I'm going away tomorrow. So it's just for tonight.'

'That's OK,' he said. 'I understand.'

He put his arm around her. 'You're a wonderful girl. I'm going to make it good for you.'

They turned and went upstairs together.

He'd gone by the time she woke in the morning. There was a note on the kitchen table. 'I made myself breakfast. I'll call you from the office. Thanks for a wonderful evening. Dick.' He'd drawn a silly moon face with a big smile by his signature. It made her smile back. He'd been good for her; a thoughtful and sensitive lover who remembered to tell her how terrific she was and let her fall asleep in his arms. He had a reputation with women. Rosa could see why. He was nice and he had a lot of charm. She was very grateful for the night they'd spent together, but now it was morning and she had to pack for her journey.

She chose simple, elegant clothes for the evening, casual shirts and trousers. She took her few pieces of jewellery, some of it was very expensive. The legacy of James' first fever of romantic love. She dialled Parker at his office.

'I'm going in half an hour,' she said. 'I spent the night with a man last night. I thought I'd better tell you. I gave him the same story about a holiday.'

'Good idea,' Parker said. 'Feeling a bit nervous, were you?'

'Yes, I was. How did you know?'

He had a dry little laugh, like a catch in the throat.

'I'd be worried if you weren't. You did the right thing. Took your mind off it. Is he a boyfriend?'

'No. I've known him casually for some time. There's nothing in it. I just felt like company. I'm fine today, looking forward to the job. I'll call Marian when I get down.'

Marian was the in-house telephone contact she used to report in. Parker was for an emergency.

'Good luck, Rosa. And mind yourself.'

She put the phone down, looked round to see she hadn't forgotten anything, checked her bag for keys to the house and the car, credit cards and wallet.

As she closed and double locked the front door, the telephone began to ring. She didn't hear it and after a while Dick Lucas hung up.

'I want you to go to London,' Harry said to Jan.

They were alone in Harry's house. The Pole looked up at him. He didn't say anything. He was nervous, Harry knew that. He hadn't done a real job for a long time. Making the contacts and getting Rilke to Geneva was not the same as setting up an operation.

'You're the best co-ordinator I ever had,' Oakham told him.

He put a hand on his shoulder and left it there, signifying his confidence and his trust.

'I want you to follow the route for Daniel, go over the timetable, see what might crop up to screw the schedule, re-work the route and the time where necessary. Make the contingency plan in case of trouble. Do the things you did for me when we worked together as a team. Bloody marvellous team we made, didn't we?'

The tension eased in him, Harry could feel it.

Jan looked at him. 'The best,' he agreed. 'If you'd been with me, they wouldn't have caught me. I often think of that.'

'Forget it,' Harry advised him. 'This'll be easy. You stay in a decent middle-range hotel, but nowhere near the Regis. That'll be crawling with Special Branch checking the place out before our target arrives. You don't need me to tell you how to do your job. Just remember, you were the best in the whole bloody outfit at putting an operation together. That's why you've got to go, Jan. Nobody else can do it.'

Jan nodded; he unclenched his hands. They'd been gripping nervously while Harry talked.

'I'll start with the whore house,' he said. 'Then work out the route for Stevenson and Daniel. When did they say he usually sends for a girl? Afternoons or evenings? The traffic will affect the timetable if it's between say five and eight at night.'

'Let's hope it's at night,' Harry answered. 'It'll be easier to make the snatch in the dark. But we can't bank on it.'

'I'll work on both schedules then,' Jan said. 'We'll need two cars. Better to buy second-hand for cash, Harry. We can dump them afterwards.'

Oakham moved away. He sat opposite Jan and listened to him with a mixture of relief and affection. He was all right, he just needed nursing along a little. He was getting fired up now with the details. Once a great pro, always a pro, Oakham thought. Those stupid bastards had thrown him on the dust heap after his release. He'd been right about Jan. They'd been wrong. As wrong as they'd been about him, when they sent him off with a lunch at the St Ermin's and a stingy handout. They thought he'd knuckle down and take it like a good fellow. Splendid fellow, Harry Oakham! Used to be a very hard type in the old days . . . Seems to have settled down quite happily now. Runs a hotel somewhere, so I heard.

Like fuck! Harry murmured in his mind, listening to Jan talking himself through the plan of operation. You shoot us, if you've any sense. You don't just leave us wandering loose.

'When do you want me to go, Harry?'

'Tomorrow morning,' was the answer. 'Stay with it till the job's done. Then get the others rounded up and back here.'

'When are they coming up?'

'Give it two days after the target arrives,' Oakham suggested. 'Then call me. I'll give a final briefing just before they go.'

'Tomorrow then,' Jan said. He looked at Oakham for a moment. 'You really have faith in me, don't you? I'm glad about that. I won't let you down, Harry.'

'Of course you won't. Want a nightcap?'

'No thanks. I'll sleep better. I'm looking forward to this. I'm looking forward to it.'

He went out and Harry Oakham poured himself a brandy. They'd worked out the plan as a team and it was based on Vassily Zarubin's outline.

Daniel had filled in his part, Stevenson had been told what to do and didn't argue with it and Monika had sat there waiting for her role to be fleshed out, with a smile on her beautiful face.

An Arab prince, guarded night and day by his own tribal bodyguards and the strong-arm goons of the Special Branch.

They'd search his suite. They'd double check the guest list. He'd bring a food taster with him, that was customary, to shield him against poison. He'd travel in a bullet-proof limousine with armed men on either side of him and a plain-clothes police car behind. There'd be protection when he gambled, when he went to see the eye specialist who was treating him for cataract. Wherever he went and whatever he did, he would have a human shield. Except when he was in bed with a woman.

Hakim's contact had given him the name of the agency the Prince used when he wanted a girl. Or sometimes two girls. He had one particular favourite. He asked for Denise, and Denise was collected by one of his cars driven by one of his Arab drivers and brought to him at the hotel. She was tall and blonde. He'd given her an expensive present last time he was over and she'd visited him most evenings when he wasn't playing roulette at the Claremont Club. The contact said that no whore ever spent the night. They left as soon as the Prince had finished with them. And returned in the same car with the driver who'd been waiting to take them back home. Denise usually wore a gauze scarf and modestly covered her face when she came and went.

He finished his brandy. What a coup, if they brought it off! He grinned, thinking of the panic in the Security Services. The cat among the pigeons. The sparrow hawk in the dovecot!

He went to bed and slept untroubled till his early tea was brought up in the morning.

Jan drove off after breakfast. He took a large amount of cash with him. He'd booked into the Kensington Gore Hotel under the name of Peters.

His first task was to leave his own car in a long-term car park and buy second-hand transport for cash. He would use public transport till he bought his first car. Afterwards there'd be no chance of the dealer remembering a registration number. Harry said goodbye in his office. Jan looked calm and rested; the old glint was in his eye. It warmed Harry's heart to see it.

'Good luck, you old sod,' he said fondly, and for a moment they embraced. Then Jan was gone.

On the dual carriageway that skirted Braintree, he and Rosa passed each other as he headed for London.

The journey took under two hours; Rosa was a fast driver, and the roads were clear once she left London. It was a very warm day, with bright sunshine and a few white clouds innocent of rain.

She was feeling nervous again, and it made her impatient at the wheel. She overtook a slow-moving family car and had to pull in sharply against oncoming traffic. James hated driving with her; he said she was too aggressive. Rosa slowed down after that;

she'd taken a stupid risk and she was irritated with herself.

There was no reason to be apprehensive. She was going into this on little more than Parker's gut feeling. It could very well be wrong. Harry Oakham might be exactly what he was supposed to be: a man with a violent past in his country's service, who had retired into normal life. There were dozens of examples. Parker had quoted one to her, playing the devil's advocate during their long briefing. A man renowned for dispatching enemy agents and some British doubles with a knife, had set up as a commercial film producer after the war, and died a respected old gentleman with his obituary in *The Times*.

All she had to do was trail her coat. The phrase stuck in her mind. She avoided the sequence that followed. *Does that mean I have to sleep with him . . . ? I can't answer that. That's for you to judge . . .*

It suddenly sounded so improbable, driving down a leafy road towards the hotel on a beautiful morning in rural England. She'd come home at the end of her stay and think what an incredible waste of time it had all been. And laugh at herself for those silly moments of premonition, like the cold chill in her old room at the weekend. She slowed, seeing the sign, and like Vassily Zarubin, waited for a gap in the cars coming across her path. It was a splendid house. Wonderful red brick glowing in the sunshine. She took a long, deep breath, and pulled up outside the entrance.

A young porter opened the door for her. She pressed the button to unlock her boot and asked him to bring in her cases. She was met by the receptionist in the hall. She was a pretty girl with a welcoming smile.

'Good morning,' Rosa said. 'I'm Mrs Bennet. I booked in last week.'

'Yes, of course.' Jane consulted her list. 'You have a room on the first floor looking over the rose garden. Sign here, please.'

Rosa registered. There were a lot of bookings. Somewhere a Hoover buzzed faintly. Another girl was refreshing a big flower arrangement with a watering-can and taking out faded blooms. It was friendly, busy, supremely normal.

She heard the girl say, 'Oh, there you are, Mr Oakham. This is Mrs Bennet; she's just arrived.'

Rosa's heart bumped. She turned and there he was, standing beside her, with three people at his back.

She saw him smile and hold out his hand. When she took it he gave a little bow.

'How do you do, Mrs Bennet? I hope you'll enjoy your stay. And do let us know if there's anything we can do for you.'

He had dark eyes; a little grey in the hair, a military bearing, as if he were a retired Army officer. A mouth that had lines around it as if he had laughed a lot over the years. Charm flowed at her. Magnetism was a better description. And something else, which he didn't quite conceal. He didn't want to linger. He was in a hurry.

'Thank you so much,' she answered. 'I'm sure I'll enjoy my stay with you.'

She felt the presence of the two men and the

woman who had been following him when the receptionist intervened. Rosa glanced towards them. The men looked away. They were in their thirties, she guessed, dressed inconspicuously; one wore a heavy moustache, the other had glasses. They deliberately avoided looking at her, unlike the woman. Provocatively, she stared at Rosa. Rosa looked into her eyes. They were pale. She found herself transfixed by the most chilling, hate-filled glare, and it so disconcerted Rosa that she took a step back, as if she'd been threatened with a blow.

'This way please,' Rosa heard Harry Oakham say. 'Just follow me through here.'

She waited by the reception desk. *I must have imagined it. If looks could kill.* The worn out cliché came to her mind.

She said to the receptionist, 'Are they guests here?'

Jane said cheerfully, 'Yes, but just for one night. They're going on to some sales conference. They're from Ireland. Mr Oakham's looking after them. We hope they'll recommend us. We don't get many business bookings.'

'That's where the money lies,' Rosa lingered. 'It's been such a bad time for everyone lately, hasn't it? And the hotel's just changed hands too.'

'Yes, that does put people off for a bit,' Jane confided. 'But all the staff stayed on and Mr Oakham hasn't changed anything. He takes more trouble with the guests than the other manager. Goes round every evening talking to people. And the assistant manager, Mr Pollock, does the same. He's very nice too.'

'I expect I'll meet him then,' Rosa suggested.

'He's just gone away for a few days,' Jane explained. 'His father's not too well. Now, will you be in for dinner tonight? We do get quite full on a weekend in the evenings.'

'I shan't be going anywhere for a bit. It seems so nice here, I don't think I'll want to.'

'Gino will take up your luggage. And don't forget, if there's anything you need, just ring the housekeeper.'

'Thank you,' Rosa said. 'I will.'

It was a charming room. A generous single bed, with a corona that matched the curtains and the armchair. The colour scheme was a soft yellow with touches of pale blue. Fresh flowers were arranged on the table and a dish with grapes, apples and peaches was near by.

She tipped the young Italian; he grinned broadly at her.

'Thank you, lady. Everything OK?'

He was very young, a student, she supposed, learning the hotel business from the bottom rung. He made her feel better.

'Yes, thank you.'

When the door closed she looked around the room. New magazines were laid out and a card by the fruit bowl said it came with the manager's compliments. Fine soap in the bathroom, high-quality towels. A menu for snacks by the telephone, with instructions how to reach the housekeeper, reception, the restaurant and to get an outside line. There was also a tariff. As she knew, it was very expensive.

She went to the window and looked out. The roses in the garden below were past their first blooming, but the aspect was very pleasing. She unpacked her clothes, hung them up, settled herself in.

Mr Oakham goes round every evening, talking to the guests. He hadn't wanted to spend time talking to her. He had clients from Ireland to look after. But surely there was nothing sinister in that?

She kicked off her shoes and curled up in the armchair. She lit a cigarette and smoked it slowly. Something was coming to the surface. An incident recalled after many years.

A dinner party in London where a rich Anglo-Irish victim of an IRA kidnapping described the female ringleader. The most frightening thing was the naked hatred in her captor's eyes. She'd never said a word, just looked at her. As she spoke, the elderly aristocrat had given a slight shiver. It was impossible to explain the depth of hatred the woman conveyed. Far, far worse than the men who were manhandling her at the time. The woman and the gang had been arrested and jailed. She was now dead or forgotten. But she had heirs and successors and Rosa had an instinct she might have just seen one of them in the reception hall of the hotel. Part of her equipment was a small, but highly sophisticated camera with a powerful zoom lens. They were only here for one day and a night. Somehow she had to get that girl, and the men with her, on film.

6

Hermann Rilke said, 'Now we will start with the theory of interrogation. And I am talking about sophisticated methods. Any fool can crush a man's balls. A skilled operator can crush his will and distort his mind. In that way, if he is released or exchanged at any time, he will be useless.'

The Irishman with the moustache broke in abruptly.

'We don't release suspects, or exchange them. What we want is to get information. And quick.'

He lit a cigarette. Rilke scowled. They were impatient, ignorant foot soldiers. His special talents would be wasted on them. To his surprise it was the girl in the group who contradicted her leader.

'Sean, we're not talking about informers. You kick them hard enough and they'd turn in their own mothers. But the Brits are specially trained to work under cover. We've never got anything out of the bastards by beating them. I think we could learn a lot from Mr Rilke here.'

She was young, not much past twenty-four. A quiet-spoken Dundalk girl from a respectable background. Her father was a doctor, she had a brother studying to be a priest at Maynooth.

Rilke knew all about her. She had decoyed soldiers at eighteen, leading them into ambushes, where they were gunned down without mercy. She had planted explosives in shops, and carried out reconnaissance for other bombers. She had been present at summary trials and executions of police informers.

She had served a brief prison sentence in the Maze for driving a car for the Provisionals during an attack on a police station. During her time in prison she had dominated and terrorized the other women prisoners.

The man called Sean scowled at her. Maeve O'Callaghan was the girlfriend of a top Provo political figure. When she heard about this special training course, she was determined to go on it.

And she got her way.

'I'd like to hear about these other methods,' she said to Rilke.

'Then you'd better come with me,' he said, and they filed out after him. 'Up here,' he said, climbing a short stair to the upper floor.

He unlocked a door, switched on a light. They followed him inside.

The man called Sean said under his breath, 'What the fuck?'

The room was bare and whitewashed; there were no windows. In the middle of it was something that looked like a dentist's chair. It was fitted with leather straps.

'Now,' Hermann Rilke began like a lecturer before a class of students. 'When you bring your subject into a room like this, his training will come to the forefront. He will experience fear, but he's been taught how to cope with it. He will have been provided with some information he can disclose after a certain amount of pain becomes intolerable. He knows that will buy him relief. But you don't speak to him,' Rilke instructed. 'Not a word is spoken to him from the moment he comes up for interrogation.'

'Is he hooded?' the man with glasses asked.

Rilke smiled at the idiocy of the question.

'If he was, he couldn't see the room or the chair where he expects to be tied in and tortured. *You* are hooded, all of you. Everyone he sees is faceless and voiceless. So. You place your subject in the chair; you strap him in. He is tense, waiting for his ordeal. Relying on his training to survive the first part of it. But nothing happens.

Nothing. He waits. One by one you leave the room, and the last one turns off the light and leaves the subject in complete darkness. Time passes.'

'Supposing we don't have a lot of time?' Sean demanded. He was still hostile to the whole set-up.

'Then,' Rilke said quietly, 'you advance the programme and begin immediately. You switch on.'

He pressed a switch by the door. The chair started revolving. He pressed again and the speed increased. The chair began to spin.

'The subject will vomit as his balance becomes affected,' the rasping voice went on. 'After some time he will lose control of bladder and bowels.'

'How much time?' Maeve O'Callaghan asked.

'An hour, maybe less. Some people react to the disorientation more slowly than others. When the interrogator judges that the subject is sufficiently softened, he stops the chair and asks the first questions.

'He is likely to get the permitted bits of information that might have come after days of physical assault. The subject has bought himself a little time. Or so he thinks. But before he's finished answering, the chair goes into motion again. Faster and for longer. Then it stops. No questions are asked this time. No-one comes into the room. It is dark and silent. The process begins again. I can guarantee you that, depending upon the subject, you will get everything out of them within twenty-four hours at the most. After which you can dispose of them. Or even let them go. They will have suffered permanent damage to the balancing mechanism of the brain. They'll be useless to anyone.'

He turned and gestured them to follow him out.

The short-sighted one took off his glasses and wiped them, put them back on and muttered, 'Jesus, I feel sick just lookin' at the thing.'

'Not as sick as if you were in it,' Rilke remarked. 'We can have some coffee and a general discussion. I'll be happy to answer questions.'

The man, Sean, squared up to him instead of sitting down in the pleasant sitting room. A tall, handsome blonde had brought in a tray of coffee and biscuits; she didn't speak and Rilke didn't acknowledge her.

'We're wasting time. We don't need all this sophisticated garbage! Where the hell are we going to get the props for this sort of thing?'

'You'll find it in a dentist's surgery,' Rilke said

coldly. 'Any skilled electrician can adapt it. All you need is somewhere isolated. I'm sure your organization can manage that.'

Maeve O'Callaghan swung away from Sean. She was flushed with anger at the stupid yob with his brains in his fists. Men like that would never win their kind of war. And he was a very senior area commander.

She said to Rilke, 'Of course we can use it! And a woman could operate it just as well as a man. Thank you, it's so simple it's brilliant.'

She glared at Sean. Rilke couldn't resist praise. His ego swelled and he smiled at her. She was a deadly bitch.

'Good,' he responded. 'You'll have coffee? Please help yourselves. Then I shall give a lecture on interrogation techniques accompanied by complementary drugs. Then a question-and-answer session. I will lead it with each of you in turn. Lunch is provided here. When you feel you have enough information then you can return to the hotel.'

He licked his lips, and watching him, Maeve O'Callaghan was reminded of a reptile catching flies.

He addressed himself to her. 'It's a pity your time is so short. I feel there's a lot I could teach you—'

'We can't hang around here,' Sean interrupted. 'We've got other business on the mainland.'

He swallowed his coffee, spilling some into the saucer. The bitch made him want to spit. He thought angrily, she could do with a good larraping. Making

178

him look a fool in front of that fucking queen. He had lived by the gun and the bomb. Rilke turned his stomach.

The Irish weren't in the dining room at lunch. Or at the bar. Rosa took her camera and set off to walk round the grounds. She might just spot them. The sun was high and there was no cooling breeze. As she crossed the smooth parkland, the whole idea seemed far-fetched. She must have imagined the look. Her nerves were strung up. She was spooking herself.

She saw the sign, ADVENTURE TRAIL, with an arrow pointing towards a wooded area some three hundred yards to her left, and a red skull and cross-bones that made her shudder. She changed direction. She was near enough to see some fencing and another sign when she heard the run-about chugging up behind her. She turned quickly and a man in sweat shirt and baseball cap waved to her to stop. He came level, bringing the little four-wheel-drive buggy to a halt along-side her.

She looked at him. 'Yes? Is anything the matter?'

He was young and he looked very fit; a load of gardening implements was piled up behind him.

'Afternoon, miss. You want a lift anywhere?'

'No, thank you,' Rosa frowned. 'I was just going to look at the Adventure Trail.'

'It's closed,' he said. He had watchful eyes under the shadow of the cap brim. The three Micks were having a quick tour with Stevenson. His orders were to keep the legitimate punters from getting too close.

'Hot today,' he said. 'We keep an eye out if we

see a lady walking around on her own; there're lots of underground springs here and the grounds get marshy. We had someone sink down and sprain her ankle; she was missing for hours till we found her. Better you let me run you back.'

Rosa hesitated for a moment. She didn't want to go with him. But most hotel guests would have complied. *Whatever you do, don't arouse suspicion.*

She smiled and said, 'All right then, it *is* hot, and it's quite a long way. Thank you.'

He leaned down and offered a hand.

'Hop in, then.'

He helped her up into the seat beside him.

'What can you do about the ground?' she asked.

'Drain it. Spend my life digging ditches.'

'Have you worked here long?'

'Since the new management took over.'

He had a West Country burr in his speech. She caught a whiff of sweat as he moved; it was acrid and she tried not to inch away.

'It must need a lot of gardeners to keep it properly,' she went on. 'There's so much of it.'

''Bout three hundred acres, I reckon. It's a big old place all right.'

She was a nice-looking bird, pretty tits bouncing up and down as they drove. He wished she'd shut her trap though. He didn't want to answer questions. Not that he talked much anyway. His mate was the one who loved sounding off. They were close enough to the main building; he judged he could stop and let her off.

'Have to drop you here, miss. All right?'

'Yes, that's fine, thank you.'

He let the clutch out and the buggy bombed off in the direction they'd come from. He was going too fast with all the tools rattling in the back.

Slowly Rosa walked round the gardens. Several guests were strolling round, a couple were reading in the shade. She sat down herself in a seat with a view of the main entrance.

She wasn't imagining things. There was something spine-chilling about that girl she'd seen with Oakham. And the young bruiser in the buggy hadn't wanted her to go near the so-called Adventure Trail.

I've got to get a photograph, she insisted. They're leaving tomorrow morning. The girl at reception was friendly; if she's on duty I'll try and find out exactly when they're leaving.

She went back up to her room to shower and change. There was a message to say Commander Lucas had telephoned and would call again later.

There was a different girl on the desk; Rosa tried to talk to her. 'I'm Mrs Bennet,' she said. 'I arrived this morning. Did you reserve a table for dinner for me?' The girl looked down at her list and then up at Rosa.

'Yes, it's here, Mrs Bennet. Eight o'clock? And did you get your telephone message?'

'Yes I did, thank you. You seem very full,' Rosa lingered.

'We are. Weekends are very busy.' The smile was polite but at that moment the switchboard buzzed and she said, 'Excuse me,' and went to answer it. Rosa put through a call in her room before she came down. She used the contact name Jim Parker had given her.

'Marian? Hello, it's me. Yes, lovely, terribly spoiling . . .' She carried on the conversation for a few minutes, and then added, 'I must go, but I'll give Jim a ring sometime tomorrow. I've got those photographs I meant to give him. Sorry I forgot. Bye.'

She dressed in her favourite dark blue, a simply cut silk dress and a long string of cultured pearls, twisted into a knot. She went down to the cocktail bar and chose a corner seat with a good view of the door. If the Irish woman and her companions passed, she'd get a second look at them, in case her plan for the morning failed.

'Good-evening, Mrs Bennet.'

Rosa started. She hadn't heard him come up beside her.

'Oh, good-evening.'

Harry Oakham smiled down at her.

He'd been abrupt with her that morning, anxious to get the Belfast scumbags out of everyone's sight. Now they were safely stowed away in their suite eating what the man Sean called 'tea', and drinking whisky.

Seeing Rosa sitting alone, he made a point of coming to speak to her. She was a very attractive woman, he thought; unusual colouring.

'I hope you're comfortable,' he said.

'Yes, very comfortable, thank you.'

'You haven't got a drink, let me get something for you.'

'A glass of white wine.' Her throat felt constricted.

Fear, a surge of adrenalin. She looked into his eyes and saw nothing in them but friendliness. And a hint of admiration.

'Why not champagne?' Harry suggested. 'As it's your first evening. With my compliments.' He raised his hand and the barman hurried across. 'Champagne for Mrs Bennet,' he said.

'That's very kind of you,' Rosa was in control by now. She smiled at him and said, 'But only if you'll join me.'

'I'd be delighted. Make that two, George.'

The tiger in the cat basket. Jim Parker's description came back to her as he took the chair opposite. 'Do you mind if I smoke?' he asked.

'Not if you give me one,' she answered. He laughed. 'I haven't broken the habit I'm afraid. But so many people get paranoid about it now. Passive smoking and all that rubbish.'

'I stopped for a long time.' Rosa bent to his lighter. 'But then something happened and I started again.'

'Nothing too bad I hope,' he said. Their drinks arrived.

'My husband left me.'

Harry looked at her over the glass. After a pause he said, 'I'm sorry to hear that. And if I may say so, he must be an incredible idiot. Here's to a happy stay with us.'

He was full of a curious energy even when still. He had a way of looking directly at her when he spoke, claiming complete attention. He certainly had charm, Rosa admitted, and male magnetism. Like a dangerous animal laying its head in your lap.

He said casually, 'Actually I've got a divorce coming up myself. All very amicable, and no children, thank God. I do mind about children when people split up. Oh dear, I hope I haven't said something tactless—'

He didn't look apologetic; he just wanted to know and she said quickly, 'No children. And mine was amicable too. Well, I suppose it was. We didn't fight over details. How long were you married, Mr Oakham?'

'Ten years. My wife didn't fancy coming to live down here. So—' He shrugged slightly, dismissing the subject.

'It's a lovely old house,' Rosa said. He wasn't hurrying over his drink and he showed no sign of wanting to go.

'I was born round here,' Harry signalled the barman again. 'Two more, George – if you don't mind chatting for a bit, Mrs Bennet?'

'I don't mind at all. I was feeling rather lonely when you came in.'

He shook his head, and smiled his lazy smile. 'We can't have that. Yes, it is a nice place. I used to come here to parties when I was a child. The family were running out of money even then. It's lucky to be a hotel. At least it's used and lived in, and enjoyed by people instead of falling into the hands of some developer who'd pull it down.'

'Have you always been in the hotel business?'

'No. I was a Civil Servant till I was given the push. I don't think I'd been civil to the right people.' He laughed. 'So I applied for this job and I got it. Being local helped, I suppose. I love it, it's a whole new world to me. Best of all, I enjoy meeting people. And I believe personal contact is a top priority if you're going to manage a hotel of this quality.'

'Didn't you have to train?' she asked him. 'It's a big responsibility running something like this.'

'I'd been concerned with personnel all my life,' Oakham said easily. 'And that's what this job is really all about. Keeping the clients happy and the staff contented and on their toes. If there's one thing more important than the manager, it's the chef. And we've got one of the best.' He looked at his watch and finished his drink.

'It's been a pleasure, Mrs Bennet.' He got up and held out his hand. She didn't imagine it; he held on for a fraction longer than was necessary. 'Perhaps,' he said lightly, 'I might join you for dinner one evening? It's against our policy to have a charming lady feeling lonely.'

'It's against my policy too,' she retorted. 'I'd be delighted. And thank you for the champagne.'

They brought the menu; she couldn't concentrate on it. It all sounded so genuine. The casual reference to his past career. Personnel. The wife Jim Parker had described so vividly, dismissed with that little shrug of the shoulders. The man who enthused about meeting people had killed without a qualm of conscience. The sexual invitation in his eyes and his self mockery.

It's against our policy to have a charming lady feeling lonely. Get to know him, Parker had instructed, but don't rush it.

But it wasn't her initiative any more. Oakham had made the move first. She was going into the restaurant when she was told that there was a telephone call for her. It was Dick Lucas.

'Hi there – how are you?'

'Fine thanks, Dick.' The cheerful voice was reassuring.

'How's the hotel?'

'Wonderful. I'm having a lovely rest.'

'I had a great time with you, Rosa. I called next morning but I guess you'd gone.'

She said, 'I had a great time too. You were very sweet.'

'I've got nothing to do this weekend,' he said. 'Why don't I drive down? Could you book me a room?'

It was so tempting. Let him come, let him stay. Keep Harry Oakham away. A boyfriend would put him off. And wreck her cover story of being a lonely divorcee. She found her nerve again and said, 'No, Dick, not just yet. I did say it was a one-night stand. Maybe after I've been here for a few more days I could call you?'

He sounded disappointed. 'OK, if that's the way you want it. But I don't have to stay. We could go for lunch somewhere, just spend a few hours together.' Yes, she thought, yes, it might be useful. Just a visit. Whatever they were doing in the Adventure Trail, they wouldn't be able to fob off Dick Lucas with stories about dangerous ground and broken ankles. She made up her mind quickly.

'Dick, that would be nice. I'm sorry, I didn't mean

to be so crabby. Look, I'm late for dinner, can I call you tomorrow morning?'

'Sure. Around nine thirty. Talk to you then.'

She hung up.

Jan took the tube to Earl's Court. He had the names and addresses of four dealers in the area, specializing in part-exchange and the sale of second-hand cars. Things were tight in the trade, and anyone with cash in their pocket could afford to pick and choose.

He knew what was needed, and at the second garage showroom he bought it. A two-year-old Subaru four-door saloon, painted an unobtrusive dark blue. He test drove it; it was fast, easy to manoeuvre, and gear operated. Bill Stevenson had insisted upon that. He was a highly skilled driver, and he refused to use an automatic for a job like this.

Jan liked the size of the boot. It was big enough and deep enough to take a man if he was bundled up tight enough. He paid hard cash and drove it away. He didn't park near the Kensington Gore Hotel.

The hotel was a quiet, respectable, middle-range place with a changing clientele of tourists and elderly couples spending a few days in London.

Jan melted into the background, spoke to no-one and drew little attention to himself. He never used the restaurant. He didn't want to be remembered.

For the next three days he test drove the route to the expensive West End club that fronted for a discreet and expensive call-girl agency. He drove there during the afternoon, timing himself, noting the traffic and the points of congestion on the way.

He drove back towards the Regis Hotel where the Prince was booked in, and went over the same route in the evenings. He checked on delays and peak traffic times, and made adjustments to a series of schedules.

Parked near the entrance to the club, he noticed the side door. A number of minicabs drew up during the day, and women came out of the entrance and were driven off. The evenings were busier. The girls were going out on their calls. The Arab Prince's favourite, Denise, would leave in the same way, except that the car came from the Prince's own fleet at the hotel and was driven by one of his entourage. No problem, Jan decided.

He reported back to Harry on a public pay phone. It was going well. It was up to Daniel to work out the details of where to make the snatch when he came up. Yes, he assured Harry, he was fine and in good spirits. No, no worries about anything. Like old times, he agreed, and he'd sit it out till he got word from Oakham's contact that the quarry had arrived.

Yes, he promised Harry, he'd lighten up and go off to a cinema or even a show if there was anything he felt like seeing. He was touched by his old friend's concern for him. When he rang off there were tears in his eyes. Harry had always looked out for him. He was his only friend, the one who came and saw him in the nut hospital when he was released, laughed him out of his fears and depressions, gave him the courage to start again when nobody believed in him any more. His hand shook with emotion as he wiped his eyes. He'd do the best job of his life on this one. He owed Harry Oakham everything.

Vassily Zarubin woke very early. He'd left his windows open and the curtains drawn back. He woke to the sweet shrilling of the dawn chorus, and he couldn't get back to sleep. Everything was unfamiliar to him and he didn't like the sense of alienation. He didn't like the food, he chafed at the time he had to spend pretending to be working, and he hadn't started on any computer program. Above all, he disliked his colleagues. He thought of Rilke as a deadly little insect rather than a man; the Dutchwoman repelled him with her oozing sexuality. He sensed that in spite of it, she hated men. He dismissed Daniel as a trader in human treachery and greed, incapable of loyalty to anything but his own survival. Most of all he disliked the Englishman, Harry Oakham.

Zarubin had a powerful intellect and a strong personality. He was used to lesser men around him, and used to giving orders and seeing them obeyed without question. But Oakham gave the orders, and he affronted the Russian by seeming to mock his own authority as much as he mocked all of them.

He wasn't a type Zarubin understood. He was arrogant, ruthless, and made his own rules. No servant of the State, but at all times his own man and his own master. He hadn't met his kind before. He protected the nerve-ridden Pole with his twitching hands and damaged psyche like a father with a son. But he could plan abduction and murder as coolly as Zarubin worked out a chess problem. It was another fine late summer's day, and he got up to take an early shower. He went to the open window and leaned out. The air was clean and sweet. And it was early. Early for anyone to be outside sitting on a seat in the garden. But there she was. He recognized her from the night before. She'd been sitting alone in the dining room. He'd been there too, waited upon by the restaurant manager himself, with a minion at his elbow. He was the famous author, and the restaurant manager had said in a respectful whisper that he'd been to London to see the production of the Vaclav Havel plays two months ago. Zarubin had noticed the woman eating alone because she was very pretty, and he liked pretty women. And there she was at eight o'clock in the morning, perched on a seat in front of the hotel reading a book. He didn't move away. He watched. She hadn't turned a page. Once she glanced up towards the entrance as if she was expecting someone.

Now he was motionless, drawn a little back from the window. A car was coming up the drive. He recognized the driver as Bill Stevenson, the ex-Marine. The car stopped at the hotel entrance.

Below, Stevenson had opened the rear doors of the car. A woman and two men were walking the few paces down the steps from the front door.

Zarubin knew who they were. Belfast scum, Oakham had called them. He swung back to the woman on the seat and saw the book lower for an instant. The sun glinted on something, he couldn't see what it was. Then she bent over her book again and didn't look up.

The car drove away down the drive, and she got

up, tucked the book under her arm and strolled back to the hotel.

Zarubin sat very quietly, considering what he had seen. He was sure she'd been watching, pretending to read. What had the sun caught? Or had he imagined the split-second reflection? He ordered coffee and an English breakfast, which was the only food he liked. He decided to find out about the lady for himself before he mentioned anything to Harry Oakham.

Jane was on duty at reception and she smiled when she saw him.

'Good morning, Mr Oakham. Lovely day again.' He paused for a moment.

'Morning, Jane. Any dramas? No? Good. Oh, has Mrs Bennet come down yet?' He sounded very casual.

'Yes, she's been down early for breakfast and gone out. Do you want me to tell her anything?'

'No, no. I just thought she looked a bit lost and stray last night, so I gave her a drink to cheer her up.'

She nodded. 'Funny, but I don't like going into pubs on my own,' she admitted. 'You feel a bit conspicuous. I'd hate to stay in a big place like this by myself.'

'I thought you were one of those liberated young ladies,' he teased, and she giggled.

'Oh, I am,' she protested. 'But I'm a bit old-fashioned about some things, that's all.'

'Thank God you are,' Oakham said. 'Have a good morning and remember don't make a drama out of a crisis!' She giggled again and he passed on. She was a nice kid, he thought. I'll give her a raise next month. Always got a smile for everyone.

He had nothing to do for the next couple of hours. He didn't feel like going to Croft Lodge that morning. He wasn't in the mood for Rilke and Monika playing happy families, or for Daniel to sit there eyeing the woman's big boobs. He was carefree and in a buoyant frame of mind.

He'd been thinking about the attractive Mrs Bennet and the more he thought of her, the more carefree he felt. He hadn't bothered about women for a long time. Hadn't needed one for sex, hadn't noticed the clients one way or the other. But she caught his eye. She was different. What had started as a professional courtesy had become a very pleasant interlude. He allowed himself to speculate whether he might end up in bed with her.

She was alone and admitted to being lonely. Not long divorced. He'd stepped a little over the line with her, just to see how she reacted. There was a hint of diffidence about her that appealed to him. He wasn't aroused by aggressive women, and he liked to do his own seducing. Everything was changing gear; the operation in London was within days of coming to a head; the frozen-faced Maeve O'Callaghan had elected herself spokeswoman and said how useful Rilke had been, and how she'd recommend a few more to slip in for some basic training. Life was exciting, full of challenge, just like the heady days before he took off on an assignment without any guarantee he'd come back.

That was why he was thinking of Mrs Bennet. Risk and libido went in tandem for him. He'd been idle and eaten with frustration for so long he'd lost the urge to take a woman to bed. He walked out into the sunshine and set off across the park.

He'd made love to a lot of women, but he had only been in love with one. Judith. Peggy was an aberration. He wouldn't think about her. Only Judith with her bright hair and cornflower eyes had turned his heart over when she smiled at him.

Mrs Bennet. He said it under his breath. Thick red-brown hair, not golden, deep hazel eyes, not blue . . . A small waist he could put both hands round and squeeze to excite her, soft skin and a mouth that would taste sweet inside. Why wait? Dinner tonight. He'd never believed in wasting time.

'There's something wrong here, but I don't know what it is. It's just little things. The way that woman looked at me, the odd-job man picking me up when I was out walking. I know it all sounds so vague,' Rosa went on. 'They wouldn't be putting up signposts—'

Jim Parker interrupted. 'I told you, you've got a good instinct. Rely on it. Leave the photographs at Ipswich police station. I'll put a call through now. They'll send them down to Special Branch. If there's a unit loose over here we want to know about it. Good girl, Rosa. That was good thinking. No sign of the Pole?'

'No,' she said. 'There is an assistant manager but he's away at the moment, something about his father being ill.'

'And Oakham?' he asked.

'We had a drink together last night. I think he's interested.'

'I'll bet,' Jim Parker agreed. 'Nice-looking girl like you on her own . . .' Rosa took a deep breath.

'I'm scared,' she said.

'Glad to hear it. Don't rush anything. Let him dangle a bit.'

'You know the man I spent the night with before I came, the American? I've asked him to come down for the day. I think we should get into that Adventure Trail and have a look. I *know* that pick-up was deliberate; I wasn't supposed to get in there. We might see something.'

Parker hesitated. 'This American — is he likely to catch on?'

'No,' Rosa reassured him. 'He's a naval attaché in London. Very nice, rather a playboy type. He wants a re-run of that night; I don't. But I thought he could be useful down here.'

'Don't let him persuade you,' Parker's tone was firm. 'It could put our friend Oakham off.'

'I won't,' she promised. 'I'd like to know if I was right about that girl.'

'Sorry,' he said, 'not my department. Not officially, anyway. If I hear anything when they look at the pictures, I'll let you know. Forget about it, Rosa. It's Oakham we're interested in. And be careful.'

'I will,' she said. The line cleared. She'd called from a public telephone on the road at the end of the long drive from the hotel, reversing the charges.

Ipswich police station. She hurried back to her car.

* * *

She'd been expected at the station, ushered into an interview room and handed the film over to an officer in civilian clothes. They'd said nothing but 'good-morning' and 'thank you', and she'd hurried out. Jim Parker's telephone call had a fast car with motorcycle escort speeding on its way to London minutes after she left.

She felt suddenly hungry. She'd been taut with nervous tension, waiting outside in the early morning taking the pictures, parking off the road while she talked to Parker. Then the fast run to Ipswich with its bewildering one-way system. She found a little tea room that served morning coffee and cakes. It must be anticlimax, she insisted, but her hands were shaking as she lifted the cup. *It's Oakham we're interested in.* And it was Oakham that frightened her. It was an odd feeling, and she didn't know how to come to terms with it. She had never been afraid of a man before. It made her aware of her feminine disadvantage – the physical imbalance that placed her at any man's mercy. And this man showed no mercy.

Rosa sat for a long time, while the coffee turned cold and the milk on top formed a thin brown skin.

I've only myself to blame. Parker laid it on the line for me. He didn't minimize the risks. I went into it with my eyes wide open and I can't walk away from it now. And there's a good chance I'm wrong after all. Fifty-fifty at least. I may have over-reacted to that girl in the hall, and she's nothing but a secretary or PA in the company on the way to a conference.

The ground in the parkland may be like a bog in places, and someone lying out there injured could be a nightmare for the hotel staff.

And Harry Oakham could be exactly what he says he is: a man starting a new life, with a busted marriage behind him, just like mine.

She remembered Parker playing the devil's advocate, and his example of the wartime assassin who'd retired and lived a normal life with a respectable career. Rated an obituary in *The Times*. Parker could be wrong and so could she.

She might have no more to fear from Harry Oakham than an attractive man in the first stages of sexual pursuit. And she, Rosa, could surely handle that.

She spent the afternoon touring the little villages, stopping at antique shops, where she bought a china figure because it was something she could give her mother, and on an impulse, bought a bright blue summer dress from a boutique.

The Doll's House Manor Hotel seemed like a friend as she stepped into the big reception hall. She went up to the desk. 'I'd like to book for this evening,' she said. It was the friendly girl with the bright smile.

'Mr Oakham's already done it for you,' she said. 'He left this message, Mrs Bennet.' Rosa slit the envelope. It was one of the manager's compliment cards. 'I'm off duty this evening. Please join me for dinner.'

7

Zarubin went down to the bar early. He'd spent the afternoon working out a complicated schedule on subversive techniques using micro computers, had begun a program with a special input key and fed the basic facts about Rosa Bennet into the system. He ordered himself a drink, vodka on the rocks; he was irritated to find they only had one variety, when at home there were so many flavours, and waited for her to come in. When she did, he appreciated her choice of colour and clothes. Black with a ruffle of scarlet on the shoulder. No jewellery to detract from the smooth, tanned skin of her throat, diamonds gleaming in her ears.

He stared across at her until she looked up. Then he raised himself from his seat slightly and said, 'Good-evening.'

'Good-evening,' she had a pleasant voice, but there was no invitation in it, or in the way she opened a magazine and started reading. The barman approached her.

'Champagne, madam? Mr Oakham's compliments.'

'No, thank you,' Rosa shook her head. 'Could I have a whisky instead with soda and ice?'

'Certainly,' the barman withdrew. The old man was making his mark all right. Champagne last night, same again on order, and dinner for two.

The staff were riveted. Even the restaurant manager had raised an eyebrow at the idea of the manager dining alone with one of the guests. Hotel owners could do what they liked, and often it was good policy to join important clients. But tête-à-têtes were not recommended. Jane, at reception, had been giggling over it ever since this morning.

Vassily Zarubin got up. He walked over to where Rosa was sitting and said, 'Excuse me, are you reading the evening paper?'

'No,' Rosa handed it to him. 'Please take it.'

'Thank you.' She picked up the magazine again. He went back to his place. The whisky arrived, and a few minutes later Oakham walked into the bar. He flashed her a quick smile and went up to the man who had tried to get into conversation with her.

'Good-evening, sir. Everything all right?'

'Can you order some pepper vodka?'

'I'm sure we can. Is the work going well?'

'Thank you, yes.'

'I hope you enjoy your dinner. Excuse me.' He came and sat down beside Rosa. 'I ordered champagne for you, Mrs Bennet.'

'I know. I changed it to whisky.'

'Don't you like bubbly?' It was such an odd, old-fashioned word. It dated him.

'I'm afraid I have to drink quite a lot of it socially and whisky makes a change.'

He wore a well-cut dark suit and a silk tie; his shoes were polished like a guardsman's on parade.

'Who is that man over there?' Rosa asked him. She wished she hadn't said that about drinking champagne socially. It gave him a chance to question her about herself.

'V.S. Zarubin,' Oakham told her. 'Haven't you heard of him? He's a famous Russian dissident author. He's here finishing his book on that playwright chap who is president of Czechoslovakia. Insists on peace and quiet and rattles away on his WP all day. Only comes down to eat. Why?'

Rosa dismissed it. 'Oh nothing. He tried to pick me up, or I think he did. I must have been wrong.'

'It says a lot for you.' Harry Oakham didn't flicker. 'Normally he's pretty dour, never mixes with anyone. I never realized that Russians were so morose. It's all those old movies, where they rush about doing Cossack dances and playing the balalaika – judging by him they're not a barrel of laughs. Why do you have to drink champagne socially – is your husband in the wine trade?'

'Not my husband,' Rosa said it sharper than she meant to. 'I'm in the Foreign Office. I was talking about embassy receptions.' Never lie when it's safe to tell the truth. That had been hammered into her by Parker. You'll trip yourself up if you do.

'Good God,' he said. 'Are you a very high-powered diplomat?'

'Not yet, but I hope to be.'

'I'm overawed,' he said gently.

'Don't be. It's no big deal. But I think I'm moving in the right direction. That's why I came here, I needed time to clear the cobwebs out of my brain and get my priorities right.'

'It seems to me it must have been your ex that

had the cobwebs,' Harry remarked. 'Did it hurt? The break-up, I mean. You don't mind if I ask?'

'I don't mind now,' she admitted. 'Yes, it did hurt. It hurts like hell when you've been breaking your neck to keep a balance between your husband and your job, and he walks out for someone else.' She didn't mean to say it but it came out, like a buried thorn piercing the skin. 'She was pregnant. That's what got him.' There was an awkward pause after she said it.

'Why don't we go to the table,' Oakham suggested. 'We can look at the menu there.'

'Can I really be off-duty?' He leaned a little towards her.

'I thought you were,' Rosa said. He'd drawn her out and she hated herself for letting it happen.

'Actually Saturday is our busiest night,' he admitted. 'I didn't want to wait till Wednesday before having dinner with you, so I took the time off. I haven't taken anyone out since I left my wife. I hope you don't think I'm being pushy.'

'I thought your wife left you,' she said.

'I offered her all my worldly goods, not that there was all that much, so I gave her a push, if you like. We hadn't been happy for years and it was time to make a break. Neither of us shed tears.' She almost believed him. 'Let's choose what we want to eat, and I'll pick a nice wine to go with it. You're so easy to talk to, Mrs Bennet. I could end up telling you my whole life story. Pretty boring stuff unfortunately.'

'I don't believe that,' she answered. It had to

be done. 'Why don't you call me Rosa? You *are* off-duty—'

'It suits you. It's unusual. Is it short for Rosemary?'

'Rosamund,' she corrected. 'My father loved old-fashioned historical names. Everyone calls me Rosa.'

'Your father sounds rather nice. Tell me about him.' He took the menu while she talked, leaned back, didn't open it immediately.

When she had finished he said, 'I was christened Henry Arthur George.'

'Good Lord! That is a mouthful—'

'After my father and grandfather and some god-father who coughed up a silver mug and was never heard from again. So I ended up as Harry. Now let's do some serious reading.'

It was one of the best dinners she had ever eaten. The room was splendid, with fine panelling and subdued lighting. Candles shed little pools of light on the tables; the dishes came and went and the marvellous wines he chose were poured and followed by liqueurs and coffee.

He told her about himself; he made the desk job in a stuffy office seem as funny as the brightest television sitcom. But when he spoke of boredom and frustration in his job she detected bitterness and some kind of angry grief. The food and wine were lulling her senses, blunting her judgement of the man sitting close to her now, his knee brushing her thigh under the table.

'Do you want to move into the library?' he asked. 'There'll be a lot of people there. Or shall we stay where we are?'

'I'm happy here,' Rosa said. 'You know, I just can't see you as a Civil Servant. I think of the ones I've known and I just can't imagine it.'

'I can't imagine you as a Foreign Office bluestocking,' he remarked. 'You're a beautiful woman, but a lot of people must have told you that. I'm going to have a cigar – if you don't mind.'

She shook her head. She watched his hands as he sliced the end off his cigar and drew on it; the rich smell of tobacco rose into her nostrils. It was a sensual smell, intensely male.

She saw the signet ring and asked him, 'Is that your crest?'

'Oakham's,' he answered. 'It was my father's. We had the same size finger so it didn't have to be altered.'

'We don't have anything like that. We're straight middle class.'

'I don't call a Regius Professor of History at Oxford middle class,' he countered. 'Anyway, life's all about a sense of humour and loyal friends. Even one loyal friend is enough.'

'And you have one?' She had to probe, or the situation would slide further still.

'Yes. I'm lucky, I have a friend like that. He's gone abroad now. Gone to Poland, where his family came from. I miss him like hell.'

The Pole who'd been in prison . . . Jim Parker was wrong about that. Harry Oakham was telling the truth. Why should he lie to her? Why should he mention the man at all . . . ?

'Maybe he'll come back,' she said.

'Nothing in this bloody country to come back for,' he said. 'He was a good man. I miss him,' he repeated.

'It's past twelve,' Rosa said. 'We can't sit here all night, keeping your poor staff—'

'You're a nice person, Rosa. I should have thought of that. It's time we put the hotel to bed. Thank you so much for tonight. And forgive me if I've been a bore talking about myself. I didn't think you wanted any *post mortem* of your own.'

'I've had a lovely dinner and enjoyed every moment of it. As for being a bore, Harry, don't fish for compliments.'

He laughed and took her arm. 'I won't; I'll see you to your room, and then I'll put my manager's hat on and take a quick check round before we lock up.'

They walked up the stairs together, past the Doll's House.

'Fascinating piece of history,' she said, pausing for a moment. She didn't want him to come any further.

'I'll tell you the legend some time.' Harry stood looking down at her. He seemed to read her mind. 'You go on up. I'll go down and put the hotel to bed. Thank you again.' He didn't touch her. He didn't need to; it was like a charge of naked electricity between them.

'Goodnight, Rosa. Sleep well.'

She turned and hurried up to the landing and through the door into the corridor. In her own room she kicked off her shoes and lay down on the bed in her clothes. She felt drained.

'Oh, my God,' she whispered, 'what am I getting into . . .'

'What the fucking hell are you playing at, Zarubin?'

The Russian gazed at Oakham. He had been reading when Oakham used his master key and slammed into his room at close to one in the morning.

'Playing? I don't understand you. And don't swear at me!'

'You're supposed to keep a low profile,' Harry spat the words at him. 'Not try and pick up one of the hotel guests! In the bar – I saw you—'

'No you didn't,' Zarubin countered. '*She* told you. I only asked for a newspaper. I saw you eating and drinking together. What about your profile?'

'That's my business,' he snapped back. 'If you want a fuck, then tell me and I'll find you a tart – but keep away from the hotel guests!' Zarubin threw back the bed covers. He got up, stretched and stood facing Oakham. He was taller than the Englishman.

He was tempted to tell him what he'd seen from the window. But he resisted. Not yet. Not till he had satisfied himself that she was an infiltrator. Spy was an old-fashioned word.

Was she watching the Irish terrorists? Was that the reason she was in the hotel? If it was, then she was a danger to them all. But Oakham wasn't the type of man to provoke into sudden action. He wasn't a chess player. Zarubin yawned.

'I'm not a prisoner here. I came of my own will. I was bored tonight and I felt like talking to a pretty woman. If she belongs to you, Harry, then I made a mistake. It won't happen again. Now get out and let me go to sleep.' He opened the door and stood aside.

For a moment Harry Oakham hesitated. The bastard had seen right through him *and* had the last word. He stalked out, and the door closed very quietly behind him. It wasn't just security. Zarubin was the professional's professional, and it was a crude excuse for his own jealous impulse, to accuse him of taking a risk.

He didn't want Vassily Zarubin, who was fifteen years younger and had little Jane and the girls going into a romantic swoon, chatting up Rosa Bennet. Simple. He didn't want competition. She'd excited him in a way he couldn't remember with anyone for years. Apart from the enormous sexual charge he felt when she was close, he liked her. He liked the honesty and independence, devoid of pettiness or vanity, the way she spoke her mind.

He wanted her, but he wasn't going to rush her. She wouldn't let him, and he respected her for that. They had time; time to circle each other and get a little nearer, until the chemistry was right for both of them. And there'd been something in her eyes as they stood beside the doll's house and she said good night . . .

He fell asleep and woke up sweating with a nightmare, where the naked woman he held in his arms had the face of Judith, pale and blind in death.

Security at the Regis Hotel effectively sealed off the penthouse suite and the special lift, and covered the two floors below. Special Branch had men inside the hotel and on patrol in the street, covering all entrances. A small team of sharpshooters was in place in the building opposite. The Saudi Prince had survived one assassination attempt in Paris, and as a result, chose London for medical attention and amusement because the precautions were so much better.

He arrived in a high-speed bullet-proof Mercedes limousine with opaque windows, and unmarked police cars in front and at the rear. His entourage came in a fleet of hire cars. His personal bodyguards, men of the ruling tribe, sworn to protect the Royal Family to the death, always travelled with him. The entrance was cordoned off, the lobby cleared, and the Prince was escorted up to his penthouse in the private lift. His own cook prepared his food and his taster sampled everything in case of poison.

He had an appointment with his specialist the next day. His visit was a private one, so there were no official receptions, but a private dinner given by the Foreign Secretary at his London home.

The Prince was tired after his journey and he slept. Jan kept watch outside the Conduit Street club in vain for the first twenty-four hours. On the second day he was rewarded.

A limousine with blacked-out windows drew up by the side entrance, and a tall girl shrouded in a sparkling veil, got inside. Jan followed. They turned right up St George Street and round Hanover Square. To his surprise, the limousine took a left turn down

Tenterden Street. It was a narrow, ill-lit area leading to Bond Street. Surely, he thought, puzzled, the driver was going wrong. Bond Street was one way. Then the indicators flashed right, the car turned out against the flow of traffic for a few yards and turned down Blenheim Street. Diplomatic immunity – Jan muttered to himself. The law didn't apply to *him*. As they sped up Oxford Street and turned towards the hotel, he dropped back and passed them slowly as the woman got out and walked quickly into the entrance. He drove back to Kensington Gore, bought a glass of wine in a local bar and asked to use the telephone.

He spoke quietly. He didn't identify himself to Harry. He was back in the routine of their days in the field. Never give a name, never use a name. 'We're ready,' he said. 'Send them tomorrow. My place.'

'OK,' Harry answered. 'Good man. You all right, old son?'

The scrambler switch was on. In his excitement, Jan had forgotten they couldn't possibly be overheard. 'I'm all right. It'll go well. I promise.'

'Good man,' Harry said again, and Jan rang off. He went back to his seat; he spilled a little of the wine because his hand was shaking. He was the co-ordinator. He could hand over to the Israeli tomorrow.

He didn't have to be anywhere near when they ambushed the car and Monika took the girl's place. He was to leave London and go back to Suffolk before they activated the plan. He wouldn't have to face the violence. He wouldn't think about the Saudi or what was going to happen. He hadn't even thought about the money clocking up for him in Switzerland. He was doing it for Harry.

The girl who served him with a second glass of wine asked him if he was feeling all right. He looked so ill and he was shaking all over. He said, 'Yes, fine. Bring me the bill please,' and she shrugged and went away to write it out. She'd done her best.

Rosa didn't see him for two days. She drove into Woodbridge, and bought a novel set in Provence, and a biography of Talleyrand which had just been re-issued by Penguin. She'd read it when she was a schoolgirl, and it had shaped her choice of the Foreign Office as a career. She wasted time in shops selling over-priced bric-à-brac and calling it antiques, and sat in the hotel gardens trying to read. The novel was pretentious and gloomy. She put it aside and turned to her old friend the biography. But she found her attention wandering. Where was Oakham? In the end, she asked at reception. She'd made a point of stopping to chat to Jane for a few minutes when she passed. 'I haven't seen Mr Oakham about,' she remarked on the second day. 'Is he away?'

Jane said, 'He's very busy. He told me yesterday that Mr Pollock wasn't coming back till the end of the week.' She glanced up at Rosa. 'I expect he'll be about this evening. Any message for him?' She had a mischievous gleam in her eye.

The dinner had gone on till past midnight. The restaurant staff said they'd been sitting there talking and he'd ordered the top of the wine list for her. Jane thought it was romantic. She liked Mrs Bennet. And, obviously, so did Mr Oakham.

Concentrate on Oakham. Those were Rosa's instructions. She couldn't afford to let time pass. 'Ask him if he'd like to join me in the bar after dinner,' she said, 'if he's not too busy.'

'Oh, I'm sure he won't be,' Jane beamed at her. She couldn't wait to tell the other receptionist about it. She was rather snooty, but she liked a gossip.

'Oh,' Rosa had moved on, but she turned back. 'I meant to ask. When is the Adventure Trail going to be open? I'd love to walk round it.'

'I'm not sure,' Jane answered. 'I think they're still working in there. Some time in the next couple of weeks. Not that I can see many of our clients climbing around in there. Too many business lunches!' she giggled.

'Oh, I don't know,' Rosa leaned against the desk. 'A lot of businesses are very keen on health and fitness for their executives. Perhaps it is a bit silly; a swimming pool or squash courts would have been better.'

Jane was on the defensive. She loved her job and she was very loyal by nature. 'We *are* going to have water skiing and wind surfing on the lake.'

'Really? Who's going to run that – it sounds rather fun.'

'The handymen, Bob and Ron. They're ex-Paras or Marines or something.'

The man who'd picked her up in the buggy had been built like a tank. Rosa said casually, 'I've seen one of them running about in a pick-up. Are they nice?'

Jane pulled a face. 'Hard to say. They don't mix much, not with the rest of the staff. Spend their evenings down at the Crown. Their boss is a real tartar. He's an ex-sergeant I think.'

'Where do they live?' Rosa asked. 'In the village?'

'No, there're three little workmen's cottages by Dunns Wood. Mr Oakham had them modernized. The housekeeper didn't want them living in our staff quarters. We get a lot of foreign girls here you see, working as pupils for a few months. She didn't like the idea of three tough guys let loose. Neither did Mr Oakham. In fact,' she lowered her voice, 'he actually said to the housekeeper, it'd be like putting foxes in a chicken run. Don't tell him I told you, will you? It was so funny . . . '

'Of course not.'

But Jane was in full flood now. 'Poor old Jim doesn't like them,' she confided. 'He's the old maintenance man; he worked here with the other owners. He says they're cheeky to him. They did all the electrical work at Croft Lodge and the carpentry. He was very put out about it. He said that had always been his job.'

'You've lost me,' Rosa said. 'What's Croft Lodge?'

'That's the auditor's house,' she explained. 'He and his wife live there. They're Swiss. He's got an assistant. He lives there too.'

'Do they come up to the hotel?'

'Mr and Mrs Brandt? No, they don't come in for meals or anything. We were all introduced to them when Mr Oakham took over. We haven't seen the other man yet. She was really attractive – very elegant. He wasn't much to look at. He looked just like someone who did accounts – you know what I mean. Small, not handsome or anything. Talking of handsome, Mrs Bennet, have you seen the author, Mr Zarubin?' She mispronounced the name, drawing out the first syllable.

'A tall, very dark man? He was in the bar the other evening. He's here writing a book, isn't he?'

'Yes, all about that playwright who was in jail and then elected president – Hungary, wasn't it?'

'Czechoslovakia,' Rosa corrected gently. She smiled at Jane. 'You think he's attractive?'

'He's so romantic looking.' The little blush crept up into her face. 'I keep hoping he'll ask for me if he wants any secretarial work. His room's full of computers and word processors – so the cleaners tell us. He works up there for hours, then goes off walking. They say writers are solitary.' She sighed. 'I wouldn't mind taking a walk with him! Well, I shouldn't say things like that, should I? Didn't you think he was dreamy?'

'I didn't really look,' Rosa admitted. 'But I will next time. Don't forget to give Mr Oakham my message, will you? I feel like a pot of tea. Bye, Jane.'

'Bye, Mrs Bennet.'

Rosa went upstairs, and ordered tea. She was hot and tired. She stretched out on the bed and fell asleep. The tea was ice cold when she woke up and there was a rim of darkness at the edge of the sky showing through her window. She'd slept deeply and for almost three hours. She ran a hot bath and lay in it, going over the scraps of information gleaned from the talkative Jane.

Ex-Army odd-job men who were also electricians and carpenters. Nothing sinister in that. Typical resettlement courses run for servicemen leaving the Army. They weren't popular and they didn't mix. A familiar story with élite troops cast into civilian life. They didn't fit in for a long time. The Swiss auditor and his wife and an assistant living on the estate. What was suspicious about that?

The Adventure Trail wasn't even finished, so no wonder they didn't want anyone wandering around . . .

She chose the bright blue dress she'd bought in the boutique. She painted her lips and sprayed the new Armani scent on her hair.

I'm scared, she'd confessed to Jim Parker. Scared of a man known to kill without a qualm. She faced her own reflection in the mirror. Now there was another reason, and she had to face it.

She was afraid of the way he made her feel. In exposing him, she might have to expose herself. Already her image had changed. The smart career diplomat, elegantly understated, looked very different from the girl in the vivid dress, with tanned bare shoulders, her hair hanging loose, long, sexy brown legs shown off by a short skirt. She slipped on gold high-heeled sandals. She looked much younger. No proof, just supposition. In the end it all hinged on Harry Oakham himself.

He was waiting for her when she came downstairs.

'Hello,' he said. 'I got your message. Do you mind if I say you look absolutely stunning? What a pretty colour—'

'Thank you,' Rosa looked up at him. He seemed tense, with lines round his eyes. A tiny muscle worked at the side of his jaw.

'Why should I mind? You pay very nice compliments. I got the dress in Ipswich of all places. It's a bit jazzy for me, but I liked the blue. Can we have a drink after dinner? Jane told me you were very busy.'

'We're short-staffed at the moment; it'll be easier when my assistant comes back.' Monika and Daniel were waiting for him at Croft Lodge. Bill Stevenson and his thugs were on alert for his call at the cottage, ready to join the other two. 'Are you going to have a drink at the bar, or go into dinner?'

'It's rather late. I think I'll go to the restaurant.'

He touched her arm, and it made her jump. When his hand slipped away it was like a caress on her skin. He said, 'After dinner I'm my own man. I'll meet you in the library around nine thirty. There won't be many people there tonight.'

Monika was excited; she paced the small sitting room, a glass of vodka and tonic in her hand. She looked at Daniel and smiled. She oozed sexual energy. He could hardly keep still himself, watching her. 'I wish Harry would hurry up. I can't wait to get started!'

'You're not afraid?' the Israeli asked her.

She laughed at him. 'I was never afraid. You forget, Danny, I took really big risks in the old days ... It wasn't only that old fart Ritterman. He was easy. There was a Swiss arms dealer – he disappeared in Zurich. He liked having women in the back of his car. He had me one afternoon. They found the car in the lake three months later. What was left of him was in the boot. And others, filthy capitalist swine like the one in Italy. We kidnapped him on a holiday. We kept him in a box and left him to die because the family went to the police and tried to set us up with the ransom money. Not that we'd have let him go anyway. One day, someone'll look in that *contadino*'s hut and find the box. But they haven't yet.' She laughed again. 'I've never tried it with an Arab. Is it true they like to sodomize? You'd know, wouldn't you, Danny?'

He was mesmerized by her. She didn't disgust him, she made him frantic with lust. He said, 'Do you get a climax when you kill, Monika? I've heard of women who do.'

'And men,' she pointed out. 'It's a cleansing. You feel power, release, and pleasure too. It's an experience – I can't explain.'

'You can,' he muttered. 'You make me feel it too. We'll have to celebrate when it's over. Will you celebrate with me, Monika?'

She smiled and suddenly came to him and ran her hand over the thick curly hair. She made a fist and pulled it.

'You set it up for me, Danny,' she murmured, 'and

afterwards I'll let you fuck me. Any way you like. I promise. Ah,' she let go of his hair and swung round. 'That's Harry now.'

He came in, saw the drink at her side and said, 'None of that. No booze, now or while the job's on. Are you two ready to go?'

'Yes.' Daniel got up. He rubbed the top of his head. *Any way you like*, she'd promised. He had a few surprises in store for her. 'What about Stevenson and the others?'

'They'll meet you up the road outside the entrance. Monika, how many bloody drinks have you had?' Oakham demanded.

'That was my first,' she snapped back at him. 'You think I'm a fool to take chances?'

'OK, then you drive. Jan's booked you into a bed and breakfast; Stevenson and his boys are staying up the road from you. When you get there, register and go round the corner to a pizzeria called Arturo's Pizza Pie. Jan'll be waiting for you. He's got it all mapped out. Then you take over, Daniel. Get Monika into that hotel. Then it's up to her. You can leave the press leak to me. I'll give them a tip off.'

Monika sniggered. 'Prince found dead after night of orgy. I'll get you some nice pictures to go with it—'

'Just get yourself out in one piece,' Oakham cut her short. 'Right, get on your way. And good luck.'

Daniel opened the door for her; they exchanged a conspiratorial smile. Harry didn't follow them out. He stayed in the sitting room till he heard the sound of the car starting up and fading into the darkness.

She was mad, of course. His grandfather used to talk about evil in his sermons; Harry remembered some of them from when he was a child. Possessed by the devil. Modern psychiatry would have an explanation for a phenomenon like Monika. Childhood trauma, lack of parental love, all the trendy crap that put the blame on other people. His grandfather had the right idea. There was nothing crazy about Daniel, sweating with lust for such a woman. He was just rotten. Born without feelings for anyone but himself, with the rat's savage instinct for survival.

The door opened and Hermann Rilke came in.

'They've gone?'

'Yes,' Oakham nodded. 'You didn't come and say goodbye, Hermann. They'll be hurt.'

Rilke regarded him with dislike. He hated the man's sense of humour. He had never enjoyed irony. 'I shall have the house to myself for a few days,' he remarked. 'I shall enjoy that. If it goes well, we'll get paid immediately?'

'The money's held in escrow at our bank,' Oakham answered. 'I don't give the story to the press till I hear it's been transferred. They want the scandal. They'll pay as soon as I contact Hakim. I could do with a drink. You want anything?'

'No,' Rilke looked down his nose at an invisible smell. His mother disapproved of drinking and had never encouraged it. He missed her very much. But she was well and happy in her new apartment, receiving monthly pay cheques, and getting his letters through a post restante in Geneva.

She was proud of his new job, and content to wait till he could get back and visit her. She believed he was in Uruguay, which was where he intended to buy a house and settle down with her when he had enough money.

Daniel made the first reconnaissance. He drove with Bill Stevenson from the Conduit Street brothel to the hotel, taking the route charted by Jan when he followed the Saudi driver and his passenger, but unlike the Saudi he didn't cross the traffic in Bond Street. And he studied the street map, with Stevenson looking over his shoulder. Both were silent; Stevenson was not a talker and he was going to have to drive the lead car along the chosen route.

Daniel pondered. He decided on a second test drive just to make sure that he'd picked the right spot. The two ex-soldiers would be in the back-up car with Monika. That was the one Jan had bought from the dealer.

It was a simple plan, because Daniel knew that the more complications the more risk of something going wrong. For three evenings the girl Denise had left for the Prince's hotel at the same time – eleven o'clock in the evening and the route never varied.

Harry unlocked the door into his office. He pressed the scrambler switch and dialled Georg Werner's home number in Berlin. It was time the bastard earned some of that subsidy he was getting paid in Switzerland. It rang for some time until a woman answered. Harry's German was faultless. 'Herr Werner, please?'

It was Werner's wife who answered. 'Who is calling him?'

'It's the Embassy in London,' he answered. There was a pause and he heard voices in the background. Then Werner came on the line.

'Listen,' Harry spoke rapidly in English, 'we've got a job on. It's a big one. The number two Saudi ... Yes, that's what I said ... Just listen, will you? He's in London and we're going to take him out.' He heard Werner suck in his breath. He'd be worried stiff; violence wasn't his line. Harry said brutally, 'It's time you earned your keep, Werner. Your lot in London have close ties with the Saudi Ambassador. I want you to monitor the official reaction for me. Find out what the cover story's going to be. They'll try to hush it up, and it's our job to blow the lid off. It's part of our brief. And anything else interesting you get hold of.'

Georg Werner's voice was edgy. 'I'll do my best, but how? What reason would I have for making enquiries?'

'Think of one,' was the retort. 'That's what you're drawing money for. It's scheduled for the day after tomorrow. Contact me here. And don't fail, will you?'

'No,' Werner answered. 'I won't. I'll think of something.'

He couldn't bring himself to wish them luck, so he hung up. His wife was watching television. She turned down the volume.

'What was it, darling? Anything important?'

'Just a little job the Ambassador wants me to do.' He smiled reassuringly at her. 'It's confidential.'

'Come and sit down. This is rather amusing.' She restored the sound and the room filled with the orchestrated laughter of the studio audience.

8

Harry Oakham felt better. He'd given Georg Werner a kick up the backside, and it was overdue. He'd been sitting smugly drawing his loot while everyone else did the work and put themselves on the line. It made Harry feel much better.

He drew in a deep breath. It was time to shut off. Time to pull down the shutters on what was going to happen. His part was done; it was in the hands of the professional kidnap expert and the rest of the team.

It was time to think of the lovely woman waiting for him. And she was lovely. She'd shed the cool image; the way she looked that night was an invitation to more than just coffee and brandy after dinner. He walked to the library, saying good-evening to the few guests in the bar and the main lounge.

The library was a long, oak-panelled room with a wall of leather-bound books behind a grille. He'd instructed the staff to light a fire, as the evenings were turning cool. He liked the library. It had a smell he relished, of old leather and wood and the faint must of age. As he expected, there was nobody else there. Just the table by a deep sofa close to the fire, with coffee and two balloons of brandy waiting for them.

'Hello.' She came up behind him and he turned.

'Hello,' he said and his voice was low. 'How was dinner?'

'Delicious. Are we over there?' She saw the flames licking round the logs in the grate, the table prepared.

He'd thought of everything. Her heart began to beat fast. Once more he touched her arm. 'You didn't jump this time,' he said. 'Let's sit down.'

They were close, but not touching. She poured coffee, and he watched her, holding the glass of brandy in both hands.

'I talked all about myself last time,' he said. 'Now I'd like to know about you.'

'Where do you want me to start? I was the blue-stocking, I was my father's favourite too. And my mother's I suppose, only we're not a bit alike. I went to university, did well, passed the Foreign Office exams and got married. And divorced.'

He passed her the brandy balloon. 'Are you still in love with him?'

'No,' she faced him. 'No, I'm not. I've tried very hard to see his point of view, and in a way I think it helped.'

'What was his point of view? What sort of guy was he?'

'Nice actually. I met him and we lived together for a while before we got married. And it worked. We were very happy together.'

'So what went wrong?' he asked.

'My career. I thought he understood how much it meant to me, but I don't think he really took it in. He thought marriage would change me. He wanted me to have children and settle down at home.'

'And you wouldn't,' he prompted.

'No, I wouldn't give everything up and just be a

wife. He made children the issue but it was more than that really. He was jealous. He didn't like me being independent.'

'Maybe you wouldn't have needed the job so much if he'd made you happy.'

'I don't know,' she said slowly. The brandy was warm inside her, and she felt relaxed. She turned to look at him. 'I felt the most terrible failure.'

'You shouldn't have,' Harry Oakham said. 'He just didn't know how to look after you, Rosa. My wife wanted children, the one I left. I always said no.'

'Why? Why wouldn't you?'

She had fine eyes, he thought, a clear hazel that changed in the shifting light. He could have taken the glass out of her hand and pulled her into his arms at that same moment. But he wouldn't. He wanted to talk to her. He wanted to know what went on inside.

He knew all about women's bodies and what to do to them, but with her, it wouldn't be enough. He wanted more. Why not open up to her a little? It would be a relief to lift the mask, to let her glimpse the real man for a change.

'Because I didn't want to leave my kids without a father,' he said quietly. 'Civil Servant is a pretty broad description. Part of my life involved taking a few risks. I didn't think it was fair. That's why. Not that I could tell Peggy the reason. She wouldn't have understood.'

'What were you doing?' Rosa kept her voice calm. He was confiding in her. Trusting her.

'I can't tell you that,' he said. 'And you wouldn't like me if I did. But it seemed right to me at the time. I shouldn't have got married. Not the second time, anyway.'

There was a long pause; neither of them spoke. She watched him quietly, waiting. He was staring at the fire and he was far away from the room and from her. *He wouldn't talk about her*, the ex-wife's complaint came to her mind. *She was dead, that's all I knew . . . She was too bloody precious to talk about . . .*

'Harry?' she spoke softly.

He looked up quickly, 'Sorry, I was miles away.'

'I know you were. What was your first wife like?'

'Beautiful,' he said. 'And sweet. The sweetest, funniest girl in the world. God knows why she married me.'

He looked at Rosa and she saw a lurking pain in his eyes. It shocked her. He could feel, and feel deeply, even after many years of loss.

'What happened?' she asked.

'I lost her,' he said simply. 'She was a great skier. We were on holiday in Verbier, we'd only been married a little more than a year. There was an accident. She broke her neck. I picked her up and she was dead.' He reached out for his glass and drained it.

'How terrible,' Rosa murmured. 'I'm so sorry.' He wasn't looking at Rosa, he was staring at something she couldn't see. 'Go on,' she said. 'If it helps.'

'Nothing helps,' he said. 'I tried everything, throwing myself into my work – I was the guy that never said no to an assignment, however lousy it was.' He lifted his empty brandy glass. 'This didn't help either; I tried it for quite a while, but then I stopped. It was the coward's remedy, and Judith would have hated me doing it. Then one day I picked up a girl in a café. She was very pretty, a bit like those blonde dolls that kids used to play with, Barbies weren't they?'

'I slept with her and it worked. I married her because nothing had been any use with anyone else after Judith died. I was lonely and lost and I hoped . . .' He shook his head impatiently at his own mistake.

'The worst thing I could have done. For both of us. I made her miserable, Rosa, and she made a complete jackass out of me with other men. The awful thing is, I didn't care. I didn't give a damn.'

'And you never got over Judith?' she asked the question quietly.

'No. I got on with my life, if you can call it that, but you don't forget someone like that. She was a great sport – you know? – loved life, and game for anything. My mother adored her. You couldn't help it, she was that kind of girl. God, we used to laugh about the stupidest things – she loved playing silly jokes . . .' His voice died on the last words. There was silence; one of the logs crackled and fell apart, sparks soared up the chimney.

'She was only twenty-four,' he said at last. 'She hadn't even lived . . . I brought her home and she was buried in Dedham churchyard with all the other Oakhams. I haven't been near the place since.'

There were tears pricking in Rosa's eyes; he looked at her and saw them. He said softly, 'Why you funny thing . . . Don't be upset, please.' He slipped an arm round her and for a moment drew her close to him. 'You've got a soft heart, Rosa. Don't let it get you into trouble.' He pressed his lips against her cheek. 'Thanks for listening to me. You're the first person I've been able to talk to about her.'

Then abruptly he got up. 'Anyway, it all happened a long time ago. I've no business sitting here pouring our old woes on you. We've let the coffee stew and our glasses are empty. That won't do. Let's have some more brandy and talk about something else.' He crossed over and pressed a bell-push by the fireplace. He threw more logs on the fire and poked them into a blaze.

Rosa watched him. She didn't speak. The kiss burned on her cheek. What she was doing seemed cheap and shameful. He'd trusted her with his feelings . . . and she'd been genuinely moved.

He came and stood looking down at her. 'I'd like to make love to you,' he said. 'Will you think about it?'

'Yes,' Rosa answered. 'Yes, I will.'

'Then let's enjoy the rest of our evening. Do you play backgammon?' She shook her head. 'Then I'll teach you.'

It was growing light when Rosa finally drifted into an uneasy sleep. He hadn't come up to her room. He taught her to play the gambling game and used matchsticks for money. He seemed a different man from the one who had spoken of his dead wife. The mask was back in place; he was teasing and self-assured, emanating the sexual attraction that disturbed her so much. But not as much as his grief.

He hadn't played for sympathy to get her into bed when her emotions were involved. That confirmed her view that he had his own code and stuck by it.

Everything about him was a contradiction. The callous egotist who'd abandoned his wife was the same man who'd spoken so movingly of his dead love. Loneliness and despair, the escape into what he called his 'work'. Into violence, risk and death. And finding no peace in any of it.

She couldn't sleep and she couldn't get the situation into perspective. Parker described him as a killer by trade. A dangerous maverick without commitment to society. But he'd been motivated by patriotism, nobody denied him that. The orders he carried out came from men like Jim Parker, who was setting the bloodhounds on him now. The Cold War had been fought without any rules on either side. The enemy had been ruthless and pitiless. Men like Harry Oakham had turned their weapons against them. She tossed to and fro, got up, stood by the window to watch the light creeping up from the horizon and turning a delicate tinge of pink. Then back to bed, wooing the sleep that wouldn't come.

I'd like to make love to you. Will you think about it? She was thinking about it because she wanted it for herself, not to help Parker trap his quarry. And when sleep came, she woke exhausted. There was an envelope on the carpet by her door.

The note said simply, 'Thank you for last night. If you like oysters I know a place we could go for lunch today. H.'

The phone rang beside her bed. His voice said, 'Hello, Rosa. Did you get my note?'

'Yes, I did. I love oysters.'

He laughed. He sounded happy. 'So do I. I'll meet you outside at twelve. It's a little drive, about fifteen miles. We don't have to hurry.'

Rosa put the receiver down. There was no turning back. She had to find out about Oakham for herself now. In every sense, her life and her future would depend on it.

It was a lovely drive; they idled through the country lanes. He was happy; he hummed 'Nessun dorma' as he drove. 'You must be a football fan,' Rosa teased him.

He laughed. 'The only time in my life I watched football was the World Cup because of that song. Do you like music?'

'Yes, I love it.'

He grinned mischievously at her. 'Then I'd better stop. I've been told I'm tone deaf.'

'I wouldn't disagree,' Rosa smiled at him.

He reached out and squeezed her hand. 'You were so nice to me last night, I'll forgive you for that crack. Here we are, Orford, and the best oysters in East Anglia.'

He pulled in by the little shop-fronted restaurant, jumped out of the car and helped her out. He came very close for a moment.

'You look very pretty,' he said. 'You know what oysters do to people.'

They ate a dozen oysters, sharp and salty, followed by salad and cheese; wine kept coming to the table. Oakham knew the proprietor; they joked about the drop in summer visitors, although the little place was full. Rosa felt physically drawn to him, as if she was on the end of a line, and he was slowly reeling her in. It was profoundly sexually exciting and it frightened her. For the first time in any relationship with a man, she felt she was in his control. And she didn't want to resist. She wanted to submit and let it happen.

He got the bill; they were the last couple in the place. 'I've had a lot of wine,' Rosa said.

'We both have,' he answered. 'Why don't we walk down to the beach? A breath of sea air might clear the head.'

He took hold of her hand as they came out into the street. 'Down here; it's not far.' The street was cobbled, and she smelt the tang of the sea before they came out on to the shingled beach. A few boats rocked at anchor, and the sun glowed like a child's balloon in a hot sky. They paused for a moment, and Rosa thought, If I don't turn back now, it'll be too late. Oakham didn't speak.

He turned her towards him and looked down at her.

'Have you really had too much wine?'

'No,' Rosa answered.

He said, 'I haven't either.'

He pulled her firmly towards him and began to kiss her face and eyes, the side of her neck, and finally he brushed her mouth, very gently, and then probed between her lips. She put her arms up and clasped him round the neck and the back of his head, and opened her mouth to receive him.

They walked along the beach; he stopped and threw stones into the water, skimming and skipping them along the surface.

'I could never do that,' Rosa said. 'My brother used to make them go for miles.'

'It's easy,' he told her, 'I'll show you. You take a flat stone, here, this'll do, and you hold it between your thumb and fingers like this . . .' But she let the stone drop and they were holding each other and kissing again as soon as he touched her. 'I don't want to go back to the hotel,' Oakham said. They had gone to the car and were driving aimlessly. She touched her lips with a finger. They were bruised from the fierce pressure of his mouth. Her breasts were heavy, her body was pressed against him. Her face burned from the wind that came off the sea.

'Where can we go?' she asked him.

'I don't know,' he said. 'I'd like to take you into a field and make love to you. It's wonderful in the open. Let's just drive till we find somewhere.'

She laid her hand on his thigh. I have no shame, she thought. I'd go into a ditch with him. I'm out of my mind . . .

'Don't drive for too long,' she whispered. 'I don't want to wait.' He laid his hand on hers and pressed it hard against him.

'I don't either. Let's try up here.' He swung the car up a single-track lane with a dead end sign. They bumped along between high hedgerows and then he saw a gap and he stopped. He turned to her.

He didn't kiss her. He laid both hands on her breasts and held them. 'You're sure about this, Rosa?'

She gave a little cry of urgency as he pressed harder. 'Come on then,' he whispered. They stumbled through the gap.

It was a field of golden stubble. 'You let me do everything,' he said. 'Just let me do it for you.' He stripped off her clothes and brought her down gently on her back; the corn stalks pricked her skin. She watched him as he shed his own clothes and his shadow fell on her as she held out her arms. It was over very quickly for both of them. There was no foreplay, no subtlety. They exploded together and lay gasping on the rough stubble, with the sun going down and a slight chill touching their bodies.

Rosa opened her eyes. He was lying beside her. He seemed to be asleep. She looked upward at the sky; a few clouds straggled, turning dusky grey as the sun began to slide towards the horizon. She was aching, scratched by the needles of harvested corn. She was so happy she felt like laughing out loud. He had turned his head and was looking at her.

'Hello, darling,' he said gently.

'Hello,' she answered.

'That was the most wonderful thing,' he said.

'You said it would be,' Rosa murmured. 'Out in the open.'

'You'll catch cold,' he whispered to her, and helped her up. He held her close against him. For a moment they didn't speak. 'I'll dress you,' he said. 'I don't want you to get cold.'

Then it was Rosa who pulled the shirt over his head, and buttoned it, and paused to kiss his throat at the nape, before she let him go. Holding hands, they went back to the lane and the car.

'I haven't felt so bloody marvellously happy for years,' he told her.

'I haven't felt so bloody marvellously happy in my whole life,' she corrected him. He switched the engine on, and they reversed very slowly down the lane, swerving a little from side to side.

'We mustn't lose this,' Harry Oakham said.

'No,' she answered, and then she shivered. It wasn't the chill of dusk that made her cold. 'Where are we going?'

'To find a hotel, or a bed and breakfast,' he said quietly. 'Somewhere we can be alone and spend the night. Where we can talk and make love and then talk some more if we feel like it.'

The desire had drained out of her, and the reality of what she'd done and why, was darker than the gathering clouds of dusk.

It was a pub with a sign that said 'The Haywain', and he turned and grinned at her. 'Good old Constable, what would the pubs round here do without him. Let's see what it's like.'

There was a double room and nobody seemed to mind about luggage. He looked at her in question and she nodded. 'Let's have a drink first,' he suggested. He touched her arm, running his hand along the smooth skin. 'Darling, you're freezing! Come on, let's have something to warm you up.'

The lounge was small and dark, with low black

beams and horse brasses running up either side of the fireplace, which was filled with a very dusty arrangement of dried flowers.

'Irish coffee,' Harry announced. 'That's what you need. I'll order it.' Rosa sat in the musty little room and waited. A girl came in and switched on the lamps. The shades were red, with faded gold fringe; the beer mats said 'Tolly Cobbold', and were dirty with old rings interlocking on them like some kind of puzzle.

I lost my head, she said to herself. I flipped out there. Oh, James, if you'd ever been able to do that . . . You're one cool lady, Rosa Bennet, aren't you? Like hell . . .

He came back and the glass was hot, with a thick froth of cream on the top. He made her take it and drink. He looked at her and the kindness in his eyes twisted her inside. 'What's the matter, Rosa? You look miserable. Are you sorry it happened?'

Now she found it impossible to lie. 'I don't know, Harry. Maybe it's just an anticlimax. I'm sorry, I'll drink this and I'll have a hot bath. I'll feel better then.'

He had a very gentle smile when he took hold of her hand and said, 'Sweetheart, I don't think this kind of place runs to hot water at six o'clock. But we'll see. You do want to stay with me, don't you?' His hand was warm and the fingers held hers very firmly.

'Yes,' Rosa said, 'I want to stay with you. That's the trouble.'

'Thank God for that,' he said. 'Now finish that off

and we'll go and investigate the bath. If there's no hot water, I'll see what I can do to warm you up.'

The water ran in a tepid and unwilling trickle that turned into a cold flood with the hot tap full on. The bedroom was small, with copies of Victorian prints well above eye level on the walls and a lumpy bed dressed in nylon sheets, with a mattress not an inch wider than four foot six. Harry sat down and drew her beside him.

'Get under the blankets,' he said. He wrapped her up and lay beside her. He kissed her and it was calm and gentle. 'Have a little sleep, darling. Close your eyes, go on.'

Rosa felt his warmth and the bed was like a womb; she was enveloped in the blankets, with his arms cradling her. She said, 'I don't want to fall in love with you, Harry. I can't afford it.'

'I know you can't,' he murmured. 'Not till tomorrow, anyway.'

'Harry?' He'd woken her from a dream in which he was handling her with slow subtle movements, and found that she wasn't dreaming. They took time, and she played her part in caressing and exploring him. There were no comparisons, no habits to be called upon, learned from other men. To Rosa it was the first time for everything she felt and did, and there was a terrifying sense of being one with this man, of dissolving into him as he lost himself in her.

'Harry?' she said again.

'Yes, darling? How's the anticlimax this time?'

'There isn't one. And there won't be. I don't know

why I felt like that. I wanted to tell you I was sorry about it. You were so good, you seemed to understand. I can think of a lot of men who'd have been furious.'

'Like husband James?'

'It never happened with him,' she said. 'It was lovely and I thought it couldn't be better. But it was something else with you.'

'You know the old Latin tag – *post coitum omne animal triste?*'

'All creatures are sad after making love – yes, I remember now. I asked my Latin mistress what it meant. I was put up to it, to embarrass the poor thing.'

'Were you a nasty little girl?'

'Very nasty,' she admitted.

'I don't believe a word of it,' Oakham squeezed her. He closed his eyes. Her hair was soft and it smelt sweet. She was warm to hold, and supple. 'You know something,' he said to her, 'I feel as if I've been living in a deep freeze and you've thawed me out. I don't think I've really felt anything for years till I met you. And I don't just mean this.' He ran one hand over her possessively. 'I mean this – lying together, talking. Being happy. I'd forgotten what it felt like.'

'With Judith?' she asked gently.

'With Judith,' he agreed. 'And now you. I mean it, you know. We mustn't lose this. I'm not going to let you check out of the hotel and walk out of my life.'

She lay in the crook of his arm and didn't answer. If he was innocent, if Parker's infallible instinct was wrong for once, then maybe there was a future for them. But she hadn't proved anything.

At last she said, 'I don't know what's going to happen when my leave is up. I don't even know where I'll be posted. Probably abroad. And anyway, I don't know anything about you. What your life was like, why you decided to change everything.'

'It was decided for me,' Harry Oakham answered. 'I was retired. After twenty-eight years, I was redundant.'

'Why?' Rosa made herself ask.

'Because my line of work wasn't respectable any more. People like me belonged to the bad old days. It was time to sweep us under the carpet and pretend we'd never happened.'

'What was your job, Harry?' He moved his arm and pulled himself up on the pillow.

'I used to go after double agents. You know what a double agent is?'

'Of course I know. A traitor, working for both sides.'

'They don't just sell secrets,' he spoke softly. He reached out and switched on the bedside light. It was yellow parchment with roses painted up one side. 'They sell people. Philby did a lot of that. We lost some good people because of him. I wish they'd put me on to him. He wouldn't have ended up in a cosy flat in Moscow.' He stretched out a hand for his cigarettes, lit one and then said, 'You want one, Rosa?'

'No. No thanks. What would you have done about him, Harry?'

'I'd have killed the bastard. So now you know.'

She felt the tension in him. She swallowed. Her throat felt tight. 'Like the people who shot those terrorists in Gibraltar?'

'Yes, only we were all civilians. There were only a few of us; we'd all had experience in the field. I used to go on missions when I was married to Judith, making contacts, picking up information, or helping someone to get back if they were in trouble. It was exciting stuff. I loved it. And I had languages' – he stubbed out the cigarette half smoked – 'I speak German with a Westphalian accent. I was very good at languages. I could manage Polish, and that's difficult, but not Russian. That's a bitch of a language . . . Judith didn't know what I was doing. I could have told her because she was the right sort of girl. She'd never have told anyone else. But I'd signed the Act and I was one of those silly sods that believed in keeping promises in defence of Queen and country, that sort of rubbish.'

'I don't think it's rubbish,' Rosa said. 'I don't believe you think so either.'

He looked down at her, and there was a slight smile on his mouth. 'We won't argue about it. After I lost Judith I joined the special section. So now you know all about me. Has it changed things?'

'No,' Rosa answered. 'It hasn't changed anything. I'm glad you told me.'

'I'm glad too,' he answered. 'Are you hungry, darling?'

'Are you?' She felt flooded with relief.

'Yes; it won't be *nouvelle cuisine*, but I could settle for a steak.'

'So could I,' Rosa said. 'Actually, I'm starving!'

'Then we'd better go before they run out of chips.' He got up, half in shadow except for the sickly light of the one lamp. 'I love you, Rosa,' he said. 'That's why I told you. I love you for understanding and accepting me for what I am.'

'I'm begging to know what you are,' she said slowly. 'And that helps.'

Jan spent most of his time walking. He walked through Kensington Gardens and Hyde Park. He covered miles in the fine, late-summer weather, snatching a snack meal when he felt hungry, returning footsore to his room in the little hotel.

It was scheduled for the next evening, if the plan wasn't upset by a change in the Prince's itinerary. Jan stretched out on his bed; he ached from the exercise. But exercise had been prescribed for him when he got back from Poland and was fit enough to stand it. Exercise was better than tranquillizers for reducing tension.

He was so tense it hurt him to sit still. His hands were bunched into fists, his legs crossed at the knee and ankle, gripping like a vice.

And he shook inside. He kept thinking of Harry because it calmed him. Harry was his fail safe. He knew how to get him out of moods, out of the black depressions or the hunted fears that were the legacy of those ten terrible years. He loved Harry, and he was doing what Harry wanted.

Only another twenty-four hours, he told himself doggedly, and then it would be over and he'd be back at the Doll's House Hotel, walking through on the evening tour with his friend beside him. Safe and at peace. Until the next time he was needed. He refused to think about that.

It was the violence that racked his nerves. The struggle, the abduction. It was the way he'd been arrested, dragged off the street into a car, punched unconscious and waking to find himself handcuffed on the floor of a cell. It had been the beginning of the long martyrdom of question and answer. Followed by years of solitary confinement.

Sometimes his eyes filled up with tears for no reason. He didn't contact the others now. They kept apart after that initial meeting at the pizzeria. Stevenson had his car, and the one they'd driven up in from Suffolk had been fitted with false number plates. His own car waited in the long-term car park. He'd pick it up, take it to the area around the Regis, and be waiting for Monika when she came out. He was dozing when the phone rang and he sprang up immediately. He wasn't expecting any call. For a moment he stared at the stubby machine, shrilling by his bed. Then he picked it up.

'This is Hakim's friend.' It was the traitor in the Saudi entourage, Hakim's contact.

'Yes.' Jan whispered.

'He's going home tomorrow,' the voice was a harsh whisper. 'He's sending for the girl same time. You've got to do it tonight.'

Jan's damaged lungs contracted; he wheezed and

choked for a moment. The voice on the telephone hissed in his ear. 'You hear me? Tonight!'

'All right.' Jan managed to croak the few words. 'All right. Tonight.'

Then the line cleared. He coughed convulsively, fumbling in his pocket for the Ventolin inhaler he carried. Two sharp inhalations and the spasm stopped. He must tell Harry first. Then alert the others. Tonight.

He dialled the private number at the hotel. It rang. It went on ringing. Jan was sweating. Harry wasn't in his office. What a fool, of course, look at the time – he'd be in the hotel. Walking round the public rooms. It was their routine; didn't he remember? He dialled again, the main number at reception. He recognized the voice.

'Good-evening. Doll's House Manor. Can I help you?'

'Mr Oakham please. It's Mr Pollock calling.'

'Oh, good-evening, Mr Pollock. How is your father?' the girl said.

'Better,' Jan mumbled. 'Much better thank you. Get Mr Oakham for me will you?'

'I'm sorry, Mr Pollock, but he's gone out. He phoned through about an hour ago to say he won't be back till tomorrow morning. Can I leave a message?'

Jan forced himself to be calm. Harry wasn't there. Harry had gone out, was away for the night. But he didn't expect the strike till the next evening. He tried to think clearly.

'Mr Pollock? Are you there?'

'Yes. I'll be back tomorrow morning myself. A day early. I'll be there by the time he gets back.'

'We'll all be glad to see you,' she said. 'So glad to hear about your father. Good night, Mr Pollock.'

There was no time to hesitate. It was their only chance. Tomorrow the target would be gone. He had to make the decision and follow it through. Otherwise he would have failed Harry. He picked up the phone, got an outside line again, and dialled the number of Daniel's boarding house.

'You've got to go,' he said, 'he's leaving for home tomorrow. Eleven o'clock tonight.'

'Shit!' Daniel spat the word. But it was typical. They acted on impulse. Any whim was reason enough to change their plans at the last minute. Knowing this, he'd insisted on everyone staying in their rooms as the deadline approached. Lucky he had. 'OK,' he snapped back. 'OK. We do it. What did Harry say?'

Jan said, 'I couldn't find him. He's away for the night.'

'Shit—' Daniel exploded again but Jan interrupted him. He wasn't going to let him criticize Harry.

'It doesn't matter; I'll take the responsibility.'

'Don't give me that crap,' Daniel snorted. 'You won't even be here. Your job finishes, you go home—'

'I'm not going,' Jan answered. 'I'll see it through with you. I said, I'll take the responsibility. I'll answer to Harry. I always have.'

'Then let's hope we don't screw up,' Daniel muttered. 'If he doesn't have your balls, I will!'

240

Jan sat still for a few minutes. Then he got up, packed his clothes in a small suitcase and made a search of his room. Nothing was left behind. Nothing in the waste-basket, under the bed or slipped down the side of the chair. He knew the routine so well it was automatic: you came, you went and you left no personal imprint that could identify you.

He pulled on a pair of gloves and went over every surface in the room, including the outside door handle and cleaned it of fingerprints. He still wore his gloves when he paid his bill in cash and walked out into the night.

He hailed a taxi and stopped at the long-term car park. His car was on the lower level. He got in, switched on, checked oil, petrol and water. He paid in cash again at the checkout. He should drive back to Suffolk; those were Harry's firm instructions.

His role was finished on the day the plan became operational. He was to leave immediately and be safe at the hotel before it happened.

But that was impossible now. He'd committed himself to stay, to see it through. Otherwise Daniel might have refused to go ahead. He couldn't let that happen. Harry depended upon him. He'd stay till it was over.

The four men were dressed in black tracksuits and trainers; black cotton gloves and nylon stocking masks were in their pockets. They'd settled their bills and paired off. Daniel was in the car with Bill Stevenson.

*　　*　　*

Monika paid her bill in cash and asked them to order a minicab. She left wearing a long, black, one-piece evening dress, and announced that she was going to a dinner party as she said goodbye at the desk. The car dropped her at a block of flats by Marble Arch. She paid him and went into the entrance. As soon as he had driven off into the traffic, she came out and the Subaru, driven by the surly Bob, drew up by the kerb and she got in. His companion, Ron, was in the back.

They were in position in Conduit Street at ten minutes to eleven. The streets were brightly lit and passers-by strolled along in the warm evening.

Daniel was in the front of the second car beside Stevenson. He checked his watch and sucked at his teeth till Stevenson nearly lost his cool and told him to stop doing it, for Christ's sake . . . Then he dug Daniel in the ribs. The black Mercedes was turning the corner.

From their parking place, they had a clear view of the agency door. The Mercedes drew up and stopped. The door opened on to the street, showing a bright glass ceiling fitment in the hallway, and a tall blonde girl came out, draped in a sparkling red shawl.

The driver of the Mercedes got out and opened the rear passenger door for her. He was a swarthy Arab in a baggy chauffeur's uniform and a peaked cap. As she approached, the girl drew the veiling, modestly over her head and covered her face. Once inside, she was invisible behind the smoked glass.

As the Mercedes moved off, Stevenson swung out and followed it. In the rear mirror, Daniel searched for Bob and the back-up car. He sucked furiously when he couldn't see them and Stevenson glared at him.

Then he said, 'There they are – they've come in behind that fucking taxi.' He kept an anxious watch, willing them to overtake and, to his relief, the taxi pulled over to let his fare out and Bob slid in immediately behind them.

The Mercedes purred along in front, not deviating from the route the driver had taken every time they followed him. Right into St George Street. Then round Hanover Square to the short cut, Tenterden Street on the left, saving time at a set of traffic lights leading into Oxford Street, when the driver signalled left and before he had time to make the turn, Stevenson swung out and cut in front of him.

The narrow street was deserted at that time. The buildings were all shops or offices. Everything was shut. Daniel glanced behind at the Mercedes and said, 'Now!' Stevenson slammed on the brakes and the Subaru slowed to a stop.

They pulled the nylon masks over their faces. The Mercedes had no option. As it halted with a screech of tyres to avoid hitting the Subaru, Bob brought the back-up car to its tail light.

Even before it stopped, Ron was out and wrenching open the rear door of the Mercedes. He was inside as Stevenson leapt into the seat beside the chauffeur and Daniel hurled himself into the back on the other side.

The girl was pinned between them. She saw nothing but a blur of faces, distorted by the masks, and opened her mouth to scream. Daniel slammed a fist into her jaw and she fell sideways. Stevenson had a knife pricking the Arab's throat. The man sat frozen with terror.

Daniel hissed under his breath to Ron, 'Get her out!' Ron heaved the unconscious girl up and dragged her out on to the road, supporting her. One quick glance showed him there was nobody about. Her bundled her roughly into the back of the Subaru and Monika helped to pull her inside. She felt for a pulse in her neck. Then expertly, she rolled up one of the painted eyelids.

'She's out,' she said.

'Yeah,' Ron muttered. 'He hit 'er hard enough.'

Monika stripped off the shawl. She turned to the dour young man beside her. 'Here,' she said, 'fix her up.' She paused for a moment and watched while he unrolled surgical tape and wrapped it round the unconscious girl's mouth. 'Don't tape her nose,' she said sharply, 'she'll suffocate.'

He glanced up at her. He called her a filthy name under his breath. She laughed at him, then wrapping the gleaming veil around herself, she walked to the Mercedes and got into the back.

Daniel was waiting there; she looked at him and nodded. For a moment they smiled in collusion. But they didn't speak. Absolute silence was the rule. Except for Daniel. They sat waiting; it seemed a long time but it was less than two minutes when the headlights flared on the Subaru.

That was Bob's signal that the girl was tied and gagged and it was Daniel's move now. It was time to dispose of the chauffeur. Stevenson held the knife point so close it drew a bead of blood. 'Get out,' Daniel spoke in Arabic. The man whimpered.

'Don't kill me . . . Spare me . . . ' Stevenson lowered the knife, and the man scrambled out on to the road. He peed himself with terror at the sight of Daniel in his stocking mask. He didn't even know Stevenson had followed him out, or feel the rabbit punch that sent him sprawling.

Stevenson ran to the car that had blocked the Mercedes and opened the boot. He was so strong he didn't need Daniel's help.

He picked up the unconscious man and threw him inside, doubling him up. Then he slammed the lid, locked it and got into the driver's seat.

The chauffeur's cap had fallen on to the road; the man's urine had formed a pool and the crown was wet.

Daniel picked it up and grimaced. He pulled off the stocking then he put on the cap and got into the driver's seat. Stevenson was already moving. He and the Subaru had a rendezvous arranged.

Daniel had timed it to the last minute. They knew what to do. He started the Mercedes and turned right into Bond Street. The time clock on the dashboard showed eleven fifteen.

'You'll be five minutes late,' he said to Monika. He grinned, showing his uneven white teeth. He was swarthy enough to pass for an Arab, his face half hidden by the cap. 'You can tell him it was bad traffic.' He chuckled to himself. It had gone exactly to schedule. The others were on their way to the Regent's Canal. It was a quiet area at that time of night.

Harry's orders were cast iron. No killing. Dump the two of them in the second-hand car, and get the hell out, back to Suffolk in the Subaru. Daniel had tried to argue because he didn't like leaving witnesses. But the Russian, Zarubin, had agreed with Harry. A political assassination was one thing. The murder of the girl and the driver would outrage public opinion and intensify the search for them.

Neither could describe anything beyond four men in black with masked faces, one of whom spoke Arabic. There'd be no fingerprints anywhere, and if forensic picked up hairs and strands of fabric, the best of luck to them. They'd have nothing to go on.

In the back of the car, Monika arranged her veiling. She had touched nothing in the interior. All they'd find would be Denise's fingerprints.

It rode very smoothly; she glanced out of the darkened windows as they rounded Marble Arch. Not even five minutes late, the traffic was lighter than usual. She smiled in anticipation.

Memories of past triumphs came back as her excitement rose. The fear on the victim's face, the seconds while they fought for their lives, the tremendous climax of killing . . .

They turned the corner into Lancaster Place and Daniel drew up by the main entrance. It was brightly lit, with flags fluttering from the building.

Immediately a uniformed doorman hurried up, saluted and opened the rear door for Monika. She didn't hurry. She got out, nodded to Daniel who was sitting immobile in the front, and slowly walked into the foyer, her face shrouded in the veiling.

The doorman knew her; he led the way to the private lift. He winked as he pressed the button and the door slid open. He must have been on friendly terms with Denise. Monika's eyes lowered above the veil and she stepped inside.

There was only one button, and it brought the lift up to the penthouse. As the doors opened, an armed bodyguard stepped forward and peered inside. He had a dark, vulture-like face and he wore Arab dress with a scimitar at his side. He carried an automatic machine pistol.

When he saw her he stepped back, and gestured her to go forward. Another servant appeared; he didn't speak, but with a movement of his hand, signalled her to follow him.

There was a big reception room to be crossed. It was brilliantly lit by a huge chandelier. Gold-framed mirrors reflected the light; she trod on a rich Persian carpet; there were sofas and inlaid ivory tables and a strong smell of the world's most expensive scent. The Prince liked to have it sprayed round his apartments.

The servant stopped by a door, knocked and a voice from inside gave him permission to enter. He opened the door, bowed very low, and stood aside for Monika.

Jan drove up to Regent's Park. He drove several circuits before he found a space to park. He doused his lights and sat in the dark. He had been chewing his lip until it was raw. The pain preoccupied him.

He felt conspicuous sitting in the car; but he saw two women approaching, walking with the slow hip-swinging gait of the prostitute looking for customers, and sank down in the front seat, pretending to be asleep. They passed on after a glance inside.

He saw a police car in the distance, and started to shake, so he drove off again. The digital clock crept, instead of moving towards the hour. He stopped in a side street off the Marylebone Road, and calmed himself with one of his ration of cigarettes. It made him cough and his lip stung from the tobacco.

It was past eleven o'clock. He turned on the radio; the street was empty; traffic and a dwindling number of pedestrians were concentrated in Marylebone Road. He listened to some popular light music; it went through his head in a tuneless buzz. Eleven twenty. Time to move. He knew the schedule; he'd gone over it with Daniel so often.

Monika would alight at the Regis about now. She had stipulated an hour at the maximum. That would give her enough time to lull her victim and then kill him. A few minutes for photographs from the little camera concealed in her handbag; she assured them that she'd make them interesting. Then she would leave the suite, a finger to her lips to warn the waiting servants that their master was asleep. Down in the private lift and out to where Daniel in the Mercedes would be waiting, as if she were the real Denise he was taking home.

On to the rendezvous with Stevenson and his thugs, where the Mercedes could be abandoned and they would cram into Stevenson's car and head for Suffolk.

If the plan worked out, they would be in their beds a hundred miles away before anyone dared disturb the Prince.

He thought of Monika and shuddered. She had no nerves; danger thrilled her. Killing was a sexual turn-on. She believed herself invincible.

He didn't hurry; he drove carefully, pacing his journey. He turned into Lancaster Place just before midnight. He cruised round once; there was the Mercedes, with the outline of Daniel in the driver's seat, the cap on his head pulled well down, waiting near the main entrance. The hotel lights were dimmed.

Special Branch would know the Prince was staying put for the night; the look-outs would have gone home till the morning when he was due to leave for the airport. There'd be a token force in the hotel itself, but they had no reason to expect trouble.

He parked in sight of the Mercedes but in the shadow of some trees. Twelve thirty.

Any moment now and Monika would come out and Daniel would move to pick her up. Twelve thirty-five. He sweated; drops fell into his eyes. He wiped them with a hand that trembled. And then he heard the screaming sirens.

9

The Prince was seated on a couch piled with cushions at the foot of an enormous draped bed. He didn't move as Monika approached him. The door closed quietly behind her. He held out a hand and she approached. She still held the veil over her face.

He wore a loose white robe edged with gold braid, and he was naked under it. He had a dark, plump face with the big hooked nose of his family, and heavy black eyes.

He got up slowly and she stood very still in front of him, only the large mascara ringed blue eyes showing, the lids lowered slightly. He reached out a hand for the veil.

'Denise?'

Slowly, Monika let the veiling fall, it slipped off her shoulders and the Prince drew back. 'What is this?' His voice rose.

'Denise is sick, Highness,' Monika spoke in a low, seductive tone, gazing at him. 'She didn't want to disappoint you, so she sent me. I am her friend. She sent me to you as a present.' She lifted one arm high and pulled the combs out of her hair. It fell in a thick blonde curtain down to her shoulders.

His eyes were narrowed, the mouth a little slack. He had a heavy belly and womanish breasts. His hands were delicate; rings glittered when he moved them.

'You may please me,' he murmured. 'Come here.'

Monika approached him. He moved quickly for a fat man. He came up to her and ran his hands down her back, squeezing her buttocks. She faked a gasp of pleasure.

'You're beautiful.' She smelt his breath. It was sour. She smiled.

'Denise told me what pleases you, Highness,' she whispered in her throaty voice. 'That's why she sent me.'

She reached backwards with both hands. Her large breasts rose under the thin black silk. He stared at them. She unfastened the hook, and the dress fell away; she moved sensuously and it slid off her lower body. She kicked off her high-heeled shoes and stood naked in front of him. For a few seconds there was no sound in the room, no movement.

Monika moved close to him; she wet her lips with her tongue, her eyes were gleaming behind heavy lids. She was trembling a little with excitement. The Prince was staring at her; one hand groped under his robe. Monika misunderstood the meaning of the gesture and she smiled. 'I'll make you die with pleasure,' she whispered to him.

Suddenly his face contorted, he opened his mouth and shouted in Arabic. She saw snarling suspicion and fury wipe the desire off his face; the hand that had felt instinctively for the dagger he wore when he was dressed, swung out at her in a fist. She ducked the blow, and he lunged away from her towards the bed, reaching for the panic button that would bring his bodyguards bursting into the bedroom. As he did so he stepped on his robe and he stumbled. Monika flung herself at him. He wasn't expecting her to attack, he turned aggressively, his hand pressing down on the alarm. She heard it screaming in her ears, and her right arm came over the body, the hand rigid.

She struck him across the throat with all her weight behind the blow and smashed his windpipe like a rotten stick. He fell, gurgling blood and sputum. Monika heard the door burst open, a fierce shouting, and swung round. It was over in seconds; she saw the wild faces, the weapons raised as they ran towards her, and the first bullets slammed into her chest and abdomen like hammer blows, flinging her backwards on top of her victim. She felt no pain; she was dying as they dragged her off the Prince, and mercifully dead before they began to slash and stab at her body, screaming their grief for their dead master.

Daniel had parked the Mercedes in a space near the hotel entrance. He sat in the front keeping watch for Monika to come out. At twelve twenty-five he switched the engine on, ready to move forward and pick her up.

And then he heard the sirens. The wailing came from a distance, growing louder, more threatening as it came closer. Flashing blue lights winked in the darkness.

Daniel leapt out into the street. He hesitated for a moment, flattening himself against the garden railings, then as the first police car turned the corner he began to run.

Jan heard the sirens, saw the flash of blue light, knew that it had gone wrong. The hotel was suddenly illuminated, as the main switches were turned on. *Monika had been caught.* Abort the plan. The old formula shouted in his head. *Abort! Get out!* He acted as he had been trained to do in a crisis, when delay meant capture.

He wrenched the wheel and the car swung at right angles, its finely tuned engine responding instantly. He drove out of Lancaster Place before the first police car turned in. He didn't see Daniel running. *Abort and get back to base.* He didn't reason, he didn't think. He acted blindly to survive.

The Regent's Canal was deserted. Stevenson brought the car into the kerb by the water's edge. The Subaru cruised up and pulled in behind him. Bob was driving, Ron was in the back with his feet on the girl. She'd recovered consciousness and he kicked her when she tried to move. Ron liked women, but he wasn't chivalrous.

Stevenson got out. The lights were doused on both cars. He stood lighting a cigarette between cupped hands, on the look out for cars approaching or any sign of life. Nothing. Not a sound but the still lap and ripple of the black water a few feet below.

He moved up to Bob in the driver's seat and the window of the Subaru slid down. 'All right,' Stevenson said under his breath, 'let's get a move on.' He gestured to Ron in the back to put his stocking on and hide his face. Ron reached down and started pulling the girl off the floor. It was awkward because she was tied up tight as an oven-ready chicken – they never did things by halves – and she was heavy.

Bob was in the road with Stevenson lighting a cigarette, waiting for him to do the business. He had her propped on the seat; her eyes were wide with terror above the surgical tape plastered over her mouth.

Ron liked women; he took a quick look out of the window. The other two had their backs to him. He pulled the girl against him and shoved a hand up her skirt.

'Holy shit!' He threw her back against the door so hard she slid half off the seat on to the floor.

Stevenson swung round snarling at him, 'What the fuck are you doing?' Ron was out of the car.

'That's no girl,' he said. 'It's a fuckin' man in drag!'

Stevenson reached the rendevous at the junction of Bayswater Road and Notting Hill. They were on time. There was no sign of the Mercedes.

They'd left the other car by the Regent's Canal. Ron had relieved his feelings by punching the hapless transvestite unconscious before he shoved him on the floor in the back. The Arab was in the boot, too frightened to make any noise. They'd be found by the morning. Ron didn't explain that he'd broken the silence rule when he made his discovery. He'd given the queer such a bashing he probably wouldn't remember . . .

The time passed. After half an hour Stevenson shifted in his seat. 'They shouldn't be this fucking late,' he muttered. He was uneasy. He chain smoked. 'We'll give 'em another fifteen minutes,' he decided.

'You think it's gone wrong, Sarge?' Ron asked. He was sucking his sore knuckles.

'Looks like it,' Stevenson answered.

'What do we do then?' Bob was watching the digital clock on the dashboard. Nearly an hour over time.

'If the wogs have got 'er or the Israeli, they'll put the pressure on 'em – 'arry said to bail out if they didn't turn up.'

'Shit,' Bob muttered. Stevenson made up his mind. They were his lads, and old habits re-asserted themselves.

'I say we don't chance it,' he said. 'We piss off and lie low for a bit. That fuckin' hotel could be running with coppers by the mornin'. OK with you?'

'OK by us,' was the response. He switched on the engine, turned the car and headed back towards the Bermondsey area.

The steak was tough; Rosa gave up on it and ate the chips with her fingers. A couple eating at a table close by eyed her with disapproval. They had dainty manners and sipped their wine with their little fingers slightly crooked.

'If you do go abroad,' Harry pushed his plate aside and reached out to take a chip off hers, 'where do you think you'll go?'

'Maybe Brussels,' Rosa answered. 'Do you want my mushroom – I've had enough.' She speared it on her fork and fed it to him.

'This is like that film, *Tom Jones*,' she said. 'Did you ever see it?'

'No. Why?'

'They kept feeding each other titbits – it was the sexiest thing you've ever seen.'

'Why Brussels?'

'I'm due to go there as Second Secretary. But things can change very quickly now. Something else may be on offer by the time I get back to the office.'

'I hope it's Brussels,' he said. 'Then I can come over and be with you. I'm not letting you go, darling. I was serious about that.'

'You'd leave the hotel?' She stared at him.

'I don't see myself going on forever,' he admitted. He called the waiter. 'Irish coffee for two please. Or do you want some of that summer pudding stuff I see over there?'

'I don't think so,' Rosa shook her head. 'Irish coffee will be fine. If you leave, what would you do? Go on to another hotel?'

He lit a cigarette and passed it to her, taking a fresh one for himself. 'I've got a business scheme going,' he said and smiled at her. 'Something on the side. It's making quite a bit of money. I might take early retirement for the second time.'

The coffee came and Rosa held the glass in both hands and didn't look at him. 'What sort of business? Nobody's making money out of anything these days.' She could feel her heart jumping. Oh God, please God, don't let Parker be right. Don't let him be mixed up in something.

'I invested in some land in East Germany. You can pick up land there for a few pounds an acre. I've already sold some for development. So I'm piling up the Deutschmarks. It was a good tip; they've stopped foreigners investing because they woke up to the money they were making, but I got in early. It's funny, I've never made a penny out of anything before. This could make me quite well off.'

'That sounds very good.' She had heard of the scheme because James and some friends were moaning about being too late to get in on it. She remembered that clearly.

She looked into his eyes and smiled. 'I've only got another five days,' she said. 'It's happened so quickly – between us. I always thought I was so level-headed. I didn't rush into relationships or get involved without thinking it through.'

'I never get into a relationship at all,' he said. 'I had the odd affair in the last ten years, but my wife, Peggy, put me off screwing around. I didn't like the lying and the general tattiness. I'd fallen in love once, and I reckoned it wouldn't happen again.

'Then I met you. Just for the record, Rosa, your career wouldn't be a problem to me. I wouldn't want to cramp your style; it's what makes you special. Just bear that in mind. Now, shall we go upstairs, my darling? I want you very much.'

'Shush,' Rosa whispered. 'They've been listening to every word . . .'

They got up and as they passed the couple at the next table, Harry paused. The man looked uncomfortable and his wife was flushed. Harry smiled down at them. 'I do hope you've enjoyed our evening. Good night.'

Rosa was laughing as they climbed the stairs. 'Harry, you're impossible – how could you say that?'

'I meant it,' he protested. 'They looked as if they needed cheering up – not like us,' he unlocked the bedroom door and drew her inside. 'I don't need anything but you.'

'Where is he?' Hermann Rilke shouted. 'This blows up in our faces and he disappears!' He was pacing up and down, watched by Vassily Zarubin. The early TV news carried the murder of the Arab Prince as its lead item. He'd put through a call to Oakham and received no answer. When reception opened, he was told the same as Jan the night before.

Zarubin hadn't bothered to turn on the TV when he woke. Rilke's call brought him leaping out of bed and within minutes he was on his way to Croft Lodge. He thought the German looked ghastly, his face the colour of dirty sand, pulling at his lip and stamping up and down in agitation.

'It was scheduled for tonight,' he kept repeating. 'They went early – why? Why weren't we told? That creature was killed that's one good thing! If they'd caught her alive and had time to question her—'

Zarubin said coldly, 'Why don't you sit down? There's nothing we can do till Oakham gets back.'

Rilke stopped in mid step. 'You think he knew, he went up to London last night and never told us?'

'No,' the Russian shook his head, 'I don't. He doesn't work like that.'

Rilke sat down and switched on the TV to catch the nine o'clock headlines. There was no further news, just the bare details rehashed from the earlier bulletin.

The Russian got up. He stretched. He was looking out of the window. 'His car's just turned in by the back entrance,' he said. 'And there is a woman with him. Leave this to me.'

'No,' Rilke said furiously. 'Why should I sit here not knowing what's happened – a woman!' He swore in German, blasting Oakham with obscenities. 'He's wallowing with some filthy woman at a time like this!' Zarubin was at the door. 'He put that damned Israeli in charge,' he raved on. 'He's ruined everything!'

The Russian paused for a moment. 'We don't know that,' he remarked.

'Then why aren't the others back here?' Rilke swung on him.

'That's what I'm going to find out,' Zarubin said and closed the door.

They drove up to the back entrance. Harry leaned over and kissed her on the lips. 'Thank you, my darling,' he said gently. 'It was the happiest night I can remember.'

'In spite of the lumps in the mattress?' she asked softly.

'Because of them. Because everything was perfect between us. We'll go in through the service door and you can use the back stairs. I can't have your reputation tarnished.' It was such an old-fashioned phrase, it made her smile. Like calling champagne 'bubbly'.

'When will I see you?' she asked him.

'Lunch? In my house? I want to spend every minute with you.'

Make the most of today, he told himself. Enjoy this extraordinary thing that's happened to you, Oakham. Before tomorrow . . . 'I'll meet you in the garden; we'll have a drink outside and then I'll show you where I live. Twelve o'clock?'

Rosa nodded, touched his face for a moment, and then slipped through the service door into the back passageway and kitchen quarters of the hotel.

Once inside her room she stripped off her crumpled clothes and ran a hot bath. She filled it with Floris bath oil and lay, soaking, breathing in the rich scent rising on the steam, thinking of him and the night they'd spent.

She felt so different that she examined herself in the mirror when she stood naked from the bath. No change was visible. But she was changed. She would never be the same again.

'I've never even been in love,' she said aloud. 'Marriage to James was nothing, Dick Lucas, the others – they were all nothing . . . I don't give a damn what Parker says . . . I'm going to call him up and tell him he's wrong. Harry's straight; if he wasn't, I'd *know*. I'll call tomorrow morning.'

Harry faced the Russian. They were in his office. Zarubin said, 'Rilke heard the news this morning. You didn't know?'

'Christ, of course I didn't—' Oakham made a fist and punched the hard surface of his desk. 'Why – why did they go last night?' He fumbled for a cigarette; the pack was empty. He searched the desk drawers, cursing.

'They caught Monika and the bodyguards killed her. That was lucky,' Zarubin went on.

Oakham glared at him. 'Not so lucky for Monika!'

He lit the cigarette, inhaled and then said, 'There must be a message – Jan would have contacted me about the change. Wait a minute—' He called through to reception; Vassily watched him, perched on the edge of the desk, one long leg swinging. 'Yes . . . he did . . . Oh, right – thanks. Yes, great news . . .' He jerked round to the Russian. 'Jan called in,' he said, 'said he was coming back this morning early. That was to tell me the plan had been advanced . . . shit! He wasn't due till tonight—'

He'd been lying in bed with Rosa when Jan had phoned through. He could imagine how his old friend had fretted and worked himself up when he couldn't make contact. 'Shit,' he said again. 'I should have been here.'

'Rilke would agree with you,' Zarubin remarked. 'So where is he? And where are Daniel and the others? The murder was discovered at midnight, that's what the news said. So why aren't they here, as planned?'

'How the hell should I know?' Oakham snapped at him. He knew the Russian was goading him, needling him because he'd slipped up by going off for the night.

He said, 'They had a bail-out plan if anything went wrong, and Monika didn't get out – Daniel and Stevenson and the boys were to lie low and give us warning. That's what must have happened – they knew there'd been a cock–up.'

'Daniel hasn't contacted us. And he was leading the team!' Zarubin pointed out.

'He will!' Oakham insisted angrily. 'Daniel knew he had to get the hell out and not risk getting picked up. Half the bloody Special Branch must have been screaming up the road when they heard what had happened. So he ran for it. He's a pro – he's gone into hiding, but he'll get in touch.'

'But not the Pole,' Vassily said. 'You insisted he came back here. Before they made the move. And he hasn't come back.'

Harry Oakham looked at him; his eyes were hot with rage. 'I know what's best for him,' he said. 'Don't worry about Jan. He'll get back.'

'He was the weak link,' the Russian said harshly. 'I never wanted to risk using him; I said so, but you wouldn't listen. He's the one who could break down and destroy us all.'

Harry took a step towards him. Zarubin saw the clenched hands and the fury in his face. He didn't back off.

'You listen to me. Jan held out against the worst fucking interrogation your lot could put him through. He's the only one of that lousy bunch who'd die before he gave us away.'

'If you believe that,' Zarubin sneered, 'you'll believe anything! Rilke wants an urgent meeting.'

'Rilke can get stuffed,' Oakham snarled. 'I'm going to look for Jan!'

'Good-morning,' Zarubin said. Rosa turned; she was waiting for Oakham in the garden. He was late.

'Good-morning,' she said. He didn't walk on. He said, 'Have you heard the news this morning?'

'No. What news?' It was a dead month, the silly season when there was no news. Or wars broke out.

'It was on the television,' Zarubin said. 'An Arab Prince was murdered at his hotel in London.' He watched her carefully. There was the normal expression of surprise and a little shock. He guessed she was waiting for Oakham.

'How awful. Was it anyone important?' It was an instinctive Foreign Office response.

'Very important, a son of the Saudi King.'

'That could be a disaster,' Rosa said. She decided there was no harm in telling the truth. 'I'm a diplomat,' she explained. 'The Middle East isn't my area, but we all know what a powder keg it is.'

He nodded. A diplomat. It had a familiar ring to it in his experience. He smiled at her. 'You must be a very clever lady.'

'Not really.' She glanced at her watch. Oakham was fifteen minutes late.

'Are you going for a walk?' Zarubin asked her.

'No, I was actually waiting for Mr Oakham.'

'Ah,' he said. 'Perhaps we could have a talk sometime. I am working on a book. It would be nice to have a talk with someone intelligent who knows the world. It's pleasant here, but I haven't found any company that is sympathetic.'

Jane was right; he was a good-looking man, and she could see how his remoteness could appear romantic. 'It must be lonely, working on your own down here,' she said. Still Oakham hadn't come. She decided to go back to her room and call through to his office.

'I couldn't work in London,' Zarubin explained. 'I need peace. London is noisy and dirty and not safe at night. Do you live there?'

'Yes.' The criticism irritated her. 'Perhaps you should have written your book at home. It's quite safe to write books now, I believe.'

He registered the rebuke. He smiled and said, 'I apologize. It is your city. I haven't been home for many years, but one day soon I hope to go. As you say, I can write books there now. I hope you're not offended?'

Rosa relented; she was anxious to get rid of him. 'Of course I'm not. We must have a talk sometime. Excuse me.' She went back to the hotel and up to her room.

The telephone buzzed in Harry Oakham's office. He knew it must be Rosa. He didn't answer. He'd gone away with her and let Jan down. He couldn't have spoken to anyone; he couldn't think of anything but the Pole, out there on his own, the world crumbling round him as it had done before. Go and look for him, but where?

His retort to Zarubin mocked him with its futility. He could get into his car and drive the route Jan should have taken. He might be pulled up, unable to go on. Stricken by the terrible panic attacks that were the legacy of his imprisonment. It was a feeble chance, but the only one Oakham had. Just re-trace the route and hope to God that Jan was stranded somewhere on it.

Rosa. He paused on his way to the door. She'd be waiting. He scribbled on a piece of paper, addressed an envelope and stuck it down. No afternoon spent making love, no time to dream with her. The reality was a murder and a dead assassin. And the man he loved like a son, on the run for his life.

Rosa thanked reception. There was no reply from Harry's office or his house. Nobody knew where to find him.

It was twelve forty-five; she felt uneasy, troubled. Then dismissed the feeling. Something must have come up suddenly. She switched on ITV for the lunch-time bulletin.

It was the main story. Prince Abdullah Al Rashid, favourite son of the King of Saudi Arabia, had been murdered by a prostitute in his penthouse suite at the Regis. The woman had been shot dead by his body-guards. Television reporters and cameramen were camped outside the hotel which was surrounded by a police cordon.

Detectives were searching the square and the ad-joining streets for clues. Comment was tactful out of consideration for Saudi feelings. Rumours were circulating that it was a terrorist assassination, since the Prince's regular Arab chauffeur was missing and the dead woman was not known to his household. A senior police officer gave a cautious briefing and confirmed that so far they had not arrested anyone in connection with the crime. Tight security was in force round all Arab embassies and European embassies connected with the Gulf War.

A retired diplomat acted as political pundit and gave a grave view of the possible repercussions in the Muslim world.

The news ended and there was still no word from Harry Oakham.

Jan couldn't remember where he was. The sun was burning through the windscreen. He pulled down the shade to shield his eyes. He hadn't slept, he was sure of that. He'd pulled up when it was dark because he couldn't remember where he was supposed to be going.

The dark had worried him. There were no overhead lights, just trees and a black sky without stars.

He had started to panic. Sweat broke out all over his body and ran down his face, turning his hands slippery on the wheel.

His foot came off the accelerator. All he knew was he had to stop before he crashed the car. His stomach heaved and he got out, shaking and nauseous. He was in a road in the middle of a black countryside, and he couldn't think how he had got there or where he should go.

He hadn't had a memory blackout for years. He had one then and he was overwhelmed with terror. Menace was all around him. It threatened from the featureless darkness of the distance. He plunged back into the safety of the car and locked the doors. He huddled in his seat and closed his eyes against the fear. Nature let him slip away.

He slept in a comatose way until the hot sun woke him, and he remembered driving away from London, with the shrieking sirens in the background. Driving back to Harry. Running, as he had run so often in the past, through hostile streets and towns where the enemy was in control. Slowly he stretched his cramped body, and forced himself to open the door and get out.

His throat was dry and he found it hard to swallow. He told himself he was all right. He was over the worst. It was a long time since he'd suffered an attack, but it was over now. But he didn't recognize the place. Harry was waiting for him, and he didn't know how to reach him.

It had all gone wrong. He was clear about that. The sirens, the blue flashing lights, his own flight from the scene. He began to shake again. He must get to Harry. And again nature was merciful.

He remembered the telephone number. It just came into his thoughts like a bright star of salvation. Find a telephone, he told himself. Start the car, drive down the road, and find a telephone.

He didn't know how long he drove or how far before he saw a kiosk in the middle of an ugly little town, and drew up beside it. He got out, fumbling in his pocket for coins.

It wasn't vandalized. He nearly burst into tears with relief when he heard Harry Oakham's voice.

'Where are you, old son?'

Harry spoke soothingly. His free hand was clenched so tight his nails bit into the palm. The stricken voice mumbled, 'I don't know where I am.'

'Oh Christ,' Oakham muttered. *Oh Christ, he's cracked.*

'Well, don't worry about it. Are you in a call box?'

'Yes. What shall I do, Harry? Help me . . .'

'I'll help you. Look on the telephone dial. What's the exchange?'

There was an agonizing pause. If he ran out of money and they lost contact . . . 'Brentwood,' Jan said at last. Harry let his breath out. He forced confidence into his voice.

'You're nearly home, you old sod. Can you see a street sign? What's the name of the road? No, hang on, give me the number you're calling from so I can call you back if we get cut off.'

Jan was looking over his shoulder. 'Handcross Road,' he said. 'I'm in Handcross Road. Harry—'

Oakham said loudly, 'Stay put. Don't try and drive, just stay put. I'll come and get you. I'll be there in one hour. One hour, Jan. Just hang on.'

Jan said, 'Yes, yes, I'll wait,' but the line had cleared.

He got back to the car; his legs were weak and he was still shaking. But Harry was coming. All he had to do was sit in the car and wait for him. Then everything would be all right.

Harry was on his way out of the office when he remembered the note he scribbled to Rosa. He dropped it at the desk and said, 'I'll be gone a couple of hours, send that up to Mrs Bennet will you.' Then he was out of the main door and down the steps, almost at a run towards his car in the manager's reserved space.

Jan hadn't been picked up. 'Thank Christ,' he said over and over. All I've got to do is get to him, bring him home. Then I'll deal with those two bastards, Rilke and Zarubin. But Jan comes first.

He drove down the dual carriageway, touching ninety all the way. He kept the radio tuned in and got the news bulletin. The same item about the murder, a few more details creeping in.

The Prince's driver and a woman had been discovered tied up in a car by Regent's Canal. The woman had been taken to hospital. She had been badly beaten up. Oakham swore. They'd been told not to get rough. The driver said they had been ambushed by terrorists on their way to the hotel.

It was hinted that the gang were Arab extremists. The hijacked Mercedes had been found abandoned in Lancaster Place. So far no suspects had been arrested but investigations were continuing. The Government had sent messages of sympathy to the Saudi Royal Family.

No suspects had been arrested. Daniel and the others had got away. He wouldn't know what had happened till he reached Jan.

Rilke had recovered his nerve. He was very angry; Zarubin thought that it made him a dangerous man to cross. And in his view, that was what Oakham had done. He'd gone absent, and that had put them all in jeopardy. Rilke's voice was dry and snapping, like twigs underfoot.

'He could have told them to cancel the operation,' he said. 'You never, never depart from your schedule unless it's a matter of life and death. Every amateur is taught that. If it couldn't be done according to the timescale, then it should have been abandoned!'

He sat with his hands twisting in and out. 'How does he expect to find that Pole?' he demanded. Zarubin shrugged. His coolness was infuriating to Rilke, but he controlled himself.

'He doesn't know,' Vassily answered. 'It was an emotional response, not properly considered. He's not the professional I thought he was. He reacted like a fool.' He took out a pocket file and cleaned under his nails. 'If Daniel's been caught, he'll sell us to make a deal for himself. But not immediately. He'll bargain.'

'We have no way of knowing,' Rilke countered. 'We sit here, waiting to be arrested while that swine goes looking for that crazy Pole . . .'

Zarubin said, 'Is that what you're going to do, Hermann? Wait?' Rilke glanced sharply at him.

'No. I don't rely on anyone but myself. I have arrangements made if I need to get out in a hurry.'

'I thought you would,' the Russian nodded. 'I don't rely on anyone either.' He got up. 'You have some vodka?'

'In the kitchen,' Rilke answered. '*She* liked it. They'll identify her in the end, won't they? She'll be on Interpol's files.'

Zarubin said, 'If I know Arab bodyguards, they'll have to rely on fingerprints. There won't be much left to recognize.' He came back with a tumbler half full of neat vodka. 'I'm going to give it a few hours,' he said, 'no more. If Daniel doesn't call in, or if Oakham doesn't find the Pole, then I go.'

'If he does?' Rilke demanded. He answered himself. 'At least we will know what happened.'

'And maybe where the others are ...' Zarubin added. He drained the glass of vodka. He showed no effect from alcohol. 'There's one thing that bothers me,' he said slowly.

'What?' Rilke looked at him.

'One of the lady guests. The one Oakham spent the night with. When those Irish people were here, she behaved rather strangely. I'd like to find out more about her. It would occupy my time.' He smiled.

Six suspects had been taken to Cannon Row Police Station. All had been found in the area of the Regis after it was cordoned off by squad cars, and summarily arrested.

The duty officer had taken details; two were released immediately. One was a local resident walking his dog – 'Bloody fools to pick him up,' the D.O. muttered – he'd been furious and was threatening an official complaint. The dog had peed all over the squad car.

The second was a young woman walking home from the tube station; her address and credentials were verified by a telephone call. She'd been pacified by an apology and a lift home.

A couple had been found in the back of a parked Volvo estate. They weren't local, and the embarrassed alibi that they were about to have intercourse was being treated with caution. They'd been fingerprinted and put on the computer.

The fifth was a man who claimed he was jogging. He was dressed in the gear and he'd been picked up some distance from the hotel simply because he was running.

The last was a local vagrant, who'd been found sleeping in a doorway in Lancaster Place. They'd brought him in, in case he had seen anything suspicious. It was a very long shot as he was dead drunk and still snoring it off in a cell.

The jogger had objected to having his prints taken and started shouting about a lawyer. They'd dabbed him anyway, and ran the name he'd given on the computer. Nothing had come up about him or the couple. It looked like a complete dead end.

The report was duly sent through to the incident room that had been set up. The D.O. poured some hot coffee from a flask.

All hell had broken out already. It looked a dirty case, and there was no way the diplomats were going to put the wraps on what had happened. The Press were drawn up in battle order as near to the hotel as they were allowed to get, and making bloody nuisances of themselves in the station, wanting to know if anyone had been arrested. No suspects. Investigations were continuing. They weren't giving the bloodhounds anything . . .

The D.O. yawned. Fancy a woman killing the

bugger. Some lady. She'd smashed his windpipe. They'd taken her body away for identification and a post-mortem. The bodyguards had gone berserk; he'd heard somebody say the place looked like a slaughterhouse when they got in. He was finishing his coffee when his phone rang.

He listened, said, 'Yes? Right, I'll get it through right away.'

In the incident room at New Scotland Yard the phone was answered on the first ring. 'We've got something, sir!'

The Detective Chief Inspector at Special Branch in charge of the murder took the phone himself. 'What? I'll be there in ten minutes. Have a room ready.' He looked round the office. 'I think we've struck lucky,' he announced. 'One set of prints taken from the suspects matches an old friend of ours.'

When the phone rang, Rosa rushed to pick it up. 'Harry?'

'It's Dick. Dick Lucas, remember me?'

She bit back an exclamation of disappointment. 'Dick? Oh, hello—'

He sounded annoyed. He asked her how she was, and by the way, who was Harry . . .? She was irritated by the sarcasm. She ignored the question. 'I was calling,' he said, 'because I can't make our date. We've got a visiting admiral flying in from Washington. I have to be on duty. Are you busy right now – you sound busy?'

'I'm just going out,' Rosa said 'Sorry you can't come down. Never mind. I'm leaving next week anyway. Maybe we can meet up another time.'

'Don't be mad at me, Rosa.' He was conciliatory. 'I can't help it, I have a job to do. You ought to understand that. I could drive down and have dinner. Why don't I do that?'

Rosa hesitated. She had asked him to come so they could investigate the Adventure Trail. She didn't need him now.

'Rosa?'

She had the excuse ready. 'I can't, Dick, I'm sorry. I promised to join some people here. I couldn't just dump them. I'll call you before I leave. We'll fix up to meet in London. I must go now, or I'll be late.'

'I wouldn't want that.' She heard the irony creep back. 'I guess Harry wouldn't either. See you around, darling.'

'Oh, damn you,' she said as she hung up. Then she dialled reception. 'It's Mrs Bennet. Did Mr Oakham leave a message for me?'

'Oh yes, Mrs Bennet — sorry, I didn't get through to you earlier, but I've just taken over.' It was Jane, friendly Jane . . . 'I found it on the desk here and I tried your room but you were taking an outside call. One minute. Here it is. I'll send it straight up. So sorry.'

It was brief, written in a hurry. The writing sprawled across the page. 'Rosa, forgive me. A drama has turned into a crisis. I have to deal with it. I'll be back to explain. My love, H.'

Oakham braked hard, pulled the car into the kerb and jumped out. Jan was sitting slumped in the front of the parked car, close by the telephone kiosk.

Harry came to the side and tapped on the window. He saw the pale exhausted face light up. The door opened and Harry said, 'Hello, old son. Out you get.' He reached in and helped Jan step on to the road. 'You all right?' he asked him gently.

'I'm all right,' Jan answered. 'I just blanked out. I'm sorry, Harry.' His mouth trembled. Harry slipped an arm round his shoulders.

'Don't be bloody silly. You did great stuff. Now come and get into my car; give me the keys of this one.'

'They're still in it,' Jan muttered.

'OK, fine. Come on now. Nothing to worry about. We'll be home in no time. I'll get the garage to come and collect this later.' He made a light-hearted joke. 'Lucky you picked a parking zone or we'd get towed away.'

He didn't question Jan when they drove. He didn't go too fast. He let him settle, relax. He was a terrible grey colour. It was Jan who volunteered the information, and Harry didn't press him. He let him talk.

'I couldn't find you, Harry – Daniel might have backed out – I had to stay and see it through.'

'My bloody fault,' Harry muttered. 'Go on, what happened?'

'I was early so I parked where I could see Monika come out. I waited; it was quiet. The hotel was quiet by then. She was late, Harry. I began to get worried.'

'I expect you did,' Oakham said gently. He slowed

down and turned off the Ipswich dual carriageway.

'I heard sirens,' Jan said. 'They were getting louder, blue lights flashing all over the place . . . coming straight for the hotel. I didn't hang around. I aborted.'

'Thank God for that,' Oakham murmured. 'Good man, Jan. You did the right thing. No sign of Daniel?' He asked it casually. Daniel could have been in the Prince's Mercedes; waiting for Monika. The Merc had been found abandoned in Lancaster Place. Daniel must have run for it when he heard the police cars closing in.

'I didn't see him,' Jan admitted. 'I didn't wait, I just took off before they closed off the square. I made for the rendezvous with Bill Stevenson, but I must have missed the road. I found myself in the country. I panicked, Harry.' He looked at him, his face twisted in remorse. 'I couldn't remember where I was or anything. It was like the attacks I used to have in the old days . . . after they let me out . . .'

'But you remembered the number to call,' Harry comforted. 'You damn nearly got yourself home, you silly old sod, so stop talking balls. It's not like it was; you're fine. You did a great job.'

Jan was silent for a while as they drove along the country roads towards the Doll's House Manor. 'Do you know what happened, Harry?'

He asked the question, and Harry noted that his voice was steadier.

'Monika killed the bugger,' he said flatly. 'But the bodyguards shot her. It was on the news and the TV this morning. Nobody's been picked up and they're making all the right official noises for the Saudis. But they can't hush the scandal, and my guess is that the media will have a ball over the double killing. So we'll get our money from Hakim's friends.'

'Do you care about the money?' Jan asked.

'Not really. I was more worried about you than anything. Here we are. Home sweet home.' He turned and grinned at Jan encouragingly.

'What you want,' he said, 'is a hot bath, something to eat and a good long sleep. You'll be back to your old self in the morning.'

As they pulled up into the staff car park, Oakham said, 'You've got to pull yourself together now. We walk in, you say hello to the girls at the desk – everyone's so pleased about your father, remember – give a bright smile and you'll be OK. No worries.'

He didn't help Jan, he let him get out of the car, smooth down his rumpled clothes and walk towards the entrance.

And Jan didn't falter. He managed a smile and a few words, even pausing to speak to the restaurant manager who came hurrying forward. If he looked grey-faced and drawn, nobody seemed to notice. Then they were upstairs in his flat, and Harry was getting him undressed and running a bath for him.

'Sandwiches and coffee for you,' he announced. 'Then you sleep.'

'I couldn't eat,' Jan protested. 'I was sick on the road.'

'That was last night,' Harry brushed it aside. 'You're fine now. And you'll eat something. Now get in and have a good soak. If you want to talk some more then we'll talk. But only if you feel like it.'

When the Pole had gone, he called through to Zarubin's room. He must have been sitting by the telephone he answered it so quickly.

'You and Hermann can stop peeing yourselves,' Oakham said coldly. 'Jan's back, and the others got away.' He rang off.

Rosa, he remembered, and was shaken by how much he wanted to go and find her, take hold of her and forget the last few hours. Maybe I'm getting past it, he wondered. Maybe it's time to retire myself.

He had to settle Jan down first. It would take time to get his nervous system under control, but with Harry's help he'd do it. They had done it together when he came out of hospital. Maybe Jan should retire too. He considered that carefully.

There'd be enough money to make both of them comfortable and independent once Hakim's Libyans paid up. That reminded him about Werner. Werner drawing a handsome monthly retainer for doing bugger all so far. It was too early to call him. He'd have to wait till he was home. European embassies were under twenty-four hour police guard. That would include the German Embassy. Reason enough for friend Werner to start making anxious enquiries from his colleagues in London . . .

10

It was a warm day with a fresh westerly breeze; Rosa dressed in slacks and slip-on shoes, and set out to walk through the park.

She wandered round the lake; there was a small jetty and a little rowboat tied up, rocking gently. There was nobody in sight. She sat for a while, letting the sun beat down, and the breeze flutter like a caress on her face. It was peaceful and still. She could have slept.

A drama had become a crisis. It was so like him to write about a problem like that, half making fun of it. She smiled a little, thinking of him. He was older, but he didn't seem so. He was more charged with vitality than Dick Lucas, more vibrant than the city-weary James who slumped in his chair at the end of the day.

I'm not going to let you go. This is too good to lose. She leaned her head back and drifted in the heat. It was too good. He was right.

She shook herself awake. Time for a proper walk, and then when she went back, he might be there waiting for her.

She didn't mean to take the long way round, leaving the lake behind and crossing the undulating grasslands; she had no plan.

But there was the wood beckoning with its cool

shade, and the sign, ADVENTURE TRAIL, with its red skull painted on the white wood. It was a jokey skull, nothing menacing about it. She could mock her own suspicions the first time she saw it, her scared reaction to the man in the run-about who'd blocked her way and insisted on driving her back.

It was there in front of her. She didn't need Dick Lucas if she wanted to go and take a look round. The gate was padlocked. No problem; Rosa felt it challenged her to climb up and drop down inside. It wasn't difficult or high. The contrast to the bright sunlit park outside made the place seem very dark. Dark and silent. She'd forgotten that there was something daunting about dense woodland. As a child she'd been warned never to go into such places for fear of a lurking prowler. There was a little pathway. She followed it, her eyes adjusting to the dim, shifting light. On either side the trees were dense. A climbing frame over a narrow ditch. A child could have clambered over it.

She went further, following the path, guided by another silly skull with a winking eye and an arrow. All good fun for adults with a kid's mentality. Another ditch with a narrow plank across it. Not much adventure on this trail. Just to amuse herself, she tackled the next obstacle, a rope scrambler, with a low wall the other side. Easy. Ridiculous to think anyone would pay money to engage in this sort of juvenile nonsense.

She thought of some of James' friends and thought, Yes, they'd think it was great macho stuff, jumping around competing with each other and boasting in the bar afterwards ... She could almost hear the backchat and the laughter.

She decided to turn back, and leant against a tree to pull up her shoe; it had slipped down when she came off the little wall. A branch crackled above her and she looked up. A grey squirrel scuttled upwards, alarmed by her presence at the foot of the tree. It flashed through the branches like a puff of smoke. Grey squirrels were vermin. They'd killed off most of the red squirrels.

Then something happened; she heard noises. Straining to see through the thick leaves, Rosa saw the little creature suspended, struggling furiously. It was trapped in something. She reached up for a branch, heaved herself up a few feet. Above, the squirrel clawed and writhed, making a terrified chattering as it fought to get free.

'Oh, you poor thing,' she said out loud. There was a branch higher up. She stretched, reached, bracing herself and caught hold. Slowly she managed to pull herself higher still. High enough to see what had entrapped the animal. Not nearly high enough to try and free it.

Camouflage netting. Thick, rope wire netting threaded through with browns and greens and mottle shading. There was nothing she could do. No way she could save the squirrel. It would die in that netting.

She lowered herself; a branch scored her arm. Twigs were showering down on her from the tree as she released the lowest branch and dropped the last few feet.

There had been an assault course at Branksome. A very arduous and sophisticated course for people on special training. None of Rosa's colleagues were enrolled in that course. One, a rather butch young woman tried to prove herself one morning by slipping into the ground unaccompanied, and ended up with a broken ankle. They'd been given a walk round one morning with an instructor. If they thought this was difficult, he'd said, grinning at their expressions, then the real thing was up above them. They'd looked up and seen the camouflage netting floor, way over their heads. 'There's a confidence course up there,' the ex-Para explained. 'You tackle your obstacles and you don't know about the netting. That's for the real tough guys' course. When I was in the Army we didn't have netting. Can't have special people like you lot breaking your necks can we.'

The group had smiled and said no, of course not.

Rosa was out of breath. Unfit, she said to herself. Not used to climbing trees. There was dust floating down, caught in a filtered shaft of sunlight, millions and millions of tiny particles from the old dead wood in the tree overhead. Why would anyone build a commando-style Confidence Course above the children's playground obstacles below . . .? What sort of people would ever climb up there and train on it . . .? She pulled at her shoe again; the shoe had raised a blister on her heel. She began to walk slowly back along the path.

Her own words to Parker hummed in her head. *I*

think we should get into that Adventure Trail and have a look. I know that pick-up was deliberate, I wasn't supposed to go there.

She had come to the padlocked gate; she climbed over it, more awkwardly this time. Her limbs felt clumsy, and when she dropped down she landed on her hands and knees.

'Have you hurt yourself?' He came forward and bent down to help her up. 'What were you doing in there?'

'I was just walking around.' She was on her feet, avoiding his offered hand. Vassily Zarubin looked at the gate. 'It's locked,' he said. 'So you always go where you're not supposed to?' He was smiling at the oddity of her behaviour. 'In Russia nobody would do that.'

'They wouldn't do a lot of things,' Rosa retorted. She started to move off and he fell in beside her.

'What was it like?' he asked. 'What is this Adventure Trail? It is some kind of game?'

'I've no idea,' she said. 'It was very dark and overgrown, I didn't bother to go more than a few yards. I was getting scratched to pieces.'

'Have you had a pleasant walk?'

'Very pleasant.' She longed to get rid of him. She couldn't find the words for small talk.

'Do you mind if I accompany you? Are you going back to the hotel now? Perhaps you would have some tea with me?'

He had long strides and she was having to keep up. She stopped suddenly and said, 'Mr Zarubin, would you please excuse me? I'd like to finish my walk alone. I don't mean to be rude but I did come out to think about a problem and I can't do it if I'm talking to someone. You don't mind, do you?'

He stopped and inclined his head. 'As a writer,' he said solemnly, 'I understand the need to be alone. I apologize. Again!' He smiled very kindly down at her, and she blushed at her bad manners.

'I'm the one who should do that,' she said. 'Won't you join me for a drink this evening? Six thirty in the bar?'

'I will look forward to it. Now, I leave you to finish your walk.' He turned and loped off on his long legs.

'Mrs Bennet?' She had tried to hurry past the desk but Jane called out to her. 'Mr Oakham's been trying to find you.'

'I was out walking,' Rosa said. 'Thank you.'

'Mr Pollock is back,' Jane went on. 'His father's much better. I expect you'll meet him tomorrow.'

'I expect so.' She hurried up the stairs and into her room.

Harry Oakham said, 'I looked everywhere for you. I used my master key; you don't mind, do you? Where have you been? You're all dirty and you've scratched your arm . . .'

'I've been in the wood.'

'Rosa, darling,' he said gently. 'You shouldn't have gone into the wood. It's not safe, that's why we keep the gate locked.'

He'd come up to her and taken hold of her; she

said, 'I was just curious. I must change my clothes and wash my hair.'

He didn't let go. 'Why won't you look at me? What's the matter?'

'There was a squirrel,' Rosa said. 'It was caught in some netting, high up in the tree. I tried to climb up and rescue it but it was too high . . . I scraped my arm . . . I'll have a quick shower, I won't be a minute.'

'Poor little devil,' he said. 'No wonder you're upset. Nothing we can do about it; we had to put netting up, some of the trees are dangerous.' Rosa looked at him.

'Is that why? Is that what the netting is for?'

'Stop anyone getting injured by a falling branch,' he explained. 'One of the chaps building that obstacle course had a narrow escape, so I closed the place up till we could get someone from the Forestry Commission to come and see what needs to be done. And the netting was a sensible precaution in the mean time. Army surplus. Do you want me to go and find the squirrel?'

'It'll starve to death,' Rosa said. She could have cried with relief. He stroked her hair. 'You tell me where you got to and I'll go and have a look.'

'What can you do?'

'I'll have to shoot it, sweetheart. Better than leaving it there.' He lifted her face to him and kissed her gently on the lips. 'Where was the tree – what was the nearest obstacle?'

'A wall, with a rope ladder thing in front of it.'

'I'll go now,' he said. 'You have your shower. I

won't be long. Don't worry about it – promise?'

'Promise,' she agreed.

It was so simple, and it made such sense. Army surplus camouflage netting; she'd been showered with dead wood under the tree. A big branch coming down could cause serious injury. Oh you idiot, she chided herself, the warm water running over her, soaping the dust and debris out of her hair. You idiot to let your imagination run away with you like that.

When he came back she was in a dressing gown, her hair hanging down still damp from the shower.

'Did you find it?'

'I found the tree. There was a lot of stuff come down where you'd been climbing. But no squirrel. It must have got free.'

'Oh I'm glad,' Rosa said. 'What happened to you today? What was the crisis?'

He smiled and slipped his hand inside the silk robe, squeezing her breast. 'If you wanted to talk, darling, you should have got dressed.'

Rosa woke because he kicked out and mumbled loudly in his sleep. The sun was below the window ledge of her room. Oakham lay with the sheet thrown half off; his chest was glistening with sweat. He rolled sideways, exclaiming something unintelligible. Rosa shook him gently.

'Harry – Harry, wake up.'

He didn't come awake gradually. He jerked, opened his eyes and sat up immediately.

'What – what's the matter?'

'You were dreaming,' she told him. 'Very noisily. Do you talk in your sleep?'

He couldn't resist it. He laughed. 'God, darling, I hope not! It's hot, isn't it . . . What's the time?' He'd slipped his watch off when they undressed. Rosa picked it up from the bedside table.

'Six o'clock. Oh, I forgot – I said I'd meet our tame author for a drink at half past—'

'Why?' Oakham was frowning. 'Why do you want to have a drink with him? He's a bloody bore, I can tell you that.'

'I gathered that for myself,' she answered. 'But he tried to walk with me this afternoon and I told him to go away. It was very rude of me, but I was upset and I didn't want him tagging along.'

'About the squirrel. You are a softie, aren't you?'

'Yes,' Rosa stroked his shoulder. 'About the squirrel. So I suggested a drink to make up for it. He keeps criticizing things here and it irritates me. Shall I put him off?'

Oakham hesitated. What was Zarubin doing, trying to pick her up? He'd been warned off once and he was still trying. But six o'clock was seven German time. He had to call Werner in Berlin.

'All right, have the drink with him,' he said. 'I'll shower and go into the office and see if anything's been happening – I'll come and rescue you. And remember, I don't like competition!'

'Your fault for disappearing like that,' Rosa retorted. 'And you owe me an explanation. I had a boring morning and no lunch.'

'Well, I hope you haven't had a boring afternoon.'

He ran his hand down her belly and she gasped. 'Now go and have a nice drink with your writer boyfriend,' he teased, and leapt up and into the bathroom before she could retaliate.

Georg Werner spoke in a low voice; his wife was in the kitchen and out of earshot but he was still nervous.

'I talked to London,' he said. 'There's a top security alert. They've identified the woman through Interpol. They know it's Monika. They're treating it as a terrorist attack by the Fundamentalists. Whoever set it up for you,' his tone was bitter, 'they gave you very poor information.' Oakham thought of Hakim.

'Why do you say that?' he asked.

'Because Rashid was homosexual. The prostitute you kidnapped was a transvestite!'

'Jesus,' Oakham breathed. 'So that's what went wrong – Monika never had a chance—'

'You were lucky she killed him, and the body-guards panicked,' Werner went on. 'If they'd taken her alive—'

'They didn't,' Oakham cut in. He was losing patience with Werner. No guts there, he thought. A sleeper best left to sleep . . . 'What's the latest. Still no arrests, no suspects?' He kept his voice calm.

'No, not so far as London knew.'

'Well, keep in close touch,' Oakham snapped. 'And I mean close. You hear anything you call through to me at once.'

'Not from my office,' Werner protested.

'Then use a fucking outside telephone,' Oakham snarled at him, losing his temper. 'Earn your money for a change.'

Werner heard the door to the kitchen open. 'And you check your contact's information next time,' he retorted bravely.

'There won't be a next time,' Harry Oakham said and cut off. He steadied himself and lit a cigarette. No arrests, no suspects. They'd got away with it. And everything had been stacked against success because Hakim's contact thought 'Denise' was a woman. Monika never had a chance of getting out alive once she revealed herself. He put out the cigarette half smoked. It tasted bitter.

She'd been in love with death; her end was fitting. There were no regrets, no pity for the pitiless.

They'd got away with it, but only just. He looked at his watch. Rosa would be having her drink with Zarubin. He knew he couldn't trust the Russian; he had never trusted Hermann Rilke.

But first he had to check on Jan. His face softened as he thought of him. He had courage; not like that wimp Werner. The courage to sit there waiting to see Monika and Daniel come out of it safely, fighting his shattered nervous system for Harry's sake.

He went up to Jan's quarters and let himself in. He opened the bedroom door. The light was on. That was a bad sign. Jan couldn't bear being in the dark for the first year after he was released.

'You asleep?' Harry asked softly.

'I have been – what's the time?' Jan was sitting

up; he looked rumpled and bleary eyed; he tried to smile at Harry.

'How're you feeling?' Oakham came and sat on the bed.

'Better. Sorry to be such a bloody nuisance. Any news?' He blinked anxiously.

'Good news,' Harry said firmly. 'I talked to Werner, he's in touch with the Embassy in London. They haven't arrested anyone and they don't know anything except they've identified Monika. All I'm waiting for is a call from Daniel. So there's nothing to worry about.'

Jan said slowly, 'I don't want to think about it, Harry. We shouldn't have done it. She murdered that man.'

'That's what she was paid for,' Harry said quietly. 'You know what she was – she'd have done it for nothing. Just for kicks. Don't think about it any more. How about a Mogadon? Give you a proper night's sleep.'

'Why don't we stop, Harry? You don't care about the money, you said so. I don't either. Let's stop now.'

'We'll talk about it tomorrow,' Harry Oakham said. 'But you get your head down now. Here,' he unscrewed the top of the bottle and handed Jan the sleeping pill. The Pole held it for a moment.

'You will think about it? Stopping?'

'I already have,' Oakham answered.

'Why did you choose Vaclav Havel?' Rosa asked. Vassily Zarubin shrugged.

'My publishers chose him. I don't find him very convincing as a politician.'

'Then why write about him?' Zarubin wasn't dull, she decided, he wasn't a bore either; he just wasn't very appealing the more you talked to him.

'Because I was offered a lot of money,' he said, 'and all this luxury to work in. Why should I refuse?'

'It depends what sort of biography you're going to write,' she countered. 'Is it a hatchet job? If you don't think much of your subject, how can you be impartial?'

'It's easy to be impartial about someone you don't admire. Your emotions aren't engaged.'

Rosa had nearly finished her glass of wine. He was on his third vodka. 'But he is remarkable,' she couldn't help arguing with him. 'He's a playwright, a poet; he's been a political prisoner and now he's the president of his country. Maybe he's not a conventional politician, but that's surely in his favour when you look at most of them.'

'I think you should be writing my book.' He gave a narrow smile. 'I don't have heroes, Mrs Bennet.'

'How sad,' she said.

He leaned a little forward. 'Tell me about your heroes then? Are they diplomats?'

'I'm afraid not. Mine are not necessarily important or well known. Just people who believe in truth and decency, and have been willing to fight for them. Like Sakharov and Solzhenitsyn.'

'Russian heroes,' he said still smiling. 'But not unimportant or unknown.'

She looked at him. 'They stand for all the others,' she said. 'So does Vaclav Havel.'

'I really think you should write my book.'

Rosa finished her wine. She actually disliked him. Honour was satisfied. She had redeemed her bad manners outside the wood. But she didn't have to make the move. Harry Oakham was coming over to them.

'Good-evening,' he said to her, smiling, and then turned to Zarubin. 'Good-evening to you. How is the book going along?'

'I'm nearly finished,' the Russian answered. Rosa felt the antipathy between them.

'Congratulations,' Oakham said. 'Mrs Bennet, there's a telephone call for you—'

'Oh? Thank you.' She got up quickly. Zarubin got up to his full height.

'I hope you'll come back; I'm enjoying our conversation.'

'I'm afraid I can't,' Rosa didn't make an excuse. She hurried out of the bar.

Oakham didn't move. Zarubin sat down again.

'What the hell are you playing at?' Harry said very low. The Russian said, 'You spent the night with her when you should have been here. Where's Jan?'

'Jan's OK. He's asleep. You leave Jan out of it.'

'How much do you know about her?' Zarubin asked.

'What I know,' Oakham said it very quietly, 'is that she's none of your business. I told you to lay off once. This is the last time.'

'She was walking through the Adventure Trail,'

Zarubin said. 'I watched her go in. She lied about only being there a few minutes. She was inside for half an hour. I timed it. Why would she do that?'

'Because she didn't want you picking her up,' Harry snapped at him. 'She told me.'

The Russian said softly, 'And you believe her?'

Oakham stared at him. 'What are you getting at?'

Vassily hesitated; Oakham was involved with her, so involved he'd taken off during the run up to a high-risk operation. Jealous if anyone spoke to her. He couldn't share his suspicions with Oakham. 'I find her very hostile,' he said.

Oakham smiled down at him. 'That just shows what a good judge of character she is. I want a meeting with you and Rilke tomorrow.'

'Daniel has called in?' Zarubin asked. Harry Oakham made one of those snap decisions that can change the course of a lifetime.

'Yes,' he said. 'Everything's under control. I told him to stay low for a couple of days longer. I'll be at Croft Lodge around eleven thirty.' He turned and walked away. Zarubin picked up his vodka and pretended to drink while he watched him go.

'I can't stand him,' Rosa admitted.

'I told you he was boring,' Harry said. They'd taken a small corner table in the restaurant. Business was quiet mid week but he didn't feel he could absent himself for the whole evening.

'It's not that,' she disagreed. 'He seems to be sneering the whole time. He has nothing good to say about living in England for a start, and damn it, we gave him asylum if he's been here for some years. He dismissed Vaclav Havel with an airy wave of the hand — doesn't think much of him as a politician — and said he was only writing the book for money . . . I wonder if his publishers know how they've been conned!'

She was quite flushed, she was so angry. Oakham smiled at her. Full of righteous conviction. No-one had robbed her of her ideals. He loved her for it. Loved her. He hadn't thought of any woman in those terms since he held Judith's dead body in his arms and wept. Wanted, lusted after, but never loved.

'Why are you looking like that?' she demanded. 'I'm not being funny. I mean it. I hate that kind of cynicism.'

'I know you do,' Harry answered. 'You're quite fiery, aren't you? Must be a good bit of redhead in you somewhere, darling. He's on the make; a lot of the so-called political refugees we took in were rubbish. That's why the Soviets let them go. Better off without them. Stop looking belligerent and listen while I tell you something.'

'About the crisis that turned into a drama?' she reminded him.

'Other way round. Drama that turned into a crisis.' He didn't even want to lie to her. He'd forgotten to make up a story. 'It wasn't really,' he said. 'Just hotel business, very boring but immediate. Staff problems. I don't want to talk shop. I said I wanted to tell you something.'

She let it slide away. Hotel business, trouble with

the staff, so what was the big deal . . . ? 'So tell me then,' she said.

'I'm in love with you, Rosa. If I do decide to chuck this in and make a new life, will you let me share it with you? On your terms?'

She had blushed and then turned very pale. 'You really mean that?'

He said, 'I'm a bit of a joker, but not about something that matters. I mean it. And I won't make the mistake the charming James did. I won't try to own you. You're not the type to cling or be clung to; I never was either. I think we could be blissfully happy. What do you think?'

It was the moment of decision for her too. She looked at him across the table in the gentle yellow candlelight. She knew every line of his face, the contour of bone, the roughness of skin on his jaw and the firm lips she'd traced with her fingers till they opened and gently imprisoned them. She knew his eyes and the gleam of humour in them. They were dark and very warm as he held her look with his own.

'I think we could too,' she said. 'If you're sure you want to try it.'

'I'm sure,' he said quietly. 'Now why don't we go upstairs and celebrate?'

'Why not?' she answered. As they got up from the table she stopped and said to him. 'Now I'll tell *you* something. I've never been happier in my life.'

Daniel shifted his buttocks. The seat was hard. There were no bright lights, no interrogator shielded from view in semi-darkness while the light burned on his victim's face. Nothing like that. Just a room in the police station, with a plain table, even an ashtray, two upright chairs, and a rug on the floor. A policeman lurked in the background – the witness demanded by law. A small tape recorder was switched on; it stood near the empty ashtray.

'Now Danny,' the Detective Chief Inspector said patiently, 'let's go over it again. Why were you jogging at twelve o'clock at night?'

'I told you,' Daniel answered. 'I couldn't sleep.' He'd lost count of time. They'd taken his watch and there wasn't a clock in the room. The DCI hadn't mentioned the time when he started the interview and switched on the tape. It seemed as if they'd been sitting there for hours.

'Why couldn't you sleep? Something on your mind?'

'You know what was on my mind.' He gave the big, bald-headed man a sullen look.

'No, I don't. That's why I'm asking. Why'd you give a false name and address when you were picked up?'

'It's the one I've been using,' Daniel said.

'Why did you give us the slip? What have you been doing with yourself all this time?'

The same questions, slightly altered but essentially the same. Why was he out in the street at that hour? Why did he give a false name when he was arrested? Why had he gone missing when he knew he was only allowed to stay in England provided he kept out of trouble?

He had the answers ready. They were all true and

the bastard sitting opposite knew it. He was caught, but they couldn't prove anything.

He wasn't a coward; he kept his head. He'd been in much worse situations and lied his way out, or bribed his way or betrayed it. But not this time. No deals with these people. Except the deal that incriminated him. Just stay with his story line, and they'd have to release him after the statutory thirty-six hours in custody or apply to the court for a seven-day extension. On suspicion. They'd probably get it. He could last out. They'd threaten deportation, but they couldn't do that without Home Office approval. It was a game of bluff and while he cursed his luck, he kept his nerve and settled down to play them to a finish.

Monika was dead; he'd heard that much on the grapevine in the cells. If they'd picked up Stevenson or the others, they wouldn't be leaning on him without mentioning them. All he had to do was stick to his story. He spread his hands in self mockery.

'All right, all right, you want it all again, I'll give it. I got sick of being watched. It got on my nerves. I couldn't sleep – that's what started it. You were watching me like a criminal. So I got fed up with it. I gave your people a run for their money. They weren't very good,' he sneered a little. 'I went to friends. They took me in. I used a different name. I got a little peace for a change.'

'Tell me about your friends, Danny. I'm surprised you've got any friends. I thought that was your trouble. You couldn't trust anyone not to tell your old Mossad colleagues where you were . . . ' He was touching on the sore spot. Daniel looked at him. He shook his head.

'You can't hand me over,' he said. 'You've arrested me. I'm official. I'm on file.' The DCI lit a cigarette. He didn't offer one to Daniel.

'Don't count on it,' he said. 'Files can be lost. Like tapes.'

Daniel shrugged. 'Go ahead, threaten. Intimidate me. I was out jogging and I got picked up. If that's against the law, then charge me.'

'You gave false information to the arresting officer. That's a crime.'

'Carries a big sentence? Don't waste your time. I've done nothing and you know it. What about the others you picked up? How about bullying them?'

'We don't bully people,' was the answer. 'Why won't you say where you were living? Give yourself an alibi?'

Daniel snorted. 'And have you harassing my friends? I know you – I'm not doing that to them. I'm a grateful man.'

The DCI got up. He stubbed out the cigarette in the ashtray. He was stiff from sitting, and cold with rage inside. It was like butting a stone wall. No impression. Not a flicker. The same lies repeated with that brassy defiance he'd seen in men like Daniel since he started as a bobby on the streets.

'You're not grateful, Danny. You'd sell your own mother, if you even knew who she was. You're a snatch artist, the lowest scum there is. You've kidnapped people and handed them over to be tortured and murdered. You're dirt, so don't talk to me about being grateful. We let you into this country and we let you stay because you traded names with people in SIS who *deal* with dirt like you. But I don't. This stinking business has your hallmark on it. I know bloody well you were involved and I'm not going to stop till I've proved it. You understand that, Danny?'

'The best of luck to you,' Daniel said. 'I need to take a pee.'

'I'm fine,' Jan insisted. 'Let me go back to work today, Harry.'

'Don't be a bloody fool,' Oakham said. 'You need to take it easy; another day won't hurt you. I'll cover for you with the staff. Nursing your sick father, coping with your mother – they'll be crying their eyes out when I've finished!'

He laughed encouragingly at Jan. He was due to see Rilke and Zarubin in half an hour. Jan had woken late, drowsy and disorientated, but like a guilty child who was worried about skipping school. He thought Harry looked very confident and good-humoured that morning. He'd sat on the bed chatting to him, making him eat breakfast, chasing the cobwebs away. He was right, of course. Jan did feel better but still wobbly. He remembered the psychiatrist dismissing his terrible attacks as a wobble in the course of recovery.

It was clever because it robbed the panic of significance. Nobody went off their heads because of a wobble.

'I've been thinking,' Harry said, 'about what you

said last night. About stopping this lark and getting out.'

Jan looked at him; Harry smiled a little into the sunken eyes, anxiety lurking in them like unshed tears.

'You have? What do you think, Harry – can we do it?'

'We can do what we damned well like,' Oakham assured him. 'We've got a nice sum in Switzerland, enough to keep us both very comfortably for a very long time. We've got passports – they are not in the name of Oakham or Ploekewski, but they're absolutely valid. We can take off, collect the loot and settle somewhere quiet like Italy. Property's cheap; nobody gives a damn so long as you can pay. I think it sounds rather good, don't you?'

Getting out ahead of the Libyans with that money wouldn't be easy but he wasn't going to tell Jan that.

Jan said nervously, 'Why do you want to do this? It's because of me, isn't it? Because I cracked up . . .' He turned his head away to hide the tears that filled his eyes.

'No,' Harry answered. 'No, it isn't. And I'm not conning you, I wouldn't do that. It's for myself. I've met a lady, Jan. Someone very special. She's going to be working in Europe; probably Brussels. I want to be able to spend time with her. Italy's only a couple of hours away by plane.' He patted Jan's arm. 'So you see, I'm a selfish bugger after all.'

After a long pause the Pole said, 'It's not like Peggy, is it? That's how you talked about her . . .'

'No, don't worry about that,' Harry spoke firmly. 'This isn't just letch. She's a wonderful girl, very bright, independent – sweet with it. There'll be no ties for either of us. Unless she wants them. That may happen but not for quite a while . . . I don't mind. I haven't felt like this since Judith.'

There was a silence between them then. At last Jan spoke to him. 'If it's like that,' he said, 'then it's right for you. Where did you find her?'

'Right here, she's staying in the hotel. I was with her when you phoned that night. I'm sorry, old son. We went off for the day and stayed in a pub. I owe you one for that.'

'You don't owe me anything,' Jan protested. 'I'm glad, Harry. I'm really happy for you.' And then he frowned, remembering. 'Daniel?' he said. 'Any word?'

'No,' Harry Oakham answered. 'Nothing. I told Zarubin he'd called in to keep him and that little skunk Rilke quiet. But he hasn't. Werner's keeping an ear to the ground through the Embassy in London; no news from them either. But if anything breaks, they'll know. And Werner will tell us.'

'You think he could have been picked up?' Jan asked. 'That's why he hasn't called in—' He bit at his raw lip, and winced.

'Maybe,' Oakham considered. 'But if there's a definite suspect they'll let the foreign embassies know to reassure them. They're all under high-level security at the moment in case this is the first move in a terrorist campaign. The view is it's the Fundamentalists hitting at the pro-American Arabs and possibly the European nations who supported the Gulf War. Monika's Red Brigade background supports this theory. Though why they worry about the Germans God knows. They did fuck all to help – I better be on my way. I'm going to have a cosy chat at Croft Lodge. Tell you what – I'll get Jane to route all calls for me up here to you while I'm gone. Just in case Daniel surfaces. And don't worry. He's a cagey sod; he'll keep his head down till he's sure it's safe to get in touch. So you stay in here and stick by the telephone, all right?'

Jan managed a weak smile. 'All right. If he does call, shall I get on to Croft Lodge?'

'No,' Harry answered. 'The less those two know the better. I have a gut feeling they're going to run out on us. So I think we may get in first. I'll come up when I get back.'

'A spy? Here in the hotel?' Rilke's colour had changed to a pasty grey. He cursed obscenely in German. 'And you said nothing?'

'I hadn't any proof. I still haven't. But my instinct says she's wrong, Hermann. I can smell it.' Zarubin tapped the side of his nose with one finger.

He'd told Rilke he'd seen her watching the Irish; he'd mentioned the little flash of sunlight, and Rilke had exploded.

'A camera! She was photographing them? But why? Who is she working for? God in Heaven—'

'That's what I have to find out. I need to get into her room. She lied about the Adventure Trail; I tried to warn Oakham but he wouldn't listen. She's got a hold on him, Hermann, so we'll have to act without him. If she is a plant, then British Intelligence must have suspected from the beginning. If I can search her room I'll find something. And I know what to look for. Daniel has called in, so we're safe for the moment. But if I'm right about her – then the sooner we get out of here the better for both of us. Oakham is coming this morning. I want you to keep him here. Keep him talking. Give me as much time as you can. I'll go back to the hotel and think of some way to get in.'

'If it was a camera,' Rilke said, 'she may keep it with her. They're made so small they're no bigger than a box of matches.'

'Unlikely,' Zarubin countered. 'She wouldn't risk losing her bag, or pulling it out by accident. If there's a camera of the kind we're talking about, it'll be hidden in her room.'

'If you find nothing?' Rilke demanded.

Zarubin looked at him. 'I've never been wrong yet,' he answered.

'And then what do we do?'

'We ask her a few questions,' he said. 'I'll give her to you, Hermann. And we say nothing to Oakham. We can't trust him. He's gone soft. Just keep him busy. And I will come later, if things go well.'

'A spy,' Rilke was muttering; his fear was changing to rage. 'So clever, so full of himself, and there's a spy under his nose!'

'And in his bed,' Zarubin remarked. 'I'll leave now. Don't let him suspect anything.'

'I'm not a fool,' Rilke snapped. 'He's coming to

bluff his way out of his mistake and I'll let him think he's got away with it. You can leave him to me. Just get into that room!'

Rosa woke late; she was still asleep when her breakfast was brought up. The sun shone through when the curtains were drawn. She lay for a little while, propped on her pillows, thinking of Harry.

It had been better between them than before; surely impossible, but it had happened. And afterwards their mutual tenderness was as powerful as their passion.

At moments they had laughed together in pure joy, then fallen asleep locked in each other's arms as if they couldn't bear to move apart.

She raised herself and smiled in contentment with the world. The orange juice was sweet, the coffee perfect. The day was glorious. Like the future. She would go to Brussels, and he would follow her there. They'd be together; lovers, friends, bound by nothing except their love for each other. He didn't want to own her; he didn't want to be owned himself.

She got up, taking her time, pleased with herself as she stood naked in the bathroom; you look as good as you feel, she said to her reflection, and blew herself a kiss before she stepped into the water.

Harry was busy that morning; he'd promised her the evening and the night, and she could idle the day away. I was going to ring Jim Parker, she remembered, after she had dressed. Give him the bad news: Harry Oakham is straight. I've found the love of my life, but nothing sinister for you. So sorry, Jim . . .

She hadn't told Harry that Brussels wasn't a simple posting. She was bound by her signature on the Officials Secrets Act. If she ever did tell him, perhaps when her tour was up, she knew he'd be amused.

I'll drive into Dedham, wander round the souvenir shops . . . have my hair washed. Buy him a present, something silly, like a tie. Why do women always buy ties for their men, and the men never wear them because they're too dull or too gaudy? She laughed at herself; happiness was making her light-headed, foolish. I miss him so much already, and there's half a day to kill before I see him . . .

She was humming as she came downstairs. She said 'Good-morning', to Jane at the desk. 'Isn't it lovely again?'

'Yes,' Jane smiled back at her. 'You've brought it with you, Mrs Bennet – we haven't had a single bad day since you came!'

'Good-morning.'

Rosa turned. It was that persistent man again, looming up beside her. She said curtly, 'Good-morning', and started to walk towards the door.

'Are you going for another walk?' He had followed her outside on to the steps.

'No, I'm driving into Dedham. I've got to hurry, I'm late for an appointment.'

'I hope you have a nice morning,' Vassily Zarubin said, and swung away back into the hotel. Rosa glanced behind her with relief. For one moment she thought he might have been crass enough to ask for a lift. He was incredibly thick-skinned; she'd conveyed her dislike to the point of rudeness and still he refused to be snubbed. She hurried down to the car park. She got into her car and started the engine.

Zarubin came up to the reception desk. Jane looked up and blushed. 'Mrs Bennet's key please,' he said hurriedly. 'She's forgotten her purse — she asked me to bring it down to her. We're going into Dedham together.'

Jane reached up and took it off the hook. It seemed quite natural. They'd left together, he'd come rushing back . . .

'Thank you,' Zarubin said, and started up the stairs, taking them two at a time. Jane gazed after him. Lucky Mrs Bennet with Mr Oakham and that romantic Russian vying for her . . .

Outside the room Zarubin opened the door, slipped the latch on and came down immediately.

He handed the key back over to Jane, who went very pink because he brushed his hand against hers. And smiled at her. 'It's not there,' he said. 'I couldn't see it on the table. It doesn't matter. I have money. I will be glad to pay for her.'

Lucky, lucky Mrs Bennet, Jane sighed again as he hurried out and disappeared from view.

He turned left, skirting the wall under the dining room, and round by the rose garden, through the shrubbery to the back stairs. The service door was always open. And close by were the service stairs leading to all floors. He slipped inside and within a few moments he was at Rosa's door. He pushed it open and went inside. There was a 'Do Not Disturb' notice on the floor by the unmade bed.

He hung it on the handle outside and slipped the catch down, locking it. Then he began to search the room.

'I want to know they've paid the money!' Rilke repeated it.

Harry gave up trying to placate him. And besides, maybe he should check.

He'd taken it for granted that Hakim's people had honoured their agreement; there'd been scandal and world coverage enough to satisfy anyone.

He hadn't been too concerned about the money. Just as Jan pointed out, it wasn't his top priority. But the whereabouts of Daniel was worrying him now that Jan was safe.

'I want confirmation it's been paid over,' Rilke went on obstinately, his voice rising angrily. 'You may trust scum like Hakim, but I don't.'

'I don't trust anyone,' Harry pointed out. 'On principle. But a deal is a deal in our little world, Hermann, otherwise nobody survives. All right, I'll get on to Geneva.'

'Why don't you phone now?' Rilke demanded. *Keep him occupied*, Zarubin had instructed.

'Because I can use the scrambler in my office,' Harry retorted.

'It's perfectly safe to call from here,' Rilke said. 'I have a right to know what's happened.'

'What's the hurry?' Harry asked quietly. 'Thinking of backing out?' Rilke wasn't fazed by the suggestion.

'Stevenson and the others haven't contacted us;

307

even if Daniel's safe, we know nothing about them. It might be necessary to move quickly. Don't tell me you haven't thought of it yourself!'

'Bill is holed up with his friends, following my orders,' Harry dismissed it.

'You don't know the criminal element in London, Hermann. Bill's one of the boys. He'll be looked after, so will the others. I've no worries about them. All right, I'll ring Geneva. Can't have you losing beauty sleep, can we?'

Rilke gave him a look of hatred as he turned to the telephone. Rilke glanced at his watch. He'd kept Oakham talking for an hour, exploring eventualities, arguing over the money in Switzerland. When he asked where Vassily Zarubin was, Rilke said he was working on a chess problem and would come when he'd finished.

Since Daniel was safe, Zarubin wasn't worried about their security. Harry dialled and asked for their contact at the bank. He gave the agreed code name for his own account. There was a pause; Rilke came up close to him. Harry said, 'It has . . . ? Good, could you repeat that please . . . ?' and passed the phone to Rilke. Then he took it back and said 'Thank you', and to Rilke, 'Satisfied? I told you they'd pay up. And the joke is, I didn't even need to stir up the real dirt – about Denise – the Arabs don't mind homosexuals – Daniel said a lot of them prefer to bugger women . . .' He felt Rilke was due a kick in the teeth for the fuss he'd been making. Harry was pleased to see by his expression that the shaft had hit the mark.

'I'll be on my way,' he said. 'You can tell Vassily his money's in the bank if he turns up.'

'Why don't you stay for a drink?' Rilke suggested unwillingly.

Harry shook his head. 'No thanks. I've got work to do – I've got a hotel to run. Not lonely without Monika, are you?'

Rilke didn't retaliate; he had no talent for irony. He looked at Harry with a gleam of malice. He thought, If Zarubin's right, there'll be another woman here instead of Monika.

He just said coldly, 'No. I don't enjoy the company of whores.'

'I can imagine,' Harry said pleasantly. Rilke watched him stride away towards the hotel. Zarubin had been given enough time, provided he'd found the opportunity. Rilke poured himself a glass of wine and lit one of his mild cigarettes. If the woman was a spy – he felt a rush of fear mingled with rage – if Zarubin's instinct about her was right and he found confirmation in her room . . . Rilke pondered, smoking rapidly.

A worm of excitement began to stir in his belly. He hadn't smelt fear in anyone for a long time. All his frustrations, his dislike of his companions and his surroundings, concentrated into a surge of cruelty. He wiped his hands on a handkerchief and sipped at his wine.

He was sweating. Harry's mistress would pay for Harry's jibes at his expense. He let his imagination run backwards to the days when he was the most feared interrogator in the service of the State; when he was powerful and respected. Nobody dared so much as contradict him then.

Now he was the butt of that insufferable Englishman's sneers about his sexuality. He liked boys and young men, but he liked nothing better than to inflict the worst subtleties of pain upon a helpless woman.

Zarubin looked round Rosa's bedroom. Apart from the unmade bed, it was tidy. The bed had been shared, he noted. There was a diary lying on the dressing table; he left that till the last . . . He began with the chest of drawers, searching through the neatly folded underclothes. A lady of expensive tastes, he thought, fingering lace and ribbons. The next two drawers yielded nothing either.

He was skilled at his task, although he hadn't searched a suspect's room for many years. It was basic training for a KGB student to know how to strip a place down to the electric wiring for a rip-out job, or go through personal effects without leaving a trace. Zarubin hadn't forgotten the art.

He turned to her wardrobe; handbags were ranged on the top shelf. He opened them one after the other. A soiled handkerchief, a few bills, receipted with a London address on them, a sachet of soluble aspirin. Nothing. He looked in pockets of dresses and a long lightweight coat without success. Underneath, neatly stacked in rows, were half a dozen pairs of shoes.

He found what he was looking for in the toe of a casual slip-on. It was smaller than a packet of cigarettes, a narrow oblong with a tiny zoom lens, capable of taking clear-focus photographs from quite a distance. Zarubin examined it carefully. A very sophisticated accessory. No toy for an amateur taking holiday snaps. His expression was very grim. That was what he had seen flash behind her book in the morning sunshine, a reflection caught off the tiny lens in the second it was exposed. That camera was a spy's tool. His own agents used similar models, some even tinier for close up photography. He was right about Rosa Bennet.

There was a roll of unused film inside. He slipped the camera into his pocket. She wouldn't get a chance to use it again. Quickly he checked through her diary, looking for something like a disguised code. The early part was full of entries, this appointment, that embassy reception, meetings, and then – he caught his breath as he read it.

17 August. Seminar. Branksome. He knew what kind of seminar the British Intelligence Service ran jointly at Branksome.

She was a new recruit. A diplomat, yes the diary proved her official status. But attached to a specialized section. 'C', headed by Air Marshal Sir Peter Jefford. Zarubin knew the names and ranks of every senior Intelligence chief in Britain and the United States. He'd made a study of them and their methods. Like posing a chess problem and playing your opponent's part.

Someone had decided to keep Oakham under surveillance, and they'd sent a new face along to do it. And Oakham had fallen into the trap.

It must be already on file that an Irish group had paid a visit; if their faces were on the computer as known IRA suspects, then the whole operation was likely to blow up at any moment. It all depended upon how much the woman had discovered and reported back.

He glanced round him to make sure everything was as he'd found it. He felt for the camera in his pocket and his hand trembled with rage. It was time to ask Rosa Bennet a few questions. He took the 'Do Not Disturb' sign off the door, slipped the catch and let it lock behind him. He went to his room through the back corridors and put a call through to Croft Lodge. Rilke's dry voice answered. 'Yes?'

'Is he there?'

'No, he's just left. Did you find anything?'

'What I expected,' Zarubin snapped. 'Keep calm, I'm going to bring the lady down to visit you. As soon as I can. Leave it with me.'

Rilke said slowly, 'I'll be ready for her.'

Rosa couldn't find a tie, gaudy or otherwise. She changed her mind about going into the hairdressers; it was crowded and she didn't want to sit waiting for an appointment. She wandered through the lovely old village, and found herself by the handsome church.

Rosa had time to spare, and the sense of leisure that was new to her. No need to be busy, to prove she was doing something useful. Time to waste if she felt like it. This, she decided, was part of being in love for the first time.

She had no religious feeling; her parents were both liberal agnostics and they had not brought her up to believe in anything but a general code of humanist morality.

She walked round the ancient church, and paused by the memorial to Harry's ancestor. The stained-glass window glowed in the late autumn light. Poor Lieutenant Arthur David Oakham, killed on the Somme, 1916, aged twenty.

She felt a pang of sadness as if she knew the boy cut down before he had a chance to be a man. She left the church hurriedly, and found herself in the churchyard.

Jim Parker had described it to her; he'd talked about the grave of Judith Oakham. Unvisited, untended. 'I never go near the place,' Harry had said. 'I couldn't bear to think of her lying there.'

It was like a pilgrimage for Rosa. She didn't feel an intruder; curiosity wasn't her motive. She wanted to see it and be able to heal that old wound for him for ever.

There was the inscription and the date. Only twenty-four. She'd been so young to die in an accident like that. She had come alive for Rosa as Harry talked about her. Blonde, athletic, a sunshine girl who loved life. And he had carried her body down from the slopes in his arms.

If I can make him forget that, Rosa thought, standing by the grave, then I'm sure it's what you'd want.

She bought a cup of coffee in one of the many tea rooms, watching the tourists strolling by. She felt very peaceful sitting there. And the time passed till she paid her bill and went out to find the car and drive back at her leisure.

But she hadn't bought him a present. She wanted to find something for him, some token to say how much she loved him. She found a corn dolly in a souvenir shop. It wore a yokel's felt hat, and had a silly face crudely painted on the knobby yellow head beneath. They were pagan symbols, Rosa remembered, something to do with the Harvest Festival. They warded off evil spirits, or nonsense like that.

'I'll take this one,' Rosa said, pointing, and the girl slipped the little figure off its hook.

'He is rather sweet, isn't he?' she said. 'Three pounds twenty-nine please. Shall I wrap it, madam?'

'No thank you.' She had the exact money in her bag. He would make Harry smile. That was what she wanted. She drove back and her heart was so light that she sang in tune to a popular song on the tape.

11

'Any messages — any crises turning into dramas?' Oakham cracked the same joke and the girl who'd taken over the afternoon shift from Jane, laughed dutifully. She wasn't his favourite and she knew it, but she played along with the routine.

'No messages, Mr Oakham.' She glanced down. 'I have a note here to transfer your calls to Mr Pollock. But nothing's come in.'

'Good,' Harry turned away.

'But,' she said, making the most of it, 'I'm afraid we do have a problem.' She irritated him; she was the type that enjoyed bad news.

'What kind of problem?'

'The main boiler's gone on the blink. The kitchen can't get any hot water, and Jim says he can't find Ron or Bob anywhere. He said would you please come down and have a look.'

'Not that I'll be much help,' Harry said. 'But I'll certainly go and see . . . '

'I wonder where they've got to?' she said.

He shrugged, making little of it. 'Out in the grounds somewhere. I don't know what Jim's grumbling about, he doesn't like them interfering.'

He turned and went towards the back. Better keep the old man happy. Keep him from moaning about Stevenson's boys being absent. If he couldn't fix the damned boiler, they'd have to get someone over from Ipswich . . . He disappeared down into the cellar area.

Vassily Zarubin saw Rosa drive up between the tall avenue of beech trees. He'd taken up her vantage point on the seat facing the hotel. The same seat where she had photographed the Irish woman and the two men. He watched her arrive in the car park using the same device as she had done: a book, casually lowered as she came into view. He watched her walk back into the hotel and pretended not to see her. Rosa noticed him and quickened her step in case he got up and followed her.

To her relief, he didn't move. He looked absorbed in whatever he was reading. She went into the reception hall. The receptionist looked up briefly. Unlike Jane, she didn't chat with the clients.

'Gorgeous afternoon,' Rosa said. She wanted to share her good spirits with someone, even the unresponsive girl behind the desk.

'Yes, very warm for this time of year.'

'My key please – thank you.'

The girl watched Rosa walk away to the stairs. Everyone knew she was shacked up with the manager. That silly twit Jane thought it was romantic; *she* thought it was disgraceful of him and didn't say much for her to behave like that, picking up someone working in the hotel. She'd heard about older women and young waiters in some of the London places, but down here – honestly! She got great satisfaction out of her disapproval.

Zarubin got up from the seat; he slipped the book under his arm and walked with his long, steady stride towards the car park.

It was a BMW; an expensive car and a recent model. He tried the handle; it was locked. She wasn't the careless type. He peered inside, checking. He couldn't see an alarm. He paused to look round him; the car park was shielded from the main building by a row of trees. It was just visible from the seat in the forecourt of the hotel. Nobody could see him, and there was no-one in sight.

He took out his penknife; it was an all-purpose Swiss Army model and he had carried it for years. Its intricacy pleased him. It concealed little tools for every emergency, from a pick to take a stone out of a horse's hoof, to the long thin needle blade he inserted into the BMW's lock. It took less than a minute to open the car.

Zarubin slipped inside and closed the door. He smelt her scent in the warm enclosed space. Such a pretty woman, he thought coldly. Such a pretty diplomat turned spy . . . He twisted the little stiletto in the ignition; the engine started with a quiet hum. The radio made him jump. It took him a moment to realize that there was a tape in the machine. The pretty spy had a sentimental taste in music. He pushed a button and the tape slid out. Then the radio came on; voices in a deep discussion on the merits of Classical architecture.

In the glove compartment he found the operating manual. She'd just come back from a trip to

Dedham. But just in case – he turned the blade.

He walked back to Croft Lodge and started up the Ford Harry Oakham had provided for him to replace his hire car. Zarubin had made a few trips to the village in it. He drove up to the hotel car park and slid into the vacant space beside the BMW. Mrs Bennet wouldn't be going anywhere in her smart car that night. He had disconnected the electrical system.

He looked at his watch. The sun was well up; he had a few hours to wait till he put his plan into effect. When the dusk was creeping up into the sky, he'd take Mrs Bennet for a drive in his little Ford. And introduce her to Hermann Rilke.

The door of Daniel's cell opened. He was lying on his bed reading a newspaper. He glanced at the sergeant. 'Come to release me?' he asked. The time was up, he reckoned. They couldn't hold him any longer without a court order.

The sergeant didn't answer. He jerked his head and stood to one side. When they were outside the cell he took a firm hold of Daniel's arm. Daniel tried to pull away. The grip grew tighter. 'You give me trouble,' the policeman said quietly, 'and I'll cuff you!' Daniel stopped struggling. He wasn't being freed. He knew that from the man's attitude.

The interview room again. The same routine of question and answer, threats, harassment – he didn't care, he wasn't going to move on his story.

He set his stubbly jaw in defiance and prepared to brazen it out. One last try perhaps, before they had to give in and set him free for lack of evidence. He hoped so. But he wasn't sure.

The DCI was waiting for him; there were two men with him, one a uniformed police officer, the other in plain clothes. There was no chair for Daniel this time.

The room was heavy with stale air and cigarette smoke. He looked quickly at the faces in front of him and saw a glimmer of triumph. His stomach lurched and then knotted with alarm.

The DCI spoke very calmly. 'The game's up, Danny.'

'What game?' He had to keep going, to keep bluffing, in case they were bluffing. But his fine-honed instincts didn't think they were.

'Your little game,' the answer came back. 'The game of kidnapping and murder.'

'I'm not frightened by your bullshit,' Daniel's voice grated. 'I've done nothing and you know it. You can't hang anything on me.'

'Oh, we know that,' the second man spoke. He had a more cultivated accent than the DCI. He was from a different branch; Daniel realized that too. 'We can't hang you, Mr Ishbav, but we can put you away for a very long time. Can't we Dave?' The DCI nodded. He actually smiled now. If it was an act then they were giving a class performance. Daniel's heart was thudding.

'You were in Lancaster Place the night that Arab was murdered,' he said. 'And you weren't jogging, Danny. You were sitting in the Prince's Merc, wearing a chauffeur's cap.' He waited; he saw Daniel lose colour. He said softly, 'I told you, the game's up. We've got a witness. He saw you in the car, he saw you get out, throw the cap into the bushes, and run for it. A positive identification, Danny. That's what we've got.'

Daniel managed to say, 'Nobody saw me. I wasn't there.'

'Our witness says you were,' the second man insisted.

The DCI turned his head and spoke to the constable, 'Bring up a chair for him, will you?' Daniel stayed on his feet.

'What witness? I don't believe you.'

'Not a very impressive one,' the DCI admitted. 'A vagrant, well known round the area. He was sitting in a doorway, getting ready for the night. He saw the car and he saw you. There was a street light quite close; he had a really good look at you. He said he'd been thinking of going to the window and asking for a cigarette or a few bob. The usual driver always gave him something. Blessed is the alms giver – good Muslims never say no to a beggar. You know that. He saw you jump out when the sirens started up; you threw the cap away and he realized you weren't the normal driver. And under that street light he saw enough to make a positive I.D.'

Daniel could feel the chair at the back of him; his legs were rigid. 'A beggar? Some old drunk sleeping rough?' He actually forced himself to laugh. 'Try that one in court. I was nowhere near the place.'

The second man came a little closer to him. He had a cold, impassive face, but the eyes were mocking him. 'We sent the cap to forensic,' he said. 'Some of the hairs matched the ones we got off your pillow, Ishbav. You try telling us how they got there.'

Daniel swallowed. His eyes narrowed and then opened. He held the other man's look. 'OK,' he said. He turned and sat down in the chair. 'What's the deal?'

'No deal!' the DCI snarled at him, bristling.

'OK,' Daniel said again. 'No deal. You get me, but you don't get the others.'

The DCI raised his voice. 'I told you, I don't deal with scum like you—'

The second man came up and touched him on the arm. He swung away, grimacing in disgust. 'Mr Ishbav,' the tone was conciliatory. 'Would you like a cigarette?'

The DCI and his companion made their way down the corridor towards his office. 'I could do with a cup of coffee,' he said. 'And something in it.'

'Good idea. Funny, isn't it? Normally, once they start talking you can't get them to stop. But not this bastard. He's caught and he knows it, but he'll give as little as he can to try and make a deal for himself. You took a hell of a chance there, but it came off.'

'It was our only chance,' the DCI said. 'That poor old bugger couldn't identify his own mother, if he had to stand up in a court. But it did the trick. Jesus, what a set up, eh? Assassination to order. Wait till the Home Office hears about this one.'

They turned into his office. 'Well,' the younger

man said, 'we've got three names for a start. And he's promised more.'

'I'll put out an APB for Stevenson and the others. We'll have our coffee and let him sweat for a bit. Then we'll have him in again. Scotch or brandy?'

'Scotch would be fine, thanks. Congratulations – you did a great job.'

'Bloody boiler,' Harry Oakham muttered. The maintenance man wiped his hands on a rag.

'I told that Bob not to meddle with it,' he said. He hated the two younger men. They were a couple of roughs in his opinion, lacking respect for a man of his age. He didn't mind putting in a bad word to Mr Oakham.

Harry recognized spite when he heard it, and doubted whether Bob had even been near the boiler room, but he didn't say anything. 'The kitchen will go on strike if we don't get it fixed,' he said. 'Try again, Jim, will you? Otherwise I'll have to get on to the heating engineers in Ipswich and get them to send someone out at the double . . .'

He was sweating in the hot, smelly space. The big boiler, gleaming new, stood silent, with a little pool of oil gathering at the base. Jim shook his head. 'I've tried everything, sir,' he said. 'The old one worked all right. You always get teething troubles with these new models. I said so, but—' He shrugged again.

'I'll call Ipswich,' Harry said. 'They'll get it fixed.'

'Hope so,' said Jim, who was hoping they wouldn't. He'd never liked the new boiler; the old model was reliable and he understood it. But everything had to be done over when the old owners left. He followed Harry Oakham out and closed the door.

The heating engineers were not sure they had a man available to come at such short notice. Harry sat in his office and swore; it took twenty minutes and a direct call to the manager of the branch to get an assurance that an engineer would be on his way in half an hour. The phone rang and it was reception.

'All right to put your calls through, Mr Oakham, or are you going out?'

'I'm going across to have a shower and clean up,' Harry said. 'Mr Pollock can take anything till I come back.'

It would keep Jan occupied. He locked his office and went off to his house and the comfort of a hot shower. Then he remembered the boiler. He grinned. All right, a cold shower. Outside his door he found the corn dolly. There was a note pinned to its straw chest.

He went inside and tore the envelope open. 'My Darling, it looked so like you I couldn't resist it! I'm longing for this evening. All my deepest love, R.' The foolish face grinned at him under the lop-sided little hat. He laughed and held it for a moment. Judith would have given him something like that.

No, he corrected himself firmly. He mustn't compare her to Rosa. They weren't alike. Rosa was serious, independent, much more intelligent. And suddenly it wasn't disloyal to think like that.

It was strange to realize that Judith's memory was less sacred, her image less clear. At last he was going to bury his memories after all these years. Rosa had done that for him. He put the corn dolly on his bed. He stripped and went under the shower. The water was lukewarm and then freezing. He came out towelling himself and shivered.

He heard the rapid knocking on his door. He called out, 'Who is it?'

'It's me,' Jan's voice was hoarse. 'Let me in, for Christ's sake!'

Harry went to the door at a run and wrenched it open. Jan stood there. His face was a sick grey. 'I've been ringing,' he mumbled. 'You didn't answer . . . They said you were in your house so I came over . . .'

'I didn't hear it, I was in the shower. What is it, Jan? Come on, what's happened?'

Jan sagged at the knees on to Oakham's bed. He looked up at him. 'Werner called. They've got Daniel. And he's talking.'

Harry Oakham lit a cigarette. His hand was steady. He'd listened while Jan repeated what Georg Werner had said, ending with the anguished accusation that he was ruined along with the rest of them, before he had rung off. 'The shit,' Harry said quietly. 'The little shit.'

Jan said, 'You knew we couldn't trust him.'

'I didn't trust anyone except you,' was the answer. 'So Werner says he's making a deal . . . That means he'll try and spin it out to get the best terms for himself. Immunity from prosecution.' He laughed suddenly. 'Much bloody good it'll do him. If he stands up in a court, the Mossad boys'll be in the public gallery!'

'What are you going to do?' Jan asked. He was calmer now, because of Oakham. Oakham never panicked. Danger brought out the best in him. Jan knew that.

'Get the hell out as fast as we can. Daniel won't give them any big fish to start with. And I'll be the last. His ace. We've got our passports, cash in the hotel safe, and we can make Heathrow and get a direct flight to Switzerland. Then we disappear.'

He came over to Jan and laid a hand on his shoulder. 'We were going to do it anyway; we're just going early, that's all. So nothing to worry about.' He looked at his watch. 'I'll call up and find out the flight times. Then we'll put a few things in a bag and slip away.'

'What about Rilke and Zarubin? Aren't you going to tell them?'

Harry didn't hesitate. 'Daniel will end up by spilling his guts out. I don't have a bleeding heart for either of them. Let them take care of themselves. He travels fastest who travels alone. Now let's see about the flights.'

The time passed slowly. More slowly than Rosa could remember. Perhaps it was always like this when you waited for a lover. The hands on your watch couldn't move fast enough. She thought of James when they first met, and she had imagined herself to be in love. She was in love, but not like this. There had always been a part of her that held back. She used to think of it as independence. She accepted the reserve as natural, healthy in a modern woman.

Now she was so restless with excitement and the desire to be with Harry Oakham that she couldn't watch TV or read a book.

She went for a walk in the grounds, skirting the lake which was grey as the sun started dipping, and ruffled by a cold wind that sprang up.

The lovely autumn day was fading; winter's chill was in the clouded sky. Rosa felt cold suddenly, and hurried back to the hotel.

She wondered if he'd found the little corn dolly, and smiled at the idea. Upstairs in her room she went through her wardrobe, wondering which dress to wear that evening. Something he hadn't seen before. Love made her vain, coquettish. She felt sensual, excited by thoughts of making love to him. She brushed her hair until it shone and let it hang loose because he'd said he liked it best that way.

She dressed in a cream silk and wool dress that she'd nearly left behind because it was too smart for a country hotel. No jewellery on the dress except gold earrings. The top was cut tight to the figure, the skirt was draped at one hip and fell almost to her ankles. She twisted her cultured pearls round one wrist. She wanted to be beautiful for him. She didn't care how exotic she looked to the other guests.

The career diplomat, Rosa Bennet, always understated. She laughed out loud at her own reflection and at that moment the telephone rang. She hurried and picked it up.

'Mrs Bennet?' It was reception. Not Harry. Too early.

'Yes?'

'You've left the lights on in your car.'

'Oh damn! I'll have a flat battery . . . thanks, I'll come down right away.'

She found the car keys, picked up the bag that matched her dress and started down the stairs. The young porter could switch them off if she gave him the keys.

But he wasn't there. The boy had been summoned to Zarubin's room to bring down a locked case for safekeeping. There was nobody to take the key and go to the car park. She would have to go herself. It was cold, she thought, and hurried across the gravel, turned round the corner and passed under the trees that concealed the cars from view. It was nearly dark. How stupid to have forgotten the lights . . . but she was driving in daylight . . .

She must have turned the switch on by mistake. She reached her car and exclaimed in annoyance. No lights, nothing. And then she felt the man come up behind her, and swung round.

He loomed over her and she gasped out loud. The point of a knife touched her throat. The cry died away. 'Turn round,' Zarubin said. 'Don't make any noise. Put your hands behind your back.'

Rosa stared at him; he saw the shock in her face. 'Turn round,' he said again. 'If you do anything stupid I'll kill you.'

She moved, slowly until she faced away from him. He reached out and pulled her right arm behind her, gripping the wrist. The pearls broke and scattered on the ground. 'The other one,' he ordered. She had begun to tremble; she bent her left arm backwards and he seized it. He had a handkerchief ready with a slip knot. Her hands were tied.

She managed to whisper. 'What are you doing . . .? What do you want . . .?'

'Be quiet.'

He jabbed the knife into her back and she arched away from it. Zarubin opened the passenger door of the little Ford. He held her above the elbow and pushed her towards it. She couldn't resist. With her hands pinioned, she was off balance. 'Bend down,' he snapped at her. 'Get in.'

He forced her into the car, slamming the door shut; in a few seconds he was beside her. He looked at her; he showed her the knife and she shrank back. She saw his face in the semi-darkness and didn't dare to speak. He leaned a little towards her and brought something out of his pocket. He showed it to her on his palm.

The little camera. 'I'm taking you to see a friend,' he said softly. 'He's very interested in photography. He wants to ask you about this one. Are you going to scream, Mrs Bennet? Nobody will hear you if you do.'

Rosa shook her head. She managed to whisper. 'No.' The camera. He had been to her room and found the camera.

He'd put it away; he switched on the engine and put the car into gear, the knife was in his left hand, and the hand was close to her side.

'We haven't far to go,' he said. 'Just a little way.' She was as pale as the clothes she wore; he wondered if she would faint.

He drove carefully out of the car park, using dipped headlights, steering with one hand. He probed her with the knife when she moved in the seat and she froze. Down the drive, no on-coming car to see them; no chance of escape for her. There was a house ahead, she saw lights in the windows, felt the car slow and turn. When it stopped she found a little courage and spoke to him. 'Where are you taking me?'

'To meet my friend.' He got out, came round and opened her door. He reached in and pulled her out; she almost fell. The house was only a few paces away. She glanced round in a rising terror, wondering whether at this last moment she might scream and someone, somewhere would hear. The front door opened and she saw a man silhouetted against the light.

She wouldn't have cared if the knife was at her throat. She was overwhelmed with fear and it was focused on that black outline in the lighted doorway. Zarubin felt her go rigid and then jerk violently to get free. He sensed the scream of panic and slapped his hand over her open mouth. He bent her head brutally and forced her forward, up to the doorway into the light where the man was waiting.

'I'm ready,' Jan said. 'I packed a holdall, I left every-thing else.'

'Good man,' Oakham grinned reassuringly at him, but there was no smile in his eyes. 'We can treat ourselves when we get there. Money no object. I've booked us on the ten o'clock flight to Geneva.' He checked his watch. 'It's pushing it, but if we leave in the next fifteen minutes, we should get there in good time. You wait here. I've got something to do before I go.'

'Your lady?' Jan asked him.

'Yes.'

'She'll be questioned,' he pointed out. 'What are you going to say?'

'I'm not,' Harry answered. He had a note in his hand. A sealed envelope. 'I'm going to leave this for her. Here,' he picked up the little straw doll. 'Stick this in a bag for me will you. I'll take it with me. I won't be long.'

Jan saw the change of expression; the glimpse of pain was very brief. But very real. He loves her, Jan thought. The first woman to break Judith's spell. He said, 'Sorry, Harry.'

'Me too, but that's life,' Oakham answered. He said again, 'I won't be long.' He hurried down the stairs to the main hall.

It was warm and well lit, a huge arrangement of autumn foliage made a splash of vivid colour by the entrance. For a moment he paused, feeling a pang of regret as he saw his favourite, Jane, back on duty for the evening shift, smiling up at him as he approached. He was going to miss it all . . .

She was a nice kid; he wished her well for the future. He wondered what she'd think when the truth came out. He closed his mind to that. 'Jane,' he said and made his voice cheerful. 'Take this note up to Mrs Bennet will you?'

She took the note from him. 'Yes of course, Mr

Oakham.' Then she frowned slightly. 'But I haven't seen her come back,' she said.

'Back from where?' Harry had turned to go; he stopped and came back to her. They were due to meet in the bar. It was dark outside. Where had she gone?

'She went to the car park. Oh . . . quite a while ago. Mr Zarubin told us she'd left her lights on and I rang up to let her know. It must be nearly an hour now. I haven't seen her come in.'

Harry's old boss used to say there were people born with an instinct for danger. It was the best life insurance he knew. And Harry, a young protégé in those days, was one of the lucky ones. Zarubin. Rosa had gone to the car park because of his message nearly an hour ago and not come back. 'I'd better go and see; maybe she's trying to start the car.'

Jane watched him swing round and was surprised how quickly he crossed to the door and flew down the steps. She looked at the envelope addressed to Mrs Bennet. It was a real love affair between those two. She would have given a month's salary to know what was in that note.

12

She couldn't move. The small sallow man had strapped her in, frowning, the leather tight over her arms and across her chest. He had sour breath that sickened her as he leaned over her. The Russian stood with his back to the wall. He was leaning against it, smoking.

They'd brought her upstairs into this nightmare chamber and bound her into the dentist's chair. She'd begun to struggle wildly, and the small man had hit her across the face so hard that her senses blurred for a few moments, and her resistance ceased. Tears ran down her cheeks from the pain of the blow, and a trickle of blood joined them from her nostrils.

When it was done, the small man stepped back. He regarded her in complete silence for some time. A long, long time, it seemed to Rosa. When he spoke she jerked in nervous terror.

'You are spying on us,' he said. 'Who are you working for?' Interrogation hadn't been touched on in any depth during her training. She would never be involved in high-risk work where it was likely to occur. She was a civilized spy, listening, evaluating, passing information for analysis. Nothing frightening or dangerous. Eyes and ears open on the diplomatic circuit. Nothing like the assignment James Parker had given her.

She was so terrified she couldn't even think beyond a whispered denial. 'I'm not . . . Let me go . . . Oh, please . . .' The words died away, mocking her in the futility of their appeal.

'My friend found the camera,' Hermann Rilke spoke in his rasping high-pitched voice. 'I know you took pictures of people who came to the hotel. I want you to tell me why, and who sent you here.'

She couldn't answer. She tried to shake her head and speak but nothing came.

'You're wasting time,' Zarubin said. He could see that Rilke was enjoying the woman's distress. Sadism didn't arouse him. It didn't disgust him either. Indulging in it at the expense of getting information did.

'Get on with it,' he snapped. 'She'll break very quickly. Stop playing with her.' He turned and went to the door.

Rilke hesitated. He calmed his excitement. Zarubin was right. The woman wasn't capable of long resistance. There was no point in prolonging the process.

He spoke to Rosa. 'Very well. We're going to leave you. When I come back, I think you'll be ready to answer.' He walked to the door. Zarubin left first and he followed.

Rosa was alone. Then the room dissolved into blackness and the blackness began to spin.

Harry Oakham knew where Rosa parked her car. The area was quite full, with guests staying and restaurant bookings for dinner.

He found the BMW, with an empty space beside

it. No light, no sign of Rosa. Nothing. He moved and then stood very still. He had stepped on something. Something that crunched under his foot. He bent down, flicked his lighter.

The pearls were scattered on the ground. The broken rope lay like a silvery snake in the lighter flame. Rosa's pearls. He'd seen her wear them so often, and admired them. He remembered saying that pearls suited her skin, and then reached up to unfasten them and kiss her throat.

Zarubin had sent a false message and brought her down to the deserted car park. Her necklace had broken. A struggle . . . He went cold and rigid at what came into his mind.

Rosa, and the Russian coming on her in the darkness.

Zarubin's warning shouted in his head. 'She's hostile . . . She lied about the Adventure Trail . . .'

He'd seized her, Oakham was certain of it in those few seconds.

He didn't question, he didn't think beyond the surge of horror that swept up and over him in the chilly darkness.

Rosa . . . He was running, threading his way through the cars, out of the gravel on to the tarmac of the drive. He ran as he hadn't run since he left Bremen, with the Vopo patrol on his heels in 1982.

He ran down between the avenue of handsome beech trees, picked out by a car's headlights coming up to the hotel, swerving on to the grass to avoid it, and then back, pounding on the hard surface towards Croft Lodge.

Zarubin had taken her to Rilke.

Jan was worrying about the time. Fifteen minutes, Harry had said. Even then, they were cutting it fine to get to the airport and check in.

He tried to control his agitation. Harry knew what he was doing. Perhaps he'd met the woman, they must be together while he said goodbye . . . What a pity he had to lose her – he deserved to be happy, to put the past to rest with the dead girl in the churchyard at Dedham.

He sat down on the bed. The two holdalls were zipped up and ready. Harry was a fast driver, too fast for Jan's comfort, but even he wouldn't have a chance of getting to Heathrow unless he came back in the next few minutes.

Jan went to the tray in the sitting room and poured a drink. His nerves were playing up; his pulse rate was too fast, his breathing short.

Panic lurked in the corner of his mind, threatening to take over. He grabbed the phone and dialled reception. 'Put me through to Mrs Bennet,' he said.

What was Harry doing? Was he crazy, wasting time, losing the flight . . . He began to sweat and shake as he waited.

'I'm sorry, Mr Pollock, but there's no reply. She hasn't been in her room since about six o'clock. Mr Oakham was asking after her and I think he went to the car park to see if she was having trouble with her car.'

'Thanks,' Jan put the phone down. Something was wrong. He had never possessed Harry's magic gift for sensing danger before it materialized, but he had learned to anticipate it even if it never happened. That was part of the legacy of Cracow Special Unit.

At any hour, or any moment of the day or night, they came for you and it started all over again. You lived with fear.

Harry hadn't come. Ten o'clock was the last direct flight. He sat with the empty glass in his hand and gave way to a numb resignation. He couldn't run without Harry. He didn't even want to.

The blackness spun into a vortex. A cry that didn't sound human was torn from Rosa, without her knowing that she screamed. Long and agonizingly, as her body whirled against the force of gravity and her senses dissolved in panic, she screamed and screamed in the empty space till she lost consciousness.

Harry saw the lights on in the windows. He didn't try the front door. He flung himself at it, and burst the lock. He saw Zarubin come to the landing above him, and he heard the thin screaming like a sea bird's cry in the distance.

'Stay where you are,' the Russian said. He stood square blocking the way. Harry gathered himself. 'She's a spy,' Zarubin shouted at him. 'I found this in her room!' He threw something and instinctively Harry caught it. 'It's a camera . . . She was photographing everything. Don't make a bigger fool of yourself, Oakham. Leave it to Rilke!'

Harry looked down at the little oblong. He'd seen its like often before. He threw it aside. 'I'm coming up,' he said. 'Try and stop me and I'll kill you.'

He moved slowly now, balancing himself, ready for Zarubin to move. He had the advantage of Oakham because he was on the landing.

Zarubin slid his hand into his pocket and produced the Swiss Army knife. The blade gleamed in the overhead light. He heard Oakham laugh; it was a savage chuckle.

'That little toy doesn't frighten me. You're a desk man. Chess is your game. You know what mine is.' He was within two steps of Zarubin.

He was watching his eyes. They always signalled a move before the body acted. The sound of the cry was louder. It rose and then died suddenly. Zarubin held the knife in his right hand. He was watching Oakham's eyes.

He was fit and years younger and he had the advantage of level ground. But if he missed the first blow, he'd never live to strike a second one. He hadn't come there to die. He lowered the knife and stepped aside.

'Please yourself if you want to interfere,' he said. He shrugged in contempt. 'She's a plant,' he said. Oakham came level with him. 'They were right to retire you. You've gone soft in your old age.'

He never saw the blow. It caught him in the groin with all Oakham's weight behind it. He gasped and jack-knifed in agony, and as he bent double clutching his genitals, Harry Oakham smashed two hands down on his neck and snapped it at the base where the vertebrae ran into the spinal column. He died instantly and fell forward, his long body rolling down the stairs, the legs entangling in the banisters so that he didn't fall to the bottom. He lay caught up like a dead spider.

Rilke had stopped the chair. She'd passed out. It was time to go in and revive her. He heard the thud and bump as Zarubin crashed down the stairs and he called out sharply.

'Vassily? What are you doing?' He came down to look and met Harry Oakham face to face.

'He's dying,' Harry said softly. Rilke started back. He gasped and backed away. 'Open that door, you little bastard.' The voice was quiet, but there was a tremor in it. He looked crazy, Rilke thought, the eyes were bloodshot, mad. Rilke was not a coward but he had no chance of survival if Oakham attacked him. He kept his nerve and answered calmly.

'Zarubin was right. She was sent here to spy on you. I haven't hurt her. She's in there. See for yourself.' He pressed a knob in the wall and there was a loud click in the silence. 'It's unlocked,' he said.

Harry didn't move. 'Open it,' he ordered. Rilke moved forward and pushed the door aside. It was pitch dark inside. 'Light?' Harry came up very close to him. He said gently, 'Turn the light on, Hermann. I don't like the dark.' There was another switch.

There was a harsh fluorescent light in the ceiling. For a second or two it flared fitfully and then came fully alight.

'A spy,' Rilke's voice was close beside Oakham; he could smell the sweat off him and the acrid breath. 'She lied to you and made a fool of you, Harry. They sent her down here to watch you. It was a very old trick. There she is, if you want her . . . She's only fainted. Why don't you question her yourself?'

All he had to do was get Oakham through the door. His hand was on the panel of buttons, resting on the one that controlled the light. The locking mechanism was below it. Below that, the button that would send the chair spinning.

Rilke waited, willing Oakham to move forward, to see her tied in the chair, collapsed like a rag doll. He'd go when he saw that. He wouldn't be able to help himself.

When the telephone rang, Jan sprang up so quickly that he knocked his empty glass off the table. He gasped out 'Harry?' but it was the restaurant manager who spoke.

'Sorry to disturb you, but is Mr Oakham with you?'

'No,' Jan's lethargy lifted; the drink had worn off.

'Have you any idea where he is? He reserved a table for himself and Mrs Bennet for eight o'clock. I've been keeping it for him, but I'd like to let it go if he's not coming. I tried his house and Mrs Bennet's room but there's no reply from either. Have they gone out, do you know?'

Before Jan could answer, he went on, 'I do apologize for ringing, but I even tried Croft Lodge in case he was with Mr Brandt, but there was no-one at home.'

No-one at home. Rilke wasn't there. Rilke was always there. He never left the house to go anywhere in the evenings.

'It's one of those nights,' the restaurant manager said. He liked Jan and felt like relieving his feelings. 'I've had two dishes sent back, one noisy bugger who'd had too much to drink upsetting people at the next table, and customers trying to get in at the last minute when it's close to our last orders.

'I'll just have to give Mr Oakham's table away. And Mr Zarubin's – he hasn't shown up either and he's not in his room. I'll be glad when you're back on duty.'

The line buzzed clear before Jan put the phone down. Rilke wasn't at Croft Lodge. Zarubin had disappeared. Harry had gone out of the hotel to look for the girl and vanished.

He was in trouble. Jan stood up. His hands were sticky like his forehead with nervous sweat. Trouble. Harry wouldn't let him down, miss the flight . . . Jesus Christ, why had he wasted time, sitting there, boozing and feeling sorry for himself when Harry was in trouble?

He sprang up, stood for a moment, trying to remember where he kept it hidden.

Of course – bloody fool losing control of his memory – among the books in the shelf beside the fireplace. Which shelf? The top? He swept them all off and they clattered to the ground. Nothing there. Below then? Yes, that's where he'd put it. A small Luger, fully loaded. That was another legacy of Cracow Special Unit. He'd kept a gun ever since he was pensioned off. He'd used some of his meagre gratuity to buy it on the illegal firearms market. It made him feel safe. If anyone ever came for him again, he insisted, when the panics and the shaking started, he'd shoot himself before they got him. Not even Harry knew he had the gun.

Harry saw her in the harsh light. Her head hung to the side, strands of hair masking her face. He saw the straps biting into her arms and across her body and bloodstains on the front of the pale dress. He cried out, and as he did so, Rilke drew his right foot up, ready to kick the door shut. Harry Oakham didn't think, he launched himself into the room, calling out to her, reaching for her. He didn't even hear the door slam. 'Rosa . . . Rosa . . . Oh Christ . . .' His hands were fumbling with the straps. Before he had time to release one of them, he was almost jerked off his feet. The chair started moving, spinning against his weight. He shouted, just as the light above them flickered and died, leaving them in thick darkness.

Oakham was fighting the chair, throwing his weight against the movement, trying to slow it down, using his body as a counter weight.

The mechanism wasn't strong enough to throw him off, but his strength was taxed to the limit. The blackness disorientated him; he shut his eyes, fighting the sensory loss, straining to hold the chair in check. It juddered and rocked, and he heard a moan as Rosa regained consciousness.

He wasn't going to win. In the end, his body would tire and he'd have to let go. In the end, Rosa would die from shock.

Terror gave him a surge of strength that almost

stopped the chair; for a few seconds he halted it. If only he could do it again, he might jam the mechanism. But suddenly his muscles knotted in a vicious cramp, and his grip slackened. He lost his footing, his feet slithered on the ground. He held on in desperation, his body moving in a circle. But slower, much slower because of the double weight . . .

He hooked an arm round the back, feeling for the place where the strap joined the frame of the chair. He dug his fingers into the space, seeking a purchase strong enough to hold him. With his left arm he fumbled for the buckle that held her across the body, tearing at the strap, trying to pull it loose.

The strain on his right arm was becoming agony. The buckle was heavy, too heavy to yield without two hands. He couldn't free her.

He tried once more to bring the movement to a halt, fighting for a foothold on the floor. He couldn't get his balance; his arms and back were wrenched in pain, fighting a battle that he was slowly losing. He sobbed her name in the darkness and through the mist of nausea and terror, Rosa heard him.

Outside the door, Rilke had paused for a moment. It was a beautiful climax. A fitting finale. It would be a long time before anyone found them.

Oakham would hear her death throes, even if he couldn't see them. And he would be on his way to Portugal, and from there to Brazil.

Zarubin was right; Rilke had made his own arrangements. As soon as the team left for London, he had a private plane on standby at Ipswich Airport to fly him out if the mission failed.

From Portugal to Brazil. A new life, papers, and a lot of money transferred from Switzerland. His mother would love living in a warm climate.

He turned away and started down the stairs. Zarubin's body hampered him; he was heavy to move and Rilke heaved for some minutes, cursing with the effort. In the end he succeeded in dislodging a leg from between the banisters and the Russian slid down and fell in a heap at the bottom.

Rilke stepped over him. As he did so, Jan came through the open front door.

Croft Lodge. There had been no reply from Croft Lodge. Rilke was missing; Zarubin gone. Harry had said he wasn't going to warn them. They must have found out. And God knew what they would have done to Harry if they'd caught him unawares.

Jan reasoned it all out as he ran to the car park with Harry's car keys in one hand, and the other gripping the Luger in his pocket.

Croft Lodge was the place to look first. He drove at seventy down the long drive, crashing over the speed bumps, crouching at the wheel, just keeping control. He was too tense to notice the hideous noise. He had broken the exhaust loose when he hit a bump and the engine was roaring like an express train.

He saw the lights on at the house and brought the car to a skidding halt that half turned it round. He jumped out. The front door was open. He shook violently with nerves. Then he started to run.

*　　*　　*

Rilke looked at the gun. The Pole was holding it in both hands, pointing it at him. It wavered even so.

He was trembling, breathing hard. Panic was near, Rilke saw that. When it climaxed it could make him shoot, or drop the gun and collapse.

'Give me that!' He spoke loudly in a voice of command. 'Give me that at once!'

He took a step towards Jan. He knew all about conditioned reflexes. He had made a special study of the technique when he was breaking a man's mind and spirit. Ten years in Cracow Prison under the regime of the Special Unit would have conditioned the Pole to obey any order given in that tone of voice. Instinctively.

And that was all Rilke needed. Just one automatic reflex, and he would disarm him.

Jan looked at him. Sweat was running down his face, his eyes stung. His body felt as if it might snap with tension. It shook out of his control.

Obey. You heard the order. Obey!

The beatings followed. The kicks, the days spent lying in your own filth. He glanced down for a second at Zarubin's body, huddled awkwardly a few feet away. Harry had been there. Harry must be dead or Rilke wouldn't be alive. Dead . . .

He took a deep, deep breath and pulled the trigger. He watched Rilke fall as if it were a film scene shot in slow motion. He fired again as the body hit the floor; it twitched and the mouth opened . . .

Jan stepped close and stared down at Rilke. He had killed Harry . . . He went on shooting, and now the bullets were hitting every guard who'd beaten him and the officers who'd stood and watched them do it. The gun was empty. It was very quiet after all the noise. He slipped the Luger back into his pocket.

He filled his lungs with air. He had stopped shaking. It was strange but he felt calm. He stepped over Rilke's body. Then he heard the sound. Coming from above.

Oakham heard the shots. They were muffled, but he heard them. They cracked and cracked as if someone was letting off fireworks. He gathered his strength and shouted at the top of his voice.

'Help me,' Harry was gasping for breath. 'Help me get her out . . .' It was Jan who wrestled the biggest straps free while Harry clawed at the ones tying her arms. She fell forward and Harry caught her.

'It's all right,' he kept saying. 'It's all right, darling. Just hang on to me.' Jan helped her to stand, but her legs buckled.

'I've been sick,' she moaned. 'Oh God . . .' They held her while she retched helplessly.

'Doesn't matter,' Harry comforted, 'Don't worry, it'll stop in a minute.'

Over his head Jan said, 'Did you know about this?'

'No.' Oakham had got his breath back. He met Jan's eye. 'I didn't. It was his show, I let him get on with it. I didn't *want* to know.' He steadied Rosa. She couldn't stand. He drew her arm round his neck and supported her round the waist. He said to Jan, 'We've got to get a doctor.'

On the landing outside he whispered gently to her, 'Rosa? Darling, listen to me.'

She tried to look at him; everything was blurred, nausea threatened again as she tried to focus and stop the sensation that everything was going round and round.

'I want you to keep your eyes shut,' he said. 'Just hold tight to me, we're going downstairs but you mustn't open your eyes. Understand? Tight shut and don't worry, you won't fall.'

He didn't want her to see the dead bodies. No more shocks. He could only pray that she hadn't been tortured for too long.

He dared not think she might be permanently damaged. He held her close, guiding her carefully down the stairs with Jan ahead of them.

The Pole was heaving the bodies to one side. The floor was slippery with Rilke's blood.

On the level Harry swung Rosa up into his arms. There was pain in every joint and muscle but he didn't care. He carried her like a child out into the clean night air.

'All right,' he murmured to her, 'open your eyes now. We're outside and it's dark. We'll drive back to the hotel and get a doctor for you. It's all over. You'll be all right now.'

She didn't answer. She raised her head to look at him and it drooped as she lost consciousness.

Oakham panicked. 'Rosa! Christ . . .'

Jan said quietly, 'She's passed out. It's a good thing. Nature's remedy when it gets too much. *She's not dead*, Harry . . .'

Not like Judith, whom he'd carried down from the ski slopes in his arms, with her neck broken. He caught Harry's arm and guided him to the car. 'Put her in the front,' he suggested. 'It's easier.'

They came through the door, supporting Rosa between them. She'd recovered consciousness and was able to walk a few steps when Harry set her down outside the hotel.

Jane gasped when she saw them. 'Oh my God!' She ran from behind her desk to help. 'Mrs Bennet – what's happened?'

'She's had an accident,' Harry explained. 'Phone through for Dr Harris – tell him to come right away!'

Jane was staring at Rosa. Her face was ashen, her eyes half closed as if she was going to faint. The lovely dress was spotted with blood and streaked with sour vomit.

'Oh my God,' she said again. 'I'll get through right away.'

Jan spoke over his shoulder. 'It's not as bad as it looks, don't worry.' Harry was holding Rosa upright by the lift door. It was on an upper floor. He swore, feeling Rosa sag against him.

'Do you want me to come up?' Jane called after them; she was on the telephone waiting for an answer.

'No, I'll look after her,' Harry answered. 'Just get the doctor!'

'The surgery's closed,' Jane said. 'I'll try the emergency number. Dr Frazer's on duty . . . I just hope he's not out on a call.' They had gone into the lift, and she hesitated. Perhaps she should call an ambulance if there wasn't a doctor available for some time . . . The poor thing, she looked so dreadfully ill.

She spoke into the receiver. Dr Frazer was on a call but his wife would get him on the car phone if it was really urgent. Yes, Jane insisted, it was. One of the guests had had an accident. How long would he be . . .? The doctor's wife promised to ring back.

Upstairs Rosa felt him lift her and lay her on a bed. But everything was blurred, and the nausea came over her in waves. She knew he had undressed her; she heard him murmuring to her, telling her she was safe, to just relax, let him look after her.

She rolled on her side and retched over the edge of the bed. It was a convulsion of her empty stomach, and it ended with a rage that shook her whole body. Harry pulled the quilt off the bed and wrapped her in it. He held her in his arms, trying to warm her and minimize the shock.

Jan went into the bathroom and wrung out a towel in hot water. 'Here,' he said. 'Wipe her face with that.'

I'll shake to death, Rosa thought. The warm towel touched her swollen cheek and she winced. She was aware of Harry Oakham's strength, of the hand stroking her hair, and his voice, urging her to breathe deeply, ride it out. It would stop soon.

And then the crisis peaked and the shaking became a continuous tremble. She was safe and he was holding her. She couldn't think beyond that. Tears welled up suddenly, and she began to cry.

'Thank God for that,' Harry said, 'Good girl, cry it out.'

Jan said quietly to him, 'She'll be all right now. The worst is over.' He knew a lot about shock and what it did to people.

She didn't know how long she cried for; like the shaking fit, it was beyond her control. Then it ended in sobbing and exhaustion. And clarity of mind began returning, as her sense of balance adjusted.

She could open her eyes and her surroundings weren't spinning as if she were in a vortex. Harry had rescued her. Harry had saved her. She wanted to sleep, not think. Just shut her eyes and drift away from the horror. But something was fighting the temptation. Something that wouldn't let her escape.

Harry. Harry was part of the horror. Part of the nightmare. Rilke's face loomed up in her mind, the skin dewed with excited sweat as he wrenched the straps tight across her body.

You're a spy. Who sent you to spy on us . . . the Russian's voice echoed in her head, the words running into each other. The sudden plunging into darkness and then the terror of the whirling, spinning . . . *Harry was one of them.* She gave a low cry, and immediately he gathered her close. 'What is it, darling? Tell me . . . Is it dizziness?'

Rosa opened her eyes and looked at him. She wasn't dizzy. The room was still, his face in clear focus. She said, forcing the words from a throat racked by screaming. 'Why did you stop them?'

Harry Oakham answered gently. 'Don't try to talk. Just stay quiet. The doctor's on his way – Jan, for Christ's sake ring down and see what's keeping him!'

There was no drawing back from reality for Rosa now, no more comfort in his arms. 'Let go of me,' she whispered. 'Don't touch me.'

Jan was speaking to Jane on the telephone. He heard Rosa say it, and he saw Oakham draw into himself as if he'd been struck. Jane's voice was in his ear. 'Dr Frazer's on his way,' she was saying. 'He'll be here in half an hour – he's out at Woodbridge. Should I call an ambulance? How is she?'

'Better,' Jan answered. 'We'll wait for the doctor.'

Harry said, 'Jan – leave us a minute, will you? Why don't you go to the bar and get us both a drink?'

Jan didn't answer. He looked at Rosa. She had her head turned away from them. She said it again. 'Don't touch me. Go away, please.'

A slow flush of anger spread over Jan's face. He had never lied to Harry but he lied then. He said, 'I'm not feeling too well. I can't go downstairs. I'll watch her, you get the drinks. I could do with one . . .' He let his voice break.

'I'm sorry—' Harry was on his feet, he'd done as Rosa asked. He had laid her back on the bed and covered her with the blankets. 'I'm sorry Jan, what a stupid, selfish bugger, after what you did . . . I'll get a brandy. You sit tight, I won't be long. What did Jane say?'

'He'll be here in half an hour,' Jan answered. He knew what it meant when Harry looked like that, with the strain round his eyes and the mouth pulled tight against pain. He'd seen it so often after Judith.

The door closed. He went close to the bed and looked at Rosa.

'You shouldn't have said that. He saved your life. You don't know him. You've got no right to judge.'

He was the man Parker had told her to look out for, the Pole who had been Oakham's friend and comrade in the Service. They always worked together, Parker said.

'You're his friend, Ploekewski,' she mumbled. 'He lied about you too.'

'I'm more than his friend,' Jan answered. 'I love him the best of anyone I've ever known. You lied to *him*, didn't you? He trusted you. But that doesn't count.'

'He knows about me?' Rosa saw the anger in his face.

'He knows, but he doesn't care. He loves you. Just like he loved Judith. When you passed out tonight, he nearly cracked. He thought you were dead. Like she was. They murdered her. Did you know that?'

It was very sudden. The bed shifted under her. She cried out in distress as everything lurched.

Murdered. She heard herself repeat it. 'Murdered . . .'

He had no pity, he didn't spare her. He'd shocked her but that was what he intended.

'Yes. They were out to get Harry. The Russians played it rough in those days. She'd borrowed his ski hat. It was yellow and black. One of her jokes – she'd given it to him. They sent a man out to Verbier. He caught up with Judith on the slope. He thought it was

351

Harry. Hit her with a ski stick, broke her neck.'

He sat down on the edge of the bed. He hardly seemed to see her as he talked, or to care if she was listening, he was lost in Harry's old agony.

He went on. 'It was all hushed up, the Service didn't want any fuss. The skier just disappeared down the mountain. I took care of Harry afterwards. I stopped him drinking himself to death. He tried to shoot himself once. He was crazy with grief. Blamed himself . . . Paying them back was the only thing he wanted to live for. And it suited some people to let a man in that state loose. So they gave him the dirty, dangerous jobs and he did them. I went through the worst of it with him, and when I got caught, they put him behind a desk after a year or so.' He turned his attention to her again.

'They didn't tell you all this when they sent you down here? No, I don't suppose they would . . . Things like that are best forgotten. He'll be back in a minute. If he hadn't gone after you, we'd have been safe and out of the country by now. He killed Zarubin to save you. I killed Rilke. So you owe both of us.'

She felt numb, but the moment of panic had passed while he was talking. She lay very still, completely drained. After a moment she asked, 'What do you want me to do?'

'Make him go,' Jan answered. 'Give him a chance to get away. And take back what you said to him. If you can, it would help.'

'I'll try,' she said slowly. 'When he comes back, leave us alone.'

The door opened; Harry gave Jan a glass of brandy. 'This'll set you right,' he said. 'You cunning old sod, I never knew you had a gun – good man for shooting the swine . . .' Suddenly he flung an arm round Jan's shoulder and hugged him fiercely. 'Best back-up in the business.'

Jan swallowed a large part of the drink. The room was quiet; Oakham hesitated for a moment and then sat down in a chair.

'I'll go down and wait for the doctor,' Jan announced and before Harry could say anything, he had gone out, leaving him and Rosa alone.

'Harry?'

He got up and came slowly to stand close to her. He said, 'Yes, darling?'

With an effort Rosa drew one hand out of the covers and held it out to him. 'Sit down with me.'

He caught hold of it, clasping it between his own two hands. The fingers were cold and he rubbed them gently.

'I didn't mean that,' Rosa said. 'Forgive me. Please.'

'Nothing to forgive,' he answered. 'I deserved it.'

'I lied to you too,' her voice was very low. Tears filled her eyes and slipped down her face.

'I know, but it doesn't matter. You were only doing your job, I understand that. I always did mine, till I went wrong. Nothing matters except you're going to be all right.' He brought her hand up and kissed it. 'Silly thing, leaving the camera in your room . . . didn't train you very well, did they?' It hurt unbearably to look at him, to see the tenderness in his face. 'I'm sorry about all the lies, my darling, but I do love you. That was true. Can you forgive me?'

'Don't say that,' she said. 'I don't want you to be caught, Harry. Please, please try and get away . . . I couldn't bear it.'

'Come on now,' he chided, 'no more tears. It's all blown anyway, nothing to do with you. One of our chums got picked up and he's talking his head off to the police at this moment. I should think they're on their way here by now. I don't give a damn what happens to me, but Jan couldn't take being locked up. Not again. He was in solitary for ten years. I've got to try and get him away somewhere safe.'

'Then go now,' she forced strength into her voice. 'Tonight – don't wait! I beg of you. If you really care about me, you'll go . . .'

'Oh I really care,' he answered. 'Can you give us a little time?' She couldn't find the words. She nodded, and for a moment pressed the hand holding hers.

'They'll be watching the airports,' he said. 'Jan's buggered my car – but we just might make it. Don't hold out on them when they get here, will you? You don't want them breathing down your neck after it's over. Look out for yourself; nobody plays by the rules in the game. Promise?'

'Yes, promise,' she managed.

'Goodbye, Rosa darling,' he said. 'Pity I didn't meet you a few months ago. We might have ended up in Brussels after all. I think I hear the doctor coming.' There was a tap on the door and it opened.

Harry came to meet the young man, his medical bag in one hand, the other responding to Harry's handshake.

'Good of you to come, Doctor. Mrs Bennet's had rather a nasty experience. She'll tell you about it.'

13

'Mr Oakham?' Jane's eyes opened wide. 'Are you going somewhere? How's Mrs Bennet?' They were standing side by side, nice Mr Pollock and Mr Oakham, with overnight zip-up bags, saying good-bye to her. The doctor hadn't even come down.

'I'm afraid,' Harry smiled at her in his friendly way, 'that something has come up and we've been called away. And Mrs Bennet's fine. The Doctor says she must have eaten something and collapsed in the car park. Lucky I looked for her. But she'll be up and about by tomorrow.'

'Where are you going? When will you be back? I hope it's nothing wrong . . . ' She kept shaking her head as if she couldn't believe it. Going, just like that. Both of them. She said it again, 'But when will you be back, Mr Oakham?'

'I'll let you know,' Harry answered. 'We must go now, or we'll miss the last train. You be a good girl and look after everything for me.'

And to Jane's astonishment, he leaned across and pecked her on the cheek. Outside, as they hurried down the steps, Jan said, 'Where are we going, Harry? What train? Why did you say that?'

Oakham had left the car parked outside by the entrance. He swung into the driver's seat and started the engine. The noise swelled into a roar as they drove off.

'What exactly did you have for lunch?' the doctor asked.

She was suffering from dehydration and shock. There were a lot of ugly bruises round her chest and on her face. Food poisoning could cause a black-out. A nasty fall, severe vomiting attacks and diarrhoea might just account for her condition. *Just*. Still she insisted it was food poisoning. It was not his job to argue. She did look in a very bad way, he had to admit, although he'd expected to find something worse judging by the way the hotel had panicked. But then they would. And they did pay the practice a retainer.

'Oysters,' he heard Rosa mumble.

'Oh well, that accounts for it. You get a bad one of those and you'd really be in trouble. Now there's nothing more to do for you at the moment. I expect you've got rid of it all by now. Try to sleep and if you must drink something, only take a sip at a time or you'll be sick again. I'll pop in and see how you are in the morning.'

He'd shut his bag and gone out, irritated that she hadn't even thanked him for coming. He'd been called away from an expectant mother with grumbling labour pains. He didn't have much time for the ailments of people rich enough to stay at Doll's House Manor and stuff themselves with oysters.

When he had gone, Rosa lay with her eyes closed against the shaded bedside light. Sleep. Oblivion. A merciful reprieve till the morning. But it wouldn't come. She lay in the shell of her exhausted body and couldn't still her mind.

He'd asked her to give him time. Time to escape justice for murder and treason. And she'd given it, because he'd risked his own life to save her. And because she loved him. That was why she couldn't sleep. She waited, feeling time as a tangible thing. She fell asleep very suddenly when her last reserve of strength ran out. When she woke there was daylight outside and the light was still shining a pale yellow by the side of the bed.

She pulled herself up slowly and painfully, weaker than any kitten in the cliché, and reached out for the telephone. Then she dialled Jim Parker's direct line.

The noise of the broken exhaust made it impossible to talk. Jan shouted at him as they drove down the drive, 'Where are we going, Harry, for Christ's sake?' But Harry didn't answer. Suddenly he swung off the tarmac and on to a narrow lane across the parkland. They bumped and roared on the uneven ground in the darkness, the headlights sweeping past trees, and ahead Jan saw the glimmering water of the lake.

The ground sloped down quite steeply and Harry braked sharply and switched off the engine, dousing the lights.

'Get the bags out,' he said briskly. 'We're going to need them. Then get behind and help me push!'

'We can't get away on foot. You're crazy, Harry. Wait!'

'Haven't got time,' was the answer. 'Bags out?

Right, now get behind, I'm going to let the hand-brake off. Now – push!'

Side by side they used their weight and all their strength and after a moment the car began to move, rolling gently and then gathering momentum as it ran down the slope under its own impetus. They stood back, breathless with the effort.

The car hit the water surface. There was a loud splash as it disappeared. Harry Oakham climbed down after it and stood watching the air bubbles streaming up as the car's interior filled and sank deeper until it came to rest.

'It's twenty feet deep,' he said. 'I had it dredged out. It could sit there for a long time. Come on, Jan, grab your bag. We're going back.'

'Back there?' Jan looked over his shoulder at the outline of the hotel, the lighted windows glowing in the distance.

'The one place they won't be looking for us,' Oakham said quietly, and began to run at a long, steady pace that he knew Jan could follow.

'Keep to the back,' he hissed, and turned through the rose garden. Jan stumbled and he stopped and helped him. 'All right?'

'Yes,' the Pole whispered. The big dining-room windows were curtained, but shafts of light cut across the darkness.

Harry moved very carefully, keeping to the deepest shadows, skirting the ornamental paths, making for the thick shrubbery that led round to the rear of the hotel. He stopped, grabbing Jan, and they crouched low, sheltering behind a tall yew hedge that separated the kitchen garden. Voices. Some of the kitchen staff on their way to their cars in the staff car park. It was late, soon the last customers would leave and the residents make their way to their rooms.

'Come on,' Jan heard him whisper. He was out of breath; he wasn't fit like Harry. He was afraid and confused; his self-confidence had gone as the car sank out of sight and their only means of escape disappeared with it.

As if Oakham knew what he was feeling, he said quietly, 'Trust me, you old sod; I did a bit of forward planning. It's clear, come on.'

The service door was open. Harry whispered to him, 'We just made it. They lock up at twelve fifteen sharp.' He looked round, listening for any footfall, any sound of someone coming through from the main building. Then, beckoning Jan, he started up the service stairs.

They came from London in their unmarked cars. No flashing lights or squealing sirens to announce them.

They were all armed except Jim Parker. He didn't know how to use a gun. The sky was turning grey in the chill pre-dawn hours; a rim of crimson came up the horizon, reminding Parker of the old adage, 'Red sky at night, sailor's delight, red sky in the morning, sailor's warning.'

There wouldn't be any warning for Harry Oakham and the rest of his unholy allies. Daniel Ishbav had betrayed them all and turned Queen's evidence. Not that it guaranteed his life. But he could *try* and run from his own people. Parker's colleague had allayed the scruples of the Detective Chief Inspector at making such a deal.

He'd assured him that Ishbav hadn't a snowball's chance in hell once he was out of custody. Stevenson and his thugs had been picked up in the East End. They weren't talking, but they would when they were confronted by Daniel.

The one thing Daniel wouldn't talk about was money. Where were the payments made? Who was the paymaster? Hoping to live to enjoy it. Parker sneered at the idea.

They'd get that out of the Pole, if Oakham and the others proved obdurate. The Pole wouldn't stand up to being in a cell waiting to be questioned. He'd crack.

Rilke – Zarubin; Parker was thinking of them all as he drove along the deserted dual carriageway towards Ipswich, with his armed Special Branch in convoy.

Strange bedfellows, united by greed and inhumanity. Hermann Rilke, the loathsome product of perverted mother love.

The sadistic intelligence chief and the chess-playing KGB strategist, servants of a political tyranny that had crumbled with the wall which was its symbol. No place for such people now . . .

Perhaps we are becoming civilized at last, Parker thought, watching the sunrise and the countryside bathed in the red light. Perhaps.

It was worth hoping for, at least. They'd be there very soon.

He had refused to worry about Rosa Bennet. She'd be sleeping safely in her bed when they surrounded the place. She'd found nothing, suspected nothing. Her routine calls had established that.

An amateur dealing with supreme professionals. It would be useful experience for her. They were at the turn-off for Higham when the car phone rang. His assistant listened and then passed it back to him. 'It's for you, sir. Routed through from London. Emergency call sign. Mrs Bennet.'

Harry watched the dawn. Jan was asleep beside him, worn out, poor devil. He hadn't liked the cramped little space and the darkness.

Harry had risked lighting the torch, and taken out two of the loose bricks so he could see a bit of sky. Jan slept on, his head pillowed on the soft bag. He'd manage; Harry'd calmed him. Only a few days lying low.

After all, he was a Papist, he shouldn't be scared of a priest's hole.

They'd been cunning, those old Catholics, building a doll's house as a front, putting some dug up bones on view to frighten off the local militia when they searched for a priest on the run for his life. The curse was a nice touch. No local yokel would be bold enough to risk being struck dead by running a pike through it. Very clever of the Lisle family.

In time, the reason behind the legend was lost; the doll's house was glassed in, preserved with its lie undiscovered. The space built into the huge chimney stack was cramped enough for one man, but he and

Jan would manage. He'd found the air brick when he explored the roof, interested by the thickness of the wall and the shallow depth of the doll's house. An air brick meant exactly that. A brick that could be moved so someone could breathe fresh air. It had been cemented in by some bricklayer in the past who thought it was merely loose. Loose like the others near by, laid in the English bond pattern.

They'd all been cemented together, but the filling was old and crumbling and it hadn't been difficult for Harry to lever them out, a few at a time until he could see what was behind them.

Jan stirred uneasily and then woke. 'Harry? Harry—'

'I'm here,' he said quickly. 'It's daylight outside. Look.'

Jan stared up at the little square of rose sky. He hated the confined space. It made him sweat and shake. But Harry said it wasn't for long.

A priest's hole. Good men had hidden there to escape the dreadful Tudor penalty for treason. He shouldn't be afraid, but he was.

Harry had guided him up on the roof and taken out the bricks one by one till there was a space big enough for them to wriggle through.

Harry had talked him out of panic, made a hole that he could focus on, and told him the story of how he'd found the hiding place. And provisioned it with tins of food and drink and a torch in case history repeated itself . . . Harry thought of everything.

'You think they'll come today?' Jan whispered.

'I'd bet on it,' Harry answered. 'Any minute.

They'll look for evidence, take statements, and all they'll know is we left in a car with a busted exhaust pipe to catch a train. They won't buy the train theory, but they've nothing else to go on. And when they go to Croft Lodge, that'll concentrate their minds.'

'What about her – does she know anything?'

'No,' Harry said. 'No, nothing. I didn't ask her to lie for me, Jan. It wouldn't have been right. And she wouldn't have done it. She's very honest. That's one of the things that made her special.'

In the gloom he looked at his old friend and he managed to smile. 'A few days, that's all. Till they've gone. Then we'll slip out during the night. We've got passports, money . . . We'll get the ferry to Ireland. Fishguard to Rosslare. It's a filthy sea crossing if it's rough. But you're a good sailor . . . Look, the sun's coming up. We'll make it. Don't worry.'

'I don't need a medical check-up,' Rosa protested. 'I'm all right!'

'You let me be the judge of that,' Jim Parker stood up. 'I'm sending you down to Branksome by car. The quacks will give you a proper examination.' He always called doctors quacks. His father used the term because the medical profession tended to condescend to dentists in his time.

'When they give you a clean bill of health I'll send someone down to debrief you. I'll be busy trying to sort out this mess here for a few days. Then I'll come myself.'

He took out a packet of cigarettes. 'Could you manage one of these?'

She shook her head. 'No – no thanks.' The idea made her feel sick. She was a dreadful colour, with huge black pits under the eyes. She'd had a rough time, very rough. He put the cigarette back in the packet. He'd come back from Croft Lodge.

The room on the top floor bore witness to her ordeal. The chair turned his stomach. The dead bodies had no effect upon him.

A broken neck. That was Oakham's hallmark, but loosing off half a dozen bullets into a man already dying was someone different. The Pole, Jan Ploekewski. Found his courage and lost his head.

Oakham had changed sides. To save Rosa Bennet. That was what she'd told him, and he believed her. And he and the Pole had got clear away from the hotel in the aftermath.

She was looking a little better than when he first saw her but not much. She couldn't stand up to questioning in depth. That would come later, when she was pronounced fit enough. Someone else would do it. 'I don't want to go to Branksome,' she insisted. Her head was thudding with a headache that resisted aspirins and the weak tea she'd been given. One of Parker's men had brought it up to her with some dry biscuits. The hotel was in limbo.

The staff and the guests were being questioned in relays; the flat and the house occupied by the manager and his assistant were being taken apart by a team of experts.

'Be a good girl,' Parker said kindly, 'and don't argue. I'm still your boss and I'm not taking any chances with you after last night's little episode. You need rest and peace of mind, and Branksome's the ideal place.'

'It's a debriefing centre,' she said wearily. 'I did my course there. I know it.'

'It's also for convalescence,' he said. 'Just a week at the most, people to look after you, a total break from this . . .' he gestured with one hand. 'Get it out of your system.'

He smiled at her and leaning forward, gave her hand a little squeeze. 'You were bloody brave,' he said. 'And I'm really sorry it got so rough. I want to make it up to you.' She didn't answer.

She couldn't fight him, she was too weak. If he said she was going to Branksome, that's where she would be taken.

After a while he got up. 'Well,' he said. 'I suppose we must be thankful it's over. One dead Saudi's bad enough; God knows what they'd have pulled off next. And you never suspected, did you, Rosa?'

'No,' she said, 'I didn't. I was completely fooled.'

'And you can't think of anything else, any clue where they might have gone?' He asked it casually in a gentle tone.

'I told you. He said something about the car. That's all.'

'Yes, well,' he buttoned his jacket, pulled it straight. 'His car's gone. We've a full description. I don't think they'll get far. We've got the country sealed up tight, airports, ports, everything. But don't you think about it. You did your best. I'll send someone to give you a hand getting dressed and packing your things. Try and sleep.' He went out, closing the door quietly.

Outside he lit the cigarette. Oakham had called a doctor. She hadn't told him the truth. Food poisoning. She'd lied. She could have asked him to call Parker, but she hadn't. She'd waited till morning, till Oakham had taken off. He knew the very man to send down to Branksome to ask her why.

14

He was a quiet-spoken man. About forty, dressed in tweeds, with a slight Scots burr in his voice. He could have been a country solicitor, an estate agent, anything but what she knew he really was.

He'd introduced himself after she'd been at Branksome for five days. Peter Mackay. They'd shaken hands and he'd said how glad he was to get the medical reports. She'd recovered remarkably well from the terrible ordeal. He congratulated her on the psychiatric assessment. She had come out of it without any traumas. Rosa thanked him, and said, yes, she was still fairly shaky but she would soon be back to normal, and was quite ready to go home.

He offered her a strong mint, which she refused. He had taken to them while giving up smoking. Now *they'd* become a habit, and he smiled at his own weakness as he put the packet in his pocket.

He was a man who dealt in pauses. He had stayed quiet after talking about his addiction to mints for a long time, as if he was thinking about it. And then he looked up and said, 'Of course, the reason you got off so lightly was because Oakham interrupted the torture session. Isn't that right?'

'Yes,' Rosa answered. 'I suppose so.'

'I think you said he was trying to stop the chair using his own body weight.'

'I know he slowed it down, but I don't know what he was doing . . . it was pitch dark and I was completely disorientated. I just knew he was trying to help me.'

'Of course, he was a very strong man,' Peter Mackay remarked. 'Even so, it was remarkable that he managed to do what he did. It certainly avoided permanent damage to the balancing mechanism of your brain. Of course, it's a fact that extreme emotion can double physical strength. An angry man is far stronger than a calm one. So is someone who's desperate. And he was desperate to stop you being tortured. You did a good job, you know.'

'I failed completely,' Rosa said slowly. 'I found out nothing; I don't know why you say that.'

'Because it's true. It was a very difficult task for someone without experience. Of course, you made mistakes – like making Zarubin suspicious. And leaving your camera in such an obvious hiding place. That was a bad lapse,' he conceded. 'It could have been fatal.'

Rosa thought, He's needling me. What is this . . . ?

'Now he was the odd man out, you know. Zarubin. He didn't quite fit in with people like Rilke and Ishbav, for instance. We've been tipped off he was a KGB plant. We've a friend in their embassy. They wanted someone in Oakham's team to keep an eye on Soviet interests. Frustrate any plan that might not suit their policies. And killing a pro-American Saudi who was in line to be King, would have been good news from their point of view. So he went along with it. Helped, in fact, from what the Israeli tells

369

us. Would you like a cup of tea or something, Mrs Bennet? You're looking a bit tired.'

'No thank you, I'm fine.'

'So it looks as if that particular leopard hasn't changed too many spots. Of course your real success was identifying those Irish terrorists. Did Jim Parker mention that? Oh, no, well I expect he will, but I'd like to congratulate you on my own behalf. I've had a lot to do with that problem.

'We picked them up, thanks to your photographs. Trailed them through to an isolated cottage in Armagh. The security forces surrounded the place and they were all arrested. Plenty of evidence, detonators, Semtex, small arms buried in the garden. A room with a dentist's chair. Is this upsetting you?'

He looked concerned. 'Then let's change the subject. Sir Peter Jefford was very complimentary about you. In fact, looking on the bright side, you've done your career prospects a power of good.'

'If you say so,' Rosa answered. She thought suddenly, If he takes another mint out and starts eating it, I'm going to scream . . .

'You'll be going to Brussels, I believe, as soon as you're ready. It's a lovely city. It'll be most interesting. Tell me, how long after you arrived at the hotel did you and Oakham become lovers?'

She looked up sharply, caught off guard. 'I've already given Jim Parker a report.'

'I know,' he said cheerfully, 'I've read it. I'm just dotting the Is and crossing the Ts, that's all. You were very clever making him fall in love with you;

it can't have been easy with a man like that. Was he a good lover?'

Rosa felt a deep flush spread across her face; she felt wildly angry as she looked into the mild eyes with their friendly enquiry.

'There's no need to be embarrassed,' he went on. 'Enjoying sex is not a crime.'

'I'm not in the least embarrassed. I think the question's irrelevant and I don't intend to answer it.'

'Do sit down, Mrs Bennet,' he said. 'So I can assume that he was a good lover. Please – just a few more questions, and they are relevant, I promise you. He fell in love with you, but you didn't fall in love with him. Is that right?' He didn't wait for an answer.

'Of course you were vulnerable; marriage just broken up, a very unsettling experience for any attractive woman. He had a lot of charm, our friend Harry . . . devil-may-care, I heard someone say about him once. Nice old-fashioned description but it's apt . . . You were given a wide brief, after all. If you had to sleep with him in the line of duty, so be it. But you weren't in love with him.'

Rosa clenched both hands at her sides to stop herself slapping him across his blandly inquisitive face. 'I deny that absolutely. I object to this sort of inquisition, Mr Mackay, and I'm not going to put up with it. Will you please leave!'

He didn't move. He crossed one leg slowly over the other and settled deeper into his chair.

'If you weren't in love with him, why did you help him get away?'

She caught a breath. 'How dare you say that! How dare you accuse me!'

'Your instructions were to call Parker in a crisis,' he remarked. 'Why didn't you do it till the next morning?'

She glared at him, and tears came into her eyes. She blinked them back and said in a voice that shook with anger, 'Have you *any* idea of the state I was in after being in that chair? I'd vomited my insides out – I'd wet myself – I was half conscious! You think I could have used a telephone? Have you ever shaken so badly you thought you'd die if it didn't stop? No, I bet you haven't or you wouldn't talk to me like this!'

He said sadly, 'You were well enough to lie to the doctor . . . Dr Frazer showed us his notes. Food poisoning, oysters, isn't that what you told him? Why did you lie, Mrs Bennet? Why didn't you ask him to call Parker's number for you?'

'I told you – I was shattered, I couldn't even think straight.'

She was quieter now, seeing the trap and trying to retreat, he decided.

'You bought time for Oakham, didn't you? Was it because he'd saved your life?' He'd given her a way out.

'I don't know. I don't know . . .'

'I think you do,' he countered. 'You're a very decisive lady, and a tough one. I think you knew exactly what you were doing. You were letting him run for it.

'Do cry if you want to, don't mind me. It can

be a great help sometimes. Why not trust me, Mrs Bennet? You're an intelligent lady, and ambitious. You don't want to ruin your future for the sake of Harry Oakham. He's a liar, a traitor to his country, a murderer . . . He is a very *bad* man, even if he did have a soft spot for you at the end.'

He knew he'd won when she swung round to face him. She was white-faced.

'But not too bad for people like you to use him, was he? You talk about lying. Did Parker tell me the truth about what happened to his wife Judith? No, of course he didn't! She was murdered in mistake for Harry, and everyone knew it. But they hushed it up.

'You made full use of what that did to him, didn't you . . .? He was mad with grief, he tried to kill himself . . . He felt he was to blame. So you taught him how to kill for his country instead.

'People like you and Jim Parker made him what he was, sitting behind your desks sending other men out to do the dirty work. You bloody hypocrites, you make me sick—'

'And did he tell you this?'

'No,' she spat back at him. 'The Pole told me about it.'

'The night you were rescued,' he remarked. 'When you were so ill and confused and couldn't think straight?'

'Go to hell.' Rosa had her back to him.

'You sent him a note, didn't you, with a present. We found the note. What did you give him?'

'Find out,' she said. 'I hope you enjoyed reading what I said.'

'Not really,' he stood up. 'I just felt very sorry for you. You can go home tomorrow if you like. And by the way, a Commander Lucas from the American Embassy has been pestering the Foreign Office for news of you. They convinced him you'd left the hotel before the nastiness happened and were staying with friends. He seemed very concerned about you. No doubt he'll get in touch, so you know what the story is.'

'Don't worry,' Rosa answered. 'I've learned to lie with the best of you. I'd like to leave tonight.'

'Make it tomorrow,' he suggested. 'You've had a trying day. You'll feel better in the morning. I'll arrange a car for you. Good Lord, look at the time. I'd better be going. Thank you for being so frank with me. And good luck.'

He knew she would burst into tears when he left.

'I shouldn't have chanced it,' Jim Parker said. He'd been waiting for Mackay in the staff quarters. They were having a drink together in the library of the fine old Victorian house. It was off limits to students.

'It was my mistake. Just think how close it was to blowing up in our faces — if that bastard hadn't intervened and pulled her out in time, I don't know how we'd have explained it.'

He finished his Scotch. He was disturbed and Mackay understood why. He'd liked Rosa Bennet. He felt guilty because of what had happened to her and let down because she'd failed to measure up.

'You can't entirely blame her,' he pointed out. 'You saw that note; she was infatuated with him.'

'I don't blame her,' Parker said sourly. 'I blame myself for sending an amateur to do a professional's job. I don't think infatuation's the right word. Certainly not for him. That farewell letter he sent her – just as well she never got it.' Jane had given them Oakham's note.

Parker asked for a refill and Mackay got up and poured it for him. He was a friend as well as a colleague. They'd worked together for years. He came and sat down and gave Parker the drink.

He said, 'Thanks to her we got O'Callaghan and her pals. That was worth it on its own. We can make quite a bit of capital out of that torture chamber and the chair. Might stop the bloody Dutch from turning a blind eye to what goes on in Amsterdam.

'I wonder where he and that Pole are hiding?'

Jim Parker said angrily, 'God knows; I've had the PM's office shouting the odds . . . What progress are we making? Why haven't we found them? I got so bloody fed up, I said they were certain to be out of the country by now.

'Probably out that night by the skin of their teeth . . . Thanks to bloody Rosa Bennet. All you need is a couple of hours' start in a situation like that.'

'What are you going to do about her?' Mackay asked.

Jim Parker didn't answer. He sat with the glass of whisky in his two hands and said nothing.

Mackay liked silences, he appreciated their purpose at times of decision. Then Parker looked up at him.

'That letter he wrote,' he said. 'I think she should get it.'

'Why?' Mackay asked.

'The way she reacted to you means that she's more committed to him than she realizes. Or wants to admit. He wrote all that stuff about wishing he could put the clock back and have a second chance to be with her in Brussels. I'm going to give him that chance, Peter. We'll tell that girl at the hotel she's to send on the letter – she'll do what she's told – I want to keep this going.

'I'm going to see Bennet and tell her you behaved like a shit. We'll give her a commendation and the job as Second Secretary in Brussels.'

'You think Oakham will be tempted to get in touch?'

'He was always a risk-taker,' Parker muttered. 'And he's gone over the top about her. You read the letter same as I did. I think there's a very good chance he'll try.'

'She won't turn him in,' Mackay said flatly. 'I'll guarantee that.'

'She won't have to,' Parker answered. He lifted his glass to Peter Mackay. 'Because we'll be there waiting for him. Cheers.'

'Rosa, I wish you'd talk to me.' Dick Lucas reached out and took her hand. It was very thin; she'd lost a lot of weight.

'I can't,' she said.

'Don't you trust me?' She gripped his fingers for a moment.

'You're about the only person I do trust,' she answered. 'That was such a good dinner. You've been an angel to me, Dick. I don't deserve it.'

'I think you do,' he said. 'I'm a very domesticated guy. I like taking care of you, you know that.'

She'd been home for a day and a night when he called her. It had been a dreadful twenty-four hours. She had roamed the silent house, unable to sleep during the night, beset by memories and regrets. And afraid of putting the light out. She didn't like darkness any more.

Her mother had been easy to fob off; she'd been told the same story as Dick Lucas. Rosa wasn't anywhere near the Doll's House Manor Hotel; she'd left to visit friends some days before.

Rosa's mother had been quite cross with her for not communicating.

'You might have thought I'd be worried when all that dreadful business came out on the news. You could at least have telephoned – you're very selfish.' Rosa hadn't argued. She'd just apologized and rung off.

She couldn't escape the lonely house by going to her mother. Questions and heavy-handed hints about how ill she looked and if only she had hung on to a good husband like James . . . it would have driven Rosa mad.

She stayed at home, but she wasn't sure how long she'd be able to cope with it. And then Dick Lucas called her and came round.

She'd been so glad to see him she'd burst into tears. He'd stayed the night. There was no lovemaking between them. He went to the spare room. There was something terribly wrong and he didn't press her. He just moved in and she let him.

He went to the Embassy during the day and came back in the evening. He cooked if she didn't feel like going out, and after the first week, he sat beside her, holding her hand and asked her to tell him what was wrong.

Rosa looked at him; he was kind and thoughtful. Loving. She shied away from the word.

'What happened to you at that hotel?'

She shook her head. He went on quietly, 'I guess you're under oath, is that it?'

'Yes.'

'You got caught up in that mess, didn't you, Rosa? You were there when it all happened. What were you doing? I think I can guess that too.'

'I'm getting over it,' she said at last. 'Thanks to you. I had a shock, I can tell you that much. It takes time to adjust.'

'Whatever it was, I feel responsible,' he said. 'I didn't come down that weekend.'

'Don't be silly,' Rosa insisted. 'You were on duty, you told me.'

'Yeah, but I was jealous too. "Harry". That's what you said and it got to me. You'd met some other guy down there. I hated the idea so much . . .'

She freed her hand and got up. 'I'd like another cup of coffee, will you have one with me?'

'I'll make it.'

He started to get up and she said quickly, 'No, you

cooked dinner. I'll make more coffee. Help yourself to a drink.'

She closed the door and went into the kitchen. He was an untidy cook; he'd left a bachelor's mess behind him.

She sat down waiting for the coffee to percolate through. He'd been so good to her, so patient. Very different from James. A million miles apart from Harry Oakham. Phrases from the letter forwarded to her by Jane floated through her mind.

'I could have made sense of my life with you . . . But there are no second chances. I wish to God it had been different. My darling, believe this: I love you . . . That's the one true thing.'

She had read it and then torn it up. Into very small pieces. Parker had been the postmaster. Anything connected with Harry would have been confiscated and read. Parker wanted her to read it.

And Parker had come to see her that afternoon, with a ribbon-tied florist's bouquet, and apologized for Peter Mackay.

He'd been very solicitous, very complimentary. Sir Peter Jefford was giving her a personal commendation for what she'd done. It wouldn't be public, of course, but it would go on her Foreign Office file.

And the job at Brussels was waiting for her. It was the least they could do to show their appreciation.

The coffee bubbled, and she picked up the pot. It smelled rich. Dick got up and took it from her.

'I got myself a Scotch,' he said. 'Anything for you?'

'No thanks. Give me your cup. My boss came to see me today.'

He sipped the coffee and said, 'What did he say? Good news?'

'They've held the Brussels posting open,' she answered.

'Good news for you, bad news for me,' he remarked. 'Means I'm going to lose you to some Belgian . . .' He made it light-hearted but it wasn't.

'I'm not taking it,' Rosa said.

He couldn't help it. He grinned like a happy schoolboy. She remembered the silly moon face he'd drawn for her after the first night they spent together. 'You're not? That's great – why not?'

Go to Brussels. Go back into the world of lies and double standards. Parker had been very sincere, very open with her. Just as he'd been when he sat where Dick Lucas was sitting at that moment, and talked about the enigma that was Harry Oakham.

Go to Brussels as bait; they hoped the man who'd written the love letter would try to contact her. And that having read it, she'd encourage him. Very open and sincere.

'Why not? Why don't you want to go?' Dick asked again.

She looked at him and managed to smile. 'Because there's nothing there for me any more. I'm not sure what to put in its place, but I don't like the way my life is going. I've got a second chance . . . Not everyone is that lucky.

'I'm resigning from the Foreign Office. I told him this afternoon. He wasn't very pleased.'

Dick Lucas poured more coffee. She was changed by whatever had happened in those few weeks. She'd been through the fire and it showed.

He looked at her and after a moment he said, 'I'm in love with you, Rosa. Sometime when you're ready I want you to marry me. But I've got to ask you something. Was Harry the guy they're looking for? Harry Oakham?'

'Yes,' she answered. 'Yes, Dick, it was. But it's all over. That's all I can say. I'm sorry.'

'That's OK. If you're sure it's over.'

The parcel had arrived that morning. He was upstairs in her bedroom, his felt hat crushed down over the little straw face with its silly painted smile.

She hadn't looked for a postmark. She'd burnt the brown wrapping before Parker arrived.

He and Jan had got away.

'It's over,' she said. 'I promise you.'

'That's good enough,' Lucas answered. 'I think you'll like living in the States.'

THE END

SONS OF THE MORNING
by Jack Curtis

'Gripping . . . a superb book in all respects'
Express & Echo

Linda Bowman was the first. Nobody special, just a face in the crowd. Yet someone picked her out, someone with a high-velocity rifle, someone elated by his own dark power. Then there was the man on the train; then the young couple drinking at a riverside pub. It was every policeman's nightmare – a clever and remorseless killer choosing his victims at random.

Robin Culley is a policeman, and it's his nightmare, but his instinct tells him that, despite what they seem, the killings have a motive.

Culley's obsession with the apparently pointless slaughter leads him into worlds of fear and shadow; from the highest level of British politics – the Cabinet itself – to the world of assassins for hire and mercenaries on the run; from a sinister Arizona billionaire art collector to the dangerous secrets of the SAS. It threatens those closest to Culley; and it takes him, finally, to a heart-stopping confrontation with a psychotic killer on the storm-torn wilderness of Dartmoor . . .

0 552 13592 5

TAKE NO FAREWELL
by Robert Goddard

Geoffrey Staddon had never forgotten the house called
Clouds Frome, his first important commission and the
best thing he had ever done as an architect. Twelve years
before that day in September 1923 when a paragraph in
the newspaper made his blood run cold he had turned his
back on it for the last time, turned his back on the woman
he loved, and who loved him. But when he read that
Consuela Caswell had been charged with murder by
poisoning he knew, with a certainty that defied the great
divide of all those years, that she could not be guilty.

As the remorse and shame of his own betrayal of her came
flooding back, he knew too that he could not let matters
rest. And when she sent her own daughter to him,
pleading for help, he knew that he must return at last to
Clouds Frome and to the dark secret that it held.

Robert Goddard, the master storyteller in the tradition of
Daphne du Maurier, has written his greatest novel yet,
peopled with richly drawn characters and with a truly
baffling enigma at its heart.

'Out of the five books he has produced in as many years,
all have been hypnotizing. I spent until four in the
morning, two nights running to finish this latest'
Daily Mail

'His narrative power, strength of characterization and
superb plots, plus the ability to convey the atmosphere of
the period quite brilliantly, make him compelling reading'
Books

0 552 13562 3

A SELECTED LIST OF THRILLERS
AVAILABLE FROM CORGI BOOKS

THE PRICES SHOWN BELOW WERE CORRECT AT THE TIME OF GOING
TO PRESS. HOWEVER TRANSWORLD PUBLISHERS RESERVE THE
RIGHT TO SHOW NEW RETAIL PRICES ON COVERS WHICH MAY
DIFFER FROM THOSE PREVIOUSLY ADVERTISED IN THE TEXT OR
ELSEWHERE.

All Corgi/Bantam Books are available at your bookshop or newsagent, or can be ordered from the following address:

Corgi/Bantam Books,
Cash Sales Department,
PO Box 11, Falmouth, Cornwall TR10 9EN

UK and BFPO customers please send a cheque or postal order (no currency) and allow £1.00 for postage and packing for the first book, plus 50p for the second book, and 30p for each additional book to a maximum charge of £3.00 (7 books plus).

Overseas customers, including Eire, please allow £2.00 for postage and packing for the first book, an additional £1.00 for a second book, and an additional 50p for each subsequent title ordered.